Cannibals and Missionaries

Books by Mary McCarthy

The Company She Keeps

The Oasis

Cast a Cold Eye

The Groves of Academe

A Charmed Life

Memories of a Catholic Girlhood

Venice Observed

The Stones of Florence

On the Contrary

The Group

Mary McCarthy's Theatre Chronicles

The Writing on the Wall

Birds of America

The Seventeenth Degree

The Mask of State: Watergate Portraits

Cannibals and Missionaries

Mary McCarthy

Cannibals and Missionaries

Harcourt Brace Jovanovich

New York and London

33718

Library of Congress Cataloging in Publication Data

McCarthy, Mary Therese, date
Cannibals and missionaries.

I. Title.
PZ3.M1272Can   [PS3525.A1435]   813'.5'2   79-4869
ISBN 0-15-115387-6

First edition

B C D E

*To Rowland
and to the memory of
Will Scarlett*

Dîtes donc, ma belle,
Où est votre ami?
Il est à la Hollande,
Les hollandais l'ont pris.

ACKNOWLEDGMENTS

With so many helpers to whom my thanks go, this book seems almost like a collaboration. On the Dutch side, I'm grateful, above all, to Cees Nooteboom—poet, journalist, novelist—for repeated trips to the polder, for an inexhaustible fund of information on proper names and place names, political parties, religion, national customs, for correction of my scanty pocket-dictionary Dutch, introductions to local figures who were themselves sources of information. It was through him and the singer Liesbeth List that I conceived the love of Holland that I believe shows through in the text. Because it was not possible for him to read the manuscript, there must still be many errors, for which he bears no responsibility. I owe him, too, the notion of Holland as an imaginary country and a number of hints for the plot, some of which were acted on, some not.

Then Hans van Mierlo, till recently deputy and leader of the parliamentary fraction "Democrats '66," who aided and abetted in various ways, *inter alia* by arranging a lively visit to Parliament and introductions to notables. The novelist Harry Mulisch, who went along that day and added his own observations and suggestions both then and later. I'm very grateful to the Prime Minister of the time, Joop den Uyl, for the interest he took, the questions he answered, the hospitality at dinner he and his wife dispensed. I know of no other country where such openness and candor would have been possible and found it significant that at the entry to the Prime Minister's residence there were then no guards—how it is now I cannot say. I also thank Han Lammers, the Landdrost of the "new polder" complex, for making possible visits to two farmers' dwellings and for an amusing and instructive lunch in Lelystad. Here in Paris, I've had considerable help with Dutch words and expressions from my husband's boss, Emile van Lennep, and his charming *mevrouw*, Alexa.

This leads to James West, my husband, who, more than anyone else, saw what seemed a chimerical enterprise at the start through to the end with continuing good humor and resourcefulness. I thank him for the many car-trips to the polder, for the books on helicopters he produced, for his critical support, as a World War II navigator, of my effort to represent planes and flying in a plausible way, for reading the text in manuscript, galleys, and page proofs with a convincing show of enjoyment. I owe to him the large color reproduction of the Kenwood House Vermeer (I might have settled, myself, for a postcard), Air France schedules, a marked plan of the interior of a Boeing 747, with Smoking and No Smoking sections indicated, information on the location and business hours of the Iranian consulate in Paris, and many other details that I now forget.

For help concerning the internal politics of Iran, I thank Jonathan Randal of *The Washington Post*, who was good enough to spend a morning briefing me, also Gavin Young of *The Observer* (London), who has taken a persevering interest in the book and joined one day in a polder exploration. Concerning the market values of art, I thank William Mostyn-Owen of Christie's, also for the material he supplied on the Kenwood House Vermeer that has been put to use in the final chapter. For rather different material in the final chapter, I thank James Angleton. For medical expertise, I thank Dr. Jacques Richard d'Aulnay and Dr. Aurelia Potor; also David Jackson. For guidance on New York "social" names, I thank Nicholas King. I thank Werner Stemans for going over the bits of German that appear here and there and Thomas Quinn Curtiss for his own account of being hijacked. And I think warmly of Hannah Arendt, who heard a lecture I gave at the University of Aberdeen on "Art Values and the Value of Art" and said afterwards, "You should draw on that for a novel." To my old friend E. J. Rousuck of Wildenstein's, no longer living, I owe what I know about sporting art—see the Ramsbotham collection, Chapter 11.

More than perfunctory acknowledgments go to the Boymans-van Beuningen Museum in Rotterdam for the Philips Koninck landscape reproduced on the jacket. Mr. Frederick de Jong, reached by telephone at the museum, showed eager Dutch helpfulness in having a new transparency made and dispatching it with speed. In connection with this, I'm very grateful, too, to Alison West of the Frick Museum for rapidly hunting down a number of Dutch landscapes to choose among.

The solution to the "Cannibals and Missionaries" game I owe to Clare Dow of London, who got it from a friend and wrote it out for me. I owe the American Academy in Rome a two months' residency this past winter which allowed me to finish the book undisturbed and in nice surroundings. Finally, I owe, as always, more than I can say to William Jovanovich and Roberta Leighton for the care they have taken in both large and small matters of copy-editing, design, and production. For this, over the years, they occupy a place like that of Holland in my heart.

Cannibals and Missionaries

One

"Bless, o Lord, thy gifts to our use and us to thy service; for Christ's sake. Amen." Excited as a kid on the day of his confirmation, the Reverend Frank Barber raced through the grace and drank his orange juice. His gaze embraced his family, whose sleepy heads had slowly returned to an upright position. One chair at the long table was vacant. His eldest, he saw, had already finished his breakfast and taken his plate, cup, and saucer to the pantry. A crumpled embossed yellow paper napkin and an empty orange juice glass marked his place. "He's gone to get the car," said young Helen. Among his manifold blessings, the rector of St. Matthew's, in lovely Gracie Square, was able to count garage privileges, extended as a courtesy to the church, over on York Avenue—a brisk seven-minute walk, great for chasing the cobwebs. He twirled the Lazy Susan in the center of the table and chose a medium-boiled egg from the basket. The eggs wore snug felt hats in the shape of roosters —a wonderful idea, he always thought: they kept the eggs warm and guided your selection, dark blue for medium, yellow for soft.

He was elated that his fledglings had all got up and dressed themselves—though it was Saturday; no school—to see him off on his mission. "Gosh, it's so darned early, it's practically dark out," he marveled. On the table candles burned in two silver candelabra, a gift from the vestry for his and "old" Helen's twentieth anniversary last July. On the sideboard stood four more candles, in saucers, that the youngsters had brought in from their rooms; they were pitching in to conserve electricity, on account of the energy crisis. In the fireplace a wood fire was lit (Frank, Jr., had brought the logs down in a U-Haul from the Dutchess County wood lot of a parishioner), and when the rector had arrived in the dining-room, "old" Helen had been bent over it in her wrapper, toasting English muffins on two forks, her face pink and her hair, pinned up in a knot with a single blond bone hairpin, starting to escape.

"I made the orange juice," announced young Helen, who had a round face and long fair silky hair like her mother's, "while my cruel brothers watched. Well, to be scrupulously fair, they set the table last night." "She *counts*," protested Matthew, the youngest, who was fourteen. There was a cell of women's libbers in the sixth form at her school; in her brothers' judgment, they were making a convert of her. Young Helen tossed her hair. "Matthew knows perfectly well that I'm doing a serious study of the woman-hours expended in this family. It's a social science assignment." John, aged sixteen, raised a finger for silence. "Members of the congregation, peace! Just think, tomorrow the Reverend Frank will be in Persia. And none of us, except Mother, has even been to Europe." "Iran," corrected his brother. "And it'll be the day after tomorrow, for Father," added young Helen. "Remember the time difference." "I like to think of it as Persia still," John said.

"But *they* don't, John," the rector interposed. "We have to respect their feelings. It's their country. Like 'black.' " He shook his head, recollecting. "We've all learned our lesson on that." "Did you really call black people 'Negroes,' Father?" Matthew wanted to know. "Everybody did, Matthew. Except the ones that called them 'niggers.' You're too young to remember." He himself could remember "colored"—what a coon's age ago that seemed! He gave a rueful chuckle and emended the worn old phrase to "raccoon's age": with oppressed minorities, he guessed, you kept *re*learning your lesson.

"But if it's their country," said John, "why are you going

4

there to butt in, like a missionary?" "That's a good question, John. But I don't know that I can answer it now. Time's a-flying. Or, rather, I'm a-flying." His wife and children groaned. "Don't try to slide out of it with one of your puns, Father," said John. "If the Shah is torturing and executing people, that's an old custom in his country. If the opposition got power, they'd do the same to him. I mean, isn't this 'ad hoc' committee of yours just trying to be a salesman for Western democratic merchandise? And why pick on Persia, particularly? Why don't you look into Ethiopia and Uganda too while you're at it?"

Frank observed that his wife was waiting for his answer. She stood watching her brood and her challenged mate from her sentry post at the sideboard, the coffee-pot in her hand and her head to one side, like an alerted bird. He was on trial, he reckoned. She took the young ones' questions more to heart than they did: out of the mouth of babes. But he knew that John was only probing, testing out his father's ideas. The boy, who was the only dark one and wore big glasses, was his father's favorite and his mother's too maybe. They said you should love them all equally, yet even Our Lord had sinned in pre- ferring *His* John, the Beloved Disciple, to the other eleven, who, unless human nature had been different then, must have been jealous of seeing him like that with his head in the Saviour's bosom—had that been Judas's problem?

Removing his mind from Judas, whose problems he often sought to understand, Frank tried to sum up succinctly why he *was* going to Persia—oh, shoot, Iran! Certainly not for a joy ride. "After all," continued John, "the Shah is basically on *our* side. If you want my opinion, that's why you're going, really. I mean, you're so darned liberal that you're sort of perverse." Frank's face lightened. He jumped up and hugged the boy. "You're right, John! You're right! I'm perverse. I never thought of it that way. But isn't that being a Christian? Jesus was perverse. Everybody thought so, even His disciples." He threw back his head and laughed in delight while his family looked on with forbearing smiles. Then he went around the table, giving them each a hug and saving a special squeeze for "old" Helen, who was four months pregnant—they were still keeping it from the children, who were likely to ask what had happened to his strong position on planned parenthood and the population explosion.

The buzzer from downstairs sounded. Frank, Jr., must be getting impatient. Outside the dining-room windows it was morning now, and the January daylight filtering through the marquisette curtains made the candlelight look pale and trembly. The six cocky egg hats lay in disorder around the table. It was time to go. Frank blew the candles out, not waiting for Matthew, who as the youngest had the right, to go around with the snuffer.

Taking a last look around the cosy room, the bright focus of his family life, he strode to the dark vestibule, where his big gray suitcase, his briefcase, and his light overcoat were waiting. At this season, it would be fairly cold (median, 38°) and dry in Teheran, according to their "bible"—the 1913 *Encyclopaedia Britannica,* in which the boys had done research for him on the trip. So much of the article was out of date (the *Columbia Encyclopedia,* in one volume, which the children used for their homework, was current, thank the Lord), but he assumed that *Climate* had not changed greatly. When it came to *Fauna* and *Flora,* he was less easy in his mind: ". . . about four hundred known species of birds" had floored Matthew, the family ornithologist, and he had insisted on lending his father his field glasses. The rector hoped the boy was not in for a disappointment. The only oil mentioned in the entry came from "the castor-oil plant, sesame, linseed, and olive." They had all had a good laugh over that, not stopping to think that the oil wells of modern Iran might have done something to the 1913 bird population. It was Frank, Jr., too readily a kill-joy for his brothers, who had pointed that out.

The *Britannica,* which had come down from the Canon, Helen's father, was getting to be a bone of contention in the family. Frank, Jr., wanted them to buy the new, University of Chicago one—the clerical discount would bring the price down

—and Frank, Sr., was beginning to agree, for reasons that this *flora* and *fauna* doubt had brought home to him: the other three, like Helen, Sr., loved reading aloud from the old set, but it was giving them a false picture of the world. They were still dreaming, on his behalf, of the country described by "Ed. M.": "The Anglican mission has its work among the Nestorians of Azerbaijan." "The flamingo comes up from the south as far north as the region of Teheran; the stork abounds." "It is a strange custom with the Persian ladies to dress little girls as boys, and little boys as girls, till they reach the age of seven or eight years; this is often done for fun, or on account of some vow—oftener to avert the evil eye." It was the same problem he faced over the new prayer book, which Helen and the children still rebelled against, preferring the hallowed old words. But prejudice, to Frank's mind, was the greatest affliction you could pass on to your children, and a prejudice in favor of the past, though it looked innocent, could lead them to reject the good in modern society, along with the bad, which of course existed too.

He had been wondering whether, once he got home, he could arrange to have the *Britannica* have an accident—not a fire, because of the history of intolerance linked to book-burning, but a little flood, say, from a leaky radiator—when Helen had gone to the hospital for her lying-in. Such criminal temptations, in a good cause, were familiar to him. Back in '68, he would not have objected to having a draft-card burned in his church, before the altar, though in deference to the vestry he might have offered the sacristy as an alternative.

It was quarter of eight. In the vestibule, the children, suddenly childish, surrounded him. "Your plane isn't till ten. Why do you have to go so soon?" Young Helen wound her arms around his neck. He understood. The Barbers were not used to air travel—they were too numerous—and at the children's age you could not keep news stories of plane accidents and hijackings from them. Maybe John, with his questions just now, had been begging his Dad not to go. Frank's conscience, normally good, all at once misgave him. It pictured Helen to

7

him as a widow with four dependent youngsters and another on the way. As the statesman-philosopher wrote, he that has wife and children has given hostages to fortune. There was a lot to be said, in the end, for a celibate clergy. Because, as a man of God, he *had* to go, darn it; he could not let his family ties stand in his way now. Helen, his tall mainstay, sent him a signal over the heads of the children: be off.

Frank cleared his throat, in which a lump was rising. "We have to stop for Gus first—didn't Frankie tell you?—at the Commodore." The name Gus seemed to act on them like a tranquillizer; the retired Bishop of Missouri, a stout old man in his eighties, was their summer neighbor in the Adirondacks —they had hiked the Indian trails with him and sailed with him on Lake Champlain. He was Frank, Jr.'s godfather and he had christened young Helen. "Oh, well. You'd better hurry then, Father. The Bishop will be on the sidewalk—do you want to bet?—with his watch in his hand." They giggled. How volatile young creatures were!

John took his father's suitcase, and the three rode down with him in the elevator. Helen, in her pink tailored wool wrapper, remained behind. The wife of the pastor of the venerable old Gracie Square church had to be careful. Pewholders lived in the building, and if she went down with him to the lobby as she was, the next thing you heard she would have been on the street "undressed." Scandal-mongering was one of the little crosses of the profession, and the Episcopalians, for all their "worldliness," were as bad as the Baptists.

For travel, under his spring overcoat, he wore a gray tweed jacket, flannels, white shirt, and a big maroon-and-white polka-dot bow tie that Helen had tied for him this morning. He never used a vest, too buttoned-up and reminiscent of the cassock; on vacations he sometimes put on a chamois waistcoat that had come down, like the *Britannica,* from the Canon. In his suitcase were some pre-tied bow ties in loud colors and energetic designs that the younger boys teased him about, two changes of suit (one dark), several changes of socks and underwear, a pair of black shoes, his slippers, tartan bathrobe, and pajamas, and his clerical dickey and collar. In his briefcase were light reading-matter, an extra bridge consisting of two upper left bicuspids and a molar, extra eyeglasses, Matthew's field glasses, two heavy folders of documentation on "Torture and Illegality in Iran," a shaving and toilet kit, the *Book of Common Prayer,* and his old pocket Bible—in a Moslem country, he did not think he could count on the Gideon Society.

He was a tall man, with a large loose-limbed frame, pale skin, gray widely spaced eyes behind big loose-fitting horn-rimmed glasses, and gray-blond springy hair cut in a style conciliating a crew cut with a pompadour. In his college days, he might have been a footballer, though his movements now were somewhat awkward and flailing. His clothes, his glasses, his necktie, arms, and legs hung on him at a variety of angles, as though unsettled by a wind of change. At his waistline he had to fight the battle of the bulge: the priestly calling, though not exactly sedentary, gave a busy rector little regular exercise beyond genuflection and marching down the aisle at a measured pace behind the teetering cross while trying to keep step with the choir and the servers.

His eager boyish features, as if to compensate, were extremely active. They wore, for everyday (excluding funerals and sick calls), several galvanic changes of expression racing from inquiry to bewilderment to joyful comprehension, marked by increasingly vigorous nods. A receptive person, the Reverend Frank, a listener rather than a talker. His ear was perpetually stretching to catch messages from the outer world, which often gave him the air of a deaf person, though his hearing was good. He was also a great waver, a sender-out of greetings, as from a large craft to smaller vessels sighted in the distance. This morning, despite his preoccupation, he had already, from under the canopy of his building, perceived a neighboring janitor, a delivery boy, the stationer from around the corner, and his arm, flung up, had flagged them, transmitting salutes.

"Come on, Father," interceded Frank, Jr., from the wheel of the car. "This is a No-Standing zone." He was nineteen and destined for the ministry. His deep voice had a nasal honking sound not well suited to the pulpit or the intoning of the liturgy; unfortunately the defect had only become evident when his voice changed, and by that time his life-decision had been made. He was small and narrow-featured, with a long probing nose—different from his brothers and sister, who were tall and favored their parents. This morning, to take his father to the airport, he wore a blazer with his old school shield, blue button-down shirt, necktie, and flannels; his straight yellow hair was cut short and its cowlick subdued by water. Only his feet, in high sneakers and long for his general size, betrayed a kinship with the other three, now grouped on the sidewalk, the boys with sweetly touseled locks and slightly stooping, which gave them an air of benevolence, and all of them dressed in jeans and several layers of frayed sweaters.

As a new pewholder had exclaimed to Helen, the Barbers were an "ideal family": "Your children are straight without being square. You must give us your recipe." In his parents' eyes, that was not quite true of Frank, Jr., who was indeed what they called square nowadays but slightly off plumb. Though he was a wonderful son and a fine human being, he was at present his father's chief worry, because of that voice and some tense aggressive mannerisms that, again, raised a doubt as to whether he really had a pastoral vocation. Given his sincere religious feelings, which abided no questioning, he might have been better off as a monk, the rector sometimes thought. A conventual discipline of early rising, fasting, prayer, and penance was an option that the Episcopal communion, perhaps short-sightedly, was ceasing to offer as an alternative to missions and parish work; it would distress but not surprise his father if one day the boy were to go over to Rome.

On the other hand, the rector surmised, not for the first time, studying his son's gaunt profile as the car headed down Park, he could be worrying about masturbation—a natural habit at his age, but he might feel it was a barrier to holy orders. Frank had had many good talks on the subject with troubled acolytes who did not dare open their hearts to their parents. At home, though, he was a parent himself in his children's eyes, he guessed, despite his efforts to make them look on him as an older, understanding friend. The other morning at breakfast, finding just the three boys at table, he had tried to start a discussion on what Jesus would have said if a disciple had come to Him with Onan's problem (" 'Let him who is without sin cast the first stone' " had been John's amused response), but instead of turning into the good free-wheeling exchange he had hoped for, the conversation had died in its tracks. The two younger boys had had a giggling fit, and Frank, Jr., giving them a searing look, had asked to be excused. That was a mistake the rector was not going to make again: offering reassurance, as he ought to know, could look like prying to a kid who was already in doubt about himself. Helen thought that Frank, Jr.'s trouble, if he had one, would clear up, like his occasional acne, as soon as he found a nice girl to get engaged to. And as for the voice (women, bless them, were so down to earth), she thought maybe an adenoids operation . . .

She and Frank had agreed, in last night's pillow talk, that he ought to discuss Frank, Jr., and his vocation with the Bishop. The good old man had a lot of human wisdom, and Frank was looking forward to the long plane trip as a chance to draw him out on all sorts of matters that had been on his mind—the reforestation of the ministry, for example, the big issue that was facing the Church today and of which the question of Frank, Jr.'s vocation was only a tiny facet. Where was the Church going to find young men with deep spiritual convictions who at the same time were not mixed up and withdrawn or, to put it mildly—which was Frank, Jr.'s case—not able to deal with people on an ordinary parish level? And this raised the question of the Church's real mission in modern society.

Making another survey of the set profile beside him, Frank decided to transfer to the back seat when they reached the Commodore; that would give the Bishop a chance to get "reacquainted" with his godson on the way to Kennedy. Last summer Gus had been complaining that he had hardly had a glimpse of "young Frankie," who had gone off to work in a wilderness camp in Maine and had come back just before Labor Day with a home-made haircut, a nose ulcerated from sunburn, a cold, and what looked like a severe case of malnutrition. The youngsters had lived on wild berries, clams, seaweed, tree mushrooms, a few fish they had managed to trap, and—they were practicing survival techniques—roast slugs. The Bishop had been shocked to hear of that, till loyally reminded by the Barbers in chorus of the Baptist's diet of locusts.

There the good soul was, as predicted, on Vanderbilt Avenue, at the entrance to the Commodore, standing in the street, red-faced and with his gold watch open in his palm. An old leather suitcase with foreign hotel stickers stood beside him. Frank waved and leapt out of the car. "Gus, dear friend!" "Frankie, my boy! And young Frankie!" Behind him waited a hotel porter holding the familiar black umbrella with the cherry-wood handle and a big book bag made of needlework. It had been stitched by Rachel, the Bishop's beautiful wife, whom the children did not remember because she had died of cancer when she was only fifty, the year young Frankie was born. But they knew her from her pictures, which were all over the Bishop's house, in wood and silver frames, and John had guessed that she was the reason for Gus's unshakable faith in the hereafter—a place that he often talked about, as though it were Burlington, where he usually went for the winter.

This morning he was dressed in a thick three-piece tweed suit and, over that, a Burberry. Gus was something of an Anglophile, and most of his gear went back to the trips he used to make with Rachel in the British Isles after his retirement more than twenty years ago. They had bought that house in the Adirondacks and fixed it up, and then, just like that, a month after Frank, Jr.'s christening, she had died—a photo on "her" piano in Gus's parlor showed her holding the baby in her arms in his christening robe; she was wearing a long-sleeved light-colored dress almost like a wedding gown.

Frank saw to stowing Gus and his precious bag and umbrella comfortably in the front seat, with a lap robe over his chunky knees. He was moved, between tears and chuckles, as always happened when he saw the Bishop after an interval. Gus had ordained him, out in Missouri (which the old man still called "Missoura"), when he got out of Harvard Divinity School; he had made a liberal of him, and now it was the name Augustus Hurlbut high on the list of the "Committee of Inquiry into Iranian Justice" that had caused him to add his own when approached by the young Iranian, Sadegh, one Sunday after Holy Communion. It was the first Sunday in Advent, a day of promise for Christians, and he had been preaching on the ordination of women—a cause Gus too supported, bless him—with a text from, of all people, St. Paul. Romans, xvi, 1: "I commend unto you Phebe our sister." Obviously, with that good fight behind him, he had been in a receptive mood when the slight dark velvet-eyed young man—whom he had noticed, thanks to his new bifocals, from the pulpit—came up to him as he stood in his freshly starched surplice shaking hands and receiving congratulations at the church door: "An inspiring sermon, Rector." "Thank you for your courage, Rector." "Frank, you were cute to take St. Paul." Gus's spirit had been very much with him while he prepared the sermon, and the old man's doughty name, materializing on Sadegh's list, seemed a sign from the Lord. The irony of it was that Gus at that stage, as it turned out, had not even been contacted, and when the Iranians did get to him they used Frank's name.

Confronted with this circumstance, Sadegh had theorized that a first letter had been lost in the mails, which was possible, since the Bishop was not always prompt about having his letters forwarded when he closed up his house at Thanksgiving. He postponed making out a change-of-address card, just as he postponed having his pipes drained, hating to take definite leave of what the children called "Rachel's shrine." But even if that were so, it did not explain everything: Sadegh and his friends were still not out of the woods.

For his own impetuous signature, Frank took some of the blame on himself. On that Sabbath morning, he recollected, as his eye had traveled down the list—which included a leading

13

Jesuit, a rabbi, a senator, a representative, all good names—in the back of his mind he had wondered that Gus, at his age, had agreed to go. But instead of being alerted by the anomaly to at least call Gus in his winter quarters in Burlington, he had let it dictate his own decision: if Gus could do it, so should he.

Now he felt no resentment. He had spent enough years in committee work to know that a pious hook needed to be baited before being lowered into the small reservoir of men of good will. To get any kind of group together to fly at its own expense to some remote corner of the earth to do the Lord's business was never an easy undertaking, he imagined, and Iran was a long way from being a Biafra or a Pretoria. Though Sadegh's briefcase contained a fair number of clippings, they were mostly not current and mostly in French. The mimeographed statement accompanying them spoke of "a total news blackout," which was no great exaggeration, as Frank's own example demonstrated. The whole Barber family took a keen interest in current events, particularly those concerning human rights and oppressed minorities, yet until Sadegh had come up that morning after divine service Frank had had no awareness that the Shah was doing anything worse than giving big wasteful parties for the international jet set while his people lacked food and housing. "No more idea than the man in the moon!" he had emphasized at lunch afterwards, as Helen stood carving the roast. "Did you know, John? Did you, Helen?" And the whole family had shaken their heads. That showed what these young Iranians were up against, and he reminded himself of it whenever in his dealings with them he found himself lacking in patience.

He understood, too, that men who worked on behalf of such causes were men of passion rather than strict principle. They were also, in this case, he gathered, young and inexperienced men. Maybe some group back in Iran was directing them, but he sometimes suspected that they were acting pretty much on their own, living on modest allowances from their families, who had sent them here to study. They did not even have the wherewithal to pay a printshop for a proper letterhead. He could never learn where they lived or how many of them there were. The telephone number Sadegh gave him kept changing, which probably meant he could not pay his room rent. Yet he was always neat and well dressed. It was all a brand-new experience for the rector, and this morning, with his air ticket (Return "OPEN") and his virgin passport in his inner breast pocket, he forgave in advance any further corner-cutting he might encounter in the organization of the trip.

Sadegh's list, as Frank had reluctantly come to realize, was protean in the extreme. Each time Frank asked to see it, it had undergone an unexplained metamorphosis. Father Hesburgh had dropped from sight and turned into a woman college president; a former Solicitor General had appeared and disappeared; the congressman had gone; there was still a senator, though not the same senator; in Paris, a Spanish monsignor and other European "personalities" would join them. As for the rabbi, Frank simply could not make it out. "Is Rabbi Weill coming? Is it *definite*, Sadegh?" "Oh, yes, possible." "No, not possible. *Sure*." "Yes, surely possible. Definite." He had tried to impress on Sadegh and his shadowy friends the importance of having the group be truly representative, and it still disappointed him that they had been unable to see the urgency of including a black—Julian Bond or one of the young ministers in the Southern Christian Leadership Conference. But in any case a rabbi was vital. If he had known Rabbi Weill personally, he would have put in a call to him; his temple (Reformed) was in Denver. When he had thought of calling him anyway, Helen had counseled against it. "You mustn't let these young men *use* you, Frank. You're such a born organizer. But let *them* manage their committee." If only, Frank reflected, they knew how! But about the rabbi, she was right, probably; these inter-faith things could be tricky.

Yet he *liked* Sadegh and the other young man, Asad, who sometimes came with him, and so he could not help trying to steer them out of what he sensed might be heavier water than they counted on. Last week, for instance, he had proposed,

15

with some forcefulness, that the group meet in New York ahead of time, to get to know each other and discuss the program of action. Sadegh and Asad had agreed, with corresponding enthusiasm, yet somehow it had never come about. Now there was nothing to do but wait for whatever surprises the airport was going to produce. If the American wing of the International Committee turned out to consist of the Right Reverend Hurlbut and the Reverend Barber, it would not be the greatest of surprises.

Luckily, the good Lord had given him a sense of humor. But something else bothered him that could develop into more than a joke at his and the Bishop's expense. The fact was, he had no notion of how they were going to gain access to the Shah's prisons and his law courts. He supposed someone had a plan; in Paris, where they were to stay overnight, they would be met by lawyers, Sadegh promised—a Belgian and a don from Oxford who had a chair of jurisprudence. But had it occurred to anyone that the group might be thrown out of the Shah's territory or clapped into jail or, worst of all, denied entry when they descended in a body from the plane? When he had put the question to the young Iranians, he had been assured that this could not happen, but he wondered how they knew. He wondered too whether their mystifying vagueness about details was due to a failure in communication: had they understood *any* of his questions?

"Hey, Father," called Frank, Jr., from the front seat. "Is there going to be some guy with you that speaks the language?" This too had been on Frank's mind, but he dratted his son's lack of diplomacy. The last thing he wanted was to share these mundane worries with the Bishop: old people were prone to become fearful at the slightest suggestion of uncertainty. Thus he had seen no reason to tell Gus that Sadegh and his friends had borrowed his name without his permission; the main thing was that Gus, when finally approached, had accepted, so where was the sense of exciting him about an understandable peccadillo when they were halfway to Kennedy with Teheran as their agreed destination?

The Bishop had turned his head, which was round as a pumpkin and partly bald, in order to catch the answer. Frank considered. At one point, Sadegh had talked of a Cambridge don who spoke several of the native dialects, but then no more was said of him, and he seemed to have been replaced by the jurisprudence don from Oxford. "I'm not totally clear on that, young Frank. We can pick up an interpreter there if we need to. No problem." But there certainly was a problem, as the Bishop was capable of guessing. In a police state any interpreter was almost sure to be a spy, and Iran seemed to qualify as a police state, though any substantial evidence to the contrary would be welcome, at least to Frank. He had an inspiration. "Through the Embassy," he shouted. The old man nodded. "Or through the Church, Frankie."

Frank felt moved again. The Bishop's serene faith was a rock. And how could he himself have forgotten the Church in his reckonings? Maybe the Anglicans no longer had a mission to the Nestorians of Azerbaijan, but the Church would be there in one or more likely a dozen of its myriad forms—in these oecumenical days it made no great matter which. Of course he had known it, in his soul, if not in his mind. He had brought along his clerical gear to be able to take divine service should the need arise. That was an old habit with him, virtually automatic whenever he packed a bag. But though he never thought about it consciously, it presupposed on his part a profound conviction that wherever a man of God went, there would be Christians and an altar. Unlike Gus, however, who was a seasoned traveler, he had failed to picture the Church as a source of material help.

A pastor in that largely Moslem community, if he did not speak the language himself, would be bound to have native speakers in his flock, along, Frank supposed, with Exxon and Shell representatives, who were in need of God too. And if the pastor was a true shepherd, he would greet with joy his brothers in Christ come to look into torture, summary executions, and trials that were a mockery of justice, which he could *not* but know about granted that even a quarter of the tales in Sadegh's folders were facts. No minister of the gospel, even the most lukewarm, one of Paul's famous Laodiceans, could be unaware of the abominations suffered in those prisons not just by political hotheads but by dissident Moslems protesting the repression of their faith. In fact, there was no excuse *not* to know; prison-visiting was a duty laid on the clergy.

Frank gave an inward start. How strange that he had overlooked that point, when he imposed the duty on himself (Helen was supportive) twice a month throughout the year. Including summers: he was grimly familiar with the inside of every correctional institution in their own and neighboring counties right up to the Canadian border and he had been taking Frank, Jr., along, to instill the habit, ever since the boy had discovered his vocation. Cast your bread upon the waters: he saw himself and the Bishop in their dog-collars being introduced into the Shah's prisons by a clerical accomplice and experienced a sense of deep and sweet relief, as though a balm had been applied to all the vexations of the journey—those foreseen and those as yet unforeseeable.

He cautioned himself not to let his natural hopefulness run away with him. SAVAK, the Shah's secret police, would scarcely have the same sociable attitude as the New York State wardens and guards, who knew him and young Frank and joshed them about searching the hampers of books and magazines they carried: "Any knives or other weapons, Reverend?" But the cloth was the cloth pretty much the world over, and even brutal men, men with something to conceal (who were not entirely lacking in New York State houses of correction), were more inclined to try to deceive it, pull the wool over its eyes, if he could use the figure, than to refuse it entry to the premises. And once you were inside, it was surprising how the prisoners would talk to you, sometimes with the aid of winks and hand gestures if a guard was present. In this age supposed to be irreligious, there was more healthy fear of God and also trust in Him than the laity reckoned.

* * *

A happy torpor came over Frank. His chin sank to his chest; he dozed. A doubt shook him awake. They were nearing Kennedy; Gus and the boy were silent. Misgiving as to his own purposes had gained entry to his mind as he cat-napped and was now demanding his full attention. John's questions at the breakfast table might have been a time-bomb, he guessed. The point John had been getting at, stripped of youthful trimmings, went to the heart of the matter: did the Church, *qua* Church, have a role to play in an affair of this kind?

Frank had pretty well resolved that—he had thought—with himself, in the time available to him, what with the pressures of departure added to normal parish work, the children out of school over the holidays, extra morning and evening services, choir rehearsals, the Girls Friendly pageant, extra sermons to prepare for the Nativity and the Circumcision (Epiphany, blessedly, had fallen on a Sunday), distribution of presents to the needy, and the darned crèche and parish-house tree to set up. But two minds were better than one, and he had been counting on picking Gus's brains in the plane today over a sherry or a bourbon (Gus's preferred tipple) on the theology of what they were up to. The subject, as he roughly saw it (he found outlining helpful in his thinking), was really a sub-head under the larger topic of the Church's task in modern society. Gus, he hoped, would play the devil's advocate, bringing up arguments *against* this jaunt they were on and all the other good causes they had crusaded for; then they could change sides, with Gus assuming the defense. Frank had been looking forward to a far-reaching, hard-hitting discussion, like the old midnight bull sessions in Divinity School, that would probably not settle everything but be wonderful mental exercise and maybe useful for a sermon.

In fact he already had a pertinent sermon in the works—based on a contemporary reading of the Book of Jonah—which he had started composing in his head, from force of habit, during his spare moments. In the barber's chair yesterday and last Saturday while watching a game of touch football played by the St. Matthew's men's club against St. George's. Actually, he would not be needing it until his return ("OPEN"), but it was always well to have a sermon ripening, in prudent reserve. None of it yet was on paper; some bits, though, he knew by heart, and he might try them out on the Bishop if the plane was not too crowded. . . .

"How many of us here this morning are Jonahs, who, having heard the divine call to betake ourselves to a place far from our homes—or perhaps merely to a less favored part of our city— to prophesy or, as we might say today, to bear witness, disobey the voice of God, which to us is the voice of conscience, and take ship for a different destination?" "No, the parallels are not perfect. The city Jonah was commanded to preach against was a wicked and flourishing city, whereas the call we hear may order us to go, if only in spirit, to very poor and wretched parts of the world, which some of us may feel are less sinful, on the whole, than the part of the world we would leave. Today the voice of God may speak to us from the columns of a newspaper, from an advertisement in a magazine, from an image on our television set. . . ."

There was no need to belabor that. The congregation would understand that he was talking about Vietnam and Cambodia and South Africa and, closer to home, East Harlem. But now a section was coming that might give them new food for thought. "We may not know, today, how to recognize the call that came to Jonah. It is not always that clear and easy. There are false calls, just as in scripture there were false prophets, and perhaps poor Jonah—let's give him the benefit of the doubt —took the voice he heard for a false voice.

"We must also try to distinguish—and this is particularly true for us in holy orders—a secular call from a spiritual call. Both may be valid but they are not the same. The Bible has taught us that the spiritual has precedence; a secular need, however great, must yield to it. This indeed is a prominent article of Jesus' teaching, though not always of His practice. We see Him, as you know, in the company of the underdog, the underprivileged. But does His sympathy for these lowly ones reach out only to their spiritual part? No. Do not let yourself be deceived. The transcendent Jesus is also a warm human being. He is present at the Marriage of Cana, where there is not enough wine to go around, and, instead of accepting this unfairness of distribution as inevitable and foreordained, He *makes* wine. When He preaches to a hungry multitude, He *makes* loaves and fishes. Even more interesting, he does not offer any *spiritual* comfort, any pie in the sky, to the leper who comes to Him saying 'Lord, if thou wilt, thou canst make me clean.' He cures the man and sends him on his way. Which shows that a fleshly need did not always have a low priority with Jesus; far from it. I dare to think that a secular need equally in our day may take on a sacred character, may cry out to Heaven for remedy. Our Lord is no longer on earth today, and the day of miracles in the old sense is past. Instead, we have our own latter-day miracles of science and technology, capable of feeding and healing the multitude if we will only use them rightly."

So far, pretty telling, although the point ought to be made that poverty had been inevitable in Jesus' day, owing to primitive methods of production; this explained His doctrine of Christian resignation—appropriate in its time-frame but now in need of updating. The whole passage could be expanded when he sat down with pencil and paper. And he would have to look up the words from St. Matthew in the revised version; when drafting a sermon in his head, he fell back, perforce, on King James, which memory—like Helen and her three young allies—was always eager to supply. But he never let details get between him and a powerful idea, such as the one his inspiration had been working toward. Experience had shown him that he might lose it if he did not swiftly clothe it in words.

"And what of civil rights, you may ask, dear friends. And the right to a fair trial and to speak our minds openly? Don't they belong to the political rather than the religious sphere? Yes and no, depending. If the craving for justice and equality was put in our hearts by God (you will not tell me they came from the devil), and in all our hearts to the same measure, then it is God's business that this yearning of the spirit be recognized as belonging to all alike and be loved in all alike. . . ."

That was the real meat of the sermon, and he had been keen to hear Gus's reaction to it. It was a ground-breaking argument for the pastorate's joining in activities (exemplified by today's mission) still looked on by many, in the Church and outside, as extra-curricular. An overwhelming argument, he had thought. But somewhere along the way he had lost sight of Jonah. This morning, while shaving, he had been wondering how he could work Jonah back in. "We in the ministry, like the prophet Jonah, have accepted a special function of attending to the Lord's business, wherever and whenever it calls us. But the world is a bigger, more complex place today than it was in Jonah's time, while we, poor mortals, are still man-sized, like the prophet. We evidently cannot answer, with holy alacrity, *all* the calls that come in to our spiritual switchboard. Not long ago, for instance, on the first Sunday of Advent, the beginning of our Christian year, a young Iranian came up to your rector, after divine service. . . . What was I to tell him, dear friends? That because he was a stranger and we had our own vineyard to tend, his call, though seemingly urgent, must be placed on 'Wait'?"

Jerked awake, like Saul struck down by the questioning Saviour on the road to Damascus, Frank now had the awful suspicion that "Wait" might indeed have been the right answer. He watched the airport Hilton go by and was assailed by a crowd of tardy second thoughts. He was no longer proud of his sermon draft, which to his mind, more uncertain with every passing second, appeared as self-serving. The unfortunate switchboard metaphor pointed to what looked like a basic unwillingness to think through the question of their mission: "Those figures of speech are cop-outs, Father," John had told him. "You bring in astronauts and space modules when you don't want to say what you mean." Frank now admitted the charge. To somebody of his democratic temperament, he

22

guessed, the idea of greater and lesser as applied to other people's emergencies was troubling. Yet a man doing the Lord's business had to budget his outlay of himself.

He asked himself whether a warning—or a sorrowful reproach—could really have come to him from on high as he dozed. Or was the sinking feeling in his stomach due to unseasonably early rising and an undigested breakfast? If God had spoken in his ear, it would be something completely outside his experience. Gus was on close terms with his Maker and seemed to converse with Him intimately as a friend, but Frank, while envying this, attributed it to Rachel's loss. He himself, though he had been granted perfect faith, had never had a direct intimation of the divine presence, not even during the religious crisis that had shaken him up when he was sixteen and led him from the high-school debating squad into sacred studies. On the other side of the coin, inner division, soul struggle, likewise was outside his ken, except as he observed it in parishioners who came to him for guidance. And his only real acquaintance with the pangs of remorse was when he had hurt one of the children's feelings and sought to repair the damage—easier, he often found, in a united family than mending a broken toy. He tried to be a good man and a good pastor and was content to know God, and love Him, through the liturgy and through His commandments.

Yet now it was as if God had deserted him; this too was a new sensation for Frank. The divine guidance on which he relied, confident that it was there, though invisible, steering him on the right road, was suddenly noticeable by its absence. He no longer felt directed but, instead, irresolute as a pinball hesitating on the board. There remained natural reason, which God, who had furnished it, would expect him to use. If it was too late, as he guessed it was, to draw back from this enterprise, he could still be clear with himself on it and gain, maybe, a new perspective.

In short, to come swiftly to the point (Frank, Jr., was braking as he approached the turn-off for the airport), could it be rightly said that he and the Bishop were answering a call of

23

the kind that had come to Jonah or were they merely acting as world citizens carrying out a secular task? In his own mind, Frank noticed, he had been referring to it as a "mission," which implied, he guessed, an apostolate. But possibly that was bad doctrine. An old-time prophet sent by God on this errand would have aimed at the Shah's reclamation. Yet he and the Bishop (if he could speak for Gus) had no intention of appearing before the monarch, as early Christians, to say nothing of the old-time prophets, would have done. They were going as mere "observers" and practically by stealth. It was probably far-fetched, under modern conditions—screening, security, protocol—to think of securing an audience with the sovereign. But if they failed to make an effort to convey God's displeasure to him, would they not be guilty of Jonah's sin?

There was a big hole—Frank now forced himself to recognize —right in the middle of that confounded sermon. Jonah's sin. It was not just disobedience. His wilfulness had a strange motive. The fact was, Jonah did not want Nineveh to repent. The reason he ignored the Lord's command, indeed did his best to escape from it, was that he was afraid that Nineveh *would* and so avoid God's punishment.

To tell the truth, Frank had never been able to understand Jonah's personality structure. But it was as clear as could be in the Bible that his governing passion was to see Nineveh destroyed, rather than saved. He was a stubborn cuss, with a one-track mind. Being in the whale did not teach him anything. When he finally did preach in that iniquitous city (since the Lord by then had him in His grip), he effected a conversion that any hellfire preacher would envy. The king "arose from his throne and laid his robe from him and covered him with sackcloth and ashes" and ordered his people to turn from their evil ways and "the violence that was in their hands." So the city was saved. But Jonah was angry with God for sparing it. He sat under his gourd-vine and reviled. Why? Narrow, sectarian Judaism maybe: clannish jealousy of the Ninevehites, who were Gentiles. It almost looked as if Jonah did not want his God to be a true Christian.

There was a lesson there for Frank and Gus. "The violence that was in their hands." Change Nineveh to Teheran, and the meaning was clear: for His business, God had no need of "observers"—He knew about the torture and the illegality. What He held out to sinful men was redemption, and for that He needed bearers of His Word.

The car had drawn up at the curb in front of Air France: Frank, Jr., was opening the trunk. In the back seat, Frank sat with his head in his hands, alleging a touch of migraine. He was still thinking. No minister today, he reasoned, would aspire to make converts of Mohammed Reza Pahlavi and Nassiri, his secret-police chief. But a man of God, possessed of the living faith, would hope to bring them to serve God in their own way, as good Moslems, and obey His commandments. Naturally, he and the Bishop, unlike Jonah, did not desire their destruction, whatever Sadegh and his friends might feel on that score. Yet for Christians the mere absence of evil wishes toward a wrong-doer was not enough. As unafraid Christians, they ought not to be satisfied with conducting an investigation and when they were safely out of the country announcing the results at an airport press conference—Asad's idea—in Athens or Paris.

That still might be very much worth doing (Frank was not prepared to gainsay it), but where did the Church come in? If he and Gus did not want to open themselves to the charge of abusing their sacerdotal function, they should go as private citizens, with no handles to their names. Yet without the mantle of their calling, they were no different from Joe Zilch, in short useless to the Iranians. It was a dilemma, all right.

Taxis behind them were honking. Making signs of apology and conciliation, Frank hastily descended from the car. Gus was standing by their baggage, waving his umbrella to attract the attention of a disappearing porter. He looked fresh as a morning rose, all primed to go, without a backward thought, apparently. Still, it was one thing for Gus—who was retired—to be flying off to far lands, and another for Frank, rector of St. Matthew's, charged with the administration of the sacraments and the maintenance of Christian values in the broad community of New York. Of course he had his curates; he had considered them when making his decision. They could run the show, as they did anyway when he was taking his vacation. If he was not back by Ash Wednesday, they would get some useful practice in preaching Lenten sermons.

Yet an uneasiness still gripped him as he stood on the walk eyeing the jet-liners taking off into the overcast sky. It came home to him that, like Jonah, he might be taking evasive action and setting sail for Tarshish when Nineveh, behind him, was where the Lord meant him to be. Would he be cast, he wondered, into the belly of the whale? He thought of the children's fearfulness about air travel—so manifest to him this morning—of Frank, Jr., who had gone to park the car. How would he react when he learned that his mother was pregnant, with his father on the other side of the world and having no fixed date of return? Frank's long-standing doubts about Sadegh's competence returned, combining suddenly with his other doubts and anxieties to make him wish from the bottom of his heart (he refrained from praying) that something would yet happen so that they would not have to go.

Unworthy man, he chided himself, could it be that he was plain afraid? Having bitten off more than he could chew, he might finally be recognizing it at the airport, of all places, where retreat was cut off. But if it was unmanly fear, not the voice of conscience, that was assailing him, he was all the more obliged to quell it and abide by his commitment. There was no time left in any case to peer into his motivations or decide what, if anything, he was nervous of. He must take the plunge briskly, as he used to urge the young ones gathered shivering on the lake shore for the first dip of the season: the water always felt chillier to those who hung back, wetting a toe and getting cold feet. He could not let Sadegh down.

Gus's freckled old hand was testing the weight of Rachel's book bag, which had been placed on top of the others for fear it would get dirty or crushed. No skycap was in sight. If Gus were to have a little heart attack . . . ? The dear soul had been warned by his specialist against lifting anything heavier than a shopping bag of groceries. If he were to try to carry that bag himself, which would be like him, it could not do him any serious damage. But a few palpitations, enough to rule out the trip for both of them—no question but that Frank would have to take the patient home . . . ?

The crazy thoughts that came to you in stress situations, as if planted in your mind by the devil! It made a modern man wonder whether it was not a mistake to doubt Satan's real existence. But of course, thanks to good habits, the "Get thee behind me" followed in a flash; he had hardly felt the brush of temptation before he took the bag firmly from the old man's grasp and set it back on the pile. They had a few minutes, he admonished, before check-in. A porter would surely come. Or he would find one of those carts, like the ones they had in the supermarket. But now a new dastardly thought came to tantalize him. If the flight were to be canceled? They did that quite often these days, on account of the fuel crisis, if the plane was not full. He was certain somebody had told him that. Frank shook his head. It would be only a reprieve. His apple-cheeked old friend had his timepiece out again. "The others ought to be here, Frankie. Should I go in and have a look?"

Frank was slow to reply. If the rabbi was not there, *or* the Senator, if nobody on this blamed committee was there, *then* they would be free to go home. It would be God's will. The prayer he had not let himself pray would be answered. But if he sent Gus inside to reconnoiter and any *one* of the promised four was there, there could be no turning back. This was something, Frank decided, that he did not yet want to know. As long as he did not know, he could still hope.

"Never mind, Gus. I see a porter." In fact a skycap was wheeling a cart down the walk toward them. Preceded by their baggage, Frank and Gus went through the door. At the Air France counter for Economy class, Sadegh was waiting, alone.

To his astonishment and moral relief, Frank's instantaneous reaction was anger: faced with the fact that the committee to all appearances consisted of Gus and himself, he could not contain

27

the oath of disappointment that sprang to his lips. "God damn it, Sadegh, you *promised!*" How little the human heart knew itself! He had sinned in mistrusting his own willingness, nay, eagerness, to fight this good fight. Now that their fine, broad-based crusade was dissolving into thin air before his disbelieving eyes, he could have wept for the pity of it. There was a lesson there of some kind: to use a homely comparison, it was like tossing a coin to decide whether to go hiking or take out the canoe; often you only learned that it was heads you really wanted when the other side, tails, showed its face.

Two

"Bon vol," Aileen Simmons wrote on one of the green-printed cards distributed by the hostess; upon reflection, she added *"Service aimable."* On the line *Effectuez-vous ce voyage pour Affaires* ☐ *Tourisme* ☐ *Autres motifs_____?* she had placed a check after *Autres motifs,* without becoming more specific. Her occupation she had given simply as *"Educatrice." "Recteur d'université"* sounded a bit pompous for the president of a women's college, and the presence of the other kind of rector, across the aisle, made her hesitate to assume the title. She would have liked to see how those men of God described themselves and what they would put next to "Other" as their reason for taking the flight—like good monolingual Americans, they would use the verso, obviously, provided for English-speakers. Aileen's bump of curiosity was well developed, and it interested her, as a one-time social historian, to note how other people responded to polls and questionnaires, which for her were always a puzzle, like a multiple-choice test.

The problems of identity posed by forms to be completed were one of the perplexities of travel for a thinking reed. The majority seemed to know who and what they were and expressed it swiftly, in block letters, but a worry bird like herself could pore for half a minute over "Domicile." She never knew whether to give her tax residence, which was Fayetteville, Arkansas, her home town, or Sunnydale, Massachusetts, which was the home of Lucy Skinner College and her semi-real residence. Then, on leaving a country, she often forgot which she had decided to put down on entering, thus making herself a mystery, she supposed, to compilers of statistics if those entry and exit forms were kept and ever actually compared.

A person named Aileen, more commonly spelled Eileen, must have started out in life with an identity crisis, she reckoned, and Simmons was frequently written as Simons—she had learned that when looking herself up in *Who's Who*: "SIMMONS, see also SIMONS." In her passport her eyes were "blue," but in her old passport they had been "gray," and her height in the current one had been officially corrected from 6' 3" (a comical erratum of the U.S. Passport Office) to 5' 3". Her hair, which had had a gray or graying interval, unrecorded in a travel document, had returned to a shade she called for brevity's sake "light brown." She answered to "Dr. Simmons," "President Simmons," and, by preference, "Miss Simmons" or "Simmie." She did not care for "Ms."

She was a chameleon, she imagined. The minute she stepped into a French airplane, she was talking French with the crew, not because she was a Francophile but because she knew how, having done two years of graduate work in French universities and lived with French families. She exercised her French, as she kept up her tennis, whenever the occasion presented itself—in restaurants, chiefly, but also in meetings with her French department staff and at dinners she gave for visiting *conférenciers*. When teased, she always said she was amortizing Senator Fulbright's investment; she had been an early Fulbright scholar, at Montpellier and Strasbourg. In Strasbourg, she had also learned German, which she kept up by listening to records of *lieder* and Mozart and Strauss operas (she loved music) but she no longer tried to speak it with Germans. In Mexico, one summer, she had picked up some Spanish.

As a girl, she had hoped to be a linguist and travel widely, but her Southern accent was a handicap. She carried it over—pure Arkansas, phoneticians said—into whatever tongue she studied, which meant she could never have taught a language at the college level. History had been a *pis aller* for her, but her real field, she had soon discovered, was administration. Here her being Southern, as well as *petite* and a woman and single, was an asset; she was a friendly, outgoing chatterbox and knew how to manage people.

Her seat companion, she noticed, had not filled in the green-printed card. She had completed her landing-card and tossed the other, which was optional, with a sort of disdainful shrug onto the vacant seat between her and Aileen. She was one of those tiresome new young women, evidently, who resisted all attempts at classification and codification, as though they represented designs to "co-opt" her into the prevailing value framework. She was not going to be helpful to Air France by consenting to be an item in their information-storage system, which must answer, Aileen assumed, to some rational need in the planning of flights, though, come to think of it, she was not sure how it served the company to know whether a passenger was traveling for business or for sightseeing or for "other purposes"—she listed some: death in the family, love, health, crime, though crime, if it paid, ought to come under "Business" surely?

Aileen's mind was fond of playing games with itself when it could not find a partner, using whatever materials came to hand; this was the good luck of having been poor as a child with scarcely a new-bought toy in the house. Only rich children were bored; she had pitied them when she had them in class and still did, though with less forbearance, when they came to her now in her office with their dissatisfactions. Her seat companion's casual clothes and indifferent manner marked her as having been one of them—even though, by now, she had probably broken with her "filthy rich" parents: as a rising star of the "new journalism," she could afford that luxury. She had yawned and slept throughout most of the trip, rebuffing the Air France meal and the list of things to buy and the earphones for the movie and yesterday's *Figaro*, accepting only two cups of tea, without sugar, despite Aileen's warning that it would be eleven o'clock at night when they got to Paris, too late to get even a sandwich from room service at the hotel. She was now

31

studying herself, rather angrily, in the mirror of an old Louis Vuitton travel case and jerking a comb through her dark short springy hair which finished in a frizzy bang over her high forehead and in which Aileen had detected with interest two gray threads. On an impulse, Aileen leaned over. "Tell me, honey, how would you sum up, if you had to, our reason for being on this flight?" She was prepared for this advance to be rejected, like all her other overtures, including the kindly hint that it would be wise to take those boots off—the elegant skin-tight things she wore, all the way up the calf, were bound to make the feet swell. But this time the dour young woman smiled. "Interference with the internal affairs of another country?" she suggested. Aileen laughed. At least she had broken the ice.

The hostess came through, collecting the Air France cards. The rector, in the aisle seat, handed his and the Bishop's over, duly filled in, and thanked the girl for the flight, just as though she were a real-life hostess. "I'm glad you enjoyed it, sir." "And our compliments to the pilot," added the Bishop. "I will tell him, sir." And probably she would; the human equation still counted in a 707. Aileen's heart warmed to the two courteous Episcolopians (as they called them back home); they were her idea of old-style American liberals and not afraid of a good time either. Before lunch, they had had a couple of bourbons, and the Reverend had got slightly high, shaking his head in ceaseless wonderment and then going off into roars of laughter that shook his whole body, like somebody being tickled. When he relapsed into gravity, he was the picture of the "concerned clergyman," all frowns and thoughtfulness, as though the fall of a sparrow had suddenly registered on his radar screen, reminding him of his duty to care. Aileen had had a bourbon herself and half a bottle of wine with her meal, which had made her want to talk, so that from her window seat she would lean across her uncommunicative fellow-traveler and address remarks and questions to the Reverend, before she finally got up—when the imprisoning tray was taken away—and circulated through the plane.

But they did not like to see you drifting down the aisle or

perching on the arm of a seat. She had been sent back to her place when the "turbulence" announcement came over the loud-speaker, and after that they had shown the movie, which she had watched without the earphones, trying to analyze what was happening and who the characters were. If she had had it to do over, she would not have elected the window seat, so confining; nor would she have chosen, necessarily, to be across from the clergy. Yet in fact she was glad they were along and glad they were somewhere close by, accessible to waves and smiles and a "Cheers" as she raised her bourbon glass. During the film, when the plane was dark and quiet, she could hear the Reverend's loud carrying voice quoting from Scriptures—the Book of Jonah, it sounded like. Though she had been a hard-shell agnostic ever since leaving high school and disliked everything about organized religion except the old Methodist hymns, today it comforted her to feel that her spiritual welfare must be of interest to two experienced males, just as it would have relieved her to know that a doctor was on the trip, though she hardly ever caught anything more than a cold when traveling or a touch of "Paris tummy," for which she had pills handy in her purse.

The pair inspired trust, particularly the nice ruddy old Bishop, whom she had liked on sight when he appeared in the departure lounge. She had not been so sure at first about the Reverend, in his bow tie, semi-crew cut, and loafers—a masquerade that failed, transparently, to disguise his calling. He was carrying a swollen briefcase and a worn tapestry hold-all that looked as if a doting helpmeet or the Altar Guild had stitched it. The peppy "collegiate" tie had worked itself around to a 45-degree angle, butting against his chin. He had set down the bags to straighten it and adjust his large glasses, appearing utterly distraught as he stood like a lost parcel in the middle of the lounge, seeking someone to claim him. Discouragement and vast perplexity were written all over him, and no wonder—as she told them later, this was the most *unstructured* committee she had ever in her whole life come across.

She had hurried right up to them, in her Southern way. "You two must be Bishop Hurlbut and the Reverend Barber." The Bishop had let out a chuckle. "Well, Frank, you see? She knew us without our dog-collars." Then he had taken her hand. "And your name, my dear?" "Aileen Simmons. Lucy Skinner College." He nodded. "We nearly worked together. You came onto the ACLU board the year I stepped down. And where is your home, may I ask?" He had noticed her accent. "Down your way, Bishop, originally, and I still go back most summers." "Missoura!" he cried, his dark-brown eyes lighting up. "Think of that, Frank!" "Over the border. Arkansas. Fayetteville. But we know about you down home." That was a tiny white lie: maybe the older folks in Fayetteville were familiar with "Gus" Hurlbut's exploits as Bishop of Missouri back in the thirties (hadn't he said "God damn them" from the pulpit preaching against some mine operators?), but she had only come to hear of these ancient jousts up north—as a matter of fact, a few weeks ago, from her Professor of Religion, who had brushed her up on Frank Barber too.

"Fayetteville. Simmons." The Bishop seemed to be searching his memory. He shook his head. "And your mother's name?" "Burdick. Catherine Burdick." "Bless me. She knew my Rachel. She used to visit down there, at the University. She talked of a family named Burdick." "There are lots of Burdicks in the area," said Aileen. "But at the University," the Bishop insisted. "Rachel Mackenzie, she was then, before her first marriage." Aileen knitted her brows as if thinking. Her maternal grandfather had indeed had a connection with the University: he was the campus policeman. She was not ashamed of the fact but she doubted that her mother, who had clerked in a feed store, could have known the Bishop's "Rachel" as a girl. To go into this at the moment would only disappoint the kindly old man, so bent on establishing a bond, and it was possible that her mother had been kin to some Burdicks at the University. Most of those Southern homonyms were cousins, if not kissing cousins.

The Reverend finally had had the good sense to interrupt;

her genealogy could wait. He wanted to know whether she had seen a rabbi anywhere. "I don't know as I could spot a rabbi," Aileen said, with irritation. "Do you mean there's one joining our group?" Two religious men were already a sufficiency. And there was still a monsignor from Spain in the offing, according to what she had been told. "Oh, Lord!" said the Reverend, sighing. "The mysterious east. So our friend Sadegh didn't tell you. But I understood him to say, just now, that the rabbi's wife was here. When I asked him if the rabbi had come, he said 'Mrs. Weill is upstairs, in the departure lounge. She waits for you.' Isn't that what you heard, Gus?" The Bishop said that his hearing was not as sharp as it had been. "Maybe your rabbi is a woman," Aileen suggested. She watched the Reverend turn this over in his mind. The thought that temples and synagogues might be accepting women for the rabbinate, while his own church tarried, would be uncomfortable for him to accept.

"I was only joking," she told him. It had been naughty of her. Having consulted *Who's Who* and the *New York Times Index,* as well as her Professor of Religion, she was aware of the rector of St. Matthew's (Harvard, D.D.) as an enthusiastic position-taker, most recently identified with the ordination of women, and the impulse to tease him on that sore subject had been as natural as breathing. But he was in too much of a flurry to recognize a joke. She resolved to be more careful in the future; the fact that she knew "all" about him, starting with his birth date (two years before her own), full names of wife, parents, and children, was a temptation to her mischievous side to use its advantage over the poor minister, who knew no more about her, probably, than he did about this missing rabbi.

But who was the rabbi? What brain had he sprung from? In self-protection, Aileen made it a rule to be well armed with facts about any group she agreed to join. This applied most forcefully to omnium-gatherums such as today's delegation. As president of a leading women's college, she was asked in practically every mail to serve on a committee, sponsor a meeting, endorse legislation, sign an appeal, so that she had to pick and choose between contenders for her sympathy: "What suitors have we got this morning?" her PR man would say, riffling through her "In" box. So many of the demands were worthy and (if the unfeeling man only knew!) tore at her heartstrings. But no matter how virtuous the cause, it was the company her name would keep, if only on a letterhead, that she was obliged to bear in mind. In her position, she had to be especially wary of being tarred with a "leftist" brush; thanks to the wicked war in Vietnam, many of the old fellow-travelers had got a foot back into the door of liberal organizations, and the newer "movement" people, with youth's short memory, did not seem to care.

She had explained all that to the Iranians. This committee, she had pointed out, was in an unusually exposed position; in passing judgment on the Shah, it would be open to the charge of furthering Soviet penetration into the Middle East, which meant that its acts and membership, as well as its financing (she was glad to know they were all traveling at their own expense), must be above suspicion. She thought she had made that perfectly clear.

Yet here she was now, with her bags checked to Paris, being informed out of the blue that a rabbi of unknown provenance, whose surname she had not even heard properly, had been added—and his wife too, apparently—to this tiny committee, which would have to live and work together in a closed foreign environment under the eye of the secret police. It was true that a rabbi these days was unlikely to be pro-Soviet, but if he was over forty and a joiner, he might well have sponsored some Soviet-American Friendship rally or signed the Stockholm Peace Appeal. . . . And a pro-Zionist rabbi would be just as much of a liability, given the tone of the Shah's pronouncements on Israel. Another point, minor in comparison, but not negligible: supposing he and his wife were orthodox and ate kosher? Had anybody thought of the problems that would create? An administrative mind learned to pay attention to such things, which counted when strangers of different backgrounds were thrown together, as Lucy Skinner's experience with the Black Muslim girls could tell you.

He might be Reformed, of course, and have a clean liberal

record, but Aileen should have been allowed to check up on that herself, at her leisure, and while there was time to reconsider. *Who's Who,* for a starter, could be quite revealing when you knew how to read between the lines. Now, if he turned up, there was nothing to be done. You did not resign from a committee—because the organizers had misled you—at an airport, on the brink of departure.

She felt incensed with the Iranians but also with herself: she had been *lax.* In a way, it was understandable. They had come to her with a letter from an old friend in the drama department; before he went to Lincoln Center, where he was now, he had worked in the Persian theatre on a grant. He vouched for the group of young rebels; he had known several of them personally and their families. They were not Communists; quite the contrary. They belonged to the conservative opposition and objected to the Shah on moral and traditionalist grounds. He himself had been greatly disturbed by the reports of torture he kept hearing while in Iran and he urged Aileen to do something to help: "Go dig out the facts, darling. And the country is enchanting." Aileen had always trusted his judgment and she recognized his thinking in the list of names the young Iranians showed her, with stars opposite those that were "definite." She agreed, with one exception: "Reston won't do it," she said, and of course she was right.

Yet she ought not to have left it there. She knew that. Several times, in fact, she had been on the verge of telephoning the Reverend Barber, whose number she had found in the Manhattan directory, but then she had reflected that it was Christmas and he would be up to his neck in church doings, hard to catch at his office (she was reluctant to call him at home), and, besides, she herself had been frantic over the holidays, flying back and forth to chair two round tables, look in at the MLA meeting, talk to a Boston alumnae group—it had been as much as she could do to buy some clothes at the sales for the journey.

None of that, though, was the real reason. The truth was, she would never have said yes in the first place except for her insatiable travel urge and the monotony of the New England winter. Teheran was dull, they said, but there were wonderful remote spots to visit if she could take a little time off from the committee: Naqsh-i-Rustan, Takht-i-Jamshid, Cyrus's tomb at Pasargadae, Isfahan. . . . Once those breath-taking pictures had taken shape in her imagination (with some assistance from *The National Geographic* in the library basement), she had been unwilling, she reckoned, to hear any fresh facts about the committee that might cause her to think twice: she *had* to see the "Cube of Zoroaster," Darius's palace, the graves of the Sassanids, and the rock-hewn tombs of the Achaeminid kings.

To tell a little more truth (it was wise to be candid with oneself), there had also been the promise of getting to know the Senator, a handsome man in his photographs and recently widowed. She saw them flying to Shiraz over weekends and renting a car to explore the country together, picnicking in the ruins; the others would not be interested in antiquities, probably, and, if some were, they could come along, sharing the expenses.

"A rabbi is so darned important," the Reverend was stating, as if to himself. He had sunk down on a bench opposite her while the Bishop had gone to the men's room. Aileen made no comment. Instead, she voiced her own worries. "They should be calling our flight any minute now. What do you suppose has happened to the Senator? He was meant to be coming in on an early plane from Washington." "Oh?" That was news, evidently, to the Reverend, but, unlike him, she had not been *totally* remiss. Last week she had had her secretary call the Senator's office in Washington; his chief aide said that Iran was certainly on the boss's calendar and asked the girl to tell President Simmons that the Senator was looking forward to meeting her. This had given her the right, she thought, to call again, and yesterday the same aide had said that, yes, he was booked this morning on a flight to Kennedy. But it was typical of Miss Meloney, in many ways an excellent secretary, that she had not thought to find out *what* flight. It could have been late or canceled. But unless you knew the flight number there was no way of checking up. "Mr. Barber, do you think you could just go downstairs and ask Mr. Sadegh if there's been a message?"

"Sadegh has gone," said the minister. Aileen let out a wail and fell back in a heap on the bench. Unbelievably, while the two clerics were checking in, the Iranian had made a phone call and "discovered" he had an appointment. So he had asked the minister's son for a ride back to town. "And you let them go," said Aileen. Useless to wonder why he had not exercised some parental authority. She turned her stricken face to the Bishop, who had seated himself during this exchange and was rocking calmly back and forth with his big umbrella between his chubby knees. "If the young fellow wanted to make himself scarce, plenty of vehicles were available," he observed.

Aileen felt ready to cry. The Senator was going to be a No Show—hadn't she always had the presentiment? The Iranian, somehow, must have known it or found it out from his phone call. "Then he just couldn't face us and he ran away. Don't you agree, Bishop Hurlbut? Don't you *know* that's what's happened? I vote we go home."

"You may be right, my dear. When you've served on as many duly constituted bodies as I have, you come to expect eleventh-hour defections. But I reckon the Senator would have had the courtesy to have one of us paged here if he missed his plane for some reason. He and I are old acquaintances, though we've sometimes been on different sides of the fence. I made a long-distance call to his office the other day—to check up, don't you know—and his right-hand man told me that Iran was on his calendar all right. 'Glad you called, Bishop,' he said. 'I know the Senator is looking forward to meeting you again.' So, until we have more information, I vote we give Sadegh the benefit of the doubt." Aileen was surprised that a man of his age and reputation for godliness could be so easily soft-soaped. "That only proves that the Senator is a politician," she said.

The boarding sign went on. Passengers started filing into

the second section of the lounge, past an Air France official at a high desk. A line formed. The Reverend hesitated. He made another lingering survey of the lounge.

Aileen's attention wandered. A new group of passengers, led by an Air France hostess, had entered from a corridor at the far end of the hall and was moving past the barrier, while the line already formed was halted. First class, naturally; they were being taken straight to the plane. She caught sight of a silvery head, then a tall, erect figure, which turned and scanned the queue and the slowly emptying lounge. The Senator! He was looking for them. Aileen vigorously waved. But he did not see her; she was too small. She reached in her bag for a handkerchief and signaled with it over her head. "Here we are, Senator!" But he could not hear her either. By her side, the tall Reverend was executing crossed-arm motions, like a trainman flagging an engineer. The Senator finally grinned and waved back. Then, making a gesture of helplessness, he moved forward, into the Security section.

"Come on," urged Aileen. "Bishop, don't you think we ought to get in line now?" The minister was still worrying about his rabbi. "Should we have him paged on the loudspeaker?" " 'Rabbi and/or Mrs. Weill'?" suggested the Bishop, amused. Aileen clapped her hand to her head. Her earrings bounced. "Heavens, I thought you said 'Weiss,' Reverend. There's a *Miss* Weil over there telephoning. Or she was, a few minutes ago. But she pronounces it 'Vile' and spells it with one *l*. I was so concerned about the Senator that I didn't see the connection." She laughed to cover her confusion in making the admission, which was true but came out sounding lame, like a lie.

It was the clerics' turn to be *bouleversés*. Now they knew how it felt to hear casually, on the dawn of D-day, that a new element had been added to the troops. Open-mouthed, they looked to Aileen for explanations. "A journalist. She writes for *The New Yorker*. And *The Atlantic Monthly*." "*The Atlantic*." The Bishop nodded. "Sophie Weil." "Why, yes!" exclaimed the Reverend. "I read an article by her only last month. On Oman, was it?" Brazil, the Bishop thought. Either or both, Aileen said. "Miss Weil gets around. Brazil was another torture story." "Right! Right!" cried the Reverend. "I remember that too. Wonderful stuff!" It was as though the good religious man had totally forgotten about the "importance" of the rabbi.

"Well! I guess that clears up the mystery. Not Sadegh's fault, really. Just a little communications breakdown. The rabbi in Denver couldn't make it and instead we'll have Sophie. Coincidence of names. But why did he say 'Mrs.,' I wonder?" He shook his head. "Between ourselves, Miss Simmons, didn't you find him kind of hard to pin down sometimes? As if there was no real, frank, open exchange . . . Of course, his English! But I guess our Iranian won't be so fluent either." He bubbled on joyously.

"I didn't meet Mr. Sadegh until this morning," Aileen said. "At the check-in counter. He had Miss Weil with him, and we agreed to be seat mates. It was Mr. Asad who came up to Sunnydale to talk to me, with another young man. And we spoke French. If you mean, did they misrepresent this committee to me, no, I can't say they did, Reverend, not really. They didn't tell me a rabbi was coming, but then, apparently, you were mistaken about that, don't you think so, Bishop? I must say, Mr. Asad might have let me know sooner that a journalist would be joining us, instead of leaving me a note last night at my hotel. But then, as I understand it, she isn't to be part of our committee or sign any statement we may release. She's going along as a reporter, on an assignment. . . . Isn't that so, Miss Weil?"

Aileen's seat mate, a tall dark long-nosed young woman wearing a long suede coat, had silently come up. "Let me introduce you to the Bishop and the Reverend. I was telling them that you're going to be with us but purely as a reporter. Mr. Asad and his friends made the arrangement with you. Or was it with your editor?" Aileen raised her head brightly, prepared to listen, as she did at assemblies when presenting a student speaker. The young woman turned to the two clergymen. "It was my own idea. I've known Asad for ages and when he told me the other night about your committee, I decided I wanted to go along. I guess I ought to have cleared it with all of you, since you're the ones concerned. . . ." This was Aileen's opinion; the Bishop and the Reverend, however, were making chivalrous noises of dissent. "But there wasn't time, and the Iranians, you know, are so frightfully vague. I wasn't sure how many of you there would be or how to reach you." Lucy Skinner College was not exactly a needle in a haystack, Aileen reflected. But she only nodded, as if in thoughtful accord, as she listened to the breathy voice addressing itself gravely to the two men, who were nodding also.

"Did the Senator make it?" Aileen pointed; you could still see the back of his head in Security. "Terrific," the girl said. "I suppose they kept him in the V.I.P. pen." Aileen gave a little cry; she had not thought to ponder the implications of senatorial privilege. "Does that mean he'll be traveling first class while the rest of us stay in Economy?" Miss Weil looked at her curiously. "What difference does it make?" The men too were gazing at Aileen, as if in wonderment. "Well, I mean," she protested, "we're a group, aren't we? We have an agenda to discuss. We ought to elect a chairman. Don't you think so, Bishop?" Before the old man could answer, Miss Weil declared, with a stifled yawn, that there was no cause for worry: the Senator could not ride first class unless he had paid a first-class fare. "The V.I.P. lounge is just a courtesy." "But how do you know that?" Aileen said plaintively. "You sound so sure, honey."

In the line, the Bishop counted heads. "Five, with the Senator. But, Frankie, shouldn't there be six?" "The rabbi," Aileen reminded him. "But no"—she corrected herself—"Miss Weil is the rabbi, isn't she?" "Somebody's missing," announced the Reverend. "Don't you have a list?" Aileen said sharply. "Doesn't any of us have a list?" Miss Weil spoke up. "There's meant to be a professor with you. A Middle East specialist. From Buffalo." "Bless you!" cried the Reverend. "Right! Right! Lenz, that's the name. I must be losing my mind. You'll think we're a woolly lot of liberals, Miss Weil. With Sadegh disappearing and everything, I plain forgot about him. Lenz. Victor Lenz. Sadegh told me to add him. I have his career data here somewhere." Inexcusable. But then Aileen recalled having seen the name herself, on the emended list they had sent her during the holidays. She had found one reference to him in the *Readers' Guide*—an article or review in *The New Republic*—that she had not had time to follow up. "Well, we can't wait for him," said the Bishop. "We may find him on the plane."

But as they moved ahead, toward the barrier, a little blond man, unshaven, in a long dark overcoat, took a boarding-card from his teeth and accosted Aileen. "President Simmons? I met you once at a panel discussion. But you wouldn't remember me, I know. I asked a question from the floor. Bishop Hurlbut, Reverend Barber, glad to know you. Sorry I can't shake hands." So this apparition was Lenz. In his left hand was an open basket that held what looked like blankets and some canned goods; a man's purse and a long trailing scarf were slung around his neck; a folded tabloid protruded from an overcoat pocket; and in his right hand was a cage containing —surely?—an animal. "Sophie Weil," Aileen indicated, when no one else spoke. "Lenz. Victor Lenz. My pleasure." "Is that a cat?" said Miss Weil.

The professor nodded happily. "Sapphire, my Persian." He crouched down and spoke to it. "Yes, Sappho, nice Sappho, mustn't be scared." "You don't mean to say it's going with us?" cried Aileen. "Coals to Newcastle, yes, you may wonder. But I couldn't leave her with the nasty vet, could I, Sapphire? We came down on the bus yesterday. Domestic airlines can be tiresome about animals. But we got to bed late, and Sapphire forgot to wake me this morning. So we nearly didn't make it. I don't suppose any of you knows where to get a drink here." The smell Aileen had been noticing could not be the cat, then. In fact the professor reeked of stale alcohol.

"There must be a drinking fountain somewhere," volunteered the Reverend, stepping out of line and looking around him vaguely. The official at the barrier snapped his fingers.

43

"Please, ladies and gentlemen! *S'il vous plaît, messieurs et dames!*" "You can get a drink of water on the plane," Aileen heard the Reverend telling the professor, as the matron frisked her for weapons.

But the retired Bishop of Missouri had a keener eye. On boarding the aircraft, he halted and from one of the pockets of his thick tweed suit he brought out a good-sized silver flask. "For medicinal purposes," he said, offering it to the professor. "Get yourself a paper cup."

Aileen had questioned the Bishop's wisdom in offering a hair of the dog to somebody so evidently in need of it. It would be the last straw, she thought, if the committee were to find itself with a problem drinker, as well as a cat, on its hands. Iran, being Moslem, was dry, presumably, but that did not apply to foreigners, not in big cities, and anyway alcoholics were cunning, adept at procuring bottles and hiding them like squirrels. The Bishop and the Reverend no doubt had experience in dealing with drunkards, and perhaps they could be trusted to handle Lenz, should he start picking fights with the secret police, for instance. . . . It was not up to her to keep a watch on him; yet the habit of supervision (she had been a dean, for her sins, and before that a registrar) and foreseeing eventualities was hard to throw off.

But before she could ponder the matter, a diversion had occurred. While they were filing through first class on their way to Economy, a large pale ringed hand had gone out to intercept the Bishop: "Gus! My dear man! How lovely!" And "Charles!" the Bishop had responded. The reunion had been cut short by the steward, chivying them on to where they belonged, past the Senator, who was already installed in his shirt sleeves in the first row of Economy, with his glasses on, and papers spread out all around him—they had given him a whole block of seats to himself. He jumped up and shook hands, explaining with a smile and a pained twist of the dark eyebrows that he had work to do: he would be stopping by for a chat as soon as his "desk" was cleared. "Did our friend fix his glittering eye on you?" he said to the Bishop.

Then they were scarcely airborne when the same hand, followed by a snowy cuff, had parted the curtain that divided the sheep from the goats and the man called Charles had peered in: a long white papery face, long nose, dark eyes, dead black hair. After some debate with the steward, he was allowed to come through. He stood in the aisle, holding both the Bishop's hands in his and proclaiming his delight in a high "English" voice that caused passengers in the rows ahead to turn about in their seats, as though anticipating a show. The fluting tones, rising to a rooster's crow, suggested deafness or its social equivalent to Aileen.

He was an old man, nearly as old as the Bishop but extremely well preserved, like a thin dried haddock. The raven hair was his own but certainly dyed, and his face was powdered with talcum. He wore a suit of coffee-colored silk, with many flaps and pockets, that looked as if it had been made for a planter in Java before the First War, an elegant soft shirt, and a beige waistcoat; on his feet were black silk socks and long shoes the color of old-time stove blacking. He fitted a cigarette into an ivory holder, and his jewelry consisted of monogrammed gold cufflinks, a plain heavy gold ring, like a man's wedding band but worn on the right hand, an antique ring with an intaglio cut in some pale gem, and the latest thing in costly wristwatches. And he was on his way to Teheran.

"On a *tour*. Can you imagine it? I'm part of a first-class *package*." The Bishop's response, inaudible, could be inferred by anybody who was curious. "You too, dear boy? Isn't that glorious? I shall certainly play hookey." Charles's tour was tremendous value, Economy class heard: first-category hotels, chauffeured limousines, archaeologists serving as guides, delicious food (they *said*), all included with the air fare, for less than it would cost Charles to dine out for a week in New York. Aileen was aware of a general stir in the public that perhaps represented envy. Nobody was paying attention to the hostess in the aisle demonstrating the inflation of the life jacket. "Trust the rich to find a bargain. I had no *idea*. In my poky way, I thought package tours were what my plumber takes. But I shall pay the price in socializing. My millionaires are up there drinking alcohol already. Full of Republican sound and fury. You should have seen the faces when I spoke to Senator Carey. Charming man. You would think, wouldn't you, that collectors would be more civilized. That living with beautiful things would rub off on them. A total fallacy. By the bye, have you talked to the Senator? There in the front row; magnificent head. I suppose he's bound for Paris to attend one of those 'meetings' politicians today go in for. I found him rather taciturn, I must say. You know he lost his wife."

Charles remained oblivious of the commotion in the aisle caused by the news he had just disseminated, which was sending autograph-hunters forward with menus to be signed. "Such a joy to see you, my dear. And how splendid to know that we shall be together on the plane tomorrow. Sensible of you to go tourist class. The rich are only tolerable in their own settings. Those dreadfully named Bloody Marys they're engorging. So menstrual, I always tell them. Well, as a good Democrat, I shall have a split of champagne with my lunch."

The Bishop must have warned him that others were listening. Disappointingly, for a time nothing further could be heard. Aileen had resigned herself to yesterday's *Figaro* and was scanning the Classifieds for items of interest when Charles again became audible, expressing concern for the Bishop's health. "You're dressed much too warmly, dear fellow. These carriers are always overheated. You'll catch cold, and that will be tiresome for you. Light-weight summer suits, I find, are best for plane travel, in this natural color. It shows the dirt less than the dyed silks, despite what people tell one. Then I always travel with a shawl or two as well as a light overcoat. And you must be careful about the sun, even in winter out there. We shall have to find you a proper broad-brimmed hat. Felt, not a Panama, mind you. The tomb-towers, as you'll see, can be damp."

He had no suspicion, evidently, of the Bishop's mission "out there." The thought that any motive other than site-seeing could be operative had not crossed his mind. Aileen wondered how those two could ever have come to know each other; maybe ADA, she speculated. But if "Charles" was such a Democrat, why was he traveling with a group of rich Republicans? "Collectors," he had said. She got up to go to the ladies' room, edging past Miss Weil and giving a little wave, as she went, to the Bishop.

When she came back, with her hair fluffed out under her turban and fresh mascara, the Bishop was waiting to introduce them. "President Simmons, my old friend Charles Tennant. Won't you join us, Miss Simmons?" "Well, just for a minute." She took the vacant place between the two ancient men. Against the wall, near the serving-pantry, the Reverend was talking happily with a hostess, who was getting the drinks cart ready. "Charles is bound for Iran too," the Bishop explained. "So I gathered," said Aileen. "Did I hear you say something about collectors, Mr. Tennant? Is it a tour of *art* collectors you're with?"

It was an archaeological tour got up by a band of "proud possessors" who were discovering Iran as it threatened to make itself scarce. The energy crisis was responsible for bringing them together on a common carrier; normally they would have chartered a plane or flown in a baby jet belonging to one of their companies—two of the men in the party were company directors. The poor dears saw this as their "very last opportunity" to tour the famous ruins, visit the museums, and explore some of the new digs before the Shah raised the price of oil again. There was a curator from the Fine Arts Museum with them, who was hoping to interest them in financing new excavations—an unlikely eventuality, Charles considered. "You mean the *Boston* Museum," Aileen decided. "But why? Are you all from Boston?" She ought to have remembered that the museum was renowned for its oriental section. "Dear me, no," said Charles. "We're from New York and Pittsburgh and Cincinnati and Hartford and Worcester—the dark satanic mills." "Charles lives on Mount Vernon Street," put in the Bishop. "He has a crackerjack oriental collection." "Almost nothing from Iran, alas. A few Khabur bits and pieces I picked up fifty years ago. No, our little curator is the only knowledgeable member of our party. Like some of the ladies, I've been 'cramming' for the journey."

He turned to Aileen. "You must come to tea one day if porcelains interest you." Then he gave a screech. "But you have some lovely Chinese work in your museum!" "You *know* our little museum?" Better than she did, she perceived, as he named a "hare's fur cup" and some "priceless *blanc de Chine*" that she could not picture to herself—ages ago, in her predecessor's time, an alumna had left Lucy Skinner a lot of *chinoiserie.* "Those people with you, are they important collectors?" she said.

"*Je regrette, monsieur . . .*" The steward was telling the gentleman that he would have to return to his own class; the hostesses were about to serve drinks and needed the aisle clear. The Reverend was waiting to reoccupy his seat. "Well, that was nice!" Aileen declared, when Charles had gone. "Bishop, do you know what a hare's fur cup is?"

Back in her place, she had slowly grown pensive. The wine at lunch, probably, had done it. True to his promise, the Senator had come by, on his way back from the men's room, for a short chat. But Miss Weil had chosen that moment to sit up and take notice (she had seemed utterly deaf to Charles's incursion), so that the conversation, inevitably, was three-cornered. The Senator reported that Sapphire had lunched on salmon from the hors d'oeuvres course cut up and heated by the hostess and had declined a bowl of milk. The professor and the cat had the bank of seats opposite him, which appeared to amuse the Senator. Aileen did not dare ask him whether Lenz was continuing to drink; Miss Weil, she could not forget, was a journalist. . . . And when Aileen returned his visit, just before the film-showing, Lenz himself, shaved at last, was very much in evidence, with the caged animal beside him and a blonde hostess bending over murmuring *"Minette, minette."* The Senator was calling him "Victor" and dispensing a fund of cat stories. Then came the turbulence announcement, and she had to climb over Miss Weil again and wearily strap herself into her corner.

It had been a strategic error not to elect to sit by herself. She had wanted to take the young woman's measure, and the New York–Paris leg of the journey, she had estimated, would provide an early occasion. But almost the reverse had happened. She knew no more about Miss Weil and her intentions than when she had boarded, and the journalist, if she had cared to listen, had quite a lot of "material" on Aileen. It was sensing that girl beside her, like a silent criticism, that was inducing her to feel defensive about herself. Though she was not at all what they called "a calculating person"—much too outgoing and open to sudden impulse—she would not like a stranger to see, sometimes, the little reckonings that were going on in her head. And they showed sometimes, she feared, giving those who did not know her a bizarre impression. For instance, before lunch just now she had asked Charles too many questions—perhaps even the Bishop had noticed—which did not sound totally idle. But when she heard that there was a group of art collectors bound for Teheran up in first class and then in the next breath Lucy Skinner's art gallery was mentioned, she could not help making a connection. Now her brain was considering how she could get at them and find out *what* they collected, which was natural in somebody who had to be concerned with gifts and bequests, while a contrary thought chain was leading her to wonder how she could avoid them if they turned up at Zoroaster's Cube or the wall tombs of Naqsh-i-Rustan when she was with Senator Carey. She could not stop herself from *thinking*, any more than the average person, on being shown 2 and 2, could avoid making 4.

Her fault was only an unusual degree of mental activity. The curse of intelligence. Stupid people were unconscious of their slow-moving thought processes. But take Charles's plain gold ring: a mind like hers could not fail to perceive immediately

that it was on the "wrong" hand and be aware of what conclusions to draw. Though he must be nearly eighty and queer
in every sense, there he was, a man and unmarried. With a
fair share of worldly goods. If he owned a house on Mount
Vernon Street and collected porcelains, he could not be, as
she had first thought, some kind of gentleman guide. She could
not be blamed if in the forefront of her idling mind these
facts were turning over, along with the notation that she was
fifty this year and single.

For some time now, ever since her *affaire* with the head of
the classics department had ended, she had been looking at
men from that angle. To her shame, even the Bishop had
passed through her head this morning. The deterrent was not
the dead wife, so hard to replace, or his age, but the fact that
he was too sweet: when he died, she knew she would suffer.
She did not *mean* to be sizing up old men; it was almost cruel.
But so few men of her own age were available. Most men of
her own age were either married or queer. A married man
could always turn into a widower, but a queer remained a
queer, though an old one, if you had some interests in common, might prove to be your best hope, assuming he was no
longer very active sexually—a women's college would not offer
many fleshly temptations. Yet what if she were called upon to
be the first woman president of Harvard or Yale? In that event,
a homosexual consort would be a liability.

Her bald approach to this topic seemed to distress her friends.
"Honey," her PR man said, "you shouldn't talk that way in
front of me. I'm a *man*. You shouldn't even talk that way to
yourself. You got to leave something to fate." But Aileen had
no trust in fate. She preferred to see this as a problem for
study, researching the field of "availables" in the same spirit
as she leafed through scholarly publications in the hunt for a
candidate with the right qualifications for an expected vacancy
in one of the departments. And with luck she might kill two
birds with one stone; that was how she had found her classicist,
an excellent teacher and a grass widower. But then, when he
was settled in, with a nice house and a top salary, his mercenary

wife had returned to him. Divorced men were a mirage: they either went back to their wives or married someone much younger, the way they would turn in an old Buick for a new Volkswagen.

She was not the kind married men left their wives for; she had learned that cruel lesson in her thirties. So her choice ought to lie between widowers and bachelors, which was not a bright outlook, given the known facts that most wives outlived their husbands and that most bachelors were disguised halves of a homosexual couple.

She ought to have married when she was young, but then she had not wanted to. She had prized her independence. Making her own way up the academic ladder, she did not fancy adding the burden of a husband to be carried along; the Ph.D. candidates she met in the graduate-school mills and in the cafeterias and faculty dining-rooms of small Southern colleges were far from enticing *partis,* and the deans and department heads had their careers already made and would never forsake tenure as well as their wives and children to follow her north when the call came.

The typical academic married too early; as a student, she had taken note of this classic mistake and made up her mind to learn from it. A woman had the advantage of being able to discard an outgrown spouse without being bled for alimony, but even so, casting off a husband who had become too small for you, like a child's pair of shoes, was bound to be painful and exhausting. Aileen was careful with her energy, which she kept for her career, her family, and her friendships. From the little experience she had had of it, she wanted no truck with remorse.

If it had not been for her family, she might have married nonetheless—the inevitable childhood sweetheart, who was still in Fayetteville and a doctor. But her family gave her the emotional nourishment and sense of belonging a woman needed. She was close to her brothers and sisters, all settled in Fayetteville, and truly loved her mother, an intelligent woman (even if she had only a high-school diploma) from whom she had got her brains. Once her Papa had died, her Mamma had wonderfully grown and developed, politically as well as culturally—she had been in the local anti-Vietnam-war movement, written regular letters of support and advice to Senator Fulbright, and at the age of seventy-one had got on a bus to Washington to march in a demonstration. Aileen had been helping her family ever since she had left home. In the summers, she insisted on paying her keep, though her mother now was reasonably well fixed, with her father's life-insurance and the widow's benefits she drew from the federal government—Papa had been a mailman. Mamma owned the house free and clear, rented rooms to students during the term, and occasionally gave a hand to her former boss, who was now eighty, with the accounts and inventory in the old feed store, which had expanded into a big hardware and housewares business and was mainly run by his daughter.

It would not have surprised Aileen if her Mamma had married again; she had gentlemen friends who sat on the porch or in the "den" with her and took her out riding on Sundays. At seventy-six, she did not feel too old for sex, apparently: she had had it with Aileen's father right up to the end, she confided, and still "missed him that way." But you did not need to get married for that, fortunately. There was always somebody who wanted to sleep with you, Aileen had found. That was one of the surprises of middle age—she would never have imagined when she was young that if you put some perfume on and left your room door on the latch in the Statler Hilton during the MLA meeting, a distinguished Russian specialist would come gliding to your bed. It had happened just this Christmas.

As Aileen saw it, sex gave a woman only two problems. Contraception was no longer a worry, thanks to the menopause, which she had completed, with gratitude, last summer, but, as that problem had receded, the other—taking care with whom you did it and where—had become more acute. Permissiveness did not extend to older females—even Mamma was criticized if she pulled the shades when entertaining—still less to older heads of female institutions. Most married men could be relied on for discretion; they had their own motives for concealment. Nevertheless she had made it a rule not to be tempted by a member of the faculty, no matter how attractive, and in the case of a visiting lecturer to respect the prohibition laid down for students—not on college property. Her classicist had been an exception. The first time, it had happened in her house, and the next morning, before the maid came, she had had to wash the sheet and iron it by hand—taking it to the laundromat would have been too risky. After that they had met in Boston hotels.

In general nowadays she kept sex for vacations and the professional conferences that figured more and more on her calendar. Some of her nicest memories were of "stolen" interludes during forums and panels with interesting men whom she never expected to see again. And if sometimes their paths did cross a second time, at another round table, there was seldom any further question of sex. Yet she remembered and, meeting their eyes in the course of some boring presentation, she knew they remembered too.

Thanks to her mother, she did not have to feel tied to Lucy Skinner. Mamma had made a home for her. She had her room, with her familiar things; her old trunks were stored in the cellar; in the den were her photograph albums. There were files of her correspondence in the attic, her doctoral thesis, programs of seminars she had attended, with the papers that had been read. Her summer dresses were waiting for her, hung up in bags, with lavender. But that was another thing: her mother was getting on. When she went, Aileen would be alone, with no center to her life. A room at one of her sisters' with full-grown children under foot would not be the same at all. It was Mamma's fault that she had never been domestic. She had mastered a few French and Mexican recipes for entertaining, and her sisters had taught her to iron. But housekeeping was Mamma's sphere, so that Aileen had not been able to develop her own touch and style, except in clothes. The President's house at Lucy Skinner bore few marks of her occupancy beyond some gay pillows she had scattered about, for students to sit on the floor on, some old prints of French cities, and her record collection. Buildings and Grounds supplied flowers twice a week and arranged them—she did not have Mamma's "hand" with bouquets—and the china and glassware she used reflected the taste of old Miss Smith, her predecessor. Even if Aileen had known how, she would not have tried to make the impersonal house homey.

She spent most of her time in her office, surrounded by the clacketing of typewriters and the ringing of telephones in the anteroom. At night, when she was not invited out to dinner or entertaining officially, she would eat in one of the student dining-halls or sit down at a table in the college snack bar, where a group would immediately join her. She dropped in on classes, films, exhibitions, lectures, and could usually be counted on to rise in the audience, wrapped in a bright shawl, and ask the first question. After college events, she would have students and faculty in for drinks. These habits had made her popular; Miss Smith, a shy academic woman, had been almost a recluse.

No one would have guessed—she thought—that underneath her liveliness was an awful fear of loneliness. Though she had been living by herself for nearly thirty years, she was seldom, in practice, alone. If she had to be alone for a whole evening, she poured herself a bourbon, listened to the news, telephoned, played the phonograph. She had lost the feeling she had had as a girl that a book could be a companion, which meant that she read less and less. She hated silence and sitting still and when she sank into meditation (as now perforce, on the plane), her thoughts were a kind of noise she kept going in her head. But she was getting a bit cracked, she feared. After a few drinks recently, playing *Carmen* one night, she had danced all by herself, clicking a pair of castanets she had brought back years ago from Mexico and stamping her heels, forgetful of how grotesque she would have looked if anyone had peeked in. Fortunately, the President's house was in an isolated position, on a hillock.

Late at night often, she would pick up the telephone and

call her mother or one of her sisters; with the time difference, they would not be asleep yet. This lifeline to Arkansas, at arm's reach when all else failed, had made her neglectful of the fact that her youth had gone while she was looking the other way. Of course fifty today was not old. There were examples of women older than herself who got husbands: George Eliot was sixty when she married Mr. Cross. But George Eliot was an exception for whom the laws of probability did not count. Aileen knew herself to be no such awesome phenomenon; lacking fame and a big brain, she was subject to the ordinary hazards of competition: unlike George Eliot, she was not even exceptionally homely, which had probably been some sort of advantage. Men were not afraid of ugly women. On the other hand, she lacked the *je ne sais quoi* that came from having been a beauty; she was betwixt and between, even though her appearance had benefited from the sharpening that age and wiser make-up had brought to her features, and she had kept her pert figure. In any case, at fifty, whatever you looked like, you could not expect a *coup de foudre*; time and proximity were necessary. But meanwhile you were being crowded not only by your coevals, entering the market via death or divorce, but by the oncoming generations, who were not looking for marriage necessarily—which made it doubly unfair.

Sophie Weil, for instance. Calmly deciding to attach herself to their group, she had never given a thought probably to how Aileen as the only woman would feel. Now they were two, and Aileen's chances of "making time" with the Senator were reduced to a forlorn hope. With a glamorous journalist in her thirties available for a "flirt," he would not have a minute for a still attractive female of his own age—four whole years younger, actually. Unless he was a very unusual politician, he would soon be eagerly carrying the sullen *New Yorker* correspondent's suitcases and deploying his Irish charm. And the meanness, the waste, of it was that the girl had no need of a silver-haired widower for a husband; if she was like most of her kind, she would be opposed to the entire concept of marriage, and it would not cross her mind that she was standing in the way of somebody who felt otherwise. To her, it would be inconceivable that a fifty-year-old educator could be any kind of rival.

So that made one motive less for the voyage to Teheran. Nevertheless Aileen found herself slowly cheering up. Eliminating the Senator from her computations meant that she would be relieved of the labor of devising strategies to throw herself in his way: maneuvering to sit next to him on tomorrow's flight, lurking in the hotel lobby to catch him as he alighted from the elevator, arranging to have herself appointed the group's chairman so that she would have occasion to stop by his room on committee business, leave little notes in his box. . . . If she could swallow her disappointment now, she would be spared a host of future disappointments and humiliating setbacks. She could enjoy the time in Iran as a working vacation that might even benefit a few of her fellow-men. Not waiting for the movie to end, she opened Asad's folder and switched on the overhead light. The awful torture-descriptions made her wince as she thoughtfully turned the pages, underlining the paragraphs that seemed most promising for the committee to follow up.

It was extraordinary how altruism, a decision to focus on others, could put you at peace with yourself. Aileen was accustomed to thinking of herself as a good person (while always resolving to be better) but lately she had been having some doubts. Her quick sympathy with the Shah's victims reassured her: cruelty appalled her, and that was the main thing to watch out for in yourself—any tendency to be insensitive to suffering, if it was only a headache. Cruelty, she had read once, was the only sin a modern mind recognized as such, and she went out of her way therefore to be considerate, which was the reason her staff loved her. And want of consideration, when she observed it in someone else, could afflict her like the drilling of a tooth.

Even in little things, like her neighbor's lofty rejection of the Air France questionnaire—*"Aidez-nous à vous mieux connaître"*—which somebody had taken trouble to frame. It had actually hurt her to watch, out of the corner of her eye, as the green-printed card was tossed as if derisively onto the seat between them. She had been indignant for the card, which, like Aileen, was only asking for some innocent information: "Help us to know you better."

The pathetic fallacy at work! Cards did not have feelings. In the disdainful gesture she must have sensed a rejection of her middle-class self and her values, among which was the duty to be helpful and do as you were asked when no possible harm was involved. By her offhand act, Miss Weil was scorning Aileen for having filled *hers* out. But that scarcely explained —or did it?—the positive hatred Aileen had felt well up in her, almost like a physical thing. And now it was rising again as she tried to concentrate on the folder. *"Pig,"* she said under her breath, using one of *their* epithets. "Stupid, arrogant pig."

It was not the first time this had happened to her recently. In her office, she would watch poor harmless stolid Miss Meloney, who adored her, and catch herself thinking "Bag!" or even "Old bag!" though Miss Meloney was younger than she was and a virtuous spinster, so far as Aileen knew, and the only connection there appeared to be was that the secretary, too broad in the beam already, had the habit of bringing her lunch to her desk and wrapping the unfinished morsels—a half-eaten browning apple or a mustard-oozing sandwich—in one of those plastic tissues called "Baggies," a package of which stood next to her typewriter. She had come to hate Miss Meloney and did not know why. The sole therapy she knew for that was to hug her a great deal and smile warmly whenever she caught her eye and send thoughtful little things to the poor girl's mother, who was a shut-in.

Yet where was the common factor between Miss Meloney and Sophie? Perhaps it was just her time of life and having a silent female body so close to her in a confined space. But there had been other signs of a growing divergence between her behavior and her feelings, which she found quite upsetting, especially as there could be no question of altering one to match the other: she could not change her feelings, and if she stopped sending Miss Meloney's mother presents or struck Miss

57

Weil, it might make her a whole person but not a person she would like better. Her best hope was that actions might occasionally prompt the appropriate emotions: a hug could sometimes make her feel warm. She would try to remember that with Sophie.

The No Smoking sign went on. The plane was starting its descent. "Paree!" she called to the Bishop, who was peering out the window. Then, distinctly, they heard a hostess scream. Aileen closed her eyes tight. They were being hijacked, she supposed. She heard someone running down the aisle. A hostess raced past. A male voice was shouting angrily. Aileen peeked through her fingers. The pilot, or the co-pilot, was standing in front of the curtain that shut off first class. She could not see a hijacker. Then, toward the front, someone laughed. A word was passing along. *"Le chat!"* "It's a cat." "Sapphire," needlessly explained the Reverend. "Keep your seats, please!" the officer ordered. "Everyone be seated. *Attachez vos ceintures."* The hostesses and the steward were chasing the cat up and down the aisle.

Aileen rose half out of her seat to see what was happening. It looked as if the animal might have escaped into first class. "But *why* did he let it out of its cage, Reverend? Mr. Lenz! How could you do such a wicked, dangerous thing?" *"Asseyez-vous, madame! Et vous, monsieur, retournez à votre siège!"* Paying no heed, Lenz was creeping down the aisle, making coaxing sounds. The cat was hiding, as they did when they were frightened. *"Regagnez votre siège,"* repeated the steward, not adding *"monsieur"* this time. *"Dépêchez-vous."* A hostess came by, looking under the seats. *"Minou, minou,"* she wheedled. "Here, kitty, kitty," essayed the Reverend. "I guess it doesn't understand French," he added to the hostess with a foolish laugh. "Oh, sir," she replied, "you do not imagine the trouble that gentleman has made. He have taken *minou* from her box and hold her on his knees. I tell him he must not do that; it is forbidden. But he say the cat is crying. I have to call the steward. Then when no one is looking, he take her out again." "Totally irresponsible!" Aileen declared. "You are right," said the hostess. "And *en plus* he smoked in the toilet." Aileen clapped her hand to her head.

Sophie's boot was exploring the floor. Her long arm reached down. "Why, it's Sapphire; hello, Sapphire." She scooped up the blue Persian and set her on her lap, rubbing her cheek against the long fur. "We must find you some catnip." The passengers applauded as the hostess came to retrieve the now purring animal. The crew took their places against the wall. There was a bump, and the flight was over.

On the bulletin board, after they had cleared immigration, the Reverend discovered a message addressed to Senator James Carey et al. LOOKING FORWARD TO MEETING YOU AT HOTEL EIGHT A.M. BREAKFAST. VAN VLIET DE JONGE CAMERON. The Senator held up the missive. "Does anybody have a guess as to how many persons that is?" It could be three or two or just one. He was laughing. "Come on, et al.'" Nobody knew. As they waited for their baggage he took Aileen's arm. "Kind of a funny committee, isn't it?" he murmured. Her eyes flew up alarmed and met his. Was he thinking of quitting? But no; he was just sharing his amusement with her. He would be a set-up for anything that tickled him, as she ought to have known.

Outside, a long black car from the Embassy was waiting for him. He conferred with the chauffeur. "Bishop, ladies, step in." He clapped the Reverend on the shoulder. "You go up in front, Rector. Sapphire and I will hop a taxi with Professor Lenz." "Victor, please, Senator." "OK, Victor, so long as you keep calling me Senator." His deep soft laugh was still audible as the chauffeur closed the doors of the limousine and they drove off into the night. "A charmer, eh, Frankie?" commented the Bishop. Aileen glanced at Sophie Weil's profile, trying to read the expression there. That he should have chosen a cat in preference to either or both of them to ride into Paris with showed how elusive of commitment he would be. She sighed. "A dreamboat. As we used to say down our way, Bishop Gus, remember? Tell us, what was his wife like?" The Bishop obliged.

Three

In fact, Van Vliet de Jonge Cameron was two persons. They rose from a round table in the hotel dining-room to greet the Americans. Cameron had been drinking tea for his breakfast, which went some way to prove that the Oxford don promised by Sadegh had actually been delivered and stood holding a chair for Miss Simmons. He was a small, out-at-elbows, taciturn Scot, somewhere in his late forties—"painfully shy" was the diagnosis. "Had a good night?" he shot out and, unable to face the Yankee return fire, beat a retreat into silence, which he only broke of his own free will to ask permission to light up a pipe. Van Vliet de Jonge had been drinking *café au lait* and lit a cheroot. He was a handsome, strong-jawed, hazel-eyed, high-colored, talkative Dutchman, dressed in a whipcord suit of eccentric tailoring, with a long, well-cut, flaring jacket that had an unusual number of pocket flaps and sleeve buttons; for a tie, he wore a pale scarf folded like a stock in some ancestral portrait of a magistrate or town councilor. It was his birthday, he announced, in a cheerful voice with the sound of a tenor horn in it, and he offered a round of schnapps: he was thirty-eight years old and had already been twice a deputy in Parliament, had a Javanese wife who was a lawyer, like himself, and three children.

While the waiter waited, the majority reached a consensus of Too-early-in-the-day. The Bishop surprised them by accepting a calvados: his doctor recommended an eye-opener for dilating the arteries and, as a matter of fact, it was his birthday too this morning. The conjunction of birthdays could not fail to be felt as significant—a favorable auspice for their journey. Cameron relented, taking a small whiskey; the Senator followed; the rest raised their coffee-cups, and a toast was drunk. "We must get you a *cake*!" Aileen said with determination. "How many candles, Bishop Gus?" Eighty-three, the old man admitted, shaking his round white head. "And one to grow on," the Reverend added, bringing a pair of tears into the Bishop's eyes, which caused the others to look away sympathetically: did he doubt, poor man, that he would live out the year?

"How old is Sapphire, I wonder?" mused the Senator, creating a welcome diversion. "In human terms, I mean." "Sapphire?" Van Vliet's cigar paused alertly in mid-air; his comprehension of English was good. It was a relief too to have someone on the mission who had an ear cocked for detail. "A cat," Miss Simmons told him. "She and Professor Lenz—the other member of our delegation—must be having breakfast in their room." "A scrumptious blue Persian," declared Miss Weil, abruptly rising. She was dressed this morning in a brown turtle-neck jersey, a long string of beads, and a skirt. They watched her cross the lobby, pick up her suede coat from on top of her suitcase, and vanish into the street.

There were six left at table—a quorum. The small dining-room was empty except for themselves. "Should the meeting come to order?" inquired Miss Simmons. "Do we have any business to transact?" The rector cleared his throat. There was the business—he hated to remind them—of Monsignor Lopez de Mayo: where was he? A long story, answered Van Vliet de Jonge, but the short of it was not to expect him. "Mohammed should be here soon. He may explain. There seems to have been a misunderstanding." The Americans nodded. "Well, I can live without a monsignor!" declared Aileen. "Can't you, Bishop? Can't you, Senator Jim?" The Senator grinned. "It's our friend the rector who feels the need. But from what I gather—excuse me, Reverend—if we poke around the cathouses in the neighborhood, we can probably raise a cardinal." Aileen gave a shriek of accord. The hotel, as they could hardly avoid noticing the night before, was on the edge of the red-light district. The only excuse that she could find, in all charity, for having been put here—stained tablecloth at breakfast, dust under the beds—was that it was convenient for getting to and from the airport, being close to Châtelet, or—as the indulgent Bishop put it—from his window, by stretching, you could see the spire of Sainte-Chapelle.

"Oh, what the heck," said Frank recklessly. "I sign off on the monsignor. We're having such a wonderful time without him. Isn't this *café au lait* great?" As he helped himself to sugar, a cloud the size of a man's hand passed across the beaming expanse of his features. He had remembered torture and illegality.

Having discovered a birthday in common, they began, as strangers do when thrown together in a novel circumstance, to seek other matching data in their life histories, like players at gin rummy seeking to fill out a run or three of a kind. Senator Carey and the Dutchman were both lawyers; in addition, they had both been at school with monks—the Senator's Benedictine and the Dutchman's Dominican—and both held elective office. The Senator was still a Catholic, but Van Vliet de Jonge had disposed of his faith back at Catholic University in Nijmegen. The Bishop and the rector and Aileen had Protestant upbringings as a *trait d'union* with Cameron, who had been Church of Scotland, in other words a Presbyterian, which led Van Vliet to dilate entertainingly on the politics of Calvinism in Holland. Sophie Weil and Lenz, had they been present, might have found that they shared the Jewish faith, though with a name like Lenz you could not tell: he might equally well have been born a Catholic or a Lutheran. Van Vliet had served with the Council of Europe in Strasbourg and knew the street where Aileen had lived as a graduate student. Strasbourg brought up the subject of storks, which reminded Van Vliet of the herons' nests in the tree-tops of his garden in a suburb of Amsterdam. Reverting to the stork, Senator Carey wondered how it had displaced the cabbage-leaf as the explanation of where babies came from: was it a German carryover? He had had a German grandfather by the name of August on his mother's side, which was Bishop Hurlbut's case as well.

The rector had been wearing a look of deepening perplexity. "Excuse me, Professor Cameron, but aren't you a lawyer too? That would make three." "A lawyer? Dear me, no." Frank persisted, sensing a semantic obstacle. "But you're a professor of jurisprudence. With us, a professor of law is a lawyer. Isn't that right, Senator?" "With us too, I believe," Cameron said. "But I'm not a professor of jurisprudence, you see."

The rector fell back in his chair. He stared despondently at the Bishop and shook his head as if it had grown too heavy. "We've been misled again, Gus." "Sorry," said Cameron, swallowing. "Awfully sorry to disappoint you if you were expecting a jurisprudence man. I can drop out if you like." Apparently they had all been eyeing the poor fellow accusingly, as if he were an impostor. "Don't think of that," hastily begged the rector. "We're all in this together." He took counsel with himself and sighed. "Maybe we should have a vote on whether to go ahead or just throw in the sponge. Which I'd certainly hate to do. But these young Iranians—let's be honest with ourselves —don't seem to have our Western conception of the truth. I won't bore you with the details, Mr. Cameron and Mr. De Jonge—well, there was a rabbi they promised us who never showed up, and now the monsignor. . . ." "And Sophie," prompted Aileen, but on getting a quizzing look from the Senator she let the Reverend continue. "The kindest interpretation we can put on it is that they've tended to take shots in the dark, and the question is, do we want to proceed with what may be, darn it, a wild goose chase."

The Bishop leaned forward. "Easy, Frankie." He turned to Cameron. "And what *are* you, then, sir? What is your field of work?" "I'm a simple historian, I'm afraid." He was the author of a textbook on Pakistan after the Raj. Problems of decolonialization were his special interest. But he had done some recent work on Iran, touching mainly on the Shah's "white revolution" and his offensive against the mullahs and the bazaar. The whiskey seemed to have finally loosened Cameron's tongue. "To be sure, I know some law. Local law, that is. The historian has to, just as he has to have some acquaintance with the languages." "You know Persian?" The rector was visibly cheering up. "New Persian. And some of the dialects, in a sketchy sort of way. I've had Indo-Iranian languages as a hobby ever since I was a laddie. And I did a stint in Afghanistan before I was called to Oxford." "So you *are* at Oxford, then," Aileen summed up, nodding her approval. "That part was right." "Oh, yes. But you mustn't think I'm a professor. With us, that implies a chair. I'm just a humble lecturer." "So what do we call you?" "Dr. Cameron, if you want to be formal. But my name is Archibald—Archie." The rector chortled. "I guess we can pardon you, Archie, if your arch-sin is not being a lawyer." "There *are* some legal niceties in what I've published," said Cameron thoughtfully. "I can see how a confusion arose." There was no further question of disbanding. "Why, he's an *expert,* Reverend," marveled Aileen. "We're so lucky to have him with us."

The getting-acquainted process went forward in the lobby, where, having paid their bills, they sat surrounded by their suitcases waiting for Van Vliet's Mohammed, who lived in some student complex in an outlying part of town. Their Air France–UTA plane left at eleven-thirty from Charles de Gaulle; had they only thought of it, they might have checked their main baggage there last night. Although some had counted on the early rising to do a little sightseeing, it was now felt to be too late for even a short stroll. At nine-thirty, they began to be anxious and to consider leaving a message for Mohammed, in case he had overslept—there was no way of checking since he had no telephone, naturally. He could follow them to the airport with Sophie, unless she reappeared soon. Lenz could be summoned from his room; he was getting dressed, the Senator testified, or had been an hour ago.

Cameron demurred. Mohammed, he pointed out, was bringing them a voucher with their hotel reservations; they had better wait. "We can dispense with that, Frank," declared the Bishop, who had commenced to pace the floor with his watch out. Old people were fidgety about departures, and Frank, who had seen it in his parishioners, was moved to reflect that the fear of missing a conveyance—a train, a bus, or Elijah's chariot —played a large part in their thoughts. Seeing the old man's eagerness to be off, the others exchanged nervous glances; he was red in the face and fuming, as if on the verge of explosion. Senator Carey intervened. "The hotel situation is tight there, Gus. My people from the Embassy were amazed last night to hear that our party had got space. The hotels are packed with munitions salesmen. Same all through the Middle East, they say." Homeopathic medicine, Van Vliet noted appreciatively: anxiety, in a small dose, applied to anxiety. And in fact the Bishop subsided, sinking into an overstuffed chair.

At nine-forty Mohammed was there, with a stiff blue folder containing the voucher, further documentation, and a list of names and addresses in Teheran. In every respect, the Americans decided, he might have been Sadegh's twin brother, except that Sadegh's folders were green. With characteristic zeal, he had a fleet of taxis ordered; the first was already outside. But there was no hurry, Mohammed said: the driver had made a mistake—they were meant to be here at ten. Meanwhile, the porter could start taking out the baggage. *"Tout le monde a son visa, j'espère."*

Aileen clapped her hand to her cheek. The others were nodding, and of course she had hers, obtained well in advance from the consulate in New York during the Christmas holidays. But Lenz, who still had not come down? And Sophie? There was no reason to be alarmed on her account; her kind of journalist (Senator Carey agreed) knew about visas. Lenz was something else, though. The visa requirement had probably not crossed his mind. And anyway where would he have got one? It would be strange if there were a consulate in Buffalo.

"You'd better ring his room, Reverend, and ask him," commanded Aileen. "And tell him to hurry. Tell him the taxi is here." There might still be time to pass by the Iranian consulate; if the Senator went along with him and used rank, a tourist visa could be issued in five minutes. *"Monsieur Asad—*

oh, pardon!—Monsieur Mohammed, où se trouve votre con-
sulat?" She might have known. It was in the Sixteenth, on the
avenue d'Iéna—back in the other direction. But assuming they
left now, and assuming there was not too much traffic, they
could allow fifteen minutes, even twenty, for the detour and
yet be at the airport by ten-forty. Once they had the visa, all
they had to do was get on the *périphérique.* How fortunate,
as it had turned out, that the taxi had come early.

"Isn't human nature strange, Bishop Gus? I don't take to
Mr. Lenz one bit—I guess none of us does really—but here I
am worrying about how we can get him his visa. When I
ought to be grateful to the hand of Providence if it's stretched
out to keep him here. You just know he's going to drink and
make trouble, Mr. Van Vliet. The best thing that could have
happened to our committee would have been to have him
overlook that little formality. Now that we have wonderful
Mr. Cameron, we don't need another Middle Eastern specialist,
who probably doesn't know ten words of the language anyway.
Utterly unreliable, that's how he is, you'll see. And yet I want
desperately to help him out of the foolish trouble he's made
for himself, don't you, Senator Carey? Is it just being American
and neighborly, do you think? I wonder if there isn't something
more universal at work. As if in these few hours we've become
an organic community, like a living body, and if one part gets
cut off, all the others feel it . . . ?"

Victor's room did not answer, the rector reported. Aileen
threw up her hands. "Where can he have got to? He's found
some low *zinc,* I'll bet anything." His key was not in his box
but of course it could be in his pocket. "Strange that I didn't see
him go out, though. In the dining-room, where I sat, I had my
eye on our bags and the door the whole time. And since then,
we've all been here in the lobby. Are you sure you rang the
right room . . . ?" She checked her watch with the clock behind the desk. "Well, if he turns up in five minutes, and sober,
he can still pass by the consulate." "But it's Sunday, my dear,"
said the Bishop gently, interposing a word.

"*Sunday!* You mean the consulate will be closed?" She

wheeled on Mohammed, forgetting in her agitation to speak French. "It's not *possible*. They *must* work Sundays at your consulate. They're Moslems." Mohammed shook his head; the office was closed. He might have mentioned that sooner instead of letting her run on. When she had wanted the consulate's address, did he suppose it was to put in her memory book? And why had none of the others seen fit to remind her that it was Sunday, since they all seemed to have known it? "We weren't privy to your thoughts," said the Senator.

In the midst of this, Sophie entered, breathless, through the revolving door, bearing a ribboned box from a pastry shop. The cake, of course. "I couldn't find candles," she explained. That was why she had been so long. But she had two votive tapers from a church in her handbag. "Did you steal them or pay?" The Senator was teasing, but she considered the question gravely, knitting up her brows—like a child, Van Vliet de Jonge thought. She had put two francs in the box and yet felt like a thief. "Quite right," said the Senator. "They're consecrated." "I know." Under her long arm was a magazine with a girl in a knitted cap on the cover: *Elle*. She offered it to Van Vliet: it had a nifty horoscope column; on the plane the birthday boys could read what the stars had to tell them. But she had chosen the wrong moment. The rector took the cake box from her and placed it out of view on a side table. "Professor Lenz has disappeared."

The second and third taxis were now at the door. It was decided that the Bishop, with Dr. Cameron and the rector, should take the first one, immediately, to the airport. The others could give Lenz five minutes more, and if he was still missing, the second taxi would take Aileen, Van Vliet, and the Senator. Sophie volunteered to remain, with Mohammed.

Contrary to what might have been assumed, the dispatch of the first group did nothing to relieve the uneasiness of those remaining. For one thing, their shrunken numbers—they were only four now, not counting Mohammed—gave them a woeful look of having been abandoned, thus bearing out, Van Vliet noted, Aileen's theory of a "community." For another, now that the Bishop was out of the way, they could speak freely. "Do you think he could be dead up there?" Aileen asked before a minute had passed. "You always read about foreigners dying in sordid Paris hotel rooms." She shot a telling glance at the dusty rubber plants and unemptied ash trays in the lobby. "His color was *awful* yesterday. Like whey, as my Mamma says. Maybe one of us should go and knock on his door." "If he's dead, how will that tell us?" said the Senator. Nevertheless, he strode across the lobby and pressed the elevator button.

"If he has gone and died and on Sunday too, what a nuisance," Aileen continued. "One of us will have to stay, that's all." "Mr. Barber is the obvious candidate, isn't he?" Sophie suggested with a small smile. Aileen's face cleared momentarily. "How true. What else can the clergy do for us but marry us and bury us? Still, would it be right to go on to Teheran without him? The Bishop certainly wouldn't want to." The Senator's deep laughing voice called out. "I don't know about Victor, but the elevator has bitten the dust."

Sophie looked at the clock. "You three had better go on. I'll wait here with Mohammed. We can send the concierge up on foot with a pass-key, just to ease our minds. When you check in, ask for a message." "Well . . ." said Aileen. "It's true, Sophie, you're not one of the committee." After a moment's wavering, she followed Van Vliet and the Senator through the revolving door, reappearing promptly on the next rotation. "I have an idea. In case he still turns up. Will they maybe give him a visa at the airport in Teheran? Ask Mohammed what he thinks. A friend of mine once . . ."

The question was rendered moot by the appearance of Lenz from the carpeted staircase. He had been stuck between floors in the elevator, and a chambermaid had let him out. He was carrying the cat-container, and the maid followed with his baggage. And he had his visa. He showed it to them, folded into his passport, seeming surprised but not offended at the general stupefaction. He could not know (Van Vliet reflected, pondering the gravity-defying power of ideas to stand unsupported by evidence) that his co-nationals had been fully persuaded that he was visa-less and half-persuaded that he was dead.

Till now, it had not occurred to any of them to ask whether the cat needed papers. "Well, I'm not going to worry about that detail," said Aileen, seating herself in the taxi between Van Vliet and the Senator, then turning around to peer out the back window to make sure the others got off. As the third taxi began to move, a clerk came running out of the hotel and signaled to the driver to stop. Lenz had forgotten to pay his bill, naturally. Aileen called to their own driver to stop too. Lenz had dismounted and seemed to be arguing with the clerk about the bill, angrily indicating some item with his forefinger. "They're trying to charge him for Sappho," estimated the Senator. In the third taxi, where Sophie was waiting, a large dog had sat up in the front seat beside the driver, contributing his bark to the affray while his owner held him back. He must be trying to leap over the seat at the caged cat in the rear. "Do you say it's raining cats and dogs?" asked the Dutchman. "Or dogs and cats?" Aileen screamed. "Let's go. I can't stand it. I'm a wreck. Look! Now he's going to wait for his change." Lenz was still on the sidewalk, the dog was still barking and growling, and a fourth taxi was pulling up, when Aileen and the two men drove off.

Nevertheless, the entire party reached the airport with a few minutes to spare. Alighting from the moving belt, Van Vliet and Aileen found the Bishop and the rector in the departure satellite talking with two ladies wearing mink coats and an old powdered man in a wide-brimmed black hat whom Aileen gaily greeted as "Mr. Charles." Cameron was on the level below exploring the duty-free shops, where Lenz had stopped off too. Mohammed had been said good-bye to at the check-in counter, having earned a merit badge by remembering the cake and going back to fetch it in a fifth taxi, for which Sophie had succeeded in reimbursing him. At the head of the moving staircase, the Senator was surrounded by young admirers bound for Moscow, whom he had introduced to Sophie; a joint autographing session was in progress. Everyone was present or accounted for.

Yet Van Vliet, studying the scene from a solitary banquette where Aileen had left him, felt puzzled, like a new boy in class observing a network of relationships to which he has no clue. The old gloved party leaning on an ivory-headed stick and the mink-draped ladies—could they possibly be members of a committee of inquiry? The briefings given by the Iranian youths had left many questions unanswered. He had sensed a possible mystery in the group's financing; although he was paying his own way, he was entitled as a lawyer to wonder whether outside funds were not being supplied. Could the expensive-looking trio be what the Americans called "angels"? Van Vliet did not like it. He signaled to Aileen, who detached herself and came hurrying to his side. "Those people—are they with us too?" She laughed and patted his arm. "After this morning, you can believe anything, can't you?" But he was not to worry; they were just millionaire art collectors—part of a tour—on their way to visit archaeological sites in Iran. There was no connection, except that "Mr. Charles" was an old friend of the Bishop's. "You wouldn't guess he was an American, would you?"

Van Vliet would not have. His visual ideas about Americans were derived mainly from the movies. Though he knew England and the English well, he had not met many live Americans before this morning. He discounted the NATO generals he had shaken hands with while inspecting maneuvers; the military, like the armies of tourists who came to view the tulips, offered an unreliable index to a country's national character. In the taxi he had confessed his ignorance. Senator Carey of course was familiar to him from Dutch television as a leading dove in the Senate and he was a type, like Adlai Stevenson in the previous generation, that Europeans thought they understood. But the rest of the American delegation were novelties to a Dutchman, he admitted. If the pastor brought back memories of Harold Lloyd in *The Freshman*, no contemporary analogy for him in movieland presented itself. And there were no Old World equivalents that Van Vliet could find for these curious American liberals. The exception was the young woman, the journalist, whom he felt he knew. "Our Sophie!" Aileen cried. "Why, she's the 'new journalism'—the latest American thing." "We have many of her in Holland, believe me," Van Vliet assured her. "Dozens of Sophies, dear me!" She gave a sharp tinkle of a laugh. "Then we don't have to warn you that she'll be making all of us characters in the piece she's writing."

Van Vliet nodded; he had taken account of that prospect at breakfast. "Well, of course, you're a political man. But the sweet old Bishop and the rector don't seem to have grasped the implications at all." "What implications?" Van Vliet said blandly. "Why, of having her along with us. They can be *devastating.*" The Senator threw back his silver head and laughed, savoring his amusement as if it were a rich morsel of private food for thought. "You're used to 'exposure,' Senator," Aileen insisted. "But it's hurting, for the rest of us, to see our little foibles and mannerisms *faithfully* reproduced on the printed page. Like all our 'new' journalists, Mr. Van Vliet, Sophie Weil has a phonographic ear. That's the way they're trained nowadays. I don't mean it against her personally. Just to give you an example, there was a young man from one of the news magazines who spent five days on our campus. I had him to breakfast and dinner and I don't know what all. Then I found spread out in the magazine word for word all these things I'd told him, the way you would a friend, about myself and the problems we had at Lucy Skinner. I know he didn't see anything wrong in what he did. He *liked* me, I could tell. Of course my press man wrote a letter. But there are things you can't reply to. Like comparing my voice to Martha Mitchell's. She's from my home state, Mr. Van Vliet: Pine Bluffs, Arkansas. But they talk differently over there. And such a cruel description of my appearance: 'a sprightly weight-watcher' with 'an incipient double chin.' " She arched her neck. "Well, if you're used to that in Holland, you'll survive. We all will, of course. What I really fear is that more space will be given to us and our squabbles and divisions than to those poor torture victims." "I think we're kind of dull," said the Senator, perversely offering a ray of hope. "Unless the Reverend gets oecumenical with those Mohammedans, we're not likely to provide much copy."

"Why does he laugh so much, that long fellow?" Van Vliet inquired. "We Americans are great laughers," said the Senator. "You mean 'tall,' not 'long,'" corrected Aileen. That was a common Dutch mistake, which Van Vliet went on making, though he had been patiently set right by dozens, perhaps hundreds, of native English-speakers. His retort was to give the two a lesson in how to pronounce his surname in the correct, Dutch way. "'Fan Fleet,'" essayed the Senator. "Sounds like a name for a strip dancer." Van Vliet surprised them by catching the allusion. He was aware of Fanne Foxe. "In Amsterdam we read the *Herald Tribune*." "Does that 'van' mean you're noble?" Aileen wanted to know. The "van" in Holland, he had to explain, as so often to English people (the French and Spanish never asked), was not like the German "von." It was not a *particule de noblesse*. And "de Jonge"? No, that did not prove blue blood either; there were lots of "de Jonge"s tacked onto ordinary Dutch surnames. "Not even gentry," summed up Aileen in a regretful tone. "Sorry. I'm a commoner." "Well, aren't we all, Senator?" she sighed, making the best of it.

His Christian name, he told them, was Henk. "Oh, I like that!" she cried. "Is it short for Hendrik?" It had been once, but now it was a regular given name. "Like Harry with us," said the Senator. "They nearly named me that till one of the relatives thought of 'hari-kari.'" "What were your people, Senator Jim?" "Farmers." "But they must have been well-to-do if they sent you to a monastery to study. How long were you there?" "Four years of high school. Then I went to the seminary." He winked at Henk. "Your turn." To Van Vliet's amusement, the persistent little woman obediently turned his way. "And you, Mr. Van Vliet, do you come from a long line of lawyers?" "My father was a judge." The Senator's terse style was catching. But he lacked the heart to hold back something half the Nether-

72

lands could tell her: his paternal grandfather (1865–1935), also a magistrate, had been the author of fifty-seven popular novels—Adriaan Van Vliet de Jonge, once a household word. "Oh. Are they translated?" "Into German, two or three. We Dutch have a hermetic literature."

"But you're a poet yourself," interposed the Senator. Van Vliet was impressed. First-rate staff work, he conjectured with envy; it was never like that in The Hague. Aileen was excited. "You mean a *known* poet?" "Two impressive volumes of verse," said the Senator. "Nearly cost you your seat in Parliament." "How did you find all that out?" exclaimed Aileen, evidently envious too. The lazy-voiced man smiled. "You forget there's a Dutch Embassy in Washington. The ambassador is a friend of mine, as it happens." Aileen seized both men's arms. "The Senator writes poetry too! I know I read that somewhere. But he calls himself a 'Sunday poet,' so he doesn't publish. Another tie between you two. You mustn't laugh. Something like that—bonding—can be vital in situations of stress."

Van Vliet looked at her with greater attention. Bright wary eyes, sharp nose, soft chin—a little hawk's face. He had been taking her chatter as no more than a bad habit or a screen to mask pervasive anxiety—she was single ("Miss") and getting on. But her last words and her grip on their arms suggested that the little predator was feeling a specific alarm. Did she imagine the Shah was going to jail her? Van Vliet smiled at the innocence—or, rather, ignorance—of such a foreboding, which he could easily dispel.

None of the Americans, he gathered—except their most junior, Miss Weil—had ever taken part in an enterprise of this kind. Europeans were more used to putting their noses into the affairs of foreign police states. Before he went to Parliament, he had worked with Amnesty and sat in on trials in Spain; in Bolivia he had taken depositions from terrorized witnesses and their families. More recently, when the Dutch had raised the question of the Greek colonels in the Council of Europe, he and a Socialist deputy had been empowered by their parties to fly to Athens and try to substantiate the stories of torture and murder in the regime's prisons and penal colonies. To say it in all modesty, their mission had been rather successful: if the colonels had not fallen as a direct result, their government at least had been censured by the Council for violation of human rights as specified in the charter. A small victory, typically Dutch-sized and won by Dutch perseverance. More relevantly, neither he nor his fellow-deputy had been molested by the colonels' police. They had been obstructed but not harassed, and he did not think they had owed their immunity to their status as members of Parliament of a NATO country.

The worst this group could expect would be that they would be followed. Or that at midnight, when they arrived, they would find that their hotel reservations had vanished without a trace. Van Vliet did not share Cameron's faith in Mohammed's voucher. He assumed that the young man's organization would have been infiltrated by Parisian agents of SAVAK, who would have informed Teheran of the committee's make-up and intentions in the fullest possible detail. Unless (he reflected) poor Mohammed's network was largely imaginary, which would not be promising for the hotel voucher either.

Van Vliet was not an apprehensive subject; he had his portion of the national phlegm. Accommodations, he felt sure, would be found, one way or another, if necessary through the pastor's church or the Senator's connections with the Embassy—the Dutchmen of the Queen's Embassy would have been long since abed. Yet SAVAK engaged his interest; his imagination, though a tranquil organ, was active. Riding beside Aileen on the escalator and again on the long moving belt like a flattened *montagne suisse* bearing them up to the departure satellite, he had taken note of two dark men—one mustached—who seemed to be sticking too close for comfort and who were speaking a language that might well be Iranian. Then he had reined in his fancy: a plane going to Teheran would naturally have Iranians aboard. In any case, he did not mind being watched by secret policemen, who were easily shaken off when a real need arose; during dull moments in unfree countries, he had been able to amuse himself by picking them out in a courtroom or in a crowded café.

He did not invite Aileen to join him in that pastime as they sat together waiting for the boarding announcement. He was sympathetic to women and their gift for worry, which was curiously random in its objects, he had found in his legal practice. Perhaps the idea that the dread SAVAK could possess ubiquity had not crossed her mind. He would have liked, as a matter of fact, to have a look at his horoscope while they waited—*Elle*'s astrologer was an amazing fellow, often cited by his wife after a session at the hairdresser's. But considering his present companion, he overcame the impulse to take the magazine from his briefcase. She would be bound to read over his shoulder and, not content with Capricorn, leap ahead to her own sign—a risky procedure for one on the brink of a momentous undertaking and as susceptible as she. Van Vliet sighed. On his birthday, he should have the right to consult with the augurs while the day was still young, but chivalry, he supposed, was enjoined on him.

Besides, he had taken a liking to Aileen and he now followed her willingly when, on the pretext of locating an ash tray, she set out on her own job of espionage, stalking the first-class passengers who had cornered the two clerics. "I have an idea those women are former parishioners of the Rev's." Waving her cigarette as a *laisser-passer*, she drew Van Vliet forward, bobbing in and out of the small crowd, till they had reached a listening-post. "Did you hear that? 'Reverend Mr. Barber.' Not 'Reverend Barber,' 'Reverend *Mr.* Barber.' It's one of the clues those social people drop to let the rest of us know who they are." Her confederate showed puzzlement; there was some drama afoot, evidently, that he was failing to appreciate.

Aileen elucidated. St. Matthew's was a fashionable New York church, right on the edge of a slum, naturally. "And Reverend Barber is a fashionable preacher?" Henk re-examined the "long" dominie with the happy protruding ears and twisted bow tie and concluded that fashion in America must have to wear a democratic disguise. "Well, he *was*," said Aileen. "He got to be *too* fashionable, intellectually, for his Gracie Square flock. He invited a black revolutionary to preach from his pulpit one Sunday, and his front pews left him in a body and went over to St. James's, on Madison Avenue. These are some of the front pews, I'll bet." Van Vliet felt suddenly bored. In Holland, he told her, such "happenings" in churches were commonplace, only there it was the Catholics, following *aggiornamento,* who staged trendy masses, with guitars and rock music and student hippies and schismatic Marxists mounting to the pulpit to sermonize. "They have ships' biscuits"—he stifled a yawn—"that they pass in a basket for communion and a chalice of wine that goes from hand to hand. There's a movement to make it a beer tankard—in Holland, why not?" She nodded. "Sort of love feasts. We have that too. But this black revolutionary at St. Matthew's demanded reparations from the churches. It was all in the papers. Millions of dollars, just like war reparations. Do you have that in Holland?" Before Van Vliet could answer, she had made a silencing gesture. "*Au revoir,* dear impetuous Mr. Barber. We shall look for you in Naqsh-i-Rustan. So nice to find you again, and in mufti, after all these years." " 'Mufti'!" snorted Aileen, as the woman moved off at an unhurried pace. "You see, I was right." Van Vliet did not understand her interest in following this encounter, nor indeed where her true sympathies lay. He would have liked, though, to know whether the Reverend's church had paid reparations and, if so, how many guilders. But the plane was boarding.

It was a 747 this time and less than half full. They would be able to stretch out, after lunch had been served, and sleep or meditate till quarter of five, local time, when they were supposed to arrive in Tel Aviv—their only stop. They had agreed to sit together in the well-named (said the Senator) Salon Rouge, the middle cabin of Economy, where smoking was permitted. That little sacrifice on the part of the non-smokers would enable the group to visit back and forth without disturbing other passengers, and yet each would have a bank of two or three seats to himself. When nap-time came, the Bishop and he could lie head to head, the Reverend pointed out, all a-marvel at the discovery. He had never ridden in a jumbo jet before. Lenz, of course, was the non-conformist. Where the others were spread out within conversational range through the center portion of the cabin, he had elected to be up front beside the movie screen, and found himself next to an Israeli couple with a baby in a swinging bassinet-thing that the hostess fitted into place—an arrangement that was not going to suit Sapphire, he objected, appearing suddenly in the aisle in his long flapping overcoat when he ought to have been strapped into his seat belt.

His cat, he said, was sensitive to noise, and what was an infant doing in a section reserved for smokers? "Isn't that the parents' business?" a voice behind him demanded, and for a moment, as Lenz swung around, it looked as if there might be an incident. He was persuaded to return to his place by the steward's promise that after take-off he and the cat could move. But he had to be near a door, he stipulated, pausing on his way. "Near a door?" "Because of my claustrophobia." Someone tittered. "You can go into the Salon Jaune, sir," calmly said the steward, indicating two seats by an exit door in the front of the cabin behind. That suggestion did not please Lenz either: too close to the serving-pantry, and Sapphire was sensitive to cooking smells. "Well, sir, I cannot help you then. We cannot ask that family to move. They have reserve that place. It is near the toilets. And anyway, sir, they go only as far as Tel Aviv." "Go back and sit down, Victor," called the Senator. "We want to take off."

Ahead, the young orthodox couple (cute as two pins, it was decided; the husband wore a beard in ringlets and a black hat) seemed impervious, luckily, to the controversy; the bassinet placidly rocked. "You must excuse our friend," the Reverend told the steward, when Victor was finally out of earshot. "Do you have this type of problem often?" "Very often, sir. Especially with gentlemen. They do not wish to sit near a baby." The Bishop nodded. " 'Suffer the little children.' We humans are funny animals, aren't we? Why, bless me, if the plane had been full, our Victor would be feeling no call to be choosy.

But with all these empty seats to pick from, he'll never find one that suits him. There's a moral there, surely." "Explicate that, Gus," begged the Reverend, but the old man's rumbling tones were lost like the Sibyl's utterance in the sudden roar of the engines.

When the No Smoking sign went off, Van Vliet lit a Batavia twist. With a careful turn of his head, he established that the two dark men he had wondered about were directly behind him, on the aisle. After a moment's reflection, he unfastened his seat belt and moved across to join Aileen. If he did not join her, he considered, she was likely to come over to him—an invitation to eavesdroppers if there ever was one. In the middle bank of seats, the Senator, just ahead of her, had already stretched out, in his shirt sleeves, with his arms folded behind his head on two pillows and did not look ready for company. Cameron, a difficult conversationalist, was puffing on his pipe by a window on the Senator's left. The Bishop and the Reverend, in front of the Senator, were minding the Lord's store, reciting the service for the day—the first Sunday after Epiphany —with the Bishop taking the responses. Van Vliet recognized the Anglican rite, which the Americans called Episcopalian. The droning of voices took him back to his school days with the monks in Brabant.

In choosing Aileen, Van Vliet was obeying his good angel. While the plane was gaining altitude, he had made up his mind to pair off with President Simmons, since there was bound to be pairing in a group of this kind. He did not enjoy being unfaithful to his wife, but it happened on trips if he did not take precautions. The Weil girl—actually a woman; he estimated her age at thirty-four—was the occasion of sin to be avoided. His aversion to bright young women journalists (one of the Dutch lot had pursued him from Schiphol to Athens, with the full backing of her editor, at that time, but no longer, his friend) might fail him, he feared, in her case. She had a tense, brave way of talking, in short, breathless spurts, and an arresting face, like a Byzantine icon—Cameron had produced the comparison this morning, watching her come in with the cake. At present, she was sitting alone, in the row ahead of Cameron, by the window. As he stood up to take the lay of the land, he had picked out the curly black head leaning against the seat back's bright red antimacassar. She put up a hand to cover a yawn, and he admired the long spatulate fingers and the stretch of the long olive neck.

He set his jaw. If he left her alone, she would gravitate to the Senator or vice versa. The lines of force were predictable in these situations. He was vain of being a good-looking, well-set-up male and did not envy the American his two meters—a tall Dutchman was a gross error of Nature. In age he had the advantage of fifteen to twenty years. In mother-wit, they were about equal, he reckoned, and he suspected he was a truer poet. But in power—irresistible to some women—the leader of a minority fraction in Her Majesty's Staten-generaal was Thumbling by comparison, which would make a contest interesting to the permanent spectator in himself. He pushed away the thought: the challenge to his virility represented by a formidable U.S. lawmaker was temptation in its most infantile form. Besides, he had no doubt as to who would win; as in a fairy-tale, he had only to wish it.

He heard the rector beginning on the lesson for the day. "I beseech you, therefore, brethren, by the mercies of God, that ye present your bodies a living sacrifice. . . . And be not conformed to this world, but be ye transformed by the renewing of your mind." The shoe seemed to fit. Making a wry face, Henk crossed the aisle like a Rubicon and left the field to Carey. The die was cast. Aileen would help divert him from the other while posing no danger herself. On that score, as a male, he felt confidence. He had no sexual interest (it was cruel, but he could not help it) in women who had passed the age of child-bearing—which no doubt made him a "sexist," as somebody like Sophie, if he bedded her, would be quick to tell him.

Aileen looked up with a smile. "Mynheer Van Vliet! So you've come to talk to me!" She snatched up the long scarf she had unwound from her coppery hair and patted the seat beside her. On her lap was an archaeological guide to Persia, which the Bishop had passed back to her. " 'I'm too old, my dear, for ancient history, and we have other work to do in that unfertile soil.' That was his presentation speech. Isn't he dear?" Van Vliet took up the book, which was the property, it seemed, of "Mr. Charles." On second thought, he set it aside and went to retrieve his briefcase, reminded of the blue folder he had put in it with the list of names and addresses in Teheran. He could not leave that lying about. It occurred to him, moreover, that in view of a possible search at the airport, he would do well to commit the contents to memory and flush it down a toilet in Tel Aviv. There was also *Elle* with the horoscope, which he ought to consult soon, if only to repay Sophie for her trouble. "Oh, dear, do we have to *work?*" Aileen lamented on seeing the briefcase. He made a silencing motion. He had heard Dutch being spoken.

Behind Aileen were a tow-headed young man and woman. He directed her attention to them. "Dutch!" he whispered. Aileen turned around. "What about it?" Van Vliet drew a hand across his eyes. No foreigner would understand. It always struck him as droll, almost uncanny, to find Dutch people outside of Holland, where they properly belonged—as though they were toy people who had stepped out of the tiny see-through box they lived in with their Queen and their princesses and Prince Bernhard and Klaus and the tulips. In a poem he had tried to express the idea of Holland as an imaginary country, invented by a travel author or satirist-turned-children's-storyteller, in which he himself, poor Henk, was fated to be born and sit in a scale-model parliament and write despairing verses which nobody but another Dutchman could pronounce or understand. Being Dutch was a comical predicament, more grotesque even than being Swiss. *They* had watches and weather clocks and cheese with absurd holes, in the place of dikes and windmills and outlandish pipes, but at least they had Alps as a trademark instead of a flat country like the medieval picture of the world, which had not had scientific credibility since Columbus and the navigators.

No rational mind in this century could believe in Holland as a real place—where but in animal farmland could the Prime Minister be a Mr. Owl?—and finding Dutch people outside, in the real world, was a threat to any Dutchman's sanity. Besides, on practical as well as ontological grounds, Van Vliet did not care to be picked out like a straw from a heap by unknown sharp-eyed compatriots who had the advantage of knowing *him*. "Van Vliet de Jonge! Did you see him?" the pair behind him would be telling each other. In a small country like Holland, where the main verticals were television aerials, it was too easy to be a celebrity. As leader of a new, left-of-center grouping, he was unavoidable in most living-rooms, including his own. Behind the famous uncurtained window panes, as he drove home in the black night, he met himself seriatim in brilliant Philips color, a gesturing household dummy, framed in the box. In his real body, he could not stop at a gin shop for a glass of genever or eat a herring from a street stall without causing a mild stir of recognition. In the extended family of the Netherlands, with its characteristic long memory, that was only to be expected; before he had been the deputy, he had been the scion of his father and his grandfather.

But abroad he was nobody, which was also to be expected. A few years ago, a Dutch company had taken a poll in France and Britain and found to its own surprise that the vast majority of newspaper readers could not identify the Prime Minister of Holland, the aforesaid Mr. Owl's predecessor. Tested on other figures, older people remembered Queen Wilhelmina and, if politically conscious, Spaak—a Belgian. To be somebody and yet nobody was a typical Dutch irony, which Van Vliet when abroad preferred to relish alone and unrecognized over a dish of tripe or an *andouillette* in a bistro, pondering the sayings "a fish out of water" and "a big fish in a small pond," with a melancholy flare, typically Dutch also, of the long nostrils, in his case, by luck, finely cut.

He had studied the Netherlands countenance and its register of expressions like Narcissus staring into a pool and decided that that widening of the nostrils, amounting to a sniff often in women, expressed a deep humor, in both senses, of the national soul but probably could be traced—half of him was a materialist—to the once widespread habit of snuff-taking and to the watery atmosphere that had been irritating the sinuses for centuries. You would not find it in Germans, even those nearby ones of the Rhineland. The nose and nasal passages were the seat of Dutch mental life, and the slow peristaltic intake of the nose-holes, as of a pensive digestive tract, had doubtless been a factor in developing the cheerful horn-blare of the Dutch voice, distinct from German gutturals, rasped from the throat, just as the Dutch language was distinct from German and not, as some fools insisted, a humble country cousin on the order of *Schwyzer-dütsch.*

Being Dutch, he sadly recognized, was turning into a fixed idea with him, to which each and every experience seemed to be referring maniacally, and like any poor madman sensing himself pursued, he could not hope to find comprehension in foreigners. He heard Dutch voices over his shouder, and "What about it?" this woman said, without sympathy. The Senator, for his part, on hearing American spoken behind him, would reach for his Parker or his Waterman—no complexes there; he was used to finding a *landgenoot* under every bush. Americans had the snugger delusion of taking their country for the world.

Now she was quizzing him about the "Dutch elm disease"— some kind of tree plague, he gathered, widespread in England and America but utterly unknown in Holland, which of course she did not believe. "I'm sure it started in Holland. All your lovely elms. Our campus has been *decimated.*" With a commiserating glance at the expressionless young people behind him, for whom English must be a second language, he abruptly disengaged himself and took a turn in the aisle to regain his equability. He would never convince her that tall healthy specimens of *ulmus campestris* extended their branches a few meters from his house; she would tell him they were oaks. But she was only trying to show a friendly interest in his country and could not know that to a Dutchman it was irritating to be lumped with tree beetles, "Dutch treats," "Dutch uncles," wooden shoes, the royal family, bicycle-pedaling ("Is it true that you've all taken to your bicycles to solve the energy crisis?" "No"), and so on. On meeting a French parliamentarian, would she be reminded of frogs' legs and "French letters"?

He put his nose into the rear cabin and noted the sparsity of passengers: uneconomic for Air France, he would have thought, to keep these big planes flying during the off-season. In the pantry, he watched the hostesses preparing the drinks cart. Continuing his tour of inspection, he drifted forward to the toilets. Lenz had made his peace with the Jewish baby and was entertaining it with Sapphire's mouse. All seemed to be well. On his return, he found that Aileen had profited from his absence to move next to the Senator, now sitting upright and reknotting his tie. Sophie was absorbed in the *Monde*. He took a seat next to Cameron, who declared himself ready for a whiskey. As they waited for the cart with its freight of bottles to be wheeled up the aisle, conversation was laborious. Van Vliet regretted the loss of Aileen. He tried Scottish separatism—there were interesting parallels with Holland's Frisian minority problem—the don puffed and nodded. He mentioned a talk he had given to the Oxford Union on Surinam independence; Cameron was sorry to have missed it. "My line of country, you know." There was a long pause; he drew on his pipe, evidently expecting his companion to continue unassisted. But Van Vliet's natural volubility was failing him; this was Sisyphean work. "You were saying?" prompted Cameron. Van Vliet raised a finger. He thought he had heard a scream come from the service area.

"Oh, drat that cat!" Aileen exclaimed from the bank of seats opposite. "Those poor stewardesses! He's gone and let her out again." Cameron stiffened. "What? What? Oh, the cat; I see." The Bishop leaned back. "We had quite a saga coming over. Professor Lenz allowed his pet out of its cage. They hate the confinement, don't you know. But she led us a merry chase.

Up and down the aisle and under the seats before they could locate her. You never saw such a to-do. And now history repeats itself. Well, we must bear with Clio, an old lady with one foot in the grave, eh, Dr. Cameron?"

A hostess went forward with a determined step, ignoring the passengers' questions. "She's gone to complain to the pilot," Aileen announced. "The pilot yesterday was furious. You'd think that man would have more consideration. He's only making it harder for other people to bring their cats into the cabin with them. Most airlines make them travel in the hold. But just because Air France is nice enough to let them ride with their owner, he abuses the privilege. And now the rest of us have to wait for our drinks till they catch that pesky animal." Understanding that a cat was at large, other passengers in the vicinity were stirring, to peer circumspectly under the seats, but no one was taking action. Lenz, up front, seemed to be sitting tight. "Why doesn't he *do* something?" Aileen cried. "And where have those hostesses got to?" With a small screech, she pulled up her legs. "She's under here somewhere, I know it. Didn't you feel her slip by then, Senator?" The Senator shook his head. Aileen examined a violet stocking for damage. "Isn't anybody going to try to catch her?" she demanded. "Are we all afraid of a cat? I know I am. Did you see those claws yesterday? I don't want her jumping in *my* lap." "Here, kitty, kitty," coaxed the Reverend obediently, patting his own lap. "Here, pretty puss." There was no response. "I don't see her," he apologized. "Old Victor ought to bell her," comfortably remarked the Senator, declining to be enlisted in a chase.

Van Vliet and Cameron chuckled. They had seen neither hide nor hair of a blue Persian but were agreeable to the consensus that one was prowling about; indeed, Van Vliet could almost have sworn that a minute ago he had felt something furry brush past his trouser leg. "She's holed up somewhere, I'll be bound," said the Bishop. "Wonderful how they can make themselves small when they want to. My Rachel had a Maltese, couldn't abide the sound of a vacuum cleaner—" "Yesterday Sophie found her," Aileen interrupted. "Sophie! *You* look! Please!"

The urgency in her voice surprised Van Vliet, yet he mentally seconded the motion. The pantry area was hidden from view by a partition, but his ears told him that activity back there had been suspended. Aileen had been right: for some nonsensical reason, no drinks were going to be served while the state of emergency lasted. And he had been looking forward to a glass.

Ahead of him, Sophie slowly unfastened her seat belt, set down the paper she had been reading, and, half bent over, her narrow shoulders hunched, went creeping along the aisle. "You! Back in your seat!" a male voice shouted, in a harsh, heavy accent. Van Vliet's head turned with a jerk. At the rear of the cabin stood the pair of dark men who had been sitting behind him. The shorter and plumper had a submachine gun which he was aiming on a long diagonal in Sophie's direction; the taller, with the mustache, had two grenades slung from his belt. Behind them peered two hostesses. They were being hijacked.

Sophie's head came up. "Me?" Her bang and forehead appeared, followed by her wondering eyes. Then she must have seen the gun. Ducking for cover, she moved up the aisle, hitching along like a centipede, while the gun kept pace with her. A strangled voice inside Van Vliet pleaded with her to hurry: as in a nightmare or at a film, he could only watch—no sound came from his throat, merely a series of swallows. Across the aisle from him, Aileen had her hands to her ears, and her eyes were closed. It occurred to Van Vliet too late, when the poor girl had edged back into her place and was tremulously refastening her seat belt—a strange security measure, surely, to take under the circumstances—that he might have interposed his own body between her and the gun barrel. The realization shook him till a defense lawyer broke in to argue that flinging himself on top of her as she passed would only have succeeded in pinning them both to the floor.

Nevertheless, that he had failed to have the thought was somewhat humiliating. A sense of slight disappointment in himself merged with a sense of disappointment in the whole event. The hijacker, seeming satisfied, had lowered his gun, and the captain's voice came soothingly over the loud-speaker: passengers were to remain seated until further instructions; if every-one stayed quiet and obeyed orders, no one would be hurt. On behalf of himself and the crew, he apologized for the incon-venience. Van Vliet smiled to himself at the inadequacy of this formula, yet as he analyzed his reactions, it seemed to him that Air France had found the *mot juste*. He was conscious chiefly of irritation, as at an untoward interruption, such as might be produced by a power failure or a tiresome visitor. The irrup-tion of these men and their weapons was bound to be time-consuming, and as a busy person he already felt robbed of precious hours, which might turn into days.

He was also mystified, which added to his vexation. His in-stincts had been warning him that their committee might be followed, in fact accompanied, by the Shah's spies—nothing could be more normal. And the event was busy proving him right, so that in some childish way he was pleased. Yet why this farce of a take-over? Perhaps he was still in shock, and his mind was not working well, but to him it made no sense. If SAVAK's aim was to frighten off the committee, they ought to have waited till Teheran, where with no danger or "inconvenience" to the rest of the passengers he and his companions could be seized and loaded at gun-point onto an outgoing plane. Then, like one coming out of anesthesia, he remembered the Tel Aviv stop. Palestinians, not Iranians? The thought, dawning as a mere notion, brought him sharply to attention. He raised himself slightly in his seat and out of the corner of his eye he took fresh stock of the gunner, who had moved to the center of the cabin.

Beside him, Cameron spoke up. "Rather a bore, this, don't you find? One reads about these bloody things but one doesn't expect them to happen to oneself." Van Vliet concurred. "Pales-tinians, do you think?" Cameron supposed so. "One can't be sure of course till one hears them speak in their own language. Do you know any Arabic?" "No." "Pity. Neither do I but I can recognize the phonemes—the noises they make, you know." Van Vliet wondered why it was a pity. "You mean we might learn what they have in mind? But are they likely to talk much in front of us?" "No," patiently said Cameron, "I was thinking that if we knew their language, we could open a dialogue with them." The idea of Cameron's opening a dialogue with anyone should have been funny, but Van Vliet, from the depths of his ignorance, was prepared to be respectful. "No chance that they might be Iranians?" Cameron turned his head. "Hardly. Your Iranian's facial features and skin color set him off from the Arabs. Although there's some Semitic admixture in the southeast. Anyhow, the Shah's opposition doesn't go in for hijacking. Rather indolent chaps, on the whole."

Van Vliet felt relieved that at least he had not voiced his conviction that SAVAK must be at the bottom of this—absurd of him to have held to it with such stubbornness, when other, less egocentric, explanations lay so ready to hand. And he supposed he ought to be grateful to the hijackers for having furnished Cameron, finally, with a congenial subject. No doubt, like so many British academics, he was a reader of thrillers and detective fiction. In a cautious undertone, he speculated on the provenance of the weapons: the gun, he decided, was an American make, and gun and grenades must have been introduced into the cabin—into a lavatory, most likely—through collusion with the cleaning staff. "Mostly North Africans here, as you know, like the dustmen." He tapped out his pipe. "Where do I think they're taking us?" He spread out the book of flight maps provided in the pocket of the seat ahead, and his pipestem silently indicated the possibilities: the Libyan desert, Aden, the Syrian desert, Oman. "Depends on whether they've received training in terrorism and are executing a mission in complicity with their sponsors. If they're an As-Saiqa commando squad, for instance, they got their guerrilla training in Syria, and Syria will have to accept them. If they trained in Libya, we can expect a welcoming committee of Khaddafi's people."

In any case, on landing, the pilot would be handed the usual list of demands. "Release of their comrades from Israeli prisons, indemnities, the lot. If our two friends are linked with a serious guerrilla network, we can count on some rough moments." His burry voice dropped still another register. Van Vliet could barely hear him over the hum of the engines. His ear caught the words "brutes" and "hostages," and his gaze followed Cameron's, which was directed meaningfully toward their right. "The Senator?" Cameron nodded, with an air of satisfaction, like one who has brought a seminar to a triumphant conclusion.

Van Vliet frowned: that implied that the hijackers knew that the Senator would be on the plane. Perfectly possible, Cameron declared. On the other hand, the selection of this particular flight might have been fortuitous. "These bully-boys, like as not, are acting on their own and don't have the foggiest notion of how to proceed next. Palestinian hotheads deciding to do their wee bit in harassing air traffic to Israel while lining their own pockets. On that assumption, they boarded the first plane for Tel Aviv that their confederates—or confederate—could smuggle arms into. Sunday being Sunday, most of the regular cleaning staff would be having a lie-in this morning, leaving the coast clear. If what we have here is a nasty pair of free lances, the passenger list is of no interest to them. We're a parcel, to be turned over with the plane on delivery of x thousand pounds."

Weighing this second hypothesis, Van Vliet grew more cheerful. Far better to be in the hands of men directed by the profit-motive than in those of idealistic terrorists. He re-examined the machine-gunner, a short, fattish, gloomy young fellow who looked, in fact, more like a clerk or the policeman Van Vliet had first taken him for than like the gaunt Palestinian extremists whose photos appeared from time to time in the press. It seemed encouraging also that there were only two. Guerrillas taking over a giant plane would be more numerous, he reasoned. Ransacking his memory for precedents, he regretted that he had not paid closer attention to the hijacking phenomenon before meeting it in person. He had indistinct but unreassuring recollections of captive planes zigzagging about in the sky at the direction of a lone gunman seeking a host country that would promise him and his booty asylum. There had been an occasion in America when the hijacker had simply bailed out with his packets of dollars and taken to the woods. But that, if memory served, had been mountain country. He doubted that such a solution would be feasible in Arabia Deserta with its parching sands.

Having stated the problem, Cameron lit a second pipe and disappeared, like a deity, in a cloud of smoke. The machine-gunner, as though restless or bored with his assignment, strolled forward, picking up an illustrated magazine from one of the seats as he went. He stood at the front entry with the magazine in his left hand, leafing through the pages and raising his eyes occasionally. The grenade-carrier was no longer to be seen. Then, as if the plane had re-entered the everyday world, the hostesses appeared with menus and the drinks cart. "Are they on the house?" jested the Senator. His deep easy voice, breaking into the general hush, caused a movement of disapproval, as though he had committed an act of irreverence in church. "I can't tell you, sir," said the girl. "Would you like me to ask the steward?" "Never mind. Just give me a split of that champagne." He laid a hand on his neighbor's. "What would you like, Aileen?" When his turn came, Van Vliet took a single whiskey. But others were asking for doubles, pointing in dumb show at the miniature bottles of spirits; the Senator's awful daring had evidently made them tremble lest any convivial noise coming from them be interpreted as disrespect. Cameron, bolder, raised his whiskey glass. "Well, Dutch courage, eh?"

Van Vliet looked at his watch. If they were on course, they should be crossing the Alps. He was starting to take a serious interest in their destination. But he could not see down from the window without getting up from his seat. The Air France map indicated that the plane should be heading southeast; he tried without success to take his bearings from the sun shadows. It was his impression that they had changed direction slightly. A smell of warm food was coming from the pantries: a choice of chicken chasseur, he had learned from the menu, or *boeuf bourguignon*.

The meal, though, was slow in coming. Some passengers were ordering fresh drinks. Half of them would soon be drunk, Van Vliet estimated, which no doubt suited the hijackers' book. As alcohol did its work in releasing inhibitions, the cabin grew more vocal. They watched a hostess go forward with two trays. "Well, finally!" said Aileen, leaning into the aisle. In front of her stood three empty miniatures of bourbon. "I'm famished, aren't you, Mynheer?" When no further trays immediately followed, a grumble of protest became audible. Van Vliet's stomach, to his shame, was adding its own growl. A hostess came by, collecting glasses. Aileen tapped her sleeve. "*Mademoiselle! S'il vous plaît!* Can you tell us why a few people up there have been served while the rest of us have to wait?" "Cool it," advised the Senator, raising a pained eyebrow that sent a message of deepest sympathy—women!—to the also-suffering Van Vliet. Aileen swung about. "I'm not complaining. I just want to know. *On a le droit à savoir, je suppose.*" "It is a special order, sir," said the hostess, ignoring Aileen's upturned face. "When they book, that family have ask for our kosher service." There was a muffled explosion of laughter. "Kosher, yet!" said a voice. "Fantastic!" murmured Van Vliet. "Fantastic!" He shook his head. The Senator, he observed, was seizing the opportunity to put a low-voiced question to the girl. "May be, sir. I am not permitted to discuss the *détournement* with passengers. But you will have your luncheons soon. It is just that we serve the kosher diet first, since it is separate."

Van Vliet sighed. He would not be sorry if the energy crisis reduced Holland to the bi-plane and the glider. Even in so-called normal circumstances, he disliked being confined in an elephantine flying object while passengers and crew enacted a fantasy of ordinary earth life in its more anodyne aspects, the sole allusion to the un-earthly facts of the case being the life-jacket demonstration, which, he suddenly recognized, had been omitted from today's program—an oversight attributable to the hijacking, he supposed.

As he was lifting the foil from his *boeuf bourguignon*, a note was passed from the Senator. "Will they show us the movie? Your guess." Van Vliet gave an appreciative laugh and handed the note to Cameron, who frowned and drew out a pencil. "Unlikely," he wrote back. "If you have in mind that darkening the plane would give us our chance to overpower them, these chaps will see that too. Unless they're utter fools. Which should not be excluded. We must get word to the personnel to be ready to show the film as usual." Just then the aircraft veered. There could be no doubt about it. The pilot was banking and turning left. Van Vliet eyed Cameron, whose bushy eyebrows went up. They were heading north.

Four

"Do you have anything that might serve as a weapon?" Senator Carey stared at the new message from Cameron. He laughed and wrote out an answer: "Hell, no. I went through Security." Actually, he had a weapon on him—a multi-bladed Swiss Army pocket knife his wife had given him for his birthday when he was a young first-term Congressman (committees: patents and coins) with half-soled shoes, one suit, and lethargic political expectations. Since she had died, he carried it as a relic of her and of a time of relative innocence—those camping trips they used to take in the August recess instead of touching base with the voters in the district. It had served him mainly to gut fish for the frying pan he had given her, but you could kill a man with it. He felt no urge, however, to encourage Cameron in his fantasies of resistance. The Scot, he reckoned, had had "a good war" and was thrilling to the call of the pibroch again.

James Augustine Carey had had a moderately good war himself, having enlisted at nineteen in the U.S. Navy's air corps and seen considerable action as a navigator in the Pacific theatre. In flying school he had failed mysteriously to get his "wings"—the instructor blamed it on lack of ambition—but in fact he was quite capable of piloting a plane and had proved it more than once when the pilot beside him was wounded or hung over. They had made him a lieutenant, j.g., six months before the War ended and sent him back to teach celestial navigation to cadets. "And a star to steer her by!"—he was as out of synch with what a flier had to know nowadays as a rusty car-crank stowed in the trunk of a Mustang. Never mind; he was still able to estimate distances and wind vectors and roughly plot the course the pilot was now on. Should the pilot and the co-pilot be killed or incapacitated during this adventure, he could probably, with God's help and some coaching, assume the controls and bring the big jet down.

He trusted it was not going to come to that. This frolic had all the earmarks of a routine hijacking, no more noteworthy than a Georgetown mugging except in the venue and the size of the haul, whose worth to the lawbreakers he estimated at up to half a million dollars—a fair price for the return of the plane and the crew and passengers intact. A low-risk investment of time, nerve, and manpower, if the two could bring it off, and there was no reason visible to him why they should fail to—no sign of a security guard aboard (Air France, he understood, had a policy of not carrying any), which disposed of the possibility of a shoot-out; the crew was being cooperative, and the under-writers, as usual, would pay.

If no one rocked the boat, the affair should proceed as smoothly as any normal jet flight. He hated these big planes and the whole soft sell of air travel, designed to persuade the passenger that he was not in a thoroughly unnatural position, several thousand leagues above ground with his heart in his mouth, but instead lounging in a dream-like movie auditorium with a drink in his hand and soft music playing in his ears. He liked a real plane, without amenities, a basic tool of trans-port that made you conscious of the extraordinary *fact* of flying, with its peril and discomfort. Hijacking, for a while, had made jet travel a little more suspenseful, but now the reality had pretty well leached out of that, though the journalists still tried to make it sound like a bated-breath business with an open-ended plot. Today's "ordeal"—as it would be described—ought not to last longer than a few hours, most of which would be spent dully at an airfield, deprived of information, while negotiations went on. Waiting, characteristically, would be the main chore.

Barring accidents. And among potentials for accident, there was the human factor, represented today by the impetuous Cameron, with his fond daydreams or—more accurately—pipe-dreams of hand-to-hand combat. Responses to seizure had not yet been programmed to the point of total automatized consent, and in any group of passengers you might find individuals, usually of middle age, still programmed to resistance. Such individuals, of course, constituted a menace to the collective.

Yet there was a wee drop of Cameron in the blood of most active males. At any rate, in himself Jim Carey had already noted a certain curiosity about the morale of the hijackers and the state of readiness of their weapons, joined with a sneaking curiosity as to his own morale and his state of fitness. Not only had he asked himself whether he was capable, should the worst happen, of bringing the plane down, but he had been letting his mind go back to the training in jiu-jitsu the Navy had put him through more than thirty years ago. He wondered whether the art of judo, which he had been pretty good at, was something that came back to you when occasion arose, like being able to ride a bicycle, or whether it got away from you, like Latin or playing the piano at social events. It had occurred to him as he watched lunch being served that the gunner could be disarmed by a couple of determined men with seats on the aisle and a concerted strategy, one to trip him as he passed and the other to get hold of the weapon. This had been a disinterested speculation; his own seat was not on the aisle but cut off from it by the small bulk of Ms. Simmons. Among the males in their party with aisle seats, he eliminated the Reverend, a man of peace, and Victor, up in front and hence incommunicado. That left only the Dutchman, an alert fellow, who must have done his military training. He did not rule out the handsome, long-legged Sophie, once she regained her presence of mind—he could picture her in khakis as an Israeli girl-fighter on patrol at some border kibbutz.

In any event, the problem was not the gunner, but the grenadier. That x quantity in the equation was now out of sight, back by the serving-pantry presumably, but Jim Carey had had a view of the small deadly engines, the Queen of

Hell's pomegranates, hanging from his belt, brief but sufficient to persuade him that the pin of at least one had been pulled. Any jarring contact, even a bad landing bump, could send him and everybody in the vicinity to Persephone's domain. *Assuming the grenade was active.* On the other hand, the grenades might be dummies. In the history of hijacking, there were plenty of episodes in which water pistols and other toy weapons had served to hold a plane at bay. Unfortunately, there were also episodes featuring real weapons, in the hands of psychopaths and suicidal terrorists. These men did not look to Carey like a kamikaze squad, but appearances might be deceptive—as he was postulating of the grenades themselves, which *looked* dangerous and could well be harmless. Nevertheless, they deterred, like a nuclear capability.

At least they deterred Carey. His curiosity, though aroused, was satisfied to exercise itself in the abstract; he felt no real need to know. Cameron, he expected, was on a different track: he must be taking as a working hypothesis the conviction that the grenades were inoperative or just irrelevant to some Boy Scout ethic of action. Carey scrawled a fresh note on a paper napkin and sent it along. Van Vliet de Jonge read it as it went by him. He nodded. " 'Who steals my purse steals trash,' " Carey had written. "Keep your shirt on." Only money, filthy lucre, was at stake, after all. And it was not as if the raiders were after Cameron's life-savings, which perhaps were worth defending at knife-point. It was corporate money, "covered" by insurance, whose transfer to the hijackers' pockets nobody could feel as touching him personally in a vital spot. Except in terms of envy: a hard-working lecturer in history or, for that matter, a U.S. Senator might well see red at the thought of a fortune acquired with so little honest sweat. But that was a daily occurrence in the board rooms and offices of government procurement; Cameron could not be ignorant of the facts of modern business life.

No doubt there was a principle somewhere to be discerned in this affair that a righteous man might be inclined to do battle for—resistance to the tyranny of arms or the right to travel unharassed and unimpeded. But this right in fact was a fringe benefit of paid-up membership in the shrinking Free World and even in England, its cradle, only a couple of centuries old; to "go unarmed unharmed," as the saying went, had been far from the rule on the American frontier. Freedom of travel was conceded today in only a residual part of the globe and there hedged about by passport and visa formalities which had been unknown in most of the "civilized" world up to the First War. If air piracy represented a reversion to an age of lawlessness, when nobody could count himself safe outside his own door, it had also reintroduced illegal searches, which Americans (Carey spoke for himself and a few of his colleagues in the Senate) had begun by resenting and had quickly got used to, evidently preferring their personal safety to their constitutional rights.

As a constitutionalist, Carey was unhappy about the fact of being hijacked, to which there was no constitutional or democratic reply. Having submitted to an illegal search at the airport, he was now submitting to force while consoling himself with history and philosophy, whereas, in his mind—and not merely as a male animal, in his gut—he believed that force should always be resisted. By hook or crook; in his interior citadel, if nowhere else, James Augustine Carey ought to be saying no to power-at-the-end-of-a-gun-barrel. Yet here he sat, staring at a slab of Nesselrode pudding, and the unaccustomed sensation of lacking power was disagreeable, for there was an implication of consent. But rushing to improvised arms, even if that were feasible, would be an over-reaction, also damaging to the self-respect. Moreover, there were others to be considered. They had the right, surely, not to be blown sky-high—for once the figure was appropriate—as the result of a unilateral decision to meet force with force. An opportunity for taking a poll seemed unlikely to present itself, but if consulted, an overwhelming majority of the passengers would vote to sit tight. Your majority's chief wish was to stay out of trouble; few, if any, battles would ever have been fought if the choice had rested with the troops.

In the past, history indicated, warlike tribes had been known, and courage, if you could believe the chroniclers, could be roused by oratory. But today the citizenry grew up fearful, every man-jack a non-interventionist. Only kooks, far out on the Right and Left, were ready to take up arms for what they believed in, which was why the Founding Fathers' wisdom in assigning the power to declare war to the Congress, rather than the Executive, had been short-sighted—they had relied on a nation of minute-men. Roosevelt had had to con the people and their elected representatives into the Second World War, and Johnson had followed suit, manufacturing his own Pearl Harbor in Tonkin Gulf to get a blank check issued to him for the war in Vietnam. While Carey had approved of the first commitment and disapproved of the second, he could see that deception had been needful in both cases if intervention was what was desired, and he had often wondered whether Kennedy's handling of the missiles crisis would have been endorsed by the country if a draft of his intentions had been submitted in advance to a vote.

Cameron, evidently, was looking to *him* now to exercise leadership, and he did not care for the assignment. Vetoing hare-brained counter-insurgency schemes was easy enough, but the alternatives were not clear. Short of supine acceptance, there ought to be some middle course, involving the arts of persuasion or mere watchful waiting on opportunity, generally glimpsed too late. And it was not just Cameron who was turning to him for leadership. He sensed that he had been "elected" by his own group—and probably by a fair number of others who had got wind that he was aboard—if only to set the tone. It was mainly a question of style. Whatever he did, or failed to do, would be on the record. It was a "moment of truth" which he would have been glad to evade. But he was too experiencd politically to ignore the sensation, stiffening his spine like a chilling yardstick thrust down his collar, of being a model in a showcase: "SENATE DOVE KEEPS HIS COOL. Asked how a liberal legislator felt on being hijacked, Carey quipped 'There ought to be a law.'"

97

It irritated him to surmise that others were looking to him for guidance when, like the rest of the human cargo, he lacked the first requisite—information—on which to base a line of conduct. He was used to being briefed on any matter likely to confront him, but now no aide sat by his side to whisper in his ear or pass him a folder of vital statistics on air piracy. Of course if he were feeling inventive, he could easily devise some innocent-seeming experiments to assess these men and the lengths to which they were willing to go. But he was not feeling inventive, and the trial balloon he had idly sent up half an hour ago with his jape "Are they on the house?" had signally failed as a temperature-taker. The gunman, if he had heard, made as if he hadn't, like old Father Peter in study hall deciding not to let himself be provoked by a solitary humorist in the back rows. And Milady Simmons was still displeased with him for his ill-timed—as she saw it—levity. "What made you want to tease that poor hostess? She's scared to come near us now. You saw how she trembled when she tried to open your champagne. Why, Senator, I think you're perverse."

The passing of notes made her nervous too. "Be careful. They'll see you. They'll think you and Mr. Cameron are up to something. We don't want to make them jumpy." As she spoke, the gunman crossed in front of the movie screen and came slowly down the aisle. "He's going to make you show him what you've been writing. Oh, my God!" Carey grinned. "Shall I swallow it?" With his teeth, he tore a shred from Cameron's original missive and carefully chewed it. The machine-gunner passed by. Aileen opened an eye. "He's gone. *Please* don't try to bait them any more, Senator. You act as though this was a game. Don't you take anything seriously?" From beneath her penciled brows came a sidelong measuring look. "I never wanted to believe the stories they told—" "How I lost the nomination to McGovern." He had heard that music before. "Don't sneer. I always defended you. I said you were just being honest. But students who worked for you in Miami said you were *impossible*. You quipped and clowned when delegates asked you questions instead of taking clear stands." "My positions were known," retorted Carey. "Anyway Nixon would have clobbered me. I would have rather it happened to George."

In fact he took the hijackers as seriously, he thought, as they deserved. Since they were neither Westerners nor Africans nor Orientals, they were Arabs, one could reasonably assume. No doubt they believed they were furthering the cause of Palestinian liberation—that hornet's nest Israel had idiotically stirred up for herself when she elected not to give back the occupied territories. The only puzzle was why a French airliner had been chosen as a target; since France was a friend to the Arab cause, Air France was regarded as a "safe" company to fly with. If that was no longer so, a cleavage might be opening in French-Arab relations which no one in Washington was yet aware of—something to do, perhaps, with Mystère and Mirage deliveries. Or could France be quietly resuming shipment of parts to Israel? Seen in that light, this morning's take-over could possess some real interest; he asked himself whether the Dutch parliamentarian was considering these implications too.

On the other hand, this pair might be low-grade members of the North African underworld without awareness of the political significance of seizing a French plane. In their ignorance of larger stakes, they would have been expecting to be received with military honors in Tripoli or Damascus when in fact their arrival could only be an embarrassment. The sudden change of course, just now, favored that hypothesis; indeed, there could be no other explanation for the pilot's executing a U-turn midway to Rome than that the Arab capitals, queried by radio, had refused the plane clearance to land. For the past ten minutes—Carey checked his watch—they had been proceeding north-northwest and must now be re-crossing the Alps. It seemed odd, though, that the gunman showed no loss of aplomb. Carey could only conclude that the change of course had been negotiated with the invisible grenadier, who was probably in command of the operation and in touch with the pilot by inter-com. Unless, up front, there was a third hijacker? Across the aisle, the Scot and the Dutchman were again bent over a map. Carey scratched his head. It almost looked as if they were returning to base—Charles de Gaulle airport. But for what reason? Feeling the first trace of misgiving, he listened but could hear nothing amiss in the regular pulse of the engines. Refueling? Unnecessary, unless their next stop was to be Moscow, and the Russians did not take to hijackers. A radar failure?

The stewardesses collecting the lunch trays were giving out no flight bulletins. "I don't know, sir," said the girl, as Carey handed over his. He retained the glass of Evian—his throat was dry. The mystery was thickening, like the cloud cover outside. If it was De Gaulle they were heading for, the pilot ought to be starting his descent. But they were still at cruising speed.

A wild surmise—Erin—entered his mind. Improbable, he sharply told himself, to the last degree that this pair could be linked with breakaway IRA terrorists and be seeking a hideout on a remote farm in Galway to barter the plane and its passengers against a package composed of Bridget Rose Dugdale, the Price sisters, and the usual Palestinian guerrillas held in Israeli jails. He must have had one too many last night with his friends from the Embassy. Only an Irishman, or a hungover half-Irishman, could summon up such a bogey from the ancestral peat fires. Granted, it was no secret that ties existed between those boyos and Palestinian guerrilla units, who were training them (as if they needed it!) in terrorist techniques and supplying them with arms. But no boggy meadow or field could take a jumbo jet, and an attempt to land on a small hidden airstrip, if such existed in the Irish Republic, would result in gruesome casualties, if not certain death for all concerned. Were the hijackers to put forward such a crazy demand, the pilot would have to dissuade them and, if he failed, let them shoot him rather than carry out their orders.

Carey sighed. He repented last night's conviviality. Since Eleanor had died, he had been resorting to drink, mainly from boredom and because he was sleeping badly. If it had not been for their religion, they would have divorced long ago, and yet now he missed her. His punishment, he supposed, for not having believed her when she used to tell him "When I die, you'll be sorry." In her last illness, she had finally stopped saying that, perhaps from lack of conviction; a pity she could not be here now to enjoy her triumph or, to be fair to her many virtues, seek to console him for the loss of her.

She drank herself, like most senators' wives, but for him she had been jealous of booze: "It takes you away from us." Jealousy made her exaggerate his attachment to the bottle: "The curse of the Irish; if it weren't for me, you'd be an alcoholic." He had never been more than a sporadic drinker, while campaigning or, precisely, to get away from her after a tiresome quarrel, and in the Senate he could count as abstemious, but now he had to accord her a certain skill in divination. He rarely went to bed totally sober these days, and this morning he had broken his own golden rule—not to add alcohol, even a beer, to a hangover. The double birthday, however, had imposed a celebratory glass, and the champagne he had ordered for the panache. He had not finished it and had felt no temptation to follow up with wine. Actually, to be fair to himself, last night's overindulgence had been venial, mainly a matter of late hours, and excused by the prospect of a dull journey to Teheran. He had counted on a restorative snooze all the way to Tel Aviv, but first this little woman had come to jaw with him, then there was the false alarm on Victor's cat, and finally the hijackers had burst on the scene. If he had known he was going to be hijacked, he would have been better prepared, he hoped, but then, as the Church taught, the wise virgin always had her lamp trimmed.

In the seat ahead, he noticed, the Bishop was dozing—a display of holy sangfroid he envied. But if he himself were to take forty winks, it would only contribute to his Luciferian legend. "*Perverse!* Why, let me tell you, that man slept right through a hijacking. As soon as he saw what was happening, he ordered a bottle of champagne, and the next thing I knew he was snoring. I don't deny his intelligence or his charm, when he wants to use it, but would you want him in the White House? I mean, in a nuclear crisis . . ."

Jim Carey supposed it was his fate to be type-cast as a semi-bad apple. Being good-looking played its part in that. "He certainly is a *handsome* man," Eleanor's father, a mortician, used to comment whenever the tall law student, then known as Augie, came to take her out in his ancient salesman's coupe—a grudging professional concession that the suitor would make a nice corpse. Yet being handsome had never hurt the Kennedys or Stu Symington—no sulphurous additive suspected there. He was a better Catholic than any of the Kennedys, though few, outside his confessor, would believe that. But when he made a retreat, which he still did occasionally, it went on the debit side: the inference drawn by the gossip columns was that he was a "spoiled priest." In his last try for the Democratic nod, his backers had implored him, for Christ's sake, to stay out of monasteries; if he needed a rest from the world, he could find some island in Maine and commune with Nature—the "spoiled priest" canard was turning off not only Jews and Protestants but Catholics. When he ignored the advice and slipped into a Benedictine monastery for a weekend—with the Secret Service, assigned to him by law as a candidate, camping in a motel opposite so they could check on the monks' fire-escapes—his chief speech-writer went over to Shirley Chisholm. No great loss; he could write his own speeches. But he did not care for the golden handshake the scribe gave him on quitting: "I have great respect for Senator Carey's moral courage, but the guy doesn't want to get elected. I guess what he wants is for somebody to hand him a crown."

He could not deny having been a seminarian. His aunts and mother had seen to that. But they had not foreseen Pearl Harbor. He had enlisted in the Navy's air corps that same Christmas (to be exact, St. Stephen's day), from a mixture of motives —patriotic reflexes, a desire to avoid the draft, a desire to avoid the priesthood, from which the "sneak attack" had intervened providentially, he felt, to save him. As a seminarian, he might not have been drafted, but if his draft board had let him stay on and be ordained, he would have ended up in the Army as a chaplain—an unappealing prospect to a youngster who had been a state-wide athletic star at Saint Ben's. Besides, coming from a farm area, he had always wanted to go to sea or fly an airplane, and the Navy offered both. The choice between God and country had not involved much wrestling with his conscience: God would still be there when Hitler and the Japs had been defeated. And God had surely not meant him to be a priest. At the outside, a monk though never an abbot: often a bridesmaid but never a bride, he might have risen to be Master of Novices. But he could not have taken the discipline, unless self-imposed by the so-named scourge. Among religious callings, being a hermit might have suited him best; a loner, not a team man, was his image. And when he had started out, in the winter of '68, preaching his campaign in the New Hampshire wilderness, he had actually thought of Peter the Hermit leading his *paupères* in what was known as the first act of the first crusade. Like Peter, he had come on strong in the first act, and then the barons had moved in to take over, and he was left by the wayside with a tiny band of ragged zealots by the time they reached the Holy Land, i.e., the convention.

His arch-sin and political crime was lack of humility. It was why he could never have been fitted for the monastic life, still less for the parish circuit, though he might have starred in the confessional. In politics, on the cocktail circuit, it was a crime he was drawn and quartered for every four years during the hunting season for presidential "hopefuls." Back in the home territory, the folks did not seem to mind—the older ones still remembered him as an end on Saint Ben's famous unbeaten high-school eleven and a crack third baseman on the spring nine. Even so, as he had heard his campaign workers say, it was a miracle that such an arrogant guy kept getting elected and re-elected to the House and then the Senate; some of it could be explained by the law of inertia, but the *first time?* Some said he owed it to Eleanor, a born campaigner and particularly effective with women's groups, but most argued that it could not be all the wife, which coincided with his own view. He was proud but not vain, and each time the returns came in showing him out in front, he began by suspecting a miscount. True, it was a Democratic state with a mixed German and Irish population and a Farmer-Labor tradition, but the machine had tried more than once to unseat him in the primaries and never even come close. Natural causes, Eleanor included, were insufficient to account for the phenomenon, and he too was inclined to consider it a miracle, proof of a Divine intention that for its own inscrutable reasons had chosen him to be a legislator rather than a small-town lawyer and weekly poet for the county newspaper.

Or an actor. At Veblen's old school (where he had enrolled under the GI bill after the War), the head of the drama department had urged him to take a screen test, but Carey had thought he was too old and his mouth was too small, like a woman's. The truth was, he did not care to be an idol. Yet there was an actor somewhere in his make-up, along with the priest and the ballplayer and versifier; he was a vocational mongrel or alley cat for all his royal ways. Like his only friend in the Senate, old Sam Ervin (now, alas, retired), he was a Shakespearean and resorted mischievously to quotation. During the uproar in the '72 campaign over the question of homosexual marriage, he had fielded queries from the audience with " 'Let me not to the marriage of true minds admit impediment.' Next?" He supposed he must project a saturnine image from the depths of a private melancholy unfathomed by his conscious intellect. Though he was a ready laugher and chuckler, news photographers liked to catch him in a brown study or with an eyebrow that appeared to be wincing in cerebral pain. His silver hair (hereditary; his father had been snow-white at thirty) lit up the paradoxes of his public personality by contrasting with his soft, smooth features, unlined except for the amused wrinkles around the eyes, so that he looked like a Drama School performer made up for the role of a senator. And in fact he was detached from his simulacrum, though not totally out of sympathy with it. Like a finished actor, he observed himself playing his part and made critical notes; he was rarely satisfied with a performance and distrusted audience reaction.

According to Eleanor, his greatest liability was his unwillingness to "throw himself into" whatever he was doing. "You make it so obvious. Some part of you is just standing there coldly and watching." She was right, though "coldly" was a typical editorial injection—compared with most of his colleagues, he was an incinerator. It was something else that tempered his commitments; whether he was interrogating a witness before one of his committees or sub-committees or receiving a delegation of dairy farmers or "meeting the press" on the tube or simply copulating, there was always a playful element. It was in sports and games, as she noted too, that he was most serious and concentrated. "Anybody watching you play softball would think you really cared." But sports were playful by definition except to the pros; you could "give yourself" without equivocation to pitching or a game of poker, whereas in politics and so-called interpersonal relations, amusement was a necessary solace, like a boon companion you brought along to keep you honest.

On the other hand, he was accused of "having too high standards." He himself could never make out whether they were too high or too low—his expectations of humanity were slim. If it were not for God's grace, all would surely burn—he had no trouble in believing that. Yet God's grace was meant to be "sufficient" to each and every occasion, and on this cardinal point he doubted: judging by the evidence, there was not enough of it available for present-day needs. It was supposed to be limitless but perhaps it was running out like the underground reserves of coal and oil on this unhappy planet. A good man, like Pope John or this old Bishop, was now a museum wonder, and Jim Carey, as a born-and-bred plains democrat, could not help regarding that as a suspicious circumstance.

Since he had left the seminary, he had never taken much interest in the question of whether he himself was a good man or a bad man; that was the Lord's business, not his, to tote up. The sin of pride, in his private experience, was unconquerable: curb it here and it reared up its head there. God, who had made him intelligent, would have to allow for the incisiveness of judgment that went with it. He lacked charity. If he loved anybody, it was God, the only person to whom he could talk, who angered him (unlike his human associates, who, for all their efforts, could never fully rouse his ire), who made him happy in the contemplation of His handiwork, who filled him with a longing for union and abandoned him during long intervals. Maybe his mistake was to expect God to approve of him for his truthfulness, the only quality in himself he greatly valued. The theologians, his confessor reminded him, had not numbered that among the virtues. In their catalogue (lifted from Plato, as his confessor had forgotten), there were only prudence, justice, fortitude, and temperance. He feared he saw what his spiritual mentor was getting at. Since nothing could be concealed from Him who knew the secrets of all hearts, honesty was no virtue in His regard, and a man who laid claim to truth-telling was very likely committing the old Greek sin of hubris, aspiring to dispense a commodity that only the gods possessed. In short, his dry candor, so attractive and yet so disturbing to his adherents, was only another form of satanic pride.

President Simmons was nudging him. He opened his eyes. Across the aisle, the Dutchman's right hand was up and signaling for attention. "Please, Teacher! Can I go to the toilet?" Some nervous snickers were heard. "What the mischief?" exclaimed the Bishop, waking up. After a suspenseful moment, the gunman accorded permission. The deputy, looking now somewhat sheepish, made his way to the toilets; it was not easy to saunter with an AK trained on your back. "Whatever possessed him?" said Aileen. "Why couldn't he just *ask*? Don't you legislators ever grow up?" "He was testing," said Carey. "Like inserting a straw in a cake. You must have seen your mother do it."

The deputy, Carey estimated, must be using his promenade to get the lay of the land. It would be interesting to know what the grenade-carrier was up to, and from the vantage-point of the toilet block both the serving-pantry and the cabin behind could be inspected. But before Van Vliet could return with whatever facts he had collected, a collective gasp directed

Carey's attention forward. In the entry from the first-class cabin, a tall elegantly dressed figure stood leaning calmly on a cane. "Mr. Charles!" whispered Aileen. "So I see," said Carey. In the far aisle, the machine-gunner, intent on the rear toilets, had not noticed the new arrival. As the frail old party came abreast of him, he swung about, startled, and moved to block the way. Muttering something—an Arabic curse or an order?— he thrust the gun-barrel into Tennant's fawn-colored waistcoat, which covered a slight gentlemanly paunch. "Nonsense," they heard Tennant reply in his high piercing voice. "I don't propose to return to where I belong, as you call it." He made a deterring motion with his cane. "Don't be frightened, my dear fellow. I have no intention of harming you. I have a long-standing sympathy with the Arab cause. And if you shoot me, you will simply waste your ammunition on an eighty-two-year-old non-combatant. I am quite prepared for death. My affairs are in order, and I've already begun divesting myself of my worldly goods."

He gently deflected the gun with his elbow. "Come, let's not fence about. We both know you're not going to shoot me." Lifting his head, like a rooster getting ready to crow, he addressed a stage aside, or confidential parenthesis, to the cabin at large. "I sensed *immediately* that something was wrong. Engine trouble, I feared, when I noticed the plane was veering about, but then a little bird told me it was a hijacking. Not a word of sense to be got from the stewardesses, of course. So I decided to come back and investigate. When the steward tried to interfere, then I *knew*, and he admitted—he had to; it was obvious—that there'd been a *détournement d'avion*. Now, if you'll just let me by—I believe I see my friends back there."

The gunman let him pass. Settling his waistcoat, he lowered himself into Van Vliet de Jonge's seat. He sighed. "So much nicer, if one is going to be hijacked, to be among friends, one's own kind." The Dutchman came back from the toilet. "Oh, dear me, were you sitting here? I'm afraid we haven't met." Aileen did the introductions. "Van Vliet de Jonge . . . ? That rings a far-off bell. Adriaan van Vliet de Jonge. The novelist.

Now utterly forgotten, I suppose." "His grandfather," supplied Aileen. The old man sprang up. "How delightful. My dear boy, I *knew* your grandfather. Charming man, and so very kind to me. I was only a lad, you see. Before the First War, in Germany. I was doing my *Wanderjahre*, with my tutor. A house party, it was, in the Rhineland, near the Dutch border. I wanted to see Zutphen, in your country, where Sir Philip Sidney fell, and your grandfather arranged to take me. I believe Hugo von Hofmannsthal was staying in the house too. He had no idea of Philip Sidney's falling in Flanders. Between ourselves, I don't think he knew who Sidney *was*. When I happened to speak of the Countess of Pembroke—'Sidney's sister, Pembroke's mother'—he asked whether she was a guest in the house. But your grandfather knew. He gave me one of his books, translated into German. Splendid writer. Harvard has it now, inscribed to me of course. As I indicated to our captor, I'm divesting myself of my possessions. Two strapping young men came from the Lamont and packed up my library. Next I must part with my porcelains. At the end of one's journey, one must travel light, don't you agree?"

"You missed something, Mr. Van Vliet," interposed Aileen. "The most thrilling scene. 'I am quite prepared for death,' he said. With a gun-barrel right in his stomach, he coolly stared that hijacker down. *Chapeau, Monsieur Charles.*" The old man gave a delighted whinny of a laugh. "Well, you see, I have so little to lose. I mustn't expect to live forever, must I, and in Boston one is mugged at every corner. Then one can't get staff any more, so that at times one feels quite ready to shuffle off this mortal coil. But you mustn't let me usurp your seat, Deputy."

It was not his seat, the Dutchman explained. "I was sitting back there, in fact." He looked around with a perplexed face. "There's room here," put in Sophie Weil, turning. Before the old man could rise, she was swinging her long legs aside to let Van Vliet de Jonge pass. Jim Carey flexed an eyebrow. He had been wondering how long the handsome hazel-eyed deputy would resist this other call of Nature.

Cameron and Tennant were now seat-mates—an ill-matched pair. "A sword cane?" came the screech after a spell of quiet. "Dear me, no. In my stick collection, I have a few examples, but this isn't one. I don't believe they're permitted in airplanes. Quite right too. I should drop that line of thought if I were you. Had I been carrying a sword cane, I should have had far less moral authority with our friend up there. Unarmed, unharmed, I always say. Look at your London bobby." They heard Cameron mention a "duty to resist." Tennant cackled. "What a strange notion! I'm quite comfortable and enjoying myself, aren't you? But everybody to his own taste. If yours runs to deadly weapons, they supply razor blades in the lavatories, as I recall."

The Dutchman and Carey exchanged smiles. It was a long time since an airplane had carried complimentary razor blades, probably not since the advent of hijacking. But the Bishop's toilet kit would be well stocked, surely, with Gillette steel, perhaps even with an old-fashioned straight razor and a strop to give it an edge. In fact, Carey mused, a resourceful man would see this crate as an arsenal. The glasses they gave you these days were plastic, but the wine bottles were still made of glass; apparently Cameron had never been present at a barroom fight or he would not be asking for better than a jagged broken bottle. Or, coming on an opponent from behind, you could garrote him with a leather shoelace, such as the Bishop was wearing in his stout brogues. What to do, however, about a live grenade in an enclosed space?

"Are all of you charming people traveling together?" the fluting voice inquired of Aileen. "Dr. Cameron and Deputy Van Vliet de Jonge too? I see. Now don't tell me. I must put my thinking cap on. What can you have in common that's taking you to Teheran or is it Tel Aviv?" He counted on his white ringed fingers. "My old friend Augustus Hurlbut, the Reverend Mr. Barber (St. Matthew's, isn't it?), Senator Carey . . . Why, you must be a committee!" He looked around him triumphantly. "I see I can take silence for consent. A bishop, a senator, a parson, the president of a distinguished college. Tinker, tailor, soldier, sailor. A Dutch parliamentary leader, a don from the British Isles. A trouble-shooting young woman journalist. It's as plain as Pikes Peak. What you lack, if I may say so, is a rabbi." In the seat ahead of Aileen, the Reverend had one of his fits of merriment. He slapped his knee. With an air of contented malice, Tennant continued. "Now what can your committee be up to? Are you off to quiz Golda, poor dear? No, I remember. We agreed to meet in Teheran, didn't we, Augustus? Ah, yes, well." He sighed. "I fear I can guess your business. And the Shah started out so well. Charming man, I'm told. But a visionary, always so dangerous. And he fell under the influence of that dreadful vizier of his." "Nassiri," said Sophie. "That's it, his secret police chief! A thoroughly wicked person. My dear, the shocking things they do to those young men in prison, some of them from excellent families. Well, you know better than I, naturally. That electric grill. They slide those young bodies into the device and *toast* them. A friend in England sent me a clipping on the subject which quite put me off my feed. It came in the morning mail, which I open while I wait for my toast to pop up. I couldn't *look* at an English muffin." "St. Lawrence on the gridiron. Old idea," said Carey.

"How clever of you, James. Yes, with all our technology, we're relapsing into barbarism. One sees the proofs of it all around one. Sheer medieval savagery. I shan't live to see the dawn of a new Renaissance." "That was damned barbaric too," growled Cameron. "Yes, one can't deny that. But there were compensations—glorious art and literature. The main enemy of civilization—you'll excuse me, Augustus—has always been religion, the spirit of fanaticism. Hunting down heresy, those dreadful dogs of the Inquisition, St. Dominic's hounds, that one sees in the cloister of Santa Maria Novella. Today we find them amusing. We don't stop to think that we ourselves are living in a new age of wars of religion. Persecution of unbelievers. One thought one had seen the last of that with Hitler."

"And Stalin?" demanded Aileen. "Quite right, dear lady. One ought to have known. But I confess that for a long time I simply refused to believe in the horrors of the Soviet camps.

I opposed the cold war on principle and then, you see, I belong to a generation that taught itself not to accept atrocity stories. The 'rape of Belgium.' Now one wonders whether Kaiser Willy's troops *weren't* impaling babies on bayonets and crucifying nuns." His shrill ululating laugh caused Carey to wince and duck his head.

Though he had known Charles Tennant for years, he had seldom felt entirely easy in his company. By now, thanks to death and retirement, Carey had moved up (he reckoned) to second or third on Charles's senatorial mailing list for regular advice and remonstrance—Charles never wrote to a newspaper but to selected members of the upper house, presidents, secretaries of defense and state. Those voluminous, closely penned "epistles" on pale blue monogrammed stationery usually wound up, Carey assumed, in the burn bag, which was a pity because Charles, while long-winded, was a sharp old bird and moreover had "done his homework," as was evidenced by the quantity of heavily underscored enclosures clipped from technical journals, the *Times* of London, *Stars and Stripes*, the *Guardian, Barron's Weekly*, stockholders' reports. He was never without a silver clipping tool resembling a small pen and had a horror of photostats. As a moderately active legislator, Carey could rarely do justice to that hand-crafted correspondence (if only Charles had learned to use the typewriter or would dictate to a secretary!), but he kept a fair amount of it in a file he had marked *Vox Populi*. To his credit, the far-sighted old liberal had been an early opponent of the war in Vietnam; he boasted that his reproaches to Kennedy on that subject, though uncatalogued in the Kennedy Library, dated back to '61. And on the day Carey announced himself as an anti-war candidate against Johnson, a check from Charles W. Tennant on the State Street Trust was in the mail. "Accept a thousand 'iron men' for your 'war chest.' Gratefully . . ." Dated October 7, 1967. Carey would not forget that. When, rising from a doubtful seat and half-attainted stall (for he was taking some flak from the home front and from his old enemies, the columnists, who had hit on the word "lackluster" for his performance), he went into New Hampshire that brave winter, he would frequently find Charles, wrapped in layers of scarves, shawls, and steamer rugs, seated in a front row of the hall—generally a chilly high-school gymnasium—with a box lunch containing chicken and watercress sandwiches, a large damask napkin, and a silver Thermos of his cook's bouillon on his lap. A somewhat unwelcome cynosure of attention, as was his antique Armstrong-Siddeley stationed outside, with a chauffeur at the wheel. "All that guy lacks is finger bowls," one of the young campaign workers had commented. "What would you call him, Senator?" "A philanthropist, I guess," Carey had said shortly. "Can't you persuade him to stay away, Jim?" Eleanor had entreated. The old hedonist's shrieked observations on "the quality of life" (meaning the hotel accommodations) in rural New Hampshire were being poorly received in the hall. " 'I know not the man,' " Carey had cited sardonically. "No. I won't."

But in today's flying auditorium Charles's unabashed, intrepid old voice was tempting Carey to deny him—thrice over—if only he could. Though he was normally immune to social embarrassment (a female complaint, he considered), doubts as to the threshold of tolerance of less sophisticated passengers could not be repressed. Without ill will, with remorseful affection even, he wished their visitor would go back to first class, where, whatever he thought, he belonged.

"So you plan to spend your time in that lovely country investigating torture in the Shah's jails. And I shall be with my millionaires' tour. As Lenin said, 'From each according to his capacities.' Dear me. I must say I've felt a qualm or two about my little jaunt. Mind you, I haven't *seen* the toaster thing, but there can hardly be so much smoke without fire, can there? But then I said to myself that one would become a total shut-in if one let moral considerations dictate one's travel plans. I suppose one could still permit oneself to visit the Scandinavian countries, though there's so little to see there. And your delightful country, Mr. Van Vliet de Jonge, with its splendid museums and attractive people. The Dutch have been much maligned by their neighbors; I've never found them in the least stolid or phlegmatic. But France, Italy? Thoroughly corrupt and police-ridden, and in France you have shocking discrimination against the foreign labor force. No wonder, I say, that they have all these tiresome strikes. England? Well, one has one's friends there, but there've been some quite off-putting disclosures about English prison conditions. And I'm told that Scotland Yard—can that be true, Dr. Cameron?—uses the third degree." He laughed. "No, a peep into Portugal and perhaps into Greece, now that the colonels are gone, and then one would be forced to go virtuously home." "Hear, hear!" came a mutter from the rear, causing Charles to turn around, smiling amiably in all directions like royalty acknowledging applause. Nevertheless he slightly lowered his voice.

"I did draw the line at the colonels, but, between ourselves, my digestion was grateful for a holiday from the nasty Greek food and wine. As for Iran, well, I said to myself that it's no wickeder probably than Spain, where my liberal friends go in droves. And what would I accomplish for those poor young oppositionists by staying home? It's not as if the Shah were dependent on tourism to make ends meet, is it? I am not such a noodle as to fancy that my depreciated dollars could make the slightest difference to him. Then, too, I said, that were I to meet him, which is not beyond the bounds of possibility, I would give him a piece of my mind. 'Look here,' I would say—"

Carey softly groaned. Nobody was censuring the old duck for clinging to the pleasure principle in the few years he had left. Amnesty International would surely get its tithe from the sybarite's holiday that in his own mind he ought to be renouncing—Charles paid up regularly for his venial sins. And as for the Shah's getting "a piece of his mind," that could be forecast with utter certainty if an invitation to the palace were to be issued. No one within earshot today would expect Charles, wherever he found himself, to show a lack of gumption. But Charles was not going to meet the Shah, at least not immediately—a point that in the flush of victory he seemed to be overlooking.

Indeed the fact of that victory—and of Charles basking like a lizard in the glory of it—was starting to worry Carey. The more he pondered it, the less he liked it. The old man's naughty venturesomeness had been rewarded. He had got his way. With every captive eye watching, the hijacker had backed down. But to anyone familiar with power and its vagaries, it was obvious that consequences could be in store. Another passenger, encouraged by Charles's success, would "try something," and the hijacker would over-react, to prove himself.

For the first time, Carey felt distinctly uneasy. He had a bodily premonition of danger, such as he had known once or twice—and with justification—in the navigator's seat with an unseasoned pilot beside him, though now he could not sense, glancing about, in what quarter trouble might be lurking. He felt confident of his power to deter Cameron, who anyway was well fenced in by Charles and his lolling walking-stick. And he trusted Van Vliet de Jonge, a political animal like himself, to have the right reflexes if an emergency were to present itself. But he would feel far happier were he posted commandingly in an aisle seat to restrain any untoward moves. He meditated asking Aileen to change places with him. Yet the slightest stir among the passengers was capable, if he was right in his foreboding, of producing a volley of gunfire.

He looked at his watch again. "Jesus!" he swore. They must have already overflown Paris. He would not feel easy till they were on the ground somewhere. Once they were on the ground, the likelihood of an incident within the plane would be minimal, or so his instinct told him. Outside, the police (in what country's uniforms?) might surround the plane and, if negotiations broke down, try to take it by storm. But that would be a whole new ballgame, which the passengers would have to sit out in the grandstand, waiting for the result to declare itself.

Charles's zestful prattle had finally died down. Next to Sophie, Van Vliet de Jonge had turned his head and was scrutinizing the seats in back. He looked mystified by whatever he saw there. A note was passed along from him—addressed, surprisingly, to "Miss Symans." She opened it and turned her head too, studying the rows behind. She frowned. "Something wrong?" inquired Carey. "Well, no. But it's strange. He wants me to tell him whether some young Dutch people who were sitting back there were a figment of his imagination. Here, read it." He put on his glasses. "You have to know the context," Aileen explained. "He has this phobia about being Dutch. How they have a secret language and how Holland is an imaginary country. I didn't follow it all too well. But when he sees Dutch people, I mean outside Holland, he gets a haunted feeling, as if they were a mirage." Carey laughed sympathetically. "But the strange part is, Senator Jim, that young couple isn't there any more. Isn't that weird? Of course I don't *know* they were Dutch. I just took his word for it. I didn't pay too much attention to them. If you asked me, I couldn't describe them. But I could swear there were two young people sitting behind us, and now that whole row is empty." "Probably moved," said Carey. "Yes, but where to? I don't see them anywhere back there. Still, as I say, I might not recognize them if I did." "Well, reassure him. Tell him you saw them too." Aileen ruminated. "I suppose he missed them when he had to go to the men's room." Her sharp eyes flew open wide. "I'll bet that's *why* he went to the men's room! The secret language. He wanted to pass them a message that nobody but a Dutch person could understand. Like a code. He had some plan in mind and needed their help."

Carey held up a hand. The pilot was starting his descent. Overhead, the seat belt signs flashed on. In a few minutes, they should be able to see land below. Now, short of a crash, nothing could happen, Carey decided: the passengers were concentrating on the windows, trying to make out where they were. He held his lighter to Aileen's cigarette. "You'd better have one too," she told him. "It'll be our last for days maybe. They'll never let us smoke on an airfield." "'For days'?" he said quizzingly. "Come on, it's not that grim. The plane and the crew are all these fellows need for bargaining purposes. The odds are, they'll let the passengers go. For them, we civilians constitute a headache." She stared at him. "A 'headache'? Why,

Jim, with you aboard and the Bishop and the deputy, they've captured a real prize. Don't you think these men know that?" He reflected. "No. I don't believe they studied the passenger list." She shrugged. "Even if they didn't know in advance, by now they must realize." "How?" "Senator Carey! Do you recall giving out your autograph to a whole pack of students back in the airport lounge? Do you think you were invisible? If I saw you, these men must have. And you had Sophie giving out autographs too. Don't tell me a hijacker wouldn't be interested. Why, this is the most important international hijacking that's ever happened. Those millionaires up in first class are just the meringue on the pie."

The plane emerged from the cloud cover. A patch of water was sighted, but then a swirl of fog came in. No visibility, Cameron reported from his window. The pilot had decreased speed. "Oh, God, what now?" said Aileen. "Holding pattern," explained Carey. "Could be the fog. Or could be the pilot negotiating with the control tower for permission to land. Or could be he's just waiting his turn." "Wouldn't you think that at least we'd have priority?" Aileen exclaimed, irritably stabbing out her cigarette. Then a rift in the fog opened up. Van Vliet de Jonge rose in his seat, like a rider in stirrups. "Holland!" he called out. *"Nederland!"* Tears of laughter were running down his handsome ruddy cheeks. The fog closed in again. The plane continued to circle.

The cabin was still, as if holding its breath. Then, without warning, with Mother Earth so near, pandemonium erupted. They heard a cat's furious cries, a man's angry yells, a metallic clatter as of something falling. From the rear, two shots rang out. The plane lurched, and the lights went dim. When they came back on, passengers were ducked down in their seats; the Reverend had assumed the fetal position. Carey looked back to where the shots had come from. By the serving-pantry, a tall fair-haired young man with big round spectacles stood holding a rifle; behind him was a fair-haired young woman, wearing glasses too. There was no sign of the grenadier. Up front, the machine-gunner was half-kneeling on the carpet, reaching toward his weapon somewhere ahead while clutching his leg and groaning. Further down the aisle lay a ball of bleeding blue fur. Beside it, Victor was weeping.

As Carey sought to understand this frozen scene, the young man raised his rifle and took aim. Sapphire's back arched; she rose into the air and visibly died. Crouched next to Carey, Aileen was moaning hysterically. "Why did they have to kill Sapphire? *Why,* Senator Jim? Beautiful, beautiful Sapphire. Oh, how cruel, how terribly cruel." "To put her out of her misery," Carey said, putting an arm around her. "You could see she was horribly wounded. I don't understand who did that." " 'Who did that?' " cried Aileen. "Why *he* did!" Carey's eyes turned to the machine-gunner, who was picking himself up and retrieving his gun; he was ashy and his plump figure seemed to droop. "No!" Aileen cried, sobbing. "Not him. *Him.*" Carey's eyes went to the young fellow with the rifle. He could not sort this out. "The Dutch!" Aileen exclaimed impatiently. "Those two. Him and the girl. I thought I didn't remember what they looked like. But of course I did. I recognized them right away, the minute I heard the shots and peeked over the seat."

Carey supposed he was being exceptionally dense. "You mean, when he was shooting at *him,* he hit Sapphire too, by accident. She was in the way." "He wasn't shooting at *him.* Don't you see, they're all on the same side! The Dutch and the Arabs. They're a gang." He could not follow this reasoning. In his own mind, he had concluded that the tow-headed young man was a security guard or maybe an Interpol agent—there could have been a tip-off on this morning's operation. On Aileen's side, though, spoke the fact that the hijacker, strangely, had been allowed to repossess his gun; he held it with one hand while with the other he pulled up his trouser-leg to examine his calf, which was bleeding. "Yet *somebody* shot our friend there," protested Carey. "Look. Surface wound, probably. I guess they aimed to disable him. Shoot at the legs—good police principle." Aileen shook her head. "Nobody shot him. That was Sapphire. She clawed him. So they killed her." She began to sob again. "Oh, poor darling Sapphire. She gave her life for us."

This was an exaggeration—her Southern fancy tearily doing its embroidery. Yet in the main Aileen's reconstruction of the event and cast of characters was exact, as was swiftly demonstrated when the plane touched down. "Schiphol," declared Van Vliet de Jonge, with a doleful countenance, as the fair strapping fellow and the girl strode ahead to first class, leaving the scowling young Arab with the machine-gun in charge. Almost at once, over the loud-speaker, they heard a woman's voice speaking excellent Nordic English: passengers were to remain in their seats with their seat belts fastened; in due time, a cold snack would be served; those needing to use the toilets were to raise their hands and permission would be given but no paper was to be put in the bowl. Soon a steward came by, distributing extra blankets; the lights dimmed. Outside, dusk was gathering. It was four in the afternoon; they had been in the plane five hours.

As though to help pass the time, the steward, finally, was willing to answer questions. He confirmed that Victor had released the cat from its container but he could not say for what reason. Possibly the animal had been crying. Then he did not know whether the hijacker had kicked the poor cat when it crossed his path, causing it to strike back with its claws, or whether the cat had struck out at him first, sensing an enemy. He favored the latter notion. *"Les chats, vous savez, c'est une race mystérieuse. Très sensibilisée. Surtout les chats pur-sang. On leur prête des pouvoirs occultes."* Aileen wailed softly. The Bishop blew his nose. There was a silence. "But what happened then, steward?" Charles demanded. "One would like to hear." Badly scratched and perhaps also bitten by the animal, the hijacker had dropped his weapon; that was the metallic clatter they had heard, as the gun struck the chromium of a seat frame. "And the Dutch?" prompted Aileen. "Dutch?" The steward had supposed they were Germans: *"anarchistes de la bande Baader-Meinhof."* The deputy ruefully set him straight. *"Des hollandais pur-sang, je vous assure."* At the moment of take-over, it appeared, they had moved in concert with the Arabs and seized the two cabins behind—the woman had a small pistol in her blouse. When the machine-gunner had let his weapon fall, the grenade-carrier must have summoned them. He had been holding two stewardesses in the strategic serving-pantry block at the center of the plane. *"C'est le chef de la bande, paraît-il."*

Cameron leaned forward. "How long would you say the gun was lying there before the other thugs intervened? One minute, two?" "Perhaps half a minute, sir." "Umm. Pity Lenz didn't seize the gun while he had the chance." Aileen concurred. "Especially when you think that that was what Sapphire *intended* him to do. She gave him the opportunity, and he failed." "You mustn't attribute design to a cat," put in Sophie sharply. "They have a brain the size of a minute." "Pity the creature wasn't rabid," mused Charles with an elfin grin. " 'Rabid'?" said the steward. *"La rage,"* said Aileen. "Oh, sir, that has been taken care of. We have given the pirate an anti-tetanus injection." Carey's eyebrows went up.

They wanted to know what had been done with the body. If they stood up, they could see it, still lying in the far aisle, the steward said. The hostesses had wanted to clean the blood off its fur and put it in a box for its master. But the hijackers had refused; they intended the corpse to be left there, as an example. "What monsters," said Aileen. "Don't you think we might ask the Bishop to say a prayer for her?" "No," said Carey.

He wrapped himself in his blanket, pulling it up over his eyes. When he opened them, it was night outside. In the shadowy dimness of the cabin, he perceived Victor, huddled in his long coat, kneeling in the far aisle by his cat's side, keeping vigil. The deputy was awake too and watching. "Antigone," he whispered. Carey nodded.

He had dropped off to sleep again when two figures, one holding a flashlight, appeared—the mustached grenade-carrier and a stewardess. They went along the aisles, stopping here and there to tap a half-awake passenger on the shoulder. It reminded Carey eerily of school dormitory inspection or of the awful night-time summonses that were wont to rouse the men in sick bay. *"Prenez vos affaires. Vous pouvez sortir,"* the stewardess was murmuring as she went. The exodus had begun. Up front, the Israeli couple with their wailing baby were being ordered to get a move on. "Out! *Raus! Weg,"* the grenadier barked. From the rear cabins, men, women, and children were filing past with their hand baggage, some still struggling into their coats. A woman had forgotten her umbrella. "Later, *madame. Maintenant vous sortez."* Aileen started to rise. *"Pas vous, madame,"* the stewardess intervened. So they were separating the sheep from the goats. As the last camera-laden straggler passed through into first class, the lights went on full. Carey saw that he and his party were alone in the cabin. Victor had retreated to his place, up front. Nine little Indians, counting Charles.

In the serving-pantry there was a sudden bustle. The hostesses came forward with trays. The grenadier, yawning, undid his bristling belt and tossed it on a seat like a discarded stage prop. He settled himself and accepted a tray.

Five

A voice was speaking to Van Vliet de Jonge in Dutch. They were still at Schiphol. Outside it was full day. He looked up into the pale green eyes, enlarged by thick lenses, of the young man who had shot the cat. "You sleep too soundly, Deputy. Come along now. We want a chat with your honor." They knew him, of course. As he had been saying, Holland was a small country. For his part, he knew the accent of Groningen —not the once-moated city, but the dour, grudge-holding province. This was a lad from the grim Northeast, reared—one could be eighty per cent certain—in a "black stockings" sect of the deepest Protestant dye. The bad teeth, half-bared in a tight sarcastic smile, bore it out: the *gereformeerde kerk* looked on dentistry as devil's work. Henk adjusted his scarf and reluctantly rose. These harsh signs of election did not bode well for a Brabanter from the sweet Catholic land "below the rivers"—current political preferences and class rancors aside.

Mounting the spiral staircase to the second story, in the cockpit he found the Air France captain, his co-pilots, and yesterday's grenadier, now armed with a very realistic large pistol. The hulking northlander—Roodeschool? Stadskanaal?—dismissed the second co-pilot and took his place in the swiveling "navigator's seat" with his back to the instrument panel and his rifle across his big knees. The gunwoman, wearing a woolen peasant blouse and a miniskirt, brought in a tray with five cups of coffee and retired, presumably to guard duty in the adjoining first-class cabin. The interview was brief. Six minutes later, he was back in his place beside Sophie, who was energetically combing her hair.

The talk had gone rapidly, in English—the common language, it transpired, as at any international meeting. He and his friends were hostages. He would be treated as group leader and held responsible for its full cooperation. During the night, negotiations had begun with the criminal government in The Hague. "Why not with the French criminals at the Quai d'Orsay?" Van Vliet had inquired, in Dutch. The question had been ignored. Nor had he been able to discover what demands the hijackers were making. For the moment, they merely wanted a plane, to be supplied by the Dutch, to fly to their next destination with the hostages. "Your government, Deputy, has refused." It was not his government, he objected, with a measure of truth. "Your fraction is the accomplice of the ruling social democrats," retorted the gunwoman, reappearing in the doorway with her coffee-pot. "If Van Vliet de Jonge's fraction voted against the American stooges, they would fall." As this was a fact known to everyone in Holland, he had not denied it. Nor did he feel moved to point out—what would surely be of no interest to these people—that the consequence of such an action would be a government of the Right.

Still, if the Prime Minister—or, more likely, the Minister of Defense—was refusing to give them a plane they craved, it was hardly his fault. In any case, they were knocking at the wrong door. It was the French they ought to have been dealing with. That the 747 was now on Dutch soil was immaterial. Permission to land must have been granted at the request of the French ambassador; that was probably why the pilot had circled so long yesterday, while the request was being considered. Yet between the hijackers and France's representative no dialogue had been opened, though messages had come last night from the control tower that he was at the airport and ready to talk. At least so the co-pilot intervened to say, wearily, out of the corner of his mouth, glancing backward at Van Vliet, as if for help with these intractable people. Van Vliet turned to the rifleman: *"Is dat waar?"* "A ruse," replied that one, with contempt.

Van Vliet shook his head. He was mystified. Why pick on the Dutch? The French, he remarked, were in a position to send them any aircraft they wanted, in exchange for the one they were holding. Even the latest model of bomber, if that were their heart's desire. *"Bien sûr,"* the pilot concurred. *"Mais soyons sérieux. Plutôt un DC-8."* In any event, as he had been telling the air pirates, they were exhausting themselves here to no purpose; he had only to return them in the Boeing to De Gaulle, where their demand would be studied. "This option does not interest us," the Arab air pirate had answered.

More than once during this puzzling conversation, Van Vliet had tried to steer it into Dutch. Each time this had brought a scowl from the Arab, which yielded, at any rate, one piece of information: perfect trust did not reign among the confederates. It was the young woman who chiefly roused his curiosity. Was she the northlander's sweetheart or did she "belong" to the Arab? Or was she—despite the coffee service—their boss? If he could have got her to speak Dutch, he might have the first elements of an Identikit portrait. But not only would she not speak it, when she heard *him* speak it to her comrade-at-arms, she put on a blank face, as though waiting to be supplied with a translation. If he had not overheard the pair of them yesterday talking Dutch behind him (unfortunate that he had heard but not listened!), her show of ignorance might have convinced. She was fiercely determined, evidently, not to admit by a word or sign that she shared a mother-tongue with the enemy.

Yet for what reason, unless because he was Dutch, had he been selected as go-between or interlocutor? Were they unaware that Senator Carey was aboard? It now indeed looked as if yesterday's exploit had been based on a tip-off that a catch of notorious liberals—"your group"—would be on the Teheran flight. Mindful of SAVAK, Van Vliet de Jonge had told no one of the trip except his family and one trusted associate and he assumed that the others too had been reasonably discreet. Yet obviously there had been a leak. The young Iranians in Paris may have innocently boasted of what was afoot to their fellow-students, who would include the usual anarchists and PFLP zealots. Even more probably, the tip had come from SAVAK. Had he not cheerily estimated, in what now seemed another incarnation, that SAVAK's spies would have seen to it that this committee did not arrive unannounced in Teheran? But prevention was the better cure. What could be more fitting than that a "black" secret police should transmit a full Interpol description, down to the flight number, of an incoming party of pinks to a squad of red terrorists? Two birds with one stone, if all went well, that is to say badly. In an hour or so, the Shah and his murderous vizier would be rubbing their hands as they followed the current episode on Iranian television. Still, even SAVAK's information system, being in some degree human, was necessarily imperfect. Since the committee itself had not known, till it met itself yesterday at breakfast, who would be in the party, it was possible that Carey's identity was not yet known to the hijackers.

Eventually, Van Vliet supposed, they would think of conducting a passport check. But at present their attention was centered on the exaction of a getaway plane. Now he understood why he had been summoned: they were looking to him for counsel. "Have you told my government that you have a Dutch parliamentarian aboard?" To his amazement, they had not. "Tell them," he advised, shortly. He knew his countrymen. The stubborn fellow at Defense would resign rather than give up a single training glider *so long as no Dutch interest was involved*. To be told that Prince Philip or the Pope of Rome was among the captives would not budge him. Henk, however, was another story. As it happened, he was a good friend of the Minister's (during a late session they often lifted a glass in the parliamentary bar), but even a mortal enemy, if he sat in the Tweede Kamer, was a vital piece of Holland worth at least a Fokker Friendship to the old boy. "Say that you are holding a member of Her Majesty's Parliament," he had reiterated. Yet, watching the faces cloud over, he saw that he had failed to convince them.

He could not fathom their reluctance. How could it harm their cause to let it be known that a Dutch deputy was aboard? The psychology of terrorists was evidently a closed book to him. Did they fear that the police would storm the plane to free him? He could easily have shown them that the effect on his government would be quite the opposite—an increase in caution. But: "We have heard enough from you." The discussion was over. It was as if an instinct, impervious to reason, warned them against revealing the smallest fact to the enemy, who might find a means to profit.

In a strange way, he was disappointed. Returned to his seat, he felt crestfallen. No doubt it irked him as a lawyer to give sound advice and perceive that it would not be followed: he had begun to look on these malefactors as his clients. Yet, beyond that, there was in him a persistent desire to be helpful, even when this helpfulness, if allowed to have its way, would further some project for which he had no great sympathy. In the present case, an antipathy: he had a distaste for hijackers and hijacking which the interview just terminated had done nothing to modify. Nevertheless, he had found himself "identifying" with these poor brutes—*kapers,* as his countrymen called them, from the old word for privateers—or, rather, with the problem they confronted: the procurement of an escape plane from his old friend and parliamentary colleague. Since he had at once seen the problem's solution in the card at their disposal—himself—it had seemed urgent to get them to play it, and his failure at persuasion was somehow profoundly saddening.

He had a love of solutions and a sometimes fatal generosity in offering them. A footnote in his country's annals might one day tell how in the year 1972, when parlous elections had left Holland without a majority, the radical deputy Van Vliet de Jonge had gone to the Queen with a truly beautiful formula of his own devising to allow Mr. Owl, his political opponent, to assume the reins of government. Like a proud child speeding to the sovereign with the year's first *kievit* egg—a Dutch rite of spring. Juliana was still grateful to him; Beatrix too. He had declined his due guerdon—a post in the Cabinet. And he had no regrets: *"Paete, non dolet,"* as the Stoic's wife said, passing him the sword she had plunged into her Roman heart.

He foresaw no regrets today were the hijackers, thanks to his coaching, to finally get their plane. True, he and his fellow-hostages would be winging off with them on the next leg of a journey which was not bright with promise. But his cerebral part would feel satisfied to have broken a deadlock by the simple application of reason. The alternative was sitting it out here in dreary confinement while each side sought by threats or deceitful promises to sap the other's morale. Since immediate release seemed not to be in question, his preference, on balance, was for a change of scene.

In this, he knew, lay the best and the worst of him: disinterested, eager absorption in the thickening plot of his time and place that went with a certain lightness, not to say levity, of commitment. If he was not small-minded, neither was he—as the palace believed—"large-souled." His attempt to be helpful to the *kapers* could hardly be laid to brotherly love. The feeling that moved him was more like the friendly impatience of a bystander watching a game of bowls. A prompting instinct, such as caused his eyes, during a debate in the House, to drop to his neighbor's half-penciled-in crossword puzzle while the gallery waited for him to claim the floor. At the journalists' *Kring* in Amsterdam, he would stop in late at night, to sit behind the chess players, move on to the match at the billiard table, lend an argument to a literary dispute. Adversary situations drew him, but his interest span was short. Though his life might be at stake, his lively brain was unable to enlist in a heavy-breathing contest between hijackers and lawful authority; he was outside it, above the chessboard, looking down the bishop's diagonal, swiftly noting openings and opportunities, foreseeing moves for either side. In short, like Senator Carey (or the reputation Carey bore), he was an intellectual and political dilettante, lacking the qualities of leadership. Already wife and children, his dear vested interests, were becoming remote; they belonged to *out there,* beyond the portholes' range of vision, like blips flitting across the radar screen. If Durgie was watching television—which often she did not— they must be anxious or envious. Were they ringing Air France to ask whether *pappie* was listed as a passenger on the big plane they could see on their set? There had been several flights yesterday from Paris to Teheran. And Air France's line, it went without saying, would be busy or unresponsive. Yet from his perspective, as two-thirds of a ghost, his family and the little alarms he might be causing them seemed ghostly themselves, diminished in reality. He could not enter into their feelings, even by conjecture, and his greatest pang of remorse, on their account, came from the thought that he might have bought flight insurance at one of those vending machines at the airport. He had never been inclined to do that and always wondered at the provident souls who could—a safe landing must give rise to mixed emotions in the insured one—but the next time, he now vowed, he would: for ten francs, roughly eight guilders, Durgie might hit the jackpot. Catching himself, he laughed shortly. "The next time"! As a matter of fact, he did not recall seeing such an infernal machine at De Gaulle yesterday; perhaps they had gone out, like complimentary razor blades in the toilets, when the *kapers* came in.

Meanwhile the others had gathered some news of their own. During his absence, the talkative steward had come by; the crew had heard that the first-class passengers were about to be released. "Did those fellows tell you anything about that?" the Bishop called out. He was the only one of the group to seem spry this morning. In the toilets, the electricity was *kapot,* so that the water-closets would not flush and the outlets for electric razors were inoperative. But the Bishop had shaved, with an old-style razor evidently; Van Vliet noticed a curl of shaving cream near his capacious ear, the deafer one. On Carey's chin, there was a dark stubble that matched his mercurial eyebrows. The pastor must have tried to use the Bishop's blade, as some still bleeding cuts and white styptic-pencil marks bore witness. Charles had applied a thick dusting of powder. Victor was sleeping, finally, beneath his overcoat and a heap of blankets, his head burrowing in a pillow. The heating too had ceased to function, and it was cold in the cabin. But the Bishop, in his thick tweeds, was comfortably dressed for the occasion.

In answer to the old man's question, Henk could only shout that negotiations were going on for a Dutch plane: no mention had been made of first-class passengers. But he could report that they were still there; in the "lounge," he had seen them, being served Bloody Marys. A cry went up. Here in Economy, they had had nothing but some weak coffee the steward had brought. "Not even a Danish," sighed Sophie. "Did they give them breakfast up there too?" Aileen demanded, giving his shoulder a peremptory tap. Van Vliet could not say; he had noticed what the Americans called "nibbles" on the service wagon as he edged past, but that information, he decided, was better kept to himself. Angry patches had appeared on Aileen's sharp cheekbones; the little jaw had tightened. He was not especially hungry, and what was gnawing at this poor woman's vitals, he surmised, was principally social envy. It would do none of them harm to miss a meal. Moreover, he would feel a little ashamed, as a well-nourished man, to mention a need of food to hijackers who represented, at least in their own minds, the famished of the earth. Yet if negotiations were going to drag on, the hijackers, he judged, would do well to ask for something to eat for the hostages—a compassionate service the Dutch would not refuse.

A few rows ahead, the young woman now stood on guard, her pistol stuck into the bosom of her blue embroidered blouse. It was up to him, probably, in the interests of general harmony, to voice the suggestion. He cleared his throat, preparing to raise his hand. It went up slowly. He found he had no appetite for making a plea on behalf of these, on the whole, too corpulent bellies. Sophie looked at him inquiringly. But the gunwoman's eyes flicked past his feebly waving hand—she was not going to give him even the briefest attention—and he let it fall, like a flag of surrender. "She didn't see you," said Sophie. "No." He was a craven and grateful to be spared.

Then, by good fortune, the Bishop remembered the cake. He lifted it out of its box, on its paper-lace doily, cut it with the Senator's pocket knife, said grace, and distributed slices. They ate while the hijacker dourly watched, stroking her pistol. "Why, bless me," said the old man. "She may be hungry too." He wrapped a generous slice in his pocket handkerchief, and Sophie bore it forward. "What is this?" said the recipient in a loud, suspicious tone. "Well, it *was* a birthday cake," said Sophie. "Would your friends like some? There's plenty. We must just save a piece for *him*." Her nod indicated Victor, supine under his coverings. "Get back to your seat," replied the hijacker. Without further comment, she slowly ate the cake. The Bishop's gesture had not had any noticeable softening effect.

Once the crumbs had been cleared away, time hung heavy. There was nothing to do but guess about what was happening, and Van Vliet was the best authority the group possessed. "Is your Cabinet meeting?" Sophie wondered. Not the full Cabinet, he thought, but an emergency task force: the Minister of Justice would have been the first to be alerted; he would have called the Prime Minister, the Minister of Defense, and the Minister of Foreign Affairs; they must have met last night and again this morning. "Where?" At the Ministry of Justice, probably, so as not to give the affair undue importance. He himself wondered about the Queen. Had she been told yet? And Bernhard? The consort, he explained, had a keen interest in planes and flying; in addition, he had the title of Inspector General of the Armed Forces. "Does that mean his ideas will be listened to, because he's the Queen's husband? I thought you had a constitutional monarchy." Van Vliet was not prepared to dilate, just now, on the role of the monarchy in present-day Holland. "The Queen is listened to. Like her mother. She's respected, as a person, and strains to be progressive." But the consort, who had the outlook of a business man, was something else. His ideas, if he were to offer any, on what attitude should be taken toward the hijackers, would be conveyed to the Defense Minister and duly tabled, with thanks. "But why the Defense Minister? Why should the armed forces have a voice? When I picture Mr. Schlesinger and the Pentagon, it scares me silly." The vision of his starchy and punctilious friend in the role of Dr. Strangelove was amusing, but Van Vliet saw he had to be patient with this bony, beautiful American who construed everything on the hated paradigm of her own government—"the military industrial complex."

Because, he gently explained, an escape plane, if it were to be furnished, would have to come from the armed forces. "Not KLM?" Certainly not; the decision being weighed was a decision of state, to be implemented from national defense stocks, which could only be drawn on with the Defense Minister's consent. "It touches his budget, you see." A screech announced that Aileen had been listening. "You mean they'll transfer us to a military plane?" "Affirmative," said the Senator. She bridled. "Why, I never heard of such a thing!" Her head turned, looking to others to share her outrage. What did she expect—Prince Bernhard's private plane?

He felt suddenly depressed. The boredom of confinement was beginning to tell. Hell, as Sartre said, was others. Outside, there were no signs of action. The big plane sat by itself, as if in quarantine, evidently because an explosion was feared. Somewhere there must be fire engines, police, ambulances, cameramen, but nothing was visible but the empty tarmac; he could not even make out in which direction the terminal lay. Yet from time to time he could hear other planes taking off; the ordinary course of life had not stopped in deference to the piteous exception.

"Mynheer Van Vliet!" Aileen again. She had been thinking about those art collectors up in first class. "Don't you think you ought to *tell* these people who they are? It's not fair—honestly, is it?—for them to be let go while we sit here with a price on our head because some of us, like the Senator, are celebrities. We have an important job to do, in Iran—doesn't anybody remember?—and they're just idle rich." Carey's pained glance met

Van Vliet's. "For Christ's sake, Aileen, change the record." "The Senator doesn't agree," she persisted. "But somebody ought to let them know, before it's too late, that they have better fish to fry than us. It wouldn't hurt those millionaires a bit to be held for ransom. They could hand over their Giorgiones and Titians and priceless hare's fur cups—it's all loot anyway." "Damn it!" begged Sophie. "Keep your voice down." Aileen surveyed the gunwoman. "She's not listening. Besides, I don't care if she does hear. As a revolutionary, she ought to realize the social implications of holding us prisoner while useless members of society go free. I mean, it isn't as if they were invalids or children. I don't see why they should be entitled to my compassion. There has to be some scale of values. We should tell these liberation fighters or whatever they call themselves that holding this committee as hostages is giving direct aid to the Shah of Iran."

Van Vliet noticed that Sophie beside him was quivering. "President Simmons, I don't understand you," she exclaimed, turning around and speaking in a low trembling voice. "Are you prepared to buy our freedom in exchange for information we can furnish, or think we can furnish, on some helpless fellow-mortals? People we don't even know. What gives us the right? The word for that is delation." The vials of Sophie's scorn, emptied on the older woman, produced no effect. Aileen appeared to consider before replying and, when she did, her tone was tranquil, as though she were interviewing a delinquent student in her office. "I don't feel it would be a betrayal, if that's what you're implying, Sophie. Most of us have made sacrifices to join this committee. We've invested our time, our power of judgment, and even our savings in this work. Our loyalty should be to that, surely, rather than to a tour of millionaires with whom I, for one, have nothing in common. Perhaps you feel you have. But I don't want to insist. Shall we put it to a vote?"

"Unnecessary," observed the Senator. "You've rendered the question moot." He nodded toward the hijacker, who was heading with a rapid step toward the first-class cabin. She spoke

131

into the inter-com, and in a minute the shorter Arab, the one with the submachine gun, replaced her on guard. It looked as if Aileen had played the informer with determination and success. And Van Vliet could not wholly dislike her for it; he felt a kind of pity for the democratic demon in the little woman that had been roused to fury by the news of Bloody Marys ahead. Besides, she had sinned to no avail, probably, if benefit to herself had been her motive: the millionaires' loss was unlikely to be her gain. Instead, thanks to her intervention, both groups now qualified to be held as hostages, which meant that the hijackers would be requiring a roomier getaway craft.

Shortly, as if to test the thesis, a bus drew up. Cameron, from his window, was the first to sight it. First-class passengers were indeed being released. But Cameron's view was obstructed by a wing; he was unable to see much more than the feet and legs of some of the lucky ones and the duty-free shopping bags many were still carrying. Soon, though, the gunwoman showed her face again and beckoned to Van Vliet. He was marched once more up to the cockpit, past the first-class cabin. Many seats were now empty, but some contained passengers: Aileen's "millionaires," manifestly, to judge by the display of camel's hair and crocodile and the American tongue being spoken. The cabin was in disarray, strewn with abandoned newspapers and magazines. One lady appeared to have fainted and was being given smelling-salts by a stewardess as Van Vliet was hurried up the stairs.

How the winnowing out had been effected, he could only conjecture—probably with the aid of the crew's manifest; the tour would have been booked as a unit, he supposed. His politician's eye swiftly canvassed them—he noted the two minked women whom he had seen talking with the pastor in the departure lounge and who, he now perceived, were mother and daughter. The sexes were about equally divided; the median age was perhaps fifty, and altogether they numbered eleven. With "Mr. Charles," still back in Economy and dozing, that gave a total of twelve and, with themselves, twenty. Plus the crew. Quite a party. On the whole, he was not sorry that Aileen had "fingered" the collectors; misery loved company, and their own band of liberals could stand some diversification. Still, a last-minute increment of eleven, more than doubling the number of hostages, must be demanding some serious readjustment in their captors' thinking. He would be surprised if they had not sharply debated among themselves about taking on the additional burden. Cupidity, in St. Paul's words, was the root of all evil; the temptation to take on the collectors might have sowed the first seeds of disunity—not necessarily a welcome development.

In the cockpit, the tall northlander and the co-pilot, wearing headphones, were testing a recording device, while the Arab was busy with his grenades and a coil of wire, which he ran along the entry partition, as if readying the plane for demolition. In these menacing conditions, Van Vliet was to make a tape, he learned—in Dutch, to be relayed by radio to his government, urging prompt compliance with the latest demand. It was interesting that they were not inviting him to make a direct broadcast—a sign of mistrust he found flattering to his courage. He was curious to hear what the "latest demand" consisted of, and, true to form, the confederates hesitated. "Tell him," said the woman finally. "His knowledge cannot hurt us." The Groningener complied. They wanted a helicopter capable of transporting thirty persons. "And your lying government has answered that it does not have a helicopter of such dimensions."

Van Vliet inwardly whistled. "It is not a lie," he remarked, after a moment, concealing his surprise. Having served on a parliamentary committee of liaison with the armed forces, he could assure them that no helicopter in the Dutch squadrons had a capacity of more than ten persons. "Can we believe this?" "Yes." From their faces he saw that they were accepting his word and he pressed his advantage. Why a helicopter? Why not a regular plane? "This is not your concern," the Groninger told him. "You will simply make the tape as we instruct you." But this meant then that The Hague was aware that he was their prisoner. "Our guest, Deputy," corrected his compatriot, with a tight-lipped smile. "So you told them?" "We confirmed that you were on board."

The inference was clear. Durgie, watching television or opening her morning paper, had feared for him. And he was glad, he fondly recognized. The wise girl must have telephoned to the Prime Minister's wife, who was her friend: "Elisabeth, tell your husband. I think Henk is in that plane." "We have confirmed," resumed the *kaper*. "But the fascists have asked for proof. So we send them your voice." "Why not my ear?" Van Vliet quipped. "All in good time, Deputy. For the present, we shall let them hear your melodious voice."

Van Vliet considered. The strange thought struck him that what his government must really be asking for was proof that he was alive. A tape could not supply that. On receiving it, the cautious legalists in The Hague would feel justified in asking for further evidence, thus prolonging the wait. "If you will allow me, I will read first from the morning's weather report. You will have had it, surely, from the control tower." The *kapers* looked at each other. "That will be helpful," the woman agreed in a grudging tone. It would be too much to expect thanks.

He spoke to the recording instrument in the pilot's box, announcing the winds and the morning's temperature and the prediction of fog. Next he attested that he was Van Vliet de Jonge, that he and his fellow-hostages were unharmed and receiving correct treatment. But their continuing safety, he had been assured, depended on the delivery of a helicopter of the type already specified no later than 2:00 P.M. Interference with its fueling and departure would not be tolerated, and attempts to "tail" it would have serious consequences: "My greetings." To his own critical ear, he sounded brainwashed, like the Patricia Hearst girl or an American POW bowing from the waist. But no variation on the prescribed text was permitted. His suggestion that he might take the occasion to appeal for some food for the hostages was vetoed; the Arab explained that the authorities could seize the humanitarian pretext to introduce a paralyzing gas into a sandwich container or coffee-urn.

Only in regard to the two o'clock deadline had they agreed to a modification. Their original deadline had been noon. They did not say—and he did not inquire—what horrors lay in store if the deadline was not met. But the methodical wiring of the cabin had lent insistence to his argument that his government, typically slow and ponderous in its deliberations, would need more time.

This was a fact, but there was another pertinent fact that second thoughts caused him to withhold. On hearing the text read to him, he had been strongly tempted to offer a bit of advice: "When you next speak with the control tower, you must tell them that you believe my government when it says it doesn't have such helicopters. But then remind them of the NATO air forces." Then he had buttoned his lips firmly, forcing that counsel back. It was true that the big German brother, across the border, had helicopters capable of holding at least fifty; only last fall, with a pang of small-country envy, he had watched squads of specialists emerge from them during NATO maneuvers. But were he to voice the suggestion, as a terse word to the wise men in his government, he would have become the hijackers' ally; worse still, he would appear as such to the ministers in session. The hijackers might be sadistic enough to invite him to make it *in propria persona* on their tape. If he declined, they might shoot him, though that would be an imprudence at this stage, which would cost them a bargaining card (a fair Jack of Diamonds) with Her Majesty's government. But whoever's voice print was on the NATO reminder, Den Uyl and the rest would recognize the brain of Van Vliet de Jonge behind it, and he was too cowardly, he discovered, to face the judgment those good fellows would pass on him. To appear as privy counselor to a ruthless gang of terrorists was different from his cherished picture of himself, and he wondered whether the crisis was not opening for inspection a split or fatal crack in his character like a hidden "fault" deep in geology.

In any case, the Cabinet did not need to have the NATO air forces recalled to its memory. His stiff-necked friend at Defense was well aware of those big whirring birds nested on the other side of the Rhine. Having been told that a Dutch parliamentarian was among the captives, he must be already overcoming his resistance to borrowing from the German neighbor. In the gloomy conference chamber at Justice, he would make the decision, swallowing his national pride in a single gulp. In his mind's eye, Van Vliet already saw the convulsive movement of the spare gullet and prominent Adam's apple as it went painfully down.

But then argument was likely to be needed to convince the fellow-ministers—Dutch statesmanship required that all sides of every question be examined with due care, and the greater the urgency the more your stubborn Lowlander refused to be hurried—and still lengthier argument to convince the partner at Bonn that a loan under the circumstances was appropriate. *"Bitte, sagen Sie mir,* how does NATO enter?"—had Holland's defenses, perchance, been penetrated by a Warsaw Pact force? If the German Defense people wanted to be sticky, they could declare it their duty, *ja, sicher,* to consult the supreme NATO command, i.e., the American general in Brussels, who in turn would have to consult Washington. And if Den Uyl, foreseeing all this, were to appeal directly to Schmidt, in the name of good social-democratic relations, to get him out of this pickle, Schmidt would no doubt agree to do the favor, resigning himself to eventual questions in the Bundestag. Even then there would remain matters to be chewed over: for example, whether German pilots familiar with that class of helicopter could be borrowed from the base in Aachen—better not, in view of the risks; in Den Uyl's place, Van Vliet would ask for Dutch volunteers.

At best, assuming that Helmut was in his chancellery, in a positive mood, and available to speak to Joop, the "decision-making process" would surely take an hour or two, to which must be added the flight time from Aachen, another hour—a giant helicopter would not be much speedier than an automobile. And already it was ten o'clock. Counting up the hours of uncertainty lying ahead for his unfortunate government,

Henk rested his head on his seat back and softly groaned. He deeply repented the vagary that had sent him winging off to Iran and left the group in The Hague (assembling even now, he supposed, to listen to the obviously dictated tape) in the humiliating quandary of going next door with hat in hand to save "the esteemed delegate's" skin. He felt a sympathy, bordering on love, for his friend at the Defense helm; the others would disperse to their various departments, but his ordeal would not end till he knocked, once again, on the neighbor's door, returning the borrowed craft like a housewife's cup of sugar. In comparison, Henk recognized, his own state of mind was tranquil. Whatever was going to happen was beyond his control. No lives depended on his decisions. Ideally irresponsible, a captured pawn, he could only muse and conjecture.

In his absence, he discovered, a silver flask of whiskey, belonging to the Bishop, had been circulating. The good man had saved some for him. He swallowed the last dram and let his mind run on the interesting question: why a helicopter, why not a regular plane? The answer could only lie in the terrain that awaited them. Either a small air-strip—"liberated" from some innocent flying club—with too short a runway to take even a Friendship, or else an open field or stretch of pasture. On the screen of his memory, he sought to project the countless films on the war in Vietnam he had watched on television; brushing aside MIGs, B-52s, falling bombs, bomb craters, screaming peasants, napalm canisters, napalm victims, at length he saw the big American "Hueys" descending on rice fields, i.e., on soft marshy ground. A small helicopter could land in a jungle or on a mountain top, but the big fellows had needed space.

The Senator no doubt could tell him for sure, or Sophie from her time as a war correspondent, but it was a quirk he treasured in his character to think out a problem whenever possible unaided, using only his memory and his reasoning power, as though he were the last human on earth. . . . So (he reflected, closing his eyes) the presumption was that the gang's prepared hideaway was not in a mountainous or even hilly area, not tucked away in a narrow secluded valley, but, rather, in

137

flat country. The flying range of helicopters excluded desert sands—there were none in Europe, mercifully—and populous farm areas could be ruled out because of inquisitive neighbors. Flat terrain, sparsely inhabited. He considered the empty plain of Apulia, the huge tableland he had inspected one splendid late August while leading a Common Market delegation to the Agricultural Fair in Bari—the Fiera del Levante, it had been called. To wake up in that somber country would almost repay being a hostage: he could compose a Horatian ode. But the whiskey on an empty stomach must be addling him. Antique Apulia was nearly as distant as a stork's winter quarters in Africa. A wide lonely northern beach, such as had served for commando operations during the Second War? He rubbed his jaw. No. Hardly at this season. All along, he had perceived, like a looming fatality, that Holland was going to answer the bill of specifications. Holland, of all places, and the Dutch pair would have known it. Not the industrial tulip fields, or the thickly populated south and center, not farm-rich Friesland either, but the polders. Most likely, the New Polder. Flevoland: Eureka! He let out a cry. "What's the matter?" said Sophie. The jubilant sound issuing from him had contained a measure of pain.

The others were turning to him too. "Anything wrong?" said Carey. "Are you all right, sir?" inquired the Bishop. He was all right, Van Vliet supposed—at least not all wrong. Everything fitted. He knew at last why they were here. But how could he tell these people that tonight they would be sleeping on a polder, when none of them, probably, knew what a polder was? Some kind of mattress, most of them would think. As usual with foreigners, he would have to explain that a polder was land reclaimed from the sea. They were on one now: Schiphol. The word meant "ship-hole." The airport occupied what was formerly a wet marshy hole, made, according to legend, by a sinking ship. Wherever they looked, there had once been water. A hundred feet below them sails had billowed, and naval battles had been fought. A good third of Holland, you could say, was nothing but a collection or accretion of polders. That was why there were dikes. And, once upon a time, windmills. Nowadays their duties were performed by pumping-stations, draining off salt water so that the sea floor could be filled in and leveled and afterwards maintained in a dry state. Over the centuries, aided by a natural silting-in process, Holland had been encroaching on the sea's territory. Or, as your Dutchman liked to say, it had been "won back" from the sea.

"Jolly interesting," said Cameron, peering out the window. "Must say I never knew the extent of the operation. Though of course I'm familiar with the Zuyder Zee project." That was not a polder, Van Vliet de Jonge pointed out; in a sense, it was the opposite—a man-made lake. But from the Zuyder Zee project, polders had resulted. Cameron nodded. "Increased your arable land area." That indeed was the point. But they were slow to perceive the relevance; arable land was not created overnight. Once the sea floor had been pumped dry, it had to be de-salted, then planted with grasses for sheep-grazing. Eventually, when the sheep had done their work, it would turn into farmland, indistinguishable from the rest of Holland. "Wonderful engineers, your people," the Bishop summed up. "Now what leads you to think that these people will be taking us to a polder, as you call it? Funny word, by the way, isn't it? Any connection with poltergeists?" "A poltergeist, Gus, is a noisy spirit," remonstrated the Senator. "From the German, *Polter*, meaning uproar, plus *Geist*." The Bishop smote his head. "I'm old, James, forgive me. I must be losing my German, along with my teeth and my wits. And years back, don't you know, I had occasion to look into poltergeists. There's a school in the Church that thinks they're true cases of diabolical possession. We had a parish in the diocese—in Joplin, it was—where they claimed to have one of those prankish spirits in the organ loft; struck up ribald tunes in the middle of a baptism or when the Altar Guild was doing the flowers. Rector wanted to exorcise it with bell, book, and candle. Well, I had to put my foot down. Turned out in the end, wouldn't you know it, to be the organist's wife. My Rachel sensed it right off, the minute she laid eyes on her. 'There's your poltergeist,' she said." "Sex!" interrupted Aileen. "She was sex-starved. I expect your organist had been too busy pawing the choir boys to take care of his spouse's needs. We had a case like that at Lucy Skinner. Malicious mischief in the chemistry laboratory. Buildings and Grounds caught the woman at it. An instructor, frustrated lesbian. We had to let her go, of course. . . ."

Van Vliet de Jonge waited. "The polders," the Bishop recalled finally. "You were going to tell us, sir?" Now that he had their ears again, Van Vliet proceeded. Northeast of Amsterdam lay the two most recent examples, popularly known as the Old Polder and the New Polder, both creations of the North Sea wall or dike, which had transformed the Zuyder Zee into a fresh-water lake. The "old" one dated back to the thirties, though work on it had been halted during the War and the Nazi occupation; it was more interesting than the "new" one because it had incorporated an island—pre-war maps still showed it that way, surrounded by water, in the middle of the "Southern Sea"—with an old fishing town and trees and what was for Holland a hill, on which stood a little church that now housed a so-called shipwreck museum. But it could hardly be interesting to the hijackers, for the simple reason that it was settled, though as yet somewhat sparsely in comparison with the rest of Holland. Whereas the New Polder, to the south of it, was virtually empty—virgin territory populated mainly by shore birds. The New Polder—Flevoland—was Holland's Alaska. Roads had been laid out, an industrial town-complex projected, and a small airport too, if he recalled right, but, except for the roads, all that booming development was still a blueprint on the drawing-boards of the planners. Factories, cinema, shopping-center, art gallery, angular modern church lay in the future; the sheep had vanished, but cows had not yet taken their places. Here and there, barns, with typical orange roofs, had gone up or were in the process of construction from prefabricated elements, but the spick-and-span homes and bright flower gardens that would follow were no more than a prophecy, borne out by occasional surveyor's sticks in the sedgy

140

waste. When he had last driven through, with his family on a Sunday, bird-watching, they had noted a few isolated new farmhouses—pioneers. By now, other enterprising colonists, encouraged by government subsidies, would have made the trek and set up house under strictly uniform rooftrees as prescribed in the specifications of the central planning authority on holdings limited by law to thirty hectares: "About seventy-five acres," supplied the Senator. "The wide open spaces." And in such a dark-green-frame, neighborless house, with clothes-pole staked outside, like a settler's claim, the *kapers'* confederates were surely installed with arms and provisions to withstand a siege. . . .

"Do you believe it?" Aileen exclaimed, turning to her neighbor. "Sounds reasonable," said the Senator. "Can't think of a better explanation of why they should be wanting a chopper." He had only one objection: if a hideaway had been set up on this New Polder, why had the pilot, following the take-over, continued on a southward course, in the direction of Rome and North Africa? Van Vliet had considered this too. His answer, not wholly satisfying, was to conjecture that the polder had been prepared as a fall-back position: the hijackers' original hope had been to be welcomed in Libya or Algiers probably. Perhaps there had been disagreement among them, the Dutch pair from the start favoring the polder solution, where familiarity with the terrain and the ways of the "host" government would give them ascendancy, while the Arabs, naturally, plumped for North Africa. "Will we ever know?" sighed Sophie. "If we come out alive," Van Vliet promised her. One of his main interests in survival, he found, was precisely to know the peripeties of the drama. He did not want to die in a state of mystification.

Gradually the group fell silent, as though overcome by despondency, hitting them one by one like a powerful drug. Each sat with his private thoughts. As he brooded, Van Vliet's nostrils made out a faint new smell. The cat, he feared: Sapphire. Before long, she would stink to high heaven. And what if he had been wrong in his expectations, what if the German

141

helicopter did not come after all? By an act of will, he refrained from looking at his watch. But it must be almost noon; in The Hague and Amsterdam, deep church bells would soon be ringing. Two hours left. The common word "deadline" was taking on an uncommon significance. He thought of Faust. At two o'clock, punctually, if the helicopter failed to materialize, would the execution of hostages begin?

He heard the Bishop loudly clear his throat and hoped he was not going to lead them in prayer. But instead of addressing the Saviour, he was turning to Henk. "You mentioned a shipwreck museum, sir. Why don't you tell us about that? It will help us pass the time, don't you know." Henk groaned at the old man's simplicity: the last thing they should be wanting was to make time pass swiftly. But the others were nodding; like children at bedtime, they were ready to hear a story. A fairytale, laid in polderland, whose herald or bard he had become. "Please," urged Sophie. "Entertain them. They're scared, and you talk so well." "The Arabian Nights," remarked Carey. "Right on, friend."

Henk obliged. The Zuyder Zee museum, to give it its proper name, on the former island of Schokland, though intended for scholars and specialists, had become a popular excursion spot for Dutch families; his children preferred it to the Tropical Museum, Rembrandt's House, the Torture Museum in The Hague, and even to Aartis, the famous Amsterdam zoo with Prince Bernhard's new elephant house. It was the children who had named it the shipwreck museum. Though the cases contained all kinds of archaeological materials recently dug up on the island, what interested them was not the bones of prehistoric animals or neolithic axes but the finds made when the pumps had dried out the sea floor. Carcasses of sunken ships had been uncovered, ribbed hulls and bony masts, curving prows like necks; 156 vessels had been yielded up by the Zuyder Zee. On the hilly grounds, overlooking what was now fresh water, entire gruesome specimens—lessons in ship's anatomy— were on display. It was as though a blanket had been drawn back from Father Neptune's bed to disclose a marine graveyard. The skeletal ships had gone to eternal rest, like the ancient Egyptians and the Etruscans, with their familiar household objects for company: cooking utensils, tableware, saws, bolts and nails, cannonballs, pipe-bowls, shoes, buckles, buttons. "Doubloons?" suggested Sophie. Henk did not recall any in the showcases—probably the Nazis had got to them first—but there were Dutch coins of course in plenty, some surprisingly recent, with Queen Wilhelmina's portly head. And a curious find had been the skeleton of a drowned fisherman with coins lying beside it—circa 1600—that must have fallen out of a trusty breeches' pocket slowly eaten away by the sea.

"Shoes, you said," mused the Senator. "Wooden, of course?" "Isn't this wonderful, Gus?" cried the pastor. "The romance of the sea. Full fathom five." Van Vliet de Jonge shook his head. The interesting thing about the shipwreck museum, he confided, was its lack of romance. The detritus of a commercial people brought to light by the pumps belonged to the same industrious family as the pumps. The long salty immersion had failed to effect a metamorphosis into something rich and strange. The shards of crockery and rusty pieces of metal were stoutly recognizable, still, in their function of use-objects—as though a sumptuary law of the lowland sea had decreed against extravagance of form or fancifulness of hue in the changes wrought by the element. "Why do you keep putting your country down?" Aileen objected. She was sure there must be wonderful old Delft patterns on the china. Van Vliet shrugged. Sailing ships had not used Delft but rough earthenware and wooden bowls, as was known from the characteristically detailed inventories that had gone down with them to a watery grave. The contents of Davy Jones's locker, as laid bare by the Dutch engineering genius, ran to such "finds" as a cargo of late eighteenth-century codfish, tidily decapitated for the market.

"Sailors' knitting needles?" hazarded Carey. Van Vliet turned in his direction, startled. Here was one who understood. Their minds were meeting, as if in connivance, over the heads of the others. "Any trace of a captain's parrot?" "I should hardly think so, Senator," put in Cameron. "Bird bones and feathers would decompose quite rapidly in salt water."

"Have you written a poem about that museum?" Aileen wondered. Again Henk was startled; her perceptions were sharper than one would have guessed. "The Mariner's Knitting Needle" was one of the best-known pieces in his first collection of verse. "Recite it for us, why don't you?" "Oh, yes, do," they struck up, in choir. But he found himself demurring. He was hesitant to make his poetic self known to the other man in the presence of all these *figurants*. "Then the Senator can give us one of *his* poems," Aileen went on. He met Carey's eyes. No. The spark that had passed between them was male in gender and private. "He writes in *Dutch*, dear lady," reproved Mr. Charles. "Like his grandfather." There, of course, it was, the always valid excuse of his hermetic language; mournful experiences had taught him the truth of the saying that poetry was untranslatable. "Well, recite *something*," said Aileen. "Don't you know any poems in French or English?"

Van Vliet was tempted. In his well-stored memory, ready to hand, lay a poetic prose fragment on the shipwreck theme. By the Japanese poet Bashō (1644–1694), in an English rendering. The poet had made a journey to the eastern provinces of *his* islands; he stood on a precipice looking down to the shore of the Inland Sea, where a famous battle had taken place, in which the young lord Yoshitsune had vanquished the Taira, and all their people had perished. Standing on the historic precipice, the scene of Yoshitsune's downhill rush, the poet pictured the ancient battle and the splendid finery of the warrior court sinking to the sea bottom. On the mournful promontory of Schokland, Van Vliet had more than once declaimed the passage to Durgie and the children. Now he raised his head and began. " 'The great confusion of the day, together with other tragic incidents of the time, rose afresh in my mind, and I saw before me the aged grandmother of the young emperor taking him in her arms, his mother carrying him on her shoulders, his legs pitifully tangled in her dress, and all of them running into a boat to escape the onslaught of the enemy. Various ladies of the court followed them, and threw into the boat all kinds of things —rare musical instruments, for example—wrapped in sheets and quilts. Many things of value, however, must have fallen overboard—imperial food into the sea for the fish to feed upon—' " Suddenly, he could not go on; a lump had come into his throat and tears to his eyes. "The compacts," Carey's rich voice prompted: " '. . . and ladies' vanity boxes on to the sand to be quite forgotten among the grass.' " Van Vliet resumed: " 'This is probably why, even today after a thousand years, the waves break on the beach with such a melancholy sound.' "

There was a soft clapping of hands. The Bishop wiped his eyes. Henk's were now dry. He was moved by the fresh proof of a kinship with the American Senator but more confirmed than surprised. In the back of his mind, he must have wagered that Carey would know the Japanese poet too. He had brought out his bit of Bashō—from "Travels of a Well-worn Satchel"— like a broken coin or a single earring in an old tale, on the bold premise that Carey, if he cared to, would produce the earring's mate, the other half of the coin. And it had happened; the brothers, long separated (had Henk, the cadet, been stolen at birth by a *kabouter* and spirited to Brabant?), had recognized each other across the gulf of an aisle. Yet the witnesses of their mutual recognition, far from being wonderstruck by the marvel, seemed to feel that it was only natural that two poet-legislators should be acquainted with the same "secret" author and go on spouting him together like "To be or not to be."

The wonder came from another source. Unnoticed, the Arab guard had moved closer during the recitation. He now touched Van Vliet's elbow. "I hear this poem before. Yes. Many times. From a Japanese comrade—Japanese Red Army." Old Tennant was the first to recover his wits. "You know Japanese? How clever of you. Such a difficult language. We used to go there, porcelain-hunting, my friend and I, between the wars. Staying in the charming Japanese inns, where they took such good care of us—" "No," interrupted the Arab. "He translate." "Into Arabic? Dear me!" "English. Japanese know only English. Not

145

Arab tongues, not French." *"Vous êtes francophone, monsieur?"* Aileen asked, adopting a social tone too. "Yes. No. For us, French is colonial tongue." His face darkened. "And you, Deputy, how you know this poem? My comrade love it very much. He love this Yoshitsune." The gaze turned on Van Vliet was accusatory. In the face of that scowl—and of the submachine gun swinging from the plump shoulder—he felt unable to explain how he had come into possession of the "poem," which in fact was a travel sketch in prose. From the Arab's point of view, he had stolen it, he supposed, in his character of colonialist. And actually he could not remember where and how he had acquired the little Penguin Classic, with a wash drawing of Bashō, wearing a sort of nightcap, on the cover— probably in an airport bookstall. "How you know it?" the Arab repeated. In his terms, of course, he had the right to ask; he had established his own claim to those lines—they had come to him, by inheritance, from a comrade-at-arms. With compassion, Van Vliet pictured the circumstances: a training camp in Lebanon or Syria, tents or improvised barracks, long, cold desert nights, the moon, a homesick Japanese youngster wrapped in a burnoos or army blanket, chattering of a feudal warrior-hero betrayed, in the end, by his wicked half-brother. He looked for a soft answer to turn away wrath. The gruffness and fat were misleading; this was a youth, not a full-fledged man. "I think I must have found the book in a shop." Diplomatically he avoided the mercantile word "bought." "And you must not be surprised. We Dutch are a curious people and we are curious about Japan, which has much in common with Holland." "Sea people," said the Arab, nodding. "Sea people are imperialistic. River people not so much." Having laid down the general statement, he showed his white teeth in a large, quite friendly smile. Contact had been made.

"And your comrade?" asked Sophie. "Where is he now?" "In prison," the Arab said curtly. "They torture him." The pastor made a clucking noise indicative of sympathy. "Who?" "The Israeli." "Come now," Aileen protested. "The Israelis don't torture prisoners." "You ought to qualify that, Miss Simmons," put in the pastor, with a quick inter-faith smile for the Arab. "We don't *know* that they don't." Charges to that effect, he reminded her, had been made by the Syrians before the UN. "Charges aren't proof," she retorted. "I'll take the Israelis' word any day over the Syrians'." "I'd *prefer* to take their word," said the pastor. "I guess we all would. I mean, as a Christian, I don't want to think that anybody is torturing anybody." "What does that *mean,* Reverend?" Aileen said irritably. "Why 'as a Christian'?" The Reverend gave one of his boyish laughs. "Heck, I'm all tangled up. What I'm trying to say is that if we do incline to take the Israelis' word, it's not because we don't believe the Syrians." "Then what *is* it, man?" exclaimed Cameron. The Bishop held out an oar to his floundering disciple. "Frank means that our faith teaches us not to be over-ready to believe the worst of our fellow-men, whoever they are. In charity, until we know more, he would like to give the Israelis the benefit of the doubt."

The Arab had moved off—out of hearing, Van Vliet trusted. He wished the Americans would close the debate or adjourn it sine die. But Aileen, like a wailing echo, persisted. "I never heard that the Israelis were torturing Japanese prisoners, did you, Senator Jim?" "Let's leave it that they're just torturing Syrians—all in the family. You'd like that better, wouldn't you? And now be quiet, can't you? Our friend's flash point may be lower than you guess."

Van Vliet's fondness for the Senator was increasing by leaps and bounds. Aileen and the dominie, in their obliviousness, were illustrating the worst of what he had heard of the American character. A people given to argumentation, someone had said. And, whatever the subject, the debate was always between themselves—as though only their own opinions counted—and was settled when they reached a conclusion or simply got tired, as the world had watched them do in Vietnam. At least Sophie had held her peace; perhaps, being Jewish, she lacked the authority to pontificate conferred on the others as a birthright. No one had asked him his opinion, but his work with Amnesty had convinced him that all prisoners were tortured; the difference was one of degree. Prison itself was a torture, and especially excruciating to violent revolutionaries of today's school, who lacked the patience of the old revolutionaries; they could not accept incarceration as a stage, like puberty, in their political development. This young gunman, for example, would never be able to "mature" quietly, pent up in a Western jail while awaiting trial by authorities whose legitimacy he did not recognize. To him and his comrades, detention was per se unjust.

In that context, the committee's "mission" to Iran must appear as the height of frivolity—in the stern eyes of actionists a punishable offense. For this young hijacker, surely, the Shah's crimes against humanity were of minimal interest in comparison with the *fact* of his comrade's detention in an Israeli jail. Not to mention the honor roll of other comrades ripe for liberation: the Price sisters, held by the English, Andreas Baader, Ulrike Meinhof, Gudrun Esslin, confined in Helmut's cells, the adjutants of "Carlos" in Giscard's hands. . . . And no committee of Western liberals felt the call to investigate their conditions of detainment, though the courtroom in Stuttgart was only an hour's flight away. Instead, as the hijackers would see it, the conscience of the West was busy looking the other way, at the mote in the Shah's eye.

Henk was not sure he saw it in quite that light himself. But they had a point. One might not concur in the notion that violence in self-ordained hands was above the "bourgeois" law, but did it follow that agents of terror had forfeited all their human rights when they treated themselves as sacred instruments? That indeed seemed to be the prevailing assumption in liberal-minded circles. The capture of a terrorist could hardly be expected to produce universal grief, yet the usual reaction "Good riddance," of which he too had occasionally been guilty, had its own barbarity.

As for the charge of frivolity, you could find considerable evidence of it in this ill-starred expedition. To be honest, he had been aware from the start that curiosity had played a leading part in his decision to join: the lure of the bazaars, carpets, miniatures, minarets, rose water in the cookery, Shiraz, Persepolis if there was time. Curiosity too about the Americans—where did such a group fit in their system?—desire to know Carey in a working relationship; speculations about the Shah and his consort. And he had probably hoped for a poem or two as a by-product.

Yet he felt no strong urge to condemn himself for impurity of motives; if a good deed was able to embrace a few stolen pleasures, so much the better. He was no Calvinist. Besides, in the committee's defense, it could be argued that liberal observers could not be present in all the world's jails and courtrooms simultaneously; unlike God, the liberal was limited by ubiety. Nevertheless, why pick on the Shah? If the truth were known, Henk feared, Reza Pahlavi's enormities had been chosen for this group's attention not just because he had an attractive country with an agreeable winter climate but for a still less pardonable motive: his regime was an easy target. Every good soul was opposed to torture, but it suited the Western soul's book to be able to attest to it in a distant land ruled by an oil monarch who was neither friend nor foe. A foe would not admit your committee, and to find fault with a friend would give pain. If your committee were to find evidence of torture in Israel, it would meet with little sympathy for its "courage" on its return. And if it failed to find evidence, it would be accused of conducting a whitewash. For liberals, the Shah was ideal; only his ambassadors would write angry letters to the newspapers. And his victims, always described as youths of good middle-class families and of respectable political antecedents, were ideal victims from a liberal point of view—guilty of nothing more than advocacy. The only embarrassment, for the committee, would be to discover a few terrorists among them—unlikely, as domestic terrorists were executed there with great promptitude.

Henk sighed. Involuntarily, he looked at his watch. Fifteen minutes before one. He hoped that these young bandits were not going to become his surrogate conscience for the duration, however that was to be reckoned, in hours, days, or weeks. It occurred to him that he might be experiencing in his own person a thing he had read about with slight disgust in the newspapers: the incredible tendency on the part of hostages—bank tellers, air stewardesses, motherly middle-aged passengers—to "see the good side" of their kidnappers: "They behaved to us like perfect gentlemen," "He was as sweet as he could be." Some carried it to the point of actually falling in love with them; he remembered the Swedish bank employee who greeted her release by announcing her engagement to the leading criminal. Henk would not say that his own symptoms were in any way amorous. Nor did he think that he was in the process of being converted to a terrorist outlook: observing terror at close quarters, he felt more than ever the futility and waste of it. But, being at close quarters, he could not fail to glimpse their point of view, which caused him to turn about and look at his own party with freshened eyes.

Yet he was feeling something else: pity for the hijackers. Their brief life-expectancy moved him as he studied the moony countenance of the machine-gunner, the soft baby-fat cheeks and incipient dewlaps. Within a year, in all likelihood, this boy would be dead; prison would only be an unwelcome reprieve—if held too long, he would hang himself. There were no active middle-aged terrorists or grizzled retired terrorists. He was a warrior, born to a short life, like the sulky Achilles or his friend's idol Yoshitsune. And, whatever he had been taught in his training camp, he would not really expect his ideas to live after him. Today's arch-revolutionaries had no faith in a future life for their ideas; it was gone, like the Christian faith in God's design.

If, thanks to this calfish specimen, Henk's own days or minutes were now numbered, at least he had had his full share of life's rewards and amusements. The fact that he had just celebrated, after a fashion, his thirty-eighth birthday (where, by the way, was that magazine with the horoscope?) suddenly seemed rather indecent, an actuarial disproportion that was like being overweight in a time of world hunger. And the pity he felt for the *kapers,* even that brute of a woman, was sharpened by irritation with the sheer folly of their enterprise. The optimum result they could hope for would be to gain the release of a few fellow-terrorists, to engage in more hijackings, daring raids, and kidnappings—a vicious circle, for most would be shot or returned to jail. The ransom money they might extort could only serve to finance a new round of suicidal operations; unlike the normal criminal, they knew of no other use for it. A food distribution, were they to include it in their demands, would turn into a grotesque scene from Brueghel.

Could reason make them see the vicious circle they were spinning in? That they were all doomed to violent and pointless extinction, on the model of their hero, Che? They would hardly be open to dissuasion at this stage. It would be pointless to make the effort, even if he were summoned again. A plea coming from him addressed to their own self-interest would not be recognized as such, however feelingly it was expressed. But later a time might come. If they got their helicopter and were put down with their freight of captives on the lonely polder, a new chapter could open. Under those circumstances, it might not be impossible, for example, to "reach" the machine-gunner, evidently the most susceptible member of the team. Bashō, as had been demonstrated, was the soft spot in his warrior's carapace. The cluster of tender sentiment surrounding the poet and the Japanese guerrilla might be the point of entry.

If the youth was responsive to poetry, in principle he was salvageable, though it was true, Henk sadly recalled, that here in Holland some of the worst SS men had been lovers of Rilke and Hölderlin—his father, the magistrate, had cited the fact ironically when he had gone to witness against them at their trials. Still, poetry, as a frail *trait d'union,* the thin edge of the wedge, was a hope—the only one available. That Henk had been led by a queer chain of coincidences to recite those lines could be taken for a sign from Heaven, showing him the right way. But the plump gloomy boy, however open to softer influences he might prove to be, was subordinate to the others. Even if he could be gently detached from them, at night as he stood watch, how in fact could he help? He had only the one weapon.

And should one aim after all at corrupting a minor? That was what it would amount to. Henk shook his head, feeling distaste for the train of thought he had been pursuing. Once again he despaired.

Sophie gripped his hand; he raised his eyes. The woman was standing in the doorway, her pistol peeping from her blouse. She had an announcement to make. A light meal was going to be served. As soon as they had eaten, the prisoners were to gather their hand baggage and proceed to the first-class cabin, where disembarkation would take place. A helicopter was standing by. "And Sapphire?" asked Victor hoarsely, speaking for the first time today; there were cake-crumbs in his two-day-old beard. "You will leave your cat," said the woman. "The hostesses will dispose of it. And you will not be needing the carrier."

Before Van Vliet de Jonge left the cabin, he retrieved the copy of *Elle*. In captivity he would have time, finally, to peruse his birthday horoscope. But in the aisle the young Arab abruptly took the magazine from him and stood frowning at the cover, which showed a pretty blonde girl wearing a blue-and-white crocheted cap—the winter sports number. His eyes slowly rose and met Van Vliet's with a look of childish mischief—was he inviting the deputy to a hand-to-hand struggle for possession of a French cover girl? Then with a grunt, as if to denote relinquishment, he handed the fashion magazine back. His white teeth flashed in a broadening, still mischievous smile as he helped himself instead to a cigar from the deputy's pocket.

Six

Human nature, they decided, was contrary. One would have supposed that they would have been grateful for practically any change, anything to break the monotony—more than a day in the jumbo at that point without even a cribbage-board. Yet the first-class hostages had not welcomed the arrival of a slew of hostages from Economy in their midst. Utterly unannounced: up to the minute the curtain had parted and that procession had filed in, one had thought one was alone in one's glory; it had stood to reason that when the separation of the sheep from the goats had taken place, eons ago, the whole Economy contingent would have been released. So that it had been a shock to see these people appear and to learn that one was going to have them for company on the next leg of the journey, for no sooner had they made their appearance than the loud-speaker had blared: everyone was to collect his belongings and stand ready to board another aircraft.

But then a long wait had followed, and in the interval one had had time to sort out who was who, more or less, among one's future companions. The gangling, bow-tied minister (Lily knew him from ages back) had got himself quite a name for being the worst type of bleeding heart—sad for his sweet wife and family and for his church, which was paying the price; nobody had a pew there any more. The stout tweedy old party with him, who looked quite a dear really with his apple cheeks and his "brolly," had been a bishop somewhere out west, but he was tarred with the same brush: he had been close to Eleanor, it seemed, though Franklin could never abide him. And dear silly Charles, turning up like a bad penny after his "slumming" tour; one forgave him because one was used to his prattle. He was a nice old thing at heart, wouldn't hurt a fly. He knew what it was to live with beautiful things. But clinging to him was a little rouged woman with dangling earrings and a screechy voice who could not stop talking—some sort of menopausal cause-person probably that he had picked up for his sins on one of his pinko boards. And there was a red-eyed unshaven creature draped in a filthy scarf and with a basket of cat food and "kitty-litter" who was evidently one of the flock; he had helped himself to several miniatures of vodka from the serving-pantry as he went by, and the steward had just shrugged. What the lot of them had been doing on a flight to Teheran was rather hard to imagine; there was nothing in that part of the world but oil and archaeology, and neither, one would think, was their dish of tea.

But it fitted that that Senator Carey was with them, a maverick even in his own party. He was a well-groomed man at any rate, rather actorish like so many of his trade but handsome in a theatrical way. He probably used a rinse on that silver hair and dyed his eyebrows. And of course he would be odoriferous of toilet lotion—the Irish in him coming out. He was exchanging witticisms with a younger man, quite handsome too, with a trench coat slung over his shoulders and got up in a flaring whipcord suit coat that must have been "bespoke"; he wore a folded-over scarf for a tie and did not seem like an American. With them was a tall, frowning girl with a long Jewish nose that Beryl said she knew—another lefty, needless to say. Bringing up the rear had been a short bristly man, who looked like a professor, with a pipe. Most of them could have done with a freshening-up in the lavatory.

Luckily, though, there was room in the helicopter for the two parties to keep their distance. Beryl, right away, had wanted to fraternize, but Lily, exercising a mother's rights, had made her stay put. Until they had actually laid eyes on the "whirlybird" they were going to have to board—quite a feat for a woman of Margaret's girth—they had been fearing a tight squeeze. Some of the ladies had armed themselves with atomizers from their toilet cases to ward off odors, and clever Mrs. Chadwick had improvised quite a pretty fan from the Air France menu. But there was space, and to spare, for everybody, including two of the cabin crew. The steward told them that the giant helicopter had been flown in from Germany (West), which was the reason for the long delay, but Harold Chadwick was sure it was an American jobbie—they did not make them that size over here. And one certainly need not have worried about lack of air. In fact, it was awfully drafty. Noisy as well; you could hardly hear yourself think. Johnnie Ramsbotham, who was up front, had kept shouting at the pilot to ask where they were bound for, but any answers he might have got were lost in the din of the propeller-blades. The stewardess—the nice one, with the smelling-salts—had no idea where they might be going. Lapland, it felt like, from the interior temperature. The high-colored, strong-jawed fellow in the whipcord seemed to know; he was standing up, rather dangerously, and pointing out landmarks to the Senator.

But it was useless to call out and ask him; he would not be able to hear. That was the disadvantage of having stayed with one's own group, leaving a no man's land of empty seats in between. Johnnie, who was a sailor and knew how to take his bearings, thought they must still be over Holland. But they had not seen any windmills. And not a sign of a landing field. That had made poor Harold anxious, as the sun was already setting. He flew his own plane, so he understood these things. According to him, the pilot would not dare to put down in the dark, just like that, without ground flares to guide him. They could count on half an hour of light after sunset; after that, they would have to find a proper landing field or crash.

It was unnerving to have to hear that, considering all they had been through already; it would be the last straw to die at this point in a common ordinary plane crash. So far, except for the little curator, everybody had been amazingly brave, treating it as a lark and fortifying the inner man with drinks; Helen Potter was quite tiddly. They had agreed to be philosophical about their baggage—Air France could keep it for them in Amsterdam, hopefully under lock and key—you could hardly expect hijackers to be interested in whether you had your nighties or clean shirts. On seeing the new additions to the party, the men, typically, had been concerned about rations: wherever they were headed for, there would be a great many mouths to feed, and the lefties, they feared, would get the lion's share. Foresighted Johnnie, before quitting the jumbo, had stuffed his pockets with Air France candies from the tray. Still, it would not hurt most of the males to tighten their belts a bit; they could make believe they were at one of their "fat farms." Yet now, with dusk gathering, all the bravely hidden worries peeked out.

First, the mystifying fact of having been singled out as "hostage material" (Beryl's funny phrase) when the rest of the first-class passengers had been sent packing. "Do we look so prosperous?" Johnnie had innocently wondered. Well, obviously they did. Johnnie Ramsbotham was one of the two hundred richest men in America. But how could the hijackers know that? Unless Charles had been naughty. The old tease loved to talk about "my millionaires" and "my Republicans." Of course he would never stop to think that hijackers too had ears. And next there were the collections, which was the point that they all—multi-millionaires or just making ends meet—had in common. Could a little bird have told the hijackers about those? Helen's Vermeer was famous, and she had been generous —or foolish—enough to share it with the public by letting it hang on loan in a show for one of her charities. And Harold's Cézannes were in all the books. Johnnie collected only sporting art, but his Stubbses and Degas were worth fortunes, not to mention his Dufy sailing subjects and his great Ward. As for Lily, some authorities thought her English water-colors, though fewer in number, were every bit as fine as Paul Mellon's.

Then of course there was the "couple" little Mr. Walton, the curator, had included on his own say-so—they were of his ilk, evidently. They had joined the tour at the airport, having driven up from their villa in the south of France: that was in the winter; the rest of the time they lived in Duxbury, outside of Boston. No one knew yet what they collected. Prints, one might guess, since, to judge from their battered attaché cases sporting ancient hotel stickers, they belonged to the category of "more taste than money." But prints, these days, were "in" and could fetch enormous prices. Eventually one could ask.

Yet even if the hijackers had somehow got wind of this tour of collectors, how could that serve their purposes? All those treasures were back in America, protected by the latest burglar-alarm systems and fully insured. Nobody traveled with their valuables these days. Years ago, Wintie Thorp, before he be-came a vegetable, used to take his Byzantine ivories with him on the steamer to Europe and set one up in his hotel dressing-room every morning on the shaving-stand, so that he could look at it while shaving, start the day right, but there were no old-fashioned steamers any more and no shaving-stands, unless maybe at Claridge's, and Margaret had sold the collection—*too* portable. Today someone feeling the pinch and having been stung once too often at Sotheby Parke Bernet might hand-carry a little pair of icons or a Book of Hours to Christie's in London for appraisal, but if the insurance company knew about it, the premiums would be prohibitive. Of the present group, only Charles, apparently, could not learn to move with the times; he insisted on wearing that intaglio ring—crystal, with *"amor fati"* incised in it—that he said had belonged to some Lord Acton, and if you turned out his pockets you would be bound to find a few of his "trinkets," a rare Babylonian shekel or a sweet little Twelfth Dynasty Horus. At least his fabulous porcelains were safe with his couple on Mount Vernon Street. So that the collections should be the least of anybody's worries now; there was no earthly reason to fear on their behalf.

And yet she did, roared Margaret, and doubtless they all did in their hearts. The penalty of owning great works of art, or even itsy-bitsy ones, was that the minute anything out-of-the-way happened, your thoughts flew to them like a mother bird to the nest. Most of the time, unless you were showing the collection to visitors, you hardly *saw* the master works hanging on your walls or mounted in cases, the way you ceased to hear a clock ticking after awhile—it was something about the attention-span. That was why experts advised one to keep changing their positions. If Helen looked at her Vermeer more than once a week, it would be unusual; her maid, dusting the frame with a special soft brush, spent more time, probably, "communing" with it than she did. It was a privilege to be a domestic in a house like that, where practically every stick of furniture was signed by a great cabinet-maker; they said beauty was contagious if you were exposed to it long enough, but sometimes one wondered—look at Harold. In any case, rub off on you or not, beautiful things were a heavy responsibility. Worse than children, who eventually grew up and found their own way. Whenever you went off for a weekend, or even downtown to the hairdresser, a part of you stayed home with your treasures, and your first thought, on opening the door after an absence, was to make sure they were still there. They said you could store them in a vault, like your jewelry, when you went away, but what was the point of having beautiful things if you had to keep coming home to blank spaces on the walls and a constant traffic of bonded moving-men on the carpets? Then there was the burden of caring for them, seeing that they had the right temperature and humidity, protecting them from the sun, making certain that they were dusted, or not dusted, as the case might be. At least, unlike an animal, they did not have to be exercised.

Lily, by the bye, had a funny story about this bolshie minister when he was a curate. She had had him to one of her musical teas—that was when she still had the house on Fifth Avenue—and in those days there was a little Augustus John in the morning-room that had come down to her from an aunt. People always asked to see it, because of the subject—Churchill's beautiful American mother—though it was a flashy thing and she finally put it up for auction. Anyway, that day there was a new butler, and when this Reverend Mr. Barber turned up, just out of Divinity School, he asked him "Where is the John?" In an undertone, because the music had already started. So the butler said "Here, sir," and showed him to the toilet. The curate was so mortified that he went in and did his business and turned tail and left. Lily only heard later, from the butler, what had happened. "He asked me for the john, madam, and I directed him."

"I don't know why Mother insists on telling that story," loudly complained Beryl, an overweight child in her late thirties who was always picking quarrels with Lily. For weeks, they gathered, she had been refusing to come on this tour and then, characteristically, changed her mind at the last minute—such a bother for Lily, who had to pull strings with the Iranian ambassador in Washington, so that the girl could have her visa in time. He could not have been more charming, and yet Beryl would not even write him a little note of thanks. Now she was tickled that they had been hijacked; it had "made" her winter, she announced. She would say anything of course to be different, but perhaps in a pitiful way it was true. Her life with Lily in that apartment was rather barren; she had so few interests of her own and refused to share in her mother's: she had hated art from the cradle and had her own queer little collections of inartistic objects, such as antique false teeth and poison labels for medicine bottles—quite amusingly arranged, it had to be admitted; she had the family knack.

If only she had not had that figure problem, which was not glands but plain over-eating—stuffing herself to fill an aching inner void—she could have been rather stunning. She had a real porcelain complexion (proof of perfect elimination, considering what she ate!), which she had to disfigure with big circus patches of rouge. Her hair was thick and naturally blond, and she wore it in a wide Dutch bang that came down to a point in the middle over the family nose—a twenties style called the "Sweetheart" that she had found in some cheap magazine. Her best feature was her eyes, bluer than Lily's and glittering like sapphires, which too often she hid behind huge dark glasses, as though she thought she was Jacqueline Bouvier or a film star. And she would not let Lily dress her. Instead, she had a passion for "separates"—billowy skirts and assorted bright-colored blouses that recalled whole choruses of buxom villagers in an opera. Johnnie commented that Beryl's outfits always looked as if she had bought each item in a different Thrift shop and then thrown them all together in a hopper. For the flight she had not wanted to wear her lovely long mink—Lily's Christmas offering. Instead, there was a cherished junk-fur jacket dyed a brilliant blue that she had planned to put on over slacks. Lily had had to insist, and now, in this freezing cabin, Beryl could be grateful.

Her trouble, of course, was that she dressed to get attention, from men, obviously (the idea that women dressed for other women certainly did not apply in her case), and she succeeded; that is, she made herself conspicuous, which was not hard, given her size. She might have taken a leaf from Margaret's book, but Margaret was all in scale; her height and deep booming voice carried her weight, and the mannish *tailleurs* she wore (always Captain Molyneux) made her look redoubtable, like a monument, which would stand out naturally in a crowd. You could not call the Statue of Liberty conspicuous. And nice men, as anyone could have told Beryl, did not care to be seen with conspicuous women, while the other kind, who would have been attracted anyway by her inherited wealth, seemed to find her an embarrassment themselves in the long run. An heiress who looked like something out of the five-and-ten (there had been Woolworth money, be it said, on Joe's side) and would not be caught dead in a smart supper club, only the lowest of low dives, must be a chore to run about with, even in Mother's chauffeured old Rolls. At any rate her "pashes" were always letting her down, and she cried in her bedroom and had orders sent in from the drugstore, rejecting Lily's trays. Naturally, as with the clothes she set her heart on, she was fatally drawn to men who were crude and common, men who were bound to hurt her. It would not be beyond Beryl to set her cap at one of the hijackers before this was over. The young Arab was *rather* interested; that was clear already. Mohammedans admired fat women, and that milk-white skin and yellow hair had an appeal for the dark-skinned races, as poor Lily had reason to know: a few years ago, there had been a Negro delivery boy who was learning to play the trumpet, but when Beryl had paid for enough lessons he had got a job with a band and skipped out. Even undesirables had their sticking-point—surprising but true. And, however one viewed her appearance, Beryl could be impossibly rude and overbearing.

Yet she could be a sweet child too. Johnnie, who liked to spar with her, was convinced that she was still a virgin. It was a case, he argued, of arrested adolescence; one of his wives had been the same—you could see it in their chubby upper arms. If she could just cut loose from Lily's apron-strings, she would mature fast, he thought; as it was, her mind had developed, but her body had not kept pace with it. As proof that she had a head on her shoulders he would cite the fact that she had never played around with drugs; she was still in the milkshake stage and did not even like alcohol, except gin alexanders and sweet liqueurs. If Beryl's sitting-room, as Lily maintained, had a permanent sweet reek of marijuana—damned hard to get out of the draperies, as Johnnie knew from his own progeny's "dens"—it was only her friends smoking the weed. Milkshakes and crushes and a yen to be different from Mamma, that was all that was the matter with Beryl. She held it against Lily that they were rich (though Lily only had her widow's portion); that seemed to be the chief grievance, which Johnnie said he could understand—he had faced the problem himself as a young man. She would have to learn to live with it, like everybody else, and stop feeling that it was a "curse" and her mother's fault. No wonder, though, that she had got a kick out of being hijacked. "Serves us right," she had repeated, back in the Air France jet, with a triumphant shake of her yellow locks. *"C'est bien fait pour nous,"* she had proceeded to translate, beaming up at the plump young Arab. *"N'est-ce pas, monsieur?"* But the wary youth had had the grace to be evasive. *"Sais pas, madame."*

161

Well, doubtless it was lucky that someone in the party, for whatever disloyal reason, was enjoying the experience. Beryl's total fearlessness, you could say, was good for the general morale, which needed some bolstering now that the drinks had worn off. The little curator was shivering in his thin coat; if it had not been for that constant whirring noise, one could surely have heard his teeth chatter—the stewardess ought to have thought to bring some Air France blankets along. And the sun was rapidly setting. They watched it sink like a plummet off to the left of the "chopper," as Harold called it. To the left and slightly astern. So they were heading northeast. In the glass bubble, beside the pilot, the big tow-headed Teutonic hijacker—they had decided to nickname him "Hans" and his girl friend "Gretel"—was leaning forward and scanning the ground. Were they nearing their destination? The pilot flew lower. He hovered. But below there was no sign of life, nothing to be seen but a ruler-straight highway running through flat unimproved land. No cars, no houses with lights in them, even though they had passed big pylons that must be for electricity. After a long pause, seemingly for inspection, the pilot continued on course, flying low above the empty highway. Far off to the left, where the sun had set, there was a gleam that was probably water, and on the right there appeared to be water too. They must be skimming over an island or a peninsula. Beside the road there were thick bushes and small, evenly planted leafless trees and what might be ditches for drainage or irrigation, but only an occasional shadowy structure that could be a house or a barn—in the gathering dusk, it was hard to tell. Yet there were no animals about, not a single cow or a sheep. "What the hell?" said Henry Potter, speaking his first word in several hours.

All at once, some lights went on below—lanterns, probably, for they were moving back and forth, as though signaling. In reply, the pilot put on his landing-lights. The "chopper" came slowly down, grazing the tree-tops. It landed. Right in the middle of a four-lane concrete highway. And they were expected to get out. The side-doors opened. "Welcome to Flevoland!" said the cheerful fellow in the whipcord. He had jumped off first, without a by-your-leave, and stood helping the others to descend. He gave a hand to the creaky old Bishop and then aided Margaret Thorp, who managed to look majestic despite her vast circumference as she was hoisted by the steward and the stewardess into his extended arms. Beryl leapt off quite nimbly, like the equestrienne she had been in her teens, and turned back to assist her mother. The "wife" of the couple—Warren's friends—helped the older "husband."

Meanwhile the team of hijackers stood by, grinning contemptuously at these simple displays of courtesy and doing nothing themselves to be useful. Beyond the bright circle made by the helicopter's landing-lights, other figures could be seen, armed with rifles. Until everyone was out of the helicopter, they too merely watched, making no move. One had the impression they were counting the hostages. The crew, as was proper, stayed aboard till the last and occupied themselves with the hand baggage; impatient looks passed among the hijackers as overnight cases from Gucci and Hermès were carefully lowered. "Hans" snapped his thick fingers and shouted at the crew to hurry up, setting an example by seizing a Louis Vuitton case and hurling it to the pavement—in the stillness, you could distinctly hear the sound of breaking glass. Then the rest of the baggage tumbled out in a heap, followed by the steward and the stewardess and the co-pilot, who was in military uniform, like the pilot. This was a military aircraft, evidently, which helped explain the lack of amenities; Harold said it must be used to carry paratroopers. The pilot was taking his time, methodically collecting papers and checking the equipment; he passed a Red Cross kit down to the stewardess. "Hans" barked an order; the lights went out, and the pilot scrambled down.

In the thick dusk, you could hardly make out anything. The lanterns of the reception committee had been shaded or doused. Impossible to tell where one was or how many of these lurking figures there were. All one knew was that one had been dumped without explanation on a highway that seemed to run through an absolute wilderness. Perhaps vehicles would appear to take them on the next lap of the dreadful journey—cars or, more likely, a truck. Yet, whichever way one looked, there was no faint beam of approaching headlights. They heard footsteps receding, twigs snapping, and the rustle of reeds or underbrush. Were they going to trek on foot with what was left of their worldly goods to some robbers' den in the woods? Or could a motor boat be moored waiting to receive them? The water they had observed argued for that, but the thought of exchanging *terra firma* for still another unreliable element was more than reason was willing to entertain. They waited.

At last Charles—bless him—took it on himself to confront the skulking gang, whose forms could barely be discerned in the murk. "Well, my dears," he screeched, "I presume you don't plan to keep us all night on this public thoroughfare. We'd be grateful if you'd show us promptly to our accommodations. This evening damp is most unhealthy; one could easily take a chill, you see, and you don't want to turn your 'hospitality room' into an infirmary, do you?" He gave that crowing laugh. A soft, gurgling sound like a suppressed giggle came from the plump young Arab, who added a friendly nudge of his weapon at Beryl's ribs. Gretel was unamused. "You will not move from this place till we tell you. Your comfort is of no interest to us at this time. You will remain here under guard of the Palestine Liberation Army." In other words, Beryl's friend, the fatted calf, whom they had named "Ahmed," and the older one with the mustache, whom they had decided to call "Abdul." Gretel's harsh voice continued. "And if any of you is so foolish as to 'try anything' during our absence, one of your number will pay the price." She strode through the group of captives, surveying them with a swiftly produced, pencil-sized flashlight, as though taking her pick. The choice fell on the Bishop. "He will come with us." Whereupon she and Hans simply melted away into the shadows, along with their band of accomplices and the helpless old man, whom they had deprived of his brolly. They ignored the murmur of shock that rose from the hostages, and the rector's loud pleas to be taken instead (the Bishop, it seemed, had a heart condition) got only a grunt from Gretel. "And no smoking!" Her "parting shot" was delivered from somewhere in the bushes with terrifying accuracy. "Put that pipe out!" A pipe rattled to the pavement. Dear Gretel must have eyes in the back of her head.

Absurd of her, though, to think that anyone would try to escape. True, the two Arabs did not look very fit and might be overpowered by sheer force of numbers, but where did one take it from there? Quite apart from the horrid threat to shoot the Bishop—surely that was what she had implied?—at the slightest false move from the others, it would be madness to strike out into this unknown terrain in mid-January and with no proper footwear to boot. By now it was pitch-dark. The hostages' eyes, still not adjusted to the blackness, could hardly distinguish the shape of the giant helicopter a few yards away. Tomorrow it might be another story. They would be able to see the lie of the land and take their bearings from the sun. Now fog was swirling in; no guiding stars were visible overhead, and not a glimmer of a rising moon. The most they could be sure of was that this sinister, deserted spot was somewhere near the sea. "Why, for all we know, it might be the Faroe Islands," declared Lily. "My God, Mother!" Beryl chided. "Didn't they give you any geography in that finishing school of yours?" "I was speaking figuratively," said Lily. "And you know very well that Saint Tim's is not a finishing school. It offers an excellent education." Good marks for Lily! In these trying circumstances, she could have been forgiven if she had mentioned the string of schools and colleges that Beryl had been asked to leave.

The luminous dial of Johnnie's watch—the latest thing in digitals—showed 6:02. Unbelievable. It felt more like midnight. And a good half-hour anyway must have passed since they had been left standing here in a huddle like cattle, but there was no way of telling, as nobody had thought to check the time when they landed. Or had the pilot noted it in his log? In the stillness, they could hear the occasional toot of a foghorn and the cry of a night bird, hawk or kestrel. Then, in the distance, a rustling and skittering that was surely animals, squirrels or rabbits or weasels, depending on the latitude. Finally a few in the party with sharp ears became aware of another sound, dull and regular, as of far-off pistons. "Do you hear that?" Harold Chadwick whispered. His wife listened. "Yes. What on earth can it be, Chaddie?" He did not know. For some reason, that rhythmic mechanical sound, in the absence of any of the normal noises of civilization, was very unnerving, like the pulsing of an infernal engine. "Sounds like a pump," said Henry. But as they all listened, it stopped, and the night became utterly silent. Then it resumed.

"It *is* a pump." That was the man in the whipcord again; his pale scarf, folded like a stock, could just be made out. In a body, the first-class hostages turned to him; all the carefully built little social barriers came down, as of course they had to in an emergency, with everyone standing here chock-a-block. He talked with quite a strong accent, difficult to place, but he sounded like a person who was very sure of himself. What they were hearing, he said, was a pumping-station. They were in Holland. And he was Dutch himself, naturally. "But I thought you said 'Welcome to Flevoland' or some name like that," protested Beryl. She was right; it *had* been somewhat misleading. But "Flevoland," it seemed, was the name of this part of Holland. From a lake which used to be here in Roman times that the Romans had called "Lake Flavus," meaning yellow.

"I'll be darned," said Johnnie. "What happened to the lake?" Well, that was a long story, said the Dutchman, and then proceeded to tell it, as people always did when they said that. But it was interesting and gave them something to think about besides the state of their extremities and the clammy fear that was starting to creep over them like the fog. The temperature was close to freezing, and standing on the icy concrete was an ordeal, especially for the women in their thin shoes. The group was at a loss as to how to interpret Gretel's injunction not to move—did it mean stay glued to the spot or could they take a few steps to stretch their legs instead of just shifting from foot to foot?

Anyhow, to hear the Dutchman tell it, the Roman lake and the land around it had been gradually taken over by the sea; then in recent times the process had been reversed. When the Zuyder Zee had been closed in from the North Sea, the old lake bottom had been drained and made into a "polder." The highway underfoot ran along a raised dike, which was part of the system that kept the water out. But it was fresh water now, not salt—the Ijsselmeer, pronounced something like "ice," he said. And this whole place they were on was a polder. "Land reclamation," said Johnnie. "Now I get it. We're on your 'Oost Polder.'" Johnnie was amazing; one would think that he never read a book and cared for nothing but his pictures and sailing and horses, but one forgot that his financial interests brought him in touch with all sorts of remote places and people, so that he could be a mine of the strangest information. It would not be surprising if one of his companies had been researching these polders for investment. And once Johnnie got hold of a fact, it stayed with him. It was stored away in his memory for when it might come in handy. Like tonight. The Dutchman, you could tell, was pleased as Punch to meet an American who knew something about his country. If the circumstances had been more normal, one could have expected an exchange of visiting cards. As it was, they traded names. "Van Vliet de Jonge." "Ramsbotham."

The reason the area was so empty was that it was all new land, ready for development. The water they had noticed to the east of them was a lake with brand-new artificial beaches for tourism. A few miles to the north, an airport was under construction. There would be some light industry in the new towns, but Flevoland's 52,000 hectares would be used mainly for cereals, sugar beets, potatoes, and dairy-farming. "What about timber?" said Johnnie. "4000 hectares," answered the other. "About 46,000 will be in agriculture." Harold interrupted. He had had his fill of this discussion. What interested him was whether the hijackers were going to make them sleep in the chopper. The Dutchman doubted it. He supposed their hideaway would prove to be a farmhouse—a few had already been built, well set back from the road. "You may have noticed one or two from the air." A farmhouse, he guessed, and a barn, too, had been taken over and got ready by their confederates. "Hopefully," said Harold, with a short laugh. "Jesus, how many are we?" "Twenty-four, with the pilots," said the Dutchman. "You've got it all at your finger-tips, haven't you?" retorted Harold, who was clearly in one of his rude moods. He was someone who was sensitive to being left out.

"What makes you so sure anyway that it's this so-called polder of yours that they've brought us to?" "Why, he guessed it hours ago, back in the plane, didn't he, Senator, didn't you, Mynheer Van Vliet?" That was the little Economy class woman with all the rouge. "And now this pumping-station proves he was right. On a newly drained polder, he explained to us, the pumps run day and night. Maintaining the water level."

"How interesting, Mr. Van Vliet," said Lily. "Do tell us what made you guess." "Exercise of reason," spoke up the Senator. "Plus being Dutch. When they asked for a helicopter, he had all the clues in his hand." "Clues?" "Sure. The flying range of helicopters and their capability of landing in rough terrain without a runway gave him his coordinates. And being Dutch, he was aware of polder country—wide open spaces with hardly any folks around. In easy flying radius of Schiphol. Your ordinary passenger plane couldn't have put down here. Well, maybe a Piper Cub. But for that we were too many, as Father Time said." " 'Father Time'?" Lily sounded alarmed. "*Jude the Obscure,* Mother. Didn't they have that on your reading-list at Saint Tim's?"

Margaret took up the questioning. "Thank you, Beryl. Now I wonder if this gentleman will enlighten us a little further. Can you tell us, sir, how these Germans and Arabs came to be acquainted with your uninhabited polder? Is it a matter of general knowledge?" Well, you could have knocked them over with a feather: "Hans" and "Gretel" were not German; they were Dutch. "You'll have to think of some new names for them, Mother," twitted Beryl. "And you don't know any Dutch names, I bet." "Naming the animals," observed the Senator, in his dry way. "Try 'Rip' as in 'Winkle.' " "But Hans *is* a Dutch name," declared Helen. "Remember *Hans Brinker or The Silver Skates*? Mary Mapes Dodge. How I doted on that book. But I forget what his dear little sister was called." "Well, give us some Dutch given names, Mr. Van Vliet," ordered Margaret in her measured my-good-man tones. "Maarten, Willem, Adriaan . . . Liesbeth, Henriette . . ." *"Saskia!"* interrupted Helen. But who would want to call a hijackeress after Rembrandt's glorious young wife? Mr. Van Vliet was thinking. "For him, you ought to have a Groningen sort of name. Gerrit . . . ?" "Never mind this name game." Harold's voice was raised again. "What I'd like to hear is how our friend here knew the gang had asked for a helicopter."

Harold had a point. In first class they had not been told a word about a helicopter or any other kind of getaway plane. How was it that Economy seemed to know such a lot while first-class passengers had been kept totally in the dark? "Very simple. The hijackers told me," cheerily replied Mr. Van Vliet and-whatever-the-rest-of-his-name-was. Again the first-class hostages could only gasp. This man had been in the terrorists' confidence and was brazen enough to admit it. It was a horrid sensation to feel that you might have a Judas in your midst. Finally Charles, the old know-all, had the goodness to explain. Mr. Van Vliet de Jonge was a deputy in their Parliament. "The leader of his party, I believe. I knew his grandfather. Charming man. His party is in the ruling coalition, you see, and since our captors were negotiating over the wireless with the Dutch government, it was only logical that he should be chosen as intermediary. Which in turn permitted him to learn some of their demands."

"Of course, Mother," cried Beryl. "Don't you remember? There was a man they took up to the pilot's cabin. Twice, I think. That was Mr. Van Vliet de Jonge, obviously. But you people never notice anything. If you saw him, you probably thought he was another hijacker. By that time, you were all drunk anyway like most of your generation. Except Mrs. Chadwick—'just a little unseasoned tomato juice'—who was fainting."

"Manners, Beryl," interposed Johnnie. "Keep your shirt on. Unlike you, honey child, the rest of us were under a strain. And, now that you mention it, I do recall somebody's being hustled up those corkscrew steps. But I didn't take much notice. And you're right: just about then, Eloise fainted."

When he stopped, one was almost grateful for the dark. As if to bear out Beryl's allegation, a distinct smell of alcohol was reaching their nostrils. It must come from the Vuitton case that had been thrown down with such violence; a bottle of whiskey must have broken—more likely, a pair of bottles. Still, Beryl's outburst, whatever the foundation in fact, could not be dismissed as easily as her protector, Johnnie, seemed to think. To accuse your mother, in public, with strangers listening, of having been drunk was rather unforgivable. And, on top of that, to do a take-off of little Mrs. Chadwick's la-de-da way of speaking. That was cruel. Actually nobody had been what you would call drunk, except the Potters, and Henry never showed it. When once in a great while he would have to be carried out of his club and entrusted to his chauffeur, it always came as a surprise: one minute he was erect and in full possession of his faculties (as far as could be judged), and the next he swayed and toppled over like a tall tree in a forest. It could happen at any time of day but only in the club—never when ladies were present. He was a gentleman to the core; the men said that when he keeled over it was almost a noble sight, like watching a cathedral pine fall. Unfortunately Helen, who now and then took one martini too many, in order to keep him company, had no head for liquor, which led people to think that she was an alcoholic and a cross for sober Henry to bear, when the exact opposite happened to be the case.

The dark was doubly welcome because it gave them time to think about Charles's revelations, and one would not like the person in question to be aware of it. There was no real reason to doubt that he was a deputy in Parliament, even though somebody like Harold might immediately want proof. Being self-made, Harold was naturally suspicious of those who had less of this world's goods than he had acquired, and right now one could not altogether blame him; the present circumstances, so eerie, hardly conduced to an atmosphere of trust. But the fact that Charles had known this man's grandfather was some sort of testimonial: Charles was awfully well connected. On the other hand, whoever one's grandfather had been did not prevent one, these days, from crossing over to the other side—almost the contrary; a mother could scarcely be sure any more that her own children were not manufacturing bombs in the cellar. What really mattered in a critical moment such as this was not blood or the ability to get elected—look at Carey—but a sense of responsibility. Was this de Jonge a responsible person? That was what one needed to know. He might be everything that Charles claimed, a leader of his party and so on, yet he had an irresponsible air about him—insouciant perhaps was the word. As though the common peril was a matter of no concern. Of course that could be put on. In the morning one would be able to tell better; one liked to *see* the person one was talking to, in order to judge fairly. Now there was only the voice to go by, and the accent, though not his fault, did serve as a reminder that he could speak to the chief terrorists in their own language with no one the wiser. He was a great talker, clearly, and, without knowing more about him, one could not foresee what he might let drop to these compatriots of his, not necessarily meaning any harm.

It would be wisdom to warn Helen, if one could just draw her quietly aside, not to dream of mentioning her Vermeer to him, which under ordinary conditions would be the most natural thing for her to do were she to find herself traveling with a pleasant-spoken Dutchman. Vermeers, as she ought to know, seemed to have a fatal attraction for art thieves and declared enemies of society. There had been that shocking case, a few winters ago, of the Kenwood House Vermeer. The terrorists had seized the canvas, in broad daylight at gun-point, from the lovely house, partly Adam, just outside London that had been a gift of Lord Iveagh to the public. Then they had cut strips off it and mailed them to a newspaper, just like that Getty boy's ear. They threatened to "execute" it as an act of proletarian justice if their demands were not met by a certain date. Yet what was it, exactly, that they had wanted? Money, naturally, and for some Irish bombers in English jails to go free, and a food distribution, or was one getting confused with the Hearst case? There were so many of these raids and kidnappings, all alike basically, that it was hard to keep the long lists of "demands" straight. In any case, the world had waited, utterly aghast at the barbarity, for the appointed day to dawn, but then the day passed and nothing happened, and eventually the picture was found, not too much the worse for wear, in a London cemetery, propped up against a gravestone. The subject of the painting—a girl in a yellow dress trimmed with ermine holding a guitar—was very similar to Helen's; you could almost speak of a replica, though Helen's was an inch or two smaller and the landscape hanging on the wall behind the guitar-player was different. That was why so many of Helen's friends had thought it was foolish of her to let hers go on show right on the heels of the Kenwood House atrocity; it was inviting a repetition.

Before that there had been the Rijksmuseum "The Love Letter," which was stolen while on show in Belgium and savagely mistreated. They said that had been a professional "heist" but professionals were usually not interested in mutilating priceless treasures—only in collecting the ransom; they had nothing against the pictures as art. Normal criminality was a thing one could understand—the acquisitive instinct we all have, carried to wicked lengths—but the new wave of terrorism let loose on helpless works of art was beyond ordinary human comprehension. That Japanese woman spraying the "Mona Lisa" with red paint to protest the museum hours that she thought discriminated against Japanese workers or women or whatever. It was heartbreaking to read about these sprayings and gougings and hackings, which were all politically motivated at bottom, even if it was only a crazy Australian artist's grudge against Michelangelo for being an acknowledged genius when he could not get recognition himself—so he attacked the "Pietà" in St. Peter's. And you did not have to be a "proud possessor" to feel the hurt of it. The ordinary newspaper-reader, if the truth were told, had trembled far more for the Vermeer when it was threatened than for the Hearst girl or even the Getty boy.

"I have many grandchildren," old Mr. Getty had commented when he let it be known that he was not going to satisfy the kidnappers' demands. He meant that if he paid up for Paul, the gangsters would be encouraged to kidnap the rest of his descendants one after the other. But the remark had been misinterpreted: people thought a callous old man was stating that among so many grandchildren one more or less did not matter. And if you compared the average grandchild with an irreplaceable work of art, that was true in a way, though one shouldn't say it. Helen had many attractive grandchildren, who would doubtless go on breeding and multiplying on the face of the earth, but her Vermeer was one of a kind, or almost. It was like a trust she held for posterity. The pleasure owning it gave her was only the income. Rather, what *had* been the pleasure; the constant increase in burglaries, pushing up the insurance premiums, and now this wave of wanton terrorism were taking a good deal of the joy out of owning beautiful things. But to let them "go public," as business people said of old family-owned companies, was not a solution; your precious works of art were no safer in a museum, as the Kenwood House crime proved. At any rate, Helen ought to be put on her guard. And if tomorrow, after a night's sleep and a chance to look about, a council of war were held, to discuss the situation and size up the chances of escape, it would be fairer to de Jonge to manage to leave him out of it. Or if negotiation, instead, were decided on—one could always *try*—they should be chary of taking him into their confidence. One of their own group, by rights, should be the spokesman, since it was money, to put it coarsely, that would be talking. . . .

Now the moon was trying to show itself, and a few stars twinkled in and out of the clouds. The fog had lifted, and, besides, their eyes had adjusted to the darkness. It had to do with the pupils dilating or else contracting, one or the other—Harold, who had started out as a pharmacist, would probably know. They saw Beryl plump herself down on the pavement; she had plenty of padding but she would ruin her nice coat. The others had found it wiser to stay on their feet and keep exercising their limbs—the Senator was throwing imaginary pitches. The temperature was dropping; you could tell because the pavement was getting slippery—a thin glaze of ice had started to form. Along each side of the road ran a ditch, too deep to see whether it held water. Beyond, there were tall reeds or sedges, and some distance off, perhaps half a mile, in the direction from which they had heard the foghorn, they could now make out a house of sorts, distinguishable by the roofline, and a big looming shed or barn. No lights showed.

Every few minutes someone consulted Johnnie's luminous watch. What had happened to their captors? No one was talking any more. Each seemed to be wrapped in his thoughts. The younger of Warren's two friends had assumed a yoga posture. Helen's head jerked on her neck; she was falling asleep on her feet. At that point, forceful Margaret decided to take the reins in her hands. "Rector," she ordered. "Give us an evening prayer." When he launched into "Lighten our darkness, we beseech thee, O Lord," everyone had to laugh—it was so appropriate. Then, looking around like a chairwoman, she called on Van Vliet to tell them what kind of government his country had. "Wait a minute," burst in Harold. "Don't say it. Let me have one guess. Socialist." He had scored on the first try, which seemed to give him some grim satisfaction, though you would think he would rather have been wrong. "Thanks, Maggie, for asking. Now we know." "Know what?" demanded Beryl. "Know what?" echoed the woman with the wailing Southern voice. They saw the Senator turn his head to listen.

Dear Lily undertook to pour oil on the troubled waters. "There are socialists *and* socialists, Harold. One has to know which kind." "There's only one kind," retorted Harold. The Senator gave a brief laugh and went back to pitching. Johnnie came to Lily's aid. In his understanding, he said, Holland was something like England—what they liked to call a "welfare state," with the Queen and Labor. "And isn't Holland in NATO?" ventured Lily. "I feel sure I read that somewhere." "You're thinking of Belgium, Mother." But Lily was right. Indeed Holland was in NATO, Mr. Van Vliet assured them. And he tiptoed over to the "whirlybird" and tenderly patted the little tail-propeller. "The NATO shield." Even Harold had to chuckle when the humor of it was explained to him. The "chopper" was part of the NATO defense screen. Mr. Van Vliet's government had borrowed it from the Germans. To oblige a team of international terrorists. "A crazy world," summed up Lily's rector-as-was.

But after that "light moment," despondency returned. Seven o'clock came and still no sign of the main hijackers. "Abdul" and "Ahmed" were talking in low voices. Maybe they too were getting worried. Harold wondered why Dutch planes had not started looking for the party. "Christ, our course could have been plotted by radar. They ought to have pinpointed where we are. By now we should have heard some action overhead." But the partly covered sky was silent, and a new tooting of fog-horns indicated a very obvious reason: no search plane would undertake a mission in this weather. "I'm scared, Chaddie," said Eloise. In fact they were all growing frightened. Older people could perish of exposure if left standing here all night. And the odor of whiskey still emanating from the Vuitton case was tantalizing, to say the least. What a pity that Henry had not packed his private stock more carefully.

If another half-hour were to pass in this vain waiting, some initiative would have to be taken. Everyone might decide to move in a body back into the helicopter, where at least there were seats and some shelter. Or start a bonfire—there were those leafless young trees along the road that appeared to be poplars; the men could tear branches off, although the wood might be too damp to burn. But first one would have to convince the two Arabs, who must be freezing themselves, to let them disobey Gretel's order; perhaps Beryl could try.

Life was full of irony. The last thing one would have expected was that one would find oneself longing for Hans and Gretel to return. Why were they staying away so long? Had something dreadful happened back there in that house? The conspirators might have got into an argument and killed each other in a shoot-out. Or blown themselves up while wiring the place with explosives. But then one would have heard the noise. The wildest conjectures must be passing through every mind, though no one dared voice them. It was like being left by one's nurse as a child in the park with one's pail and shovel and told to stay put till she came back. The fears that rose to assail one when she did not appear for hours and one's little feet were getting cold! That she had been run over by a car, that she had got lost in the park, that the bogey-man had taken her, that she had just walked off on purpose and was never coming back. That sense of utter abandonment—it was odd to feel it now. And the same fear one had had then of disobeying by going to look for her. Nurse, as one knew now, had simply been off with some young man and when she came back, she was cross that one was frightened and made one promise not to tell the Missus. Well, most of us have had such experiences, and they leave a mark.

Of course the situations were not parallel. One had usually loved Nurse. One had wanted her never to leave. While if one was sure that Hans and Gretel had disappeared for good, it would be bliss beyond belief. It was the doubt that was so harrowing. Rather than remain a prey to useless guessing and imagining, not to mention desperately hungry and chilled to the bone, almost anybody, actually, would prefer to see their scowling faces. It was normal to be silently pleading for them to come back soon: *"Please,* Hans and Gretel, where are you?" And the Bishop, too, of course. How strange to have almost forgotten about him.

Seven

It would be an exaggeration to say that these people had never been so glad to see anyone in their lives. More exactly (Sophie estimated), no sound of footsteps had ever been so welcome to them as the purposeful tread advancing almost in march-time—the leaders had changed their footwear and were wearing thick boots. All too soon, naturally, they were perceived again in their true colors—hardly had they shown their faces when it was obvious that the leopard had not changed his spots. Absent, they had been idealized: it was curious how, within the mere space of an anxious hour or so, the group huddled here had succeeded in forgetting what their captors had been like. Apprehension as to what was coming next would have been the rational emotion. Instead, if her own feelings were an index, the nearing steps of the *kapers*, heralded by a distant snapping of twigs, had evoked simple gratitude: they were a rescue party.

Their return meant food, shelter, sleep, possibly a blanket—civilization. At any rate, to Sophie: she had been picturing the shadowy house off there as a sort of canteen or mess, with cauldrons of hot soup, bread, Dutch cheese, coffee. She had not eaten a full meal for seventy-two hours. And for the older people, people of her parents' age, all this must have been much harder. She was hungry, and her legs, encased like sausages in these elegant leather boots, had lost all feeling. Yet as a journalist she was familiar with rough assignments—she had humped about in army trucks and slept in a cave alongside guerrillas eager to be interviewed; she had lived for days on a diet of black beans and rice—and furthermore she was thirty-six, still young. The older people, with their hardening arteries and poor circulation, not to mention proneness to worry, could only be objects of compassion to someone so junior and so far ahead in experience. For their sake, she tried to picture army cots in the house or barn or at least rows of mattresses; if this was to last long, sleep would become essential for keeping a steady head. For her, hay or the floor would do, if only she could get these boots off—a razor, she feared, might be required.

She felt sorriest for the art collectors. A millionaire's life was no preparation for the trials of being a hostage. Perhaps, in the light of present-day trends, they should be getting special training courses to harden them up for the eventuality. But in fact the collectors had borne up remarkably well, and she wondered whether her parents could have equaled them—they had the double handicap of being semi-rich and Jewish, which taken together seemed to soften the fibre. These super-rich Wasps had been lambs on the whole: no complaints, no moans, just the stately silliness proper to their station in life. The only black sheep among them had been the quarrelsome man with the Midwestern accent and the younger wife; it was hard to imagine what art he collected—cock-fighting subjects? On the fringe, as if not quite accepted among the super-rich, was a pair of queens with the usual age difference between them. They were bearing up well too, considering the fact that they *were* on the fringe. She tried to guess what the parched old one collected—the other probably cooked, drove the car, and generally catered—prints, she thought: Beardsley first impressions, Klimmt, Cocteau, Japanese erotica.

The fat girl, Beryl Somebody, Sophie remembered from school; she was the one who had appeared in the sixth-form year with a trunkful of incredible clothes that she had cut to pieces with a pinking shears on a dreary Sunday afternoon in a fit of misery or boredom while her roommate looked on. It was easy to sympathize with the act, which had contrived to get her expelled—a thing that almost never happened at Putney and caused her to stand out in the memory as someone who had put Mrs. H.'s progressiveness to the supreme test. She deserved a commemorative plaque, really, for exposing the hypocrisy of the place. It had been odd to find her again, traveling with her mother and dressed in a long lustrous matronly mink coat but otherwise not much changed from the old Beryl. She was still fat and flaxen with made-up electric blue eyes that blinked like a china doll's and still a disciplinary problem, or so it sounded. Sophie saw that she could not have changed greatly herself, for it was clear that Beryl remembered her too. "Hi, there," she had muttered over her shoulder as they were boarding the helicopter. Later they might have a chat, dormitory style, when Sophie's boots were off and the older generation would be snoozing, having taken its Valium or sleeping-pill.

But something was wrong with that picture. They were not going to be bedded down yet. And where was the Bishop? The hijackers had not brought him back with them. The realization seemed to steal over the whole group of hostages in the course of an instant, as though they were one body that had been nudged to attention. What had this pair done with the nice old man? Near her, eyebrows shot up, making points of interrogation; shrugging shoulders replied in dumb show. Nobody, Sophie supposed, wished to be the one to ask, partly for fear of learning the answer but mostly for fear of angering their hosts —if that was the right word for these redoubtable people. In any case, for the moment the leaders were unapproachable— they were over by the helicopter arguing heatedly with the pilot; their voices were raised—and the Arabs, though available, could claim not to know. If other members of the band had come back with the leaders, they were waiting silently in the bushes.

Sophie told herself that there could be an innocent explanation for the Bishop's disappearance, and no doubt her fellow-hostages were telling themselves the same thing. He might be asleep, for instance. Yet this sop she was offering her conscience for not speaking up—"Where is the Bishop?" she was free to shout, or "Please, where is Bishop Hurlbut?"—failed to be effective, since from long experience she recognized it as a sop. She sensed in herself a reluctance to antagonize that she knew too well, a disabling reluctance for someone in her profession. She had proof of her physical courage and the courage of her pen, but spoken words, for her, were different. It was not mere dread of offending a powerful person but embarrassment: she did not like to ask a point-blank question when the anticipated reply, or evasion, was something only a prosecuting attorney could pounce on with joy. She had given long thought to this subject; was it tact or shyness or femininity that inhibited her? She was sure that if she had had the bad fate to interview Nixon, she would have helped him cover up, at least while she sat in his office under his shifty eye. Poor girl (she sighed to herself), she wanted to be "clean." She always pitied confessors, who in their stuffy intimate boxes had to hear and wash away such a lot of dirty sins. And tonight, added to that squeamishness was a plain, weak, selfish desire not to incur the special hostility of "Hans" and "Gretel," as the collectors were calling them—naming the animals, the Senator had observed. She was the only Jew, she guessed, in this whole caboodle; why should it fall to her to speak up?

But the parson, thank God, had recognized his duty. They watched him approach the Arab guard and secure a permission, apparently. Then he brought out a pocket handkerchief—plaid, but in the dark it could pass for white—and holding it up as a truce flag he manfully crossed the open ground to the helicopter, where the second pilot had joined the loud debate. Two flashlight beams played over the tall missionary form. "He's asking," Simmons marveled. "I wouldn't have the courage; honestly, would you? But then he has to. Being his brother's keeper, I mean." "He's getting the bum's rush," commented Harold. It was true. In two shakes of a lamb's tail, the parson was hurtling back toward his companions; a rough final shove from the older Arab caused him to slip on the icy pavement—he fell. "I guess they mean business," he said, trying to laugh as he picked himself up. He applied the flag of truce, groaning, to his shin. But it was only a scrape. "And so what did they tell you?" Sophie demanded. "Nothing. Not a darned thing. She just gave me a piece of her mind for butting in. Quite a scold, she is. A regular martinet." Soon the woman herself strode up, as if to enforce the lesson poor Mr. Barber had got. The dispute with the pilots—whatever it had been about—seemed to be over. But something had left her in a vicious humor. "We are not here to answer your questions. We are not accountable to you swine. You were ordered not to disperse, and one of you has disobeyed. Now you will form a line, quickly. We have no time to waste."

The erect old collector reached for his wife's dressing-case. "Here you are, Helen. Margaret, my dear, where's yours?" "Drop that case!" exclaimed the woman. "And form a line, I said." "But we need our things," protested Harold's wife. "Our night things, don't you see, so as to go to bed." She might have been explaining matters to a child, Sophie thought. " 'Beddy-bye,' 'do-do,' " the mincing voice went on. "Forget do-do, Mrs. Parasite," said the woman. "You are going to be put to work." "Me?" "Some of you. All of you. We will decide." What work could she mean? Uncertainly, the hostages lined up and faced the two confederates. Like confused recruits, they did not understand the order and were too frightened to ask more. All that was clear to Sophie was that the leaders were making a selection. They went down the long line using their little flashlights like methodical probes. After a brief appearance the moon had gone in again, and the last few stars were covered. The dancing rays of light made the dark seem darker. Sophie was glad to know, anyway, that she had Henk on her right side and on her left Jim Carey, who laced his fingers firmly in hers and murmured "Whatever's coming, let's the three of us try to stay together." On his other side was Simmons; a faint shriek came from that quarter. "He was *feeling* me, Jim," the wailing voice confided. "What part of you?" asked the Senator. "I guess you'd call it my biceps," she admitted, raising a laugh. "Auschwitz," muttered Sophie, not finding this very funny. Paranoia, perhaps, but it did seem to her that a Nazi-style sifting of those fit to work was going on. What would they do with the others—kill them or save the ammunition and leave them to die of exposure? She asked herself what it meant that neither of the two had bothered to test *her* muscles. Again she considered the fact of being Jewish: did that classify her as fit to work or the opposite? Hunger was making her light-headed. If she was slightly delirious, that would account for the somber imaginings that were assailing her—her own special pink elephants; her parents had got out of Frankfurt early, but distant relatives from the French branch had died in the ovens. "Fall out," barked the woman. Sophie jumped. "Ahmed, take him away." It was Charles the woman was speaking of. How shameful to feel relief.

Yet the elimination of Charles threw a new and terribly clear light on the Bishop's disappearance. In a flash the confusion in her head was replaced by hyper-lucidity. The old and the unfit. "Take him away"—a code expression, most likely, on the model of "the final solution" or "Waste 'em" in Vietnam. At the same time, in another part of her mind she was finding it wildly comical that "Ahmed's" name was Ahmed. And in still a different compartment, her brain was working on a hideous new theory: the Bishop had died of a heart attack, *or* they had killed him, and they were picking a burial squad. Sophie could not stand it. "I'm going to *demand* that they tell us. If they won't say where he is, it means they've done away with him." "What good will it do us to know, Sophie?" Carey said gently, stroking her cold fingers. "It *always* does good to know," Sophie said passionately, pushing his hand away. "No talking there!" shouted the man's voice. A flashlight was turned in their direction. In its path Sophie distinctly saw—unless it was a hallucination—a figure carrying a shovel crossing the road. Her knees began to buckle. "Henk!" she appealed, in a whisper. He was not there. It was like waking up from a bad dream and finding the place beside you empty. But he had merely stepped forward, without saying a word. The leaders saw him. "Back in line there, Deputy. Take your place."

He was not going to obey. He stood there quite coolly (she

could tell from his profile and the tilt of his chin), his head thrown back as if idly contemplating the sky. As she watched, he calmly folded his arms and continued to gaze upward, like the musing figure of a poet in a German Romantic painting— all he lacked was a black cloak wrapped around him. Sophie smiled; in this half-minute she had grown uncannily calm herself. No doubt it was the advent of real danger that had done it. She ought to tremble at his daring; instead, she was content —perhaps the true word was "thrilled"—that he was standing his ground.

If Henk did not move, she reasoned, they would come over to him themselves. The odds were that they would not shoot him unless they had to. A little plume of white vapor, like smoke, came from the nostril she could see and made her think of a bull-god snorting. And of course he was not a political animal for nothing; the bold strategy was working. First the man and then the woman materialized from the shadows, drawn as if by a magnet or by common, normal curiosity—an underrated force of attraction. Henk shifted his head in their direction, like somebody who thought he had heard visitors. The man said something in Dutch. Henk answered with a word that sounded like "Nay." Stepping up rather too close to him, the woman pointed her flashlight into his face. He ignored it and started talking to the man. Then he made an irritable gesture, as if to ward off the beam of light, like a buzzing fly, from his eyes. The man's hand suddenly closed over the woman's; he clicked her flashlight off. His own he kept pointed at the pavement, lighting up patches of ice. Henk continued. "He's asking about the Bishop," Sophie murmured to Carey. "I heard him say 'bisschop.'" They strained their ears to follow. Carey caught the words "oud man," which must be "old man." But as the rapid exchange went on, they could pick up less and less. Their German was not much help; the pronunciation was too different. The recurring "Nay," a nasal sound, was evidently "No" or "Nein," and the woman kept interrupting with what sounded like "haast hebben," which might be kin to German "Die Hast" and English "hurry."

If so, she was not the only impatient one. From the far end of the line, the unmistakable voice of Harold called out. "What's going on? What are you telling them, de Jonge?" He must have received a cuff or a sharp poke from an Arab gun butt, for there was a loud grunt and he subsided. The discussion in Dutch went on. The word "helicopter," however spelled, was being pronounced. Sophie turned quickly to Carey. He had got it too. He emitted a soft whistle. She could not guess what he was surmising, but for her part Sophie had just had a sudden joyful suspicion. Was the Bishop going to be evacuated, as an act of mercy—"medevac," the Army would have called it in Vietnam—and Charles too? "Bishop," "old man," "helicopter," even *"hebben haast"*—it all added up to that. As for the work-detail the leaders had been choosing, that could be for ordinary chores; collecting firewood, for instance, or KP—nothing would make her happier now than to be set to peeling potatoes, especially if she knew than an ailing old cleric and his ancient crony were going to be flown out. She blessed Henk for his gift of persuasion. The hulking man, she estimated, was more than half convinced; at least he was listening and nodding his head up and down, as if pondering. And the woman was staying out of it. Her restless flashlight was on again, playing over the pavement. Sophie's eye absently followed it. She froze. Lying by the edge of the road were *two* shovels.

"Nay," Van Vliet was saying. Just down the row, another voice, pleasanter than Harold's, intervened—Beryl's mother. "Dear Mr. Van Vliet, don't argue with them. You're only making them cross. Let's just do as we're told and get it over with." "Can it, Mother. We're not meant to be talking, don't you realize that?"

But Henk answered, and the big fellow did not stop him. Sophie tried to listen, but her attention kept wandering. Had no one else noticed the shovels? She touched Carey's sleeve and pointed. He shrugged. He was more interested in what Henk was saying—something about being a lawyer and advice being his profession. Could she be wrong in the dire conclusion she had leapt to? Leaping to conclusions was a bad habit with her.

184

Wouldn't they be spades rather than shovels if a grave was to be dug? She ordered herself to listen. Henk was telling the hostages in English what he had told the two leaders in Dutch. "They have said that they are not accountable to us. In strict power terms that is true. But I counsel them that it is in their own interest not to keep us in ignorance when they need our cooperation." Sophie bridled. "Cooperation?" she muttered to Carey. What did that mean? They were in a no-choice situation; they *had* to cooperate. He was a charming, absurd Dutchman, over-trained in coalition politics. Nevertheless, she reminded herself, softening, he was brave, and for that she owed him some attention. Slave labor, he was saying, was always inefficient. "That is known from the camps. But in the gulag there were millions, so the low productivity of each individual unit was unimportant; in the scale of things it did not matter." Why was Henk telling all this to the hostages, half of whom could not care less? Then slowly she understood: he was really addressing himself to the *kapers,* taking advantage of having the floor to repeat an argument that he had been making in camera. It was a parliamentary trick, to use an attentive gallery to make your point sink in, as though doubling the size of the audience doubled the force of your words. And possibly it did. "Here tonight," he continued cheerily, "the labor force is very small. Perhaps thirty persons. They need the full productivity of thirty persons and therefore they must pay for it." " 'Pay'? That's a bit stiff, isn't it, under the circs?" The collector called Ramsbotham laughed in a worldly way, as if he thought poor Henk quite mad or in need of a business education. Henk took his meaning. "I am not a 'simple,' as we say in Dutch. No. Ask yourself a question. What have our friends here got that we haven't?" "Guns," yelled Harold. "Evidently," said Henk. "But what else?" No one knew. "Information," answered Henk. "They must pay us in information."

"Your Bishop is alive," the woman said abruptly. "He has not been harmed. No one will be harmed at this stage of the operation that behaves himself. He is too old, simply, for the work, and we have told him so. He will only be in the way."

"The work?" echoed Beryl's mother. "You will see," said the man. "Now fall out, madam. Fall out again, funny old gentleman." That was Charles, who had slipped back into line—doubtless to hear better. "And you, Deputy, fall in."

It ought to have been plain as a pikestaff. It was a question of moving the helicopter. Henk had guessed it before they told him. Jim Carey had guessed it. That was the "work." As soon as the fog cleared, or in the morning at the very latest, search planes would come looking for them. That man Harold had been griping, half an hour ago, that none had come yet. The helicopter would have to be hidden. It could not be left standing here all night in plain view.

That *of course* they could not leave it parked on the highway was a fact of life too obvious to have escaped Sophie's attention; she would have had to be a total idiot not to see that. But she had given no consideration to the mechanics of its removal; when they were ready, the pilot, she had assumed, would taxi it off the road to some nearby hiding-place. All that would have been thought through. But in the dark she had failed to notice something that the men had seen at once: the helicopter did not have wheels; it had skids. Yet why claim the dark as an excuse? The truth was that she had not used her eyes, while the men had. And even if at some point she had vaguely taken note of the skids, she would probably have failed to grasp the implications: without wheels, the craft could not taxi. Having to hear that explained to her now, jointly, by Henk and Jim made her blush for herself as a journalist. She would fire herself had she been here on assignment, charged with "covering" the event. She hated imperceptiveness, most of all in herself. And being a woman, alas, had something to do with this particular lapse from grace; women did not think about machinery.

Henk said that the hijackers themselves had failed to notice the skids at Schiphol. They had become aware of them here. And right away they had got angry at the pilots. But it was not the pilots who had flown the aircraft in from Germany. They were Dutch Air Force men and the Germans who had brought

186

it had turned it over as it stood, complete with the operations manual for the Dutchmen to figure out. Still, commented Sophie, you would think that these Dutch would have *mentioned* the skids while the helicopter was still at Schiphol and it would not have been too late to change them. No point, Henk retorted: there was not a set of wheels in Holland that would fit this model. His placid tone irritated her; she wanted blame to be assigned. Then why in the world, she said crossly, did the Germans send one with skids? Henk shrugged. At this time of year the craft was probably used for paratrooper training exercises on snow and ice; when the order came down from the Ministry, nobody at the base had thought to put on wheels. Very natural, too, said Carey. "These birds should have sent their specifications along. Hell, they might have got pontoons." The two men laughed. Being males, they found the quandary amusing.

So, since the helicopter could not taxi, it was going to have to be pushed or pulled. The road was icing up nicely, Carey estimated, testing it with his feet. "But that's impossible," Sophie protested. "Why can't the pilot fly it to wherever they want it to go?" That was the idea of the *kapers*, Henk said. But the pilot had refused. The argument just now had been about that. "You could hear it all?" said Carey. "Enough," Henk said, "to seize the drift. Or do you say 'catch the drift'?" " 'Get the drift,' " said Sophie, feeling quite impatient. "But go on. Why did the pilot refuse?" "Not enough room for maneuver," answered the Senator. "If he took it up and tried to turn it on a dime in these conditions, there'd be a fair chance of a foul-up." "And he was unwilling to take the chance," observed Sophie. "Why didn't they ask the co-pilot if he was so afraid?" Henk said that the co-pilot had agreed with the pilot. "These fellows are Dutch and stubborn." He held up a finger, recommending quiet. Over by the helicopter, the argument with the pilots had resumed. And no wonder, Sophie thought. A fresh survey of this band of hostages ought to have convinced them that the job could not be done by manpower—sheer madness even to consider it. "They are telling that the helicopter is the property of the German air arm," Henk reported. "And they say the Royal Dutch Air Force has responsibility for this property." "Kind of funny," said Carey. "I mean to be harping on property and responsibility when you want to make an anarchist see your point."

Then all at once the discussion was over. The big hijacker and the co-pilot were underneath the helicopter, looking up at something. The pilots had won their point. Carey said he was not surprised. On balance, he guessed, the hijackers could not have been too eager to see the helicopter take off with the Royal Dutch Air Force at the controls. "Nothing much to prevent them from flying it back to Schiphol, wouldn't you say, Henk? Then good-bye getaway craft." "But why do they *need* a getaway craft?" Sophie demanded. "Psychological," said Carey, and let it go at that. The pilot was now inside the helicopter. From the bottom he was letting out a long cable. "Standard equipment," said Carey. "A hoist, they call it. Used for making drops and pick-ups normally. He has a winch in there that's operated by a motor." He had been a flyer, Sophie remembered, in the Second World War. The cable unwound and lay on the pavement, in coils, like a thin black snake. "But I thought we were going to push," said Sophie. "They'll try the hoist for now," Carey said. "But I expect the time for pushing will come."

The lazy voice broke off. Suddenly there was a great deal of action. It was as though a whistle had been blown. First, the male hostages were quickly separated from the women and formed into a squad, which was set to work unwinding the cable. Then, from the periphery, four new figures appeared. All were dressed in windbreakers and baggy pants, but one might be a woman—she was too far off still to tell. Two stayed by the cable, watching it play out, and two ran off to a point several yards up the highway. They had brought lanterns with them, and now you could see better. But without Carey to brief her, Sophie felt at a loss. She could not make out what was happening, exactly. The pair up the highway was shouting in rapid German. *"Ja!" "Nein," "Doch, das stimmt," "Nein. Es stimmt nicht."* Eventually it dawned on her: they were looking for a tree to fix the cable to. But the trees along the road were just big saplings—willows, Sophie thought, and she tried to remember from her parents' property whether willow was a soft wood or a hard wood. There could not be any full-grown trees anywhere here; the polder was too new. In the thicket were only tall bushes. And along the road no telephone poles. Nothing stout and fixed to anchor onto. And no hope of a big jutting rock; the land was perfectly flat—level sea-bottom. She was not surprised that Carey had sounded skeptical. Yet the confederates, apparently, had found a tree, several yards further up the road, that they thought would suit the purpose, for one of them called out "Jeroen! *Ja, ja! Hier!*" and the tall Dutch hijacker—they were big, Henk said, in the fen-lands he came from—went up to consult with them. Then an order was given, and the hostages hoisted the cable onto their shoulders and marching in step, spaced out in single file, carried it up the road till the order to halt came. The frieze of toiling figures with the cable stretched between them looked curiously like a chain gang silhouetted against the night sky.

The end of the cable reached, but there could not be much slack, because a wait followed while the men tried to hook it to the tree trunk, cursing in a babel of tongues (*"Merde!"* cried the voice of Henk). Finally the laborers fell back. There was a sound of cranking and groaning as the winch turned and the cable tautened. The helicopter moved. It was proceeding on a diagonal to the highway's edge. The problem, of course, was the skids. The thin glaze of ice on the highway was uneven, and halfway along the great hulk seemed to balk. You could hear the skids scrape on the pavement. "Halt!" called the co-pilot and went over to inspect.

There was a consultation. No damage seemed to have been done, and the hijackers, apparently, had been prepared for a setback. An emollient of some kind, Sophie guessed, was needed to grease the skids; the ice was too patchy. She thought madly of Dutch butter. But mud, it seemed, was the answer, and there was no shortage of it in the ditch beside the highway. That was where the shovels fitted in.

Now the women were put to work. Pails were produced, and two groups were formed, one to carry the pails, which "Gretel" was rapidly filling, and the other to apply the contents by hand to the stretch of pavement in front of the runners. The new confederate, who was in fact a woman, pale, thin, German, and young, seized the second shovel and followed Gretel's example. While this was going on, the men took places at the rear of the helicopter, to start pushing when the word came —they would push in concert with the turning winch. Having lost—or wasted—so much time, the hijackers were now in a great hurry. But the pails were small, almost like children's pails, and the mud was cold; actually there were splinters of ice in it. Sophie's hands ached, and she looked with pity at the manicured fingernails of Harold's wife, which showed a black-ish red in the lantern light. In Sophie's view, it would have made sense to let the hostages use a shovel to smooth the mud onto the pavement rather than have them slather it on like cold cream with their bare hands. But the shovels were re-served for the use of Gretel and the other. Rather than trust the captives with them, they leaned on them during pauses to watch contemptuously, like forewomen, while the feeble carriers bore off their dripping loads.

At length the leadership was satisfied with the slippery state of the pavement, and the pilot resumed his place. The winch turned, the men pushed, but, instead of advancing, the heli-copter was sliding backward. The cable was pulling the tree, which slowly rose, turned a sort of somersault, exposing its roots, and was dragged along the road. A sound of clucking came from the women. "Sheer vandalism," Sophie's nearest neighbor pronounced. "Don't you agree? When one thinks of the money this government must have spent planting those trees . . ." Yet they were going to try again, with another tree—still frailer in appearance, Sophie considered. She rather sympathized with her neighbor: before they were through, they would have ripped up every tree in the area. But at least this next one, unlike its predecessor, had not been weakened by a first assault. And the hijackers this time were trying a new strategy. A rope was brought from the helicopter and tied to the tree trunk. The workers were redistributed. Males, both hostages and hijackers, were assigned to pull on the rope, to hold the tree steady when the winch started its counter-pull, while the women, all of them, were to push the helicopter from the rear. They practiced, then "One, two, *three!*" the fen-land giant counted. The cable tightened. The helicopter moved forward. They had done it.

But the job was not yet over. The ditch they had been digging in constituted a new hazard. It was not very wide; nevertheless there was the danger that one of the skids could slip into it and tip the helicopter over on its side. "Jeroen"—at any rate they now knew his name, which rhymed with "shoon"; was it Dutch for "Jerome"?—stood with his hands on his hips, studying the ditch. He measured the skids and shook his head. Then he called to Ahmed, who brought him a small ax, of the kind used for cutting firewood. Seizing it in his huge hands, he set to work to chop branches off the young willows till he had enough to fill in the ditch at the point the helicopter would cross. Here there was no question of using the winch. Again the women got behind to push; in front, the work-gang of men pulled on the cable. Without gloves, their hands slipped; it was hard to get a purchase. But the bed of twigs and branches was wet and slimy; in half a minute the helicopter was across.

Now there was less hurry. Even though the helicopter was still visible, it was not blocking the road to a truck or car that wanted to pass—there must be maintenance men at that pumping-station and if they worked in shifts, some could be arriving or leaving at any hour of the night. This highway must connect with the mainland, where people lived, and to Sophie it was a miracle that no vehicle so far had appeared. And if one had, what would the hijackers have done? Taken whoever was in it prisoner, she supposed. But then the car would have to be hidden too. At any rate it would have had wheels. And if the night-shift worker had had a family, wouldn't somebody have given the alarm when he failed to come home? All the time they had been pushing and shoving she had been worrying, she realized, that a car would come before they finished, and now that that danger no longer mattered much—in the dark a driver would be concentrating on the road and not looking to see what was beside it—she pushed the damp fringe back from her forehead and breathed easier.

There remained the thick underbrush to be dealt with. A sort of path or track, she noticed, already ran through it, and the vegetation was crushed and trampled in places. But the track was too narrow for the helicopter to pass. It would have to be widened. Otherwise, she guessed, the rotor blades might get tangled in the tall reeds. Or some other damage could befall its vital parts. Fatigue was making her unmechanical brain even more hazy: in Vietnam she had ridden in dozens of helicopters and actually come under fire from the ground once, yet now she could not even remember where their engines were exactly. But she was right about widening the path.

While the teams of hostages rested and the men mopped their brows ("Wonderful exercise!" she heard the minister proclaim), Ahmed busied himself with the ax. His progress along the thicket's encroaching edges was maddeningly slow, and behind him he left masses of snarled reeds and prickly branches, which the others, following in his wake, had to clear away. Carey, walking beside her and watching the young man's clumsy efforts, was manifestly losing patience. "Here, let me have that," he said and proceeded to cut a clean swath, rapidly felling bushes on either side as he went. There came a piercing whistle. "Put that ax down!" It was strange how these people, though they must be even more tired than the hostages, could be so alert. They must have their wits about them to be instantly conscious of the deadly-weapon potential latent in an ax or a mere shovel.

Or was it not, rather, dim-witted on their part to be so fiercely suspicious? One thing they were incapable of divining, it seemed, was the impulse to be helpful common to most Americans—other people had it but not to the same degree. In America, if you were not born with it, they taught it to you in school. Carey's was just a reflex reaction to the sight of incompetence; it hurt the American farm boy in him to watch somebody use an ax that badly. Nor was it only the Senator. Sophie had noticed that the task of moving this oversize helicopter to safety had produced something like a team spirit even in the bystanders. Once indignation over the tree-uprooting had subsided, there had been a quick shower of advice, to which Simmons of course had contributed but also the queenly mammoth they called Margaret: "You will have more traction, I think, Harold, if you shift your position somewhat more to the right." More remarkable: a pair of pale yellow gloves had been silently tendered to the cable-pullers, relayed—too late, as it happened—from Charles, banished to the shadows but evidently taking an active interest. And now poor Ahmed had managed to cut his thumb; instead of letting it bleed, the Air France stewardess promptly came forward with her first-aid kit. These little occurrences touched Sophie. Of course it was in the stewardess's training. And of course Ahmed was by way of becoming everybody's pet hijacker. But something more was at work, Sophie felt—an endearing, irrational, human tendency to make common cause. Nothing could be more foreign to the hostages' self-interest than the project of hiding this helicopter.

Finally the path was declared to be wide enough. Ahmed's place had been taken by a gaunt new Palestinian even less adept. "I guess in the desert they don't get much use for an ax," summed up Carey. Henk had gone ahead merrily at the wood-chopper's side, and now he reported what he had been able to see: a typical gabled Dutch farmhouse, two stories high, and near it a barn in construction—it lacked one wall and a roof. The helicopter was ready to move. There was no need for fresh mud; the ground here, being marshy and half-frozen, was naturally slippery—a point the pastor had demonstrated by another sorry tumble. There were also, Henk said, crusted remnants of a snowfall in the open space around the barn, where the helicopter would obviously go. From now on the job would be easy. And in fact that was so. The only difficulties were interposed by the pilots. The track was still on the narrow side—either thanks to Ahmed and his successor or because the hijackers had not wanted to make it too wide, in case it would be noticeable from the air—and to keep the helicopter straight on course, free of interference from protruding briars and branch-ends, seemed to have become a point of honor with the flyers, who from time to time shouted *"Halt!"* and brought everything to a standstill, as though a few scratches on the German paint job would matter. It was their training, Sophie supposed. But the *kapers* were humoring them, and the helicopter made it to the barn.

Urging it in, finally, was the simplest part. It really looked as though Providence were working on the hijackers' behalf. That the barn lacked a wall and a roof could not have been better for their purposes. If the roof had been on, the helicopter could not possibly have fitted under it, and the open side was a made-to-order portal. The unfinished barn was a perfect berth; you would almost think it had been designed by a builder to function as a hangar. And lying around, as though in readiness, were sheets of builders' tar paper and a carpenter's ladder. It was quick work for the more able-bodied hostages, following the northlander's instructions, to climb up and fit the tar paper loosely over the top, like a tent, resting on the outspread blades. When the job was finished, the lanterns were put away, and everyone stood back to admire. As though at the command of a stage electrician, the moon came out, to provide a ghostly lighting. Standing back, you would never know that a helicopter was garaged here unless you were directly in front, facing the open side. And from the air, that would not matter; from the air, the illusion would be complete. A search plane would see only a typical barn in the process of construction, and the tar paper might have been laid over the top to keep the damp out. No jungle camouflage, Sophie decided, could ever have been so naturalistic. "A light blanket of snow would add a touch," commented Jim. He himself was a wet blanket, Sophie told him. Her legs had regained feeling, and she momentarily forgot being hungry

in a general glow of satisfaction—Veblen's pride of workmanship, it must be, though her own part had been small.

The other hostages, too, had been reanimated; interest had
shifted to the dark farmhouse and what it might contain by
way of amenities. "Will there be a toilet?" Simmons wondered.
Beryl's mother was hoping for a "bathe"—even a sponge bath.
The men's thoughts ran to food and heating: better not be
counting on steaks, though, and Ramsbotham understood that
Holland had an oil shortage. Henk, as the authority, was be- ·
sieged with eager questions: would they heat with gas maybe,
how many rooms in a farmer's house, any hope of a frigidaire?
For these poor souls, merely naming those "necessities of life"
—warmth, food, running water—even with cautious pessimism,
could not fail to bring on a mood of anticipation. "Will they
let us get our things now?" said Harold's wife.

Certainly by now they had earned a good night's rest and
something hot to eat. But the hijackers did not see it that way.
From their point of view, there was still work to be done.
Obviously the path that had just been widened would have to
be restored to at least a semblance of its earlier state, so that
from the air it would look as if nothing more than a builder's
truck had used it, to bring in materials. They could not just
quit and go to bed. With reluctance, Sophie conceded that,
and Jim Carey, beside her, was nodding his agreement as the
leader, leaning against the barn wall, went down the list of
tasks that remained. A squad of hostages was to collect sedge,
lopped-off branches, and so on, to fill in the sides of the path.
The uprooted tree was to be put back in place and all traces
of disturbance cleared off the highway. To Sophie, it was as
if a stage were about to be set, with the hostages as scene-
shifters, and she asked herself whether so much verisimilitude
was really necessary—could there be an element of sadistic
enjoyment? "And our toilet cases?" prompted Harold's wife,
whose chief interest probably lay in her eight-hour cream.
Curious, though, that the hijackers had omitted to mention
the detail of the hostages' "things"; now that the helicopter

was gone, the pile of cases on the highway was the most conspicuous item for miles around. The question annoyed Gretel. "We have not forgotten, Mrs. Moneybags. A squad will be assigned to place them in the ditch until we are ready." That was a cruel blow; some of the women gasped and some emitted piteous bleats. Sophie caught Henk's eye. He cleared his throat. *"Neen!"* he called out. Again he was going to come to the rescue. Over by the barn, he talked rapidly to the two in Dutch; Sophie watched his gestures—he seemed to be counting on his fingers, as a demonstration of something. And almost at once Jeroen was making an announcement: for "compassionate reasons," a group of hostages would be permitted to collect their "hand baggages" and proceed to the house; the others would finish the work.

"How did you pull that off?" inquired Carey when Henk was back among them. "Yes, how?" said Sophie. "I said that here are too many persons. For them, it must be dangerous. And most are not needed." Whenever he had been speaking Dutch, she noticed, his English got worse, as though he were trying to be his own interpreter at some summit meeting—he had pronounced "said" as "sayed." Or was it a sign of strain? He was certainly a gifted negotiator.

It was the first-class passengers who reaped the immediate benefit. With the exception of Beryl and the curator, they were being sent off to bed, which was only fair, Sophie thought: most of them were well past fifty. It was a relief to see them set forth, guarded by two Arabs and clutching their cases. "But *I'm* fifty," cried Simmons. "Why should they be privileged?" "You don't look it, Aileen," said Carey. "Let them have their shut-eye. Be good now and stay with us liberals." "But they'll eat up all the food, Jim." Nevertheless, she complied. In a minute she was helping him pick up branches.

As it turned out, everyone's baggage was promptly transported to the house. The steward and stewardess saw to it, and the pilots lent a hand. They did not forget the Bishop's umbrella or his old carryall—his dead wife's needlework. The squad working on the path smiled as they watched the young pilot go past with the treasured possession. "Gus'll be happy as a clam to see it again," the minister redundantly said. "Did he love her so much?" asked Simmons. "Or only after she was dead?" In the moonlight Sophie saw Carey wince. "Cult of relics," he said, roughly pushing a heap of briars into position.

Their labors were almost over. The final chore was to remove all the skid traces from the highway. In Sophie's opinion, this was overdoing it. The *kapers* were succumbing to a perfectionist temptation, unless they were plain brutes. And in their place she would have advised water, carried from their hideaway if necessary, rather than a broom. She and Beryl were alone on the empty road. They had relieved the young museum man and the silent Scottish don. The tree had been replanted, the path had been "landscaped" to the limit of possibility, and most of the weary workers had been allowed to go to the house. Only Henk and Jim remained, waiting loyally by the road's edge and strictly forbidden to help. Somewhere nearby, the leaders were keeping watch. Eventually they would come with their flashlights to assure themselves that Beryl and Sophie had not shirked. To shirk was certainly tempting, with one broom between them and the skid tracks half frozen in places. They could have used a shovel as a scraper; instead they had only the feet God had given them. Kicking at a lump of ice, Beryl hurt her big toe. Sophie commiserated, grateful, now, for her boots. Both would greatly like to know how it was that the two of them had been specially elected to perform this senseless last task by themselves. "Why us?" wondered Beryl. Sophie suspected that it was because the gang was punishing her for being Jewish but she decided not to say that; anyway, it did not explain Beryl. On that point, however, Beryl had her own theory. "Ahmed likes me," she said. "That's why."

Suddenly Sophie was bone-tired, too tired, she feared, to be able to eat. And tomorrow, she expected, would be worse, even if they were fed, because tomorrow there would be nothing to do but wait. She took the muddy broom from Beryl and gave a ferocious swipe. As she did so, Beryl's head turned. They heard the sound of a plane's motor. It was flying low. A searchlight was playing over the highway perhaps half a mile off and coming nearer. They saw a flare drop. "Cripes," said Beryl and ducked. Automatically Sophie let go of her broom; she crouched. A strange thought crossed her mind. "If it sees us," the thought said, "we are lost." She scrambled toward the road's edge, looking crazily for shelter.

"Down!" the man's voice commanded from somewhere in the underbrush. Clearly he could not see that the order was superfluous. "Down, both of you," said the woman's voice. "Into the ditch." "She loves that ditch," muttered Beryl. The icy, muddy trough was the last hiding-place either of them would have chosen; nevertheless they obeyed. Sophie hoped at least that Henk and Jim would be there, too, but they must have been told to hide in the bushes. She was by herself with her one-time classmate, the two of them crouching down, with their feet in the gelid mud. "Does she remind you of Mrs. H.?" Beryl said, under her breath. "Ssh!" said Sophie. She had remembered something. The broom. She had left it lying on the road. She asked herself whether Gretel realized that. Maybe she could not see it from where she had taken cover. Sophie straightened up and peered out. The searchlight was still some distance off, making broad sweeping arcs; she had time. Her heart raced; her knees shook, as if the plane was "enemy" with a load of bombs to release on her. She crept out. "Get back!" called the man's voice. Sophie did not answer. She inched along the highway on her hands and knees—dirt on her suede coat no longer mattered—till she could touch the tip of the broom-handle; then she pulled the broom toward her and fell back with it into the ditch. "The broom," she explained, idiotically. Beryl gripped her filthy hand. "Shake, sister." All at once, Sophie remembered a funny thing about her at Putney: the time she had told the whole form that she was changing her name to "Aventurine" and expected them all to call her that.

Now the plane was directly overhead. Another flare was dropped. Next to her, Sophie could feel Beryl holding her breath. Impossible that the plane would not see them as a motionless pair of shadows in this blinding light. The pilot was making sweeps, yet what interested him seemed to be farther up the road. Did the replanted tree look peculiar? She remembered reading a background story—was it about the Moors murders?—which said that aerial photographs could show where a grave had been dug from the way the soil looked even when the turf had been carefully replaced. Now even Beryl's breathing seemed to her too loud; she could not rid herself of the queer feeling that they could be overheard by the plane. Yet the pilot could not have noticed anything suspicious, for he had turned away from the road, in the direction of the dark house and the barn. It was safe now to peek out. He dipped, and the searchlight prowled. The peaked roofline of the house showed clearly, a quarter of a mile away. Sophie wondered what the hostages inside were feeling. She pictured Harold trying to signal from the roof. But apparently the pilot was satisfied that there was nothing there but "a typical Dutch farmhouse." In a minute the plane veered back to the highway. It went on, still flying low, toward what must be the mainland. The sound of the motor gradually died away.

The scare was over; bodies popped up, as if resurrecting, and stretched their limbs. Nothing could be heard but the distant pumping-station, the sudden rustle of bird wings, and low human voices, still pitched to an undertone. The flare petered out; everything returned to normal. Or so to speak. " 'Beddy-bye,' eh?" said Carey, and no one contradicted. As he took her arm to steady her on the homeward path, Sophie could not help feeling that she had proved quite a heroine in the broom episode—courage and initiative under fire. Yet she fought back the urge to mention it, since on the one hand objectively there had been no "fire," as a sane part of her giddy mind must always have known, and on the other the whole adventure, insofar as it was one, was best kept between herself and "Aventurine." What would the Bishop think if he heard that singlehanded and without prompting or duress Sophie Weil had foiled a powerful search plane intent on learning their whereabouts? And that she was unrepentant and unregretful, though she could not say why. He would pray for her maybe.

Eight

During the night, a thin snow had fallen. The temperature stood at −1° Celsius. The sky was empty; no plane had yet come snooping. From the air, in any case, nothing unusual would be noticed: a typical new farmhouse painted dark green in the Frisian way, its eastern window panes glittering in the rising sun, the sloping roof tiles a shiny fresh orange. Outside the main door swung a clothes-yard on which laundry hung, the only sign of habitation. Fifty meters off, there would appear to be a barn twice the size of the house in construction, loosely roofed over with tar paper or plastic sheeting and lightly blanketed with snow. Beyond, stretching to the horizon and broken only by the gleam of a canal, lay ploughed fields marked by frozen furrows like the deep wrinkles of a weathered *boer* face—on the ridges the earth color showed through where the wind had swept them bare. Around the house were dainty bird tracks but as yet no human footprints. Later the men would be led out in pairs to pee and move their bowels, if able, close to the back shed; the women would use the downstairs toilet for the time being—the toilet permission would be revoked were a breach of discipline to occur. From the air, the house should appear to be occupied but not unduly, not beyond the norm of four to six persons warranted for a settler's family.

On this day in reality it held thirty-two. Eight guards, twenty-four prisoners, which made an acceptable ratio: for every three imperialists, one people's army soldier. In the kitchen the Air France personnel was preparing a morning meal of bread, cheese, cold ham, butter, and coffee. The same meal had been distributed the night before, with the addition of pea soup and herring. If the hostages were to become constipated on this diet, it made no matter: fewer trips under guard to the outdoors and fewer stinking turds deposited. For this reason, prunes had been struck off the list of military supplies required. The logistics of this phase of the operation had been reviewed in depth; no detail of housekeeping was too small to be passed over. These people, it must be remembered, were prisoners of war. In engaging an enemy the less left to chance, the greater your flexibility in meeting the challenge of the unexpected under whatever form it might arise—"For want of a nail," as the proverb said.

Now, thanks to good planning, on this Tuesday morning, precisely forty-four hours after the launching of the assault, the innocent-looking farmhouse was an arsenal, stocked to the rafters with arms and ammunition, sandbags, explosives, canned and dried foods, smoked meat and fish, legumes and cereals, dairy products, blood plasma—all the matériel needful for a sustained auto-defense. The dwelling stood isolated, in open ground, without neighbors. As yet, no tree or shrub, which might afford cover, screened it from the wind. Any force seeking to approach would be seen immediately, at any rate by daylight. On the side away from the barn ran an entry road visible along its whole length from the big kitchen window, no doubt for the housewife's convenience; the underbrush that might have obstructed a sweeping view had been cleared and stacked in piles. The thicket near the highway on the barn side extended only a few hundred meters of protection. As noted in the initial study, the position had one small drawback, unavoidable in this terrain: the dwelling lacked a cellar, which might have been used for storage and for punishing disciplinary offenders. On the other hand, in the utility room, which occupied the shed, there was a big deep-freeze chest, and the kitchen had a frigidaire, ample shelves and cupboards and old-style bins. Outside the rear door were a chicken coop and a rabbit run. The welfare state was kind to its kulaks.

This rich farmer's house boasted eight rooms: on the ground floor, utility room, kitchen, family living-room, and *beste kamer,* plus a lavatory off the entry hall, containing shower and toilet; upstairs, the parents' room, two rooms for the children, playroom, and bathroom with tub and toilet. Above, reached by a ladder, was an attic. These *boers* had a washing-machine, a color television, a floor-waxer, a dish-washer, and central heating, fueled by oil—earth gas, the Netherlands' bragging retort to the Arab oil "boycott," had not arrived at the polder. The cookstove ran on propane. In addition, these folk had a tractor, fueled by petrol, and a new family automobile—a Ford Fiesta—as well as bicycles. On Sunday morning, bright and early, the Fiesta had carried the farmer and his butterball wife and four children to Schiphol, with six round-trip tickets (four half-fare) to the Balearics for a two weeks' winter vacation in the sun. Besides the *dreck* of capitalist technology, the family had a real eiderdown on the matrimonial bed, a child's crib painted with traditional Hindeloopen designs, and, in the *beste kamer,* genuine old-time oak-framed samplers embroidered with Old Testament mottoes, an *erfstuk* Reformed Bible bound in leather, with silver locks, a vase of peacock feathers, and three oriental carpets, one of which Yusuf declared to be genuine and at least fifty years old.

The Palestine Liberation Army had been impressed by this farmer's style of life. That was one of the negative side-effects of the decision to lease a pioneer house on the new polder as a base of operations. The Arab comrades should have been armed by their revolutionary training to resist the crude seductions of the welfare state. What they saw here, they should know, was window-dressing. The upper peasantry of the "advanced" countries of the West were a privileged caste, the same as the trade unionists, poisoned by the crumbs that fell to them from the rich man's table. All these social elements were the bribed tools of imperialism, in Marx's phrase—some of the old prophet's insights were still useful. One had thought that Hussein and Ahmed, at least, as "guest workers" in the kitchens and streets and sewers of Paris, would long ago have been demystified. They had seen with their own eyes the realities of class and race behind the façade: the HLMs and bidonvilles of Giscard's police state, alias *la belle France*. Their social origin was petty bourgeois, but in their political activity as emigrants they had shared the "quality of life" of the sweated underproletariat and did not need to be taught how to hate.

Yusuf, by contrast, was a greenhorn, detailed to the present mission from his training camp in Syria; he was an expert in explosives but still innocent of the inner workings of bourgeois democracy on its home ground. In view of that, it had seemed wiser to withhold him from the first and most dangerous phase of the operation. His physical courage was guaranteed by his Syrian sponsors, but the take-over of an airplane was a more serious affair than raiding a kibbutz or blowing up a hotel. A direct strike at the vital organs of the West called for a more seasoned militant than Yusuf, on arrival, proved to be. After a preliminary screening, in Frankfurt, it had been decided to defer him for service on the polder, where he would be able to make himself useful and profit from instruction from the other comrades. He had been conducted to a safe house in Aachen, issued a new false passport and identity papers, provided with a haircut, a suit of clothes, and a solid pair of shoes. Three days ago, with the German comrades and Carlos, the Uruguayan, he had crossed the border at Maastricht. The signal from Paris had come. The following noon, Sunday, the operation would begin; at that time the support elements arriving from Germany should already be in place, with concise directions for preparing the farmhouse to receive the commando and its prisoners, whose number was still unknown.

Coordination had been excellent. There had been no difficulty at the border with Yusuf's papers, and the trunk of the car had not even been opened. Twenty-four hours later, it might have been another story—with the capture of the plane a general alert could have gone out. Yet, despite the good functioning of the time-table and the accurate deployment of the reserves, it now looked as if there might have been an error of judgment on the human level, insofar as Yusuf was concerned. Too little was known about him; his language capacity, in particular, had been overestimated by the Syrian contact—the only Western tongue familiar to him was a rudimentary English he had picked up in a Zionist carpet factory. Inspection this morning showed that he had carried out his assignments creditably: the house had been correctly wired, the remaining stocks of explosives stored in a dry place—the choice of a flour bin was commendable. But he had no reading skill, and, once his work was completed, time, it seemed, had hung heavy on his hands.

This was a restless *knabe*, Elfride reported, and, like so many of the *fedayin*, curious, full of questions needing clear answers, which, because of the language handicap, she had been unable to give him, she feared. In the end, he had passed his Sunday silently roaming about the house, doing his laundry in the washing-machine, and watching the children's hour program from a German station on the farmer's television: Snow White and the Seven Dwarfs. On Monday he had counted the piles of starched linen sheets in the housewife's cupboard and walked over the farmer's fields. Horst and Carlos had not known what to do with him.

With the appearance last night of Ahmed and Hussein, his tongue had loosened. But Ahmed, who had his own weaknesses, was more concerned with his cut thumb—wondering whether he should not give himself an injection of blood plasma from the frigidaire—than with their comrade's political education. Like Yusuf, Ahmed and Hussein seemed bewitched by the kulak's living space and by the signs of wealth they pointed to, eagerly chattering in Arabic. Encouraged by Yusuf and his child-like excitement, they had reverted themselves to an infantile level. It became clear that there was an irritating residue of gullibility in all three comrades. Yusuf had showed them his discovery—the shower—and they got into it together, giggling and splashing each other, as though they had never met a hot-and-cold shower before. Then, having been assigned to the big bed, they climbed under the eiderdown, which they fingered with

awe, tucking it tenderly under their chins, when a mature political reaction, as Greet commented, would have been to slash
the old fetish through with a knife and let the feathers fly. The
whole disheartening performance was like an advertisement of
the benefits of capitalism. Did the sleeping patriots dream of this
fat land of milk and honey, where the merry peasant had "never
had it so good"?

Jeroen felt discouraged. Seated at the kitchen table, he spat
out a morsel of ham onto the paper plate in front of him. Then
he sought to be fair. There was a reverence for property here,
he realized, that no bourgeois could possibly feel, and it would
have to be treated with care or the Arabs could become problems. He was touched by it in a way, remembering himself
when he had first come to Amsterdam as an apprentice electrician and looked with wonder at the great houses on the canals
and the pictures in the Rijksmuseum. It had been a feeling close
to worship and had made him ask whether he should not become an artist, dedicate himself to a thing he thought he saw
represented here, which he had called to himself *"waarde."*
This "worth" or value, he imagined, was what the liberation
fighters were seeing in the farmer's housing, which was causing
them, still this morning, to open their dark eyes wide, as
though they had been given a vision of paradise.

An oriental paradise, he thought to himself, shaking his
head, and hoped the idea was not racist. A regular Garden of
Allah, sumptuously carpeted, for it was the *beste kamer,* he
perceived, that affected them most strongly—they would tire of
the shower-bath and the washing-machine. Except for the
couple's bedroom, the remainder of the dwelling was more like
a "contemporary" suburban villa than an agricultural worker's
home. The manipulative hand of some firm of Amsterdam
architects—planners for the state—was crudely evident in the
family room, where the new television throned and a stack of
religious newspapers seemed to wait for banishment. "Picture"
window, rough plaster wall with "sculpture" pattern, false
ceiling beams, synthetic-tweed floor covering, indirect lighting panels—Jeroen was sadly familiar with this alienating

mass-produced *rommel*. He had installed the identical panels and fixtures in city housing developments for workers and could look back on the shame of it as a step in his own development. Here they would name it "polder style," and where the wild sedges now grew there would be a landscaped house lot, ornamental shrubbery, a weeping willow, a rock garden, possibly a pool. But the couple had respected the old concept in furnishing the parlor.

Crossing the magic threshold, the three Arabs stared at the housewife's collection of well-watered plants blooming on window-sill and tables before the shining plate-glass window, at the framed tinted photos of the ancestors, at the harmonium in the corner, at the doilies and antimacassars, at the vase of peacock feathers; they stood silent before the deep-toned carpet, apparently the real one, that hung on the round window-table and they stepped softly, as if fearful of leaving a footprint, on the thick carpets that lay on the waxed floor.

Jeroen had watched their nostrils sensuously take in the characteristic Dutch *beste kamer* smell, of furniture polish—the good old *boenwas*, guaranteed pure from the hive—mixed with the moist hothouse fragrance of flowering plants, with a strong sniff of lye, and a damp, slightly moldy odor of upholstery fabric exuded by a rarely opened room. Yet it was pointless to explain to them, as Greet was doing, that the room was never used except for marriages and will-readings and maybe sometimes the Sabbath. That could only heighten the value of the room in their eyes; what they sensed here was something sacred. The *beste kamer* was a religious shrine, a holy of holies, with a ceremonial carpet serving as altar cloth; the predominant smell of soap and beeswax was the odor of sanctity. If it was used for everyday, it would no longer be a place of worship. To demystify them, it would be necessary to show them what god was being worshipped here and at what cost of blood and grinding toil to their brothers.

It was true that such a room occupied valuable space in a house and had no practical utility. But a mosque had no practical utility. And in Jeroen's view, which differed sharply from Greet's on this point, a revolutionary should not try to set at naught the experience of something higher, called "transcendence" in philosophy. He did not accept the position, typical of orthodox Leninism, that the philosophers had been sheer obscurantists; some of their terms, if reinterpreted and purged of ruling-class overtones, pointed to truths that the revolutionary should embrace as his own. There was a potential in man for rising above—in other words, transcending—gross material concerns that the revolutionary by his act and example sought to bring to full life in every human creature, while the bourgeois and the bourgeois revisionist sought to strangle it at birth, above all in the working masses but finally, perforce, in themselves. The argument of practicality, which Greet was invoking to disabuse the Arabs, could make no impression on them since it was essentially a bourgeois argument.

Moreover the childish reverence they showed for this standard Dutch kitsch had to be understood and allowed for in context. It reflected the oppression and deprivation of agricultural workers in their homeland. That such a house should appear to them as a palace told the whole story of imperialist exploitation of the "backward" peoples. To let oneself be impatient with the comrades' wonderment would be a fault, mirroring one's own sense of superior social development. Greet despised the *beste kamer* of her middle-class parents as the ultimate symbol of Dutch hypocrisy; to profane this farmer's parlor was seen by her as a revolutionary necessity—she was insisting, for instance, that they go back on the promise they had given to water the housewife's army of plants. With all that Jeroen did not sympathize. He had no especially vengeful feelings toward his hard-working parents' humble best room with the big black Bible and the wheezy old harmonium; the clambering "Busy Lizzies" on the window-sill, industriously flowering without care or nourishment, the lowest of the low among house plants, had been a bright joy of his childhood. To leave this woman's innocent plants to droop and die as an act of revolutionary justice would be a kind of slow execution painful to witness and, far from setting the Arabs an example of disciplined class behavior, would only confuse and hurt them. Their development in these matters should be allowed to find its own way without undue prompting or correction. Regarding Ahmed and Hussein, it had been a mistake, plainly, to assume that the lessons learned in Giscard's France would be seen to apply to the Netherlands; the West was a hydra, bearing many heads, which had to be struck off separately, even though the trunk of the beast was one and indivisible.

The fact was that Den Uyl and his allies were cleverer than their brothers of the Right. They were able to take in the working class with their skilful propaganda, which consisted not in empty slogans but in social measures speaking for themselves and to a certain degree incontestably. A revolutionary would err in saying that there was large-scale poverty in Holland and naked oppression of minorities, that the aged were harshly neglected—Jeroen's own parents, drawing their state pension and health benefits, were living proof of paternalistic "favoritism" to the old. That the pension policy was a ruse to induce early retirement and withdraw a section of the work force from the labor market, thus masking real unemployment, did not alter the facts. The noisy protests of the Right, howling against "confiscatory" taxation and blind to its own interests—in reality so well served by Den Uyl and Company—helped sustain the fiction. It was only in foreign policy that Den Uyl and his gang regularly gave their game away: was it not openly boasted that staunch little Holland was the "best friend" of Israel and the U.S. imperialist warmakers? Hand in glove with the imperialists, as their trusted lackey, Den Uyl could afford a crocodile's concern for human rights in General Pinochet's Chile and the moribund Franco's Spain. On the domestic scene, the multi-nationals flourished through shameless bribery and corruption, while land-reclamation projects, such as this polder, kept alive the national myth of sturdy self-help. That the Communist Party had no influence and the only real opposition came from the Right and the fanatic confessional parties demonstrated how effective the simulation of socialism had been. Even the Indonesians, after a period in unpublicized camps, were consenting to be "absorbed" by their former colonialist masters. Should one blame Arab patriots, born and raised in the teeming bazaars, if they were not wholly immune to the subtle indoctrination of this farmer's housing?

They were also impressed—and for the same reasons, rooted in history—by the extent of the farmer's fields. After walking them yesterday, Yusuf had concluded that they must comprise fifty hectares already ploughed, with about five, including the house lot, still unimproved. He had said to Elfride that the man here must be a big landowner, an exploiter. She had told him no, correctly. Lying to the masses was always a mistake; one had to explain and carefully expose the underlying contradictions. Being a German and unfamiliar with Dutch agrarian patterns, she could not say whether this farmer owned the land or rented it from the state, but in the end it came to the same. Narrowly speaking, he was not an exploiter, since it was clear that he used machinery rather than the labor of landless peasants to work it, yet, in a broader sense, as an instrument of imperialism, he was exploiting the resources of the Third World, in his very tractor and the diesel that fueled it, the rubber tires of his automobile, the copper-derived chromium of his wife's appliances, the nitrates of his fertilizer, and so on. On the other hand, it would be stupid to pretend that he and his wife, by Dutch standards, enjoyed great prosperity; there was too much evidence here to the contrary, though some of it might not be visible to a Palestinian eye. Even the word "kulak" was probably misplaced. In terms of the Dutch class structure, these were not moneyed people. The new furniture consisted of "suites" purchased no doubt at a discount house; there were no books, and the only picture was a cheap reproduction of a Rembrandt self-portrait tacked up in the children's playroom. Very likely the man was still paying out to the usurers of the loan companies on the car and the tractor. His wife made her own and the children's clothes, as an old Singer in the couple's room testified. But in Yusuf's eyes, a sewing-machine was a sign of affluence—another contradiction springing from historical unevenness.

The clearest proof, however, that this family's circumstances were relatively modest was the way they had jumped at the offer to vacate the premises for a two-week period. It had perhaps not even been necessary to throw in the vacation in the Balearics. Probably they would have been glad to move in with relatives on the mainland—the woman had her people in Kampen. So Jeroen had contended, but Greet, though not denying it, had argued that the cost factor must be weighed against the temptation the couple might feel to "look in" on their tenants—some trivial pretext could always be found. She did not trust the woman; to her mind, it was worth a thousand guilders for the group to have the assurance that the creature was out of Holland, safely lying on a beach and coated with sunburn lotion, during the crucial first phase of the operation. Doubtless she had been right; Jeroen knew it was inconsistent for a revolutionary to have, like him, a penny-pinching mentality inherited from peasant forebears of the deepest "black-stockings" dye.

Besides, Greet had to be deferred to for the remarkable vision she had shown in proposing the polder as a base. From the start they had all seen that for a strike of this magnitude a fall-back position would have to be prepared, since the usual ports of call, though sometimes curiously open to commercial hijackers, could not be counted on to receive a people's army commando and its prisoners of war—this was one of the sad results of factional division within the liquidation-of-the-Zionist-entity forces. That among the people's prisoners an American senator would figure made it all the more likely that a "diplomatic" attitude could be expected from the Arab capitals, to say nothing of Havana, where this senator was regarded, simplistically, as some kind of friend. Hence it had been essential to develop a serious alternative, not dependent on the whims and opportunistic calculations of national leaders, and it was Greet, at the December meeting, who had had the genius to think of the polder. Like every creative idea, it had got a lukewarm reception to begin with; all sorts of "practical" objections were raised, particularly by the German comrades. But then Jeroen himself had caught fire, and, before the meeting was over, the whole planning council was converted.

After that, a familiar law of momentum took over: the more the comrades studied the polder, the less interest they showed in the original list of sanctuaries which were to be tried before falling back, as a last resort, on a substitute. By a swift overturn, comparable to a revolution, almost overnight and yet without anyone's conscious decision, the last became first. When finally, after cautious reconnoitering and consultation of a geodetic map, this particular farmhouse had been pinpointed as most suited to their purpose, it was as if they could no longer, willingly, reverse direction, any more than a snowball rolling downhill could change course. This, at any rate, was Jeroen's analysis of the phenomenon as he looked back from today's perspective on the stages, unrolling as in a slow-motion film, from doubt to total commitment the plan had traversed. From here, like any process when looked at backward, it appeared foreordained, never to have been in doubt. Yet at the final meeting in Paris, on the eve of the great day, it had still been voted that on take-over the pilot would query the "sympathizing" Arab capitals for permission to land. But more as a matter of form—if his sense of that meeting was correct—and as a brotherly concession to the Syrian arms-suppliers than in any serious expectation of a favorable response. Jeroen did not like to think, now, what his reaction would have been if an Arab capital had surprised them. Bitter regret, surely, for the time and work and study that had gone into the polder alternative—not to mention the air fares and the rent money and the Majorca hotel outlay—but, beyond that, for Jeroen and perhaps for Greet too, there would have been almost an artistic disappointment.

Already, while it was still a blueprint, they were proud of their idea, of its simple clean lines and undeniable originality

—it owed nothing in its conception to any of the current models of revolutionary strategy. The Japanese Red Army comrades, Wadi Haddad and his PFLP contingent, even the matchless "Carlos" could only admire. And in the captive Boeing, Jeroen had needed all his schooling in indifference to keep an impassive face as they monitored the radio for answers which were strangely slow in coming, while the plane flew steadily southward and, on the polder, if all had gone well, the farmhouse stood ready and waiting. To sit dully, by contrast, in the Libyan desert, while Khaddafi's people bargained for you would have been a sorry comedown; in fact such a prospect had become unthinkable to Jeroen, and not merely because the most predictable outcome would be "administrative detention" in a Benghazi jail.

Working out the details—the bothersome minutiae, each of which required a separate inspiration to resolve—he had fallen in love with the plan. He had watched it grow under their hands, change and develop, meet and encompass obstacles or else leap over them. The sense of it as a work of art had grown in him, and not a solitary work of art fashioned by a bourgeois dreamer out of lifeless materials but an active, vital collaboration in which even the farmer and his wife and red-cheeked children played a part, albeit an unwitting one. They were the local materials to be worked in, as your architect used brick or fieldstone, according to availability, and they were also the "local color," the *oud-Hollands* camouflage serving as your disguise. And insofar as they were a part of the medium you worked in, the resistance they offered to your design had to be calculated and incorporated as an element in the overall picture. In short, they were a challenge, and here again it was Greet who had responded creatively.

The problem presented was simple, and yet everything hung on it: how to approach these people with an offer to "borrow" their property that would not excite their suspicions. Suspicion was inbred in farm-dwellers—a reflex set in motion by any novelty, by the mere sight of a stranger. Yet to take over the house by force was an option ruled out by the circumstances;

violence applied prematurely would abort the whole design. Some stratagem was needed that would disarm the pair as effectively as a weapon and yet have an innocent, indeed attractive appearance. Something familiar to them in their everyday life, something they would welcome as it crossed their threshold. A fistful of money would not do it; the sight of money in quantity would be too unfamiliar. To find an "open sesame" was not so easy; the others were almost ready to give up and look for another stronghold when Greet hit on the answer: television, of course. They would pose as a television crew doing a story on the polder.

No one doubted that this at last was the solution—an answer so obvious that it might have been overlooked, like the television aerial on the roof of the dwelling over which the eye passed without taking notice, any more than of a chimney. And the event had proved her right, as if it had been programmed: the knock on the door, footsteps inside, a pair of blue eyes peering out the window, cautious unbolting of the door, inspection of the four persons standing outside, carrying cameras and sound equipment, quick glance at the small truck parked in the entry road with large stickers "Hamburger Rundfunk" on its sides and rear, removal of apron, smoothing of hair, and "Come in, please, ladies and gentlemen, but kindly wipe your feet." Then, after the inevitable service of coffee, the housewife was ready to hear their proposition.

The truck and the stickers on it must have dispelled any lingering doubt. The stickers had been Horst's idea. Strange how, from the instant that impersonating a television crew was thought of, the details had fallen into place, like iron filings assembling around a powerful magnet. Improvements and minor corrections seemed to derive naturally from the key concept, as if it had a brain of its own. Jeroen, at the beginning, had thought of hand-lettering the trunk with the name of the German station, but Horst had showed him the risk in that if they should happen to be stopped by the highway police—stickers, which could be removed immediately on leaving the farmhouse, served the same purpose and would not be seen to be stickers unless examined close up. Similarly, the original scenario had had them coming from the Omroepstichting. But Jeroen himself had seen the flaw: it would be too easy for the couple to check up with the Dutch feature service; a simple phone call would do it. German television combined the known and the remote. It was watched regularly in Holland, yet to place a call to Hamburg to check up on a polder documentary would be beyond these people. In addition, "Hamburger Rundfunk" had the virtue of explaining the German comrades: Horst was posing as the sound-man, with Elfride as his script girl. Jeroen was the camera-man, and Greet his lighting assistant and the crew's interpreter. The dark-skinned Yusuf and Carlos would not be seen during the negotiations; they would appear later, when the family's departure from Schiphol had been confirmed by the comrade at the KLM desk.

It had been wonderful how the couple had swallowed the story. *"Dummköpfer!"* said Horst. Yet should one sneer at them for credulousness, considering the inducements to belief furnished by the stickers, the Hamburg license-plate, the paraphernalia of sound-equipment, cameras, cables, blackboard, tripod, light meter, carried into the house by the "crew"? Hundreds of feet of simulated film were turned, showing the husband seated on the tractor, the wife feeding the chickens, the children at play, and so on. An interview with the couple on polder conditions was taped—a genuine one, by good luck, since the woman's final request, when the team was already packing up, was to hear her voice played back.

They had raised fewer objections than had been anticipated in the preparatory study. The man's main concern was that he should be back in time for his spring sowing, which, given the state of the ground, could be as late as February, and he agreed, though with slight hesitation, that work on the barn should be halted when the keys were turned over—too noisy and disruptive for the crew while it was filming. He might have asked why the Germans had chosen the dead season of the year for doing a documentary on polder life—"scheduling" was the only answer Jeroen had been able to think of—but the question seemed not to have occurred to him, and the woman's questions had to do with the sleeping arrangements—were the two couples married?—with the oil and electricity bills and potential damage to the furnishings—who would pay? A generous deposit, to cover, also, wear and tear on towels and bed linen, had sufficed to quiet her.

Her only demur arose over the contract, made out in duplicate on paper bearing the letterhead of the Hamburg station, which Jeroen put in her hands, pleased to have remembered this crowning small touch of verisimilitude. She did not want it, and her man, meeting her eyes, had concurred. For a moment, Jeroen had been dumbfounded. Then he understood: taxes. Obviously the couple preferred to have the deal take place under the table, with nothing on paper to show income received. Putting the contract back in his pocket, he had nearly laughed for joy. This solved the last problem confronting the commando: how to keep the woman from talking. Were she to boast to her kin and neighbors that her house had been chosen by a German network for a documentary on the polder, the place would be surrounded by curiosity-seekers. Even the resourceful Greet had been unable to think of a means, stronger than mere persuasion, of guaranteeing the creature's silence. A reward to be placed in the couple's hands on their return if the crew had been allowed to film undisturbed by neighbors or relatives? But the promise of a reward for silence might sow a germ of doubt: respectable people, the pair might well reflect, did not pay to have no witnesses to their doings. In the group's thinking, that bridge had been still uncrossed when they had arrived at the house that first morning; they were waiting on inspiration. Then the woman's gesture, totally unexpected, of pushing back the contract, did their work for them. There could be no better insurance that the affair would remain quiet than that the couple had their own motive for concealment: cheating the tax man! And this illustrated once again the genius of the central concept: the raw materials of bourgeois life, of their own initiative, sprang forward to collaborate in a revolutionary design aimed at its destruction. Moreover it showed—to descend to the particular—how erroneous it would have been to pretend to come from Dutch television: revenue from Omroepstichting would be automatically reported to The Hague; no motive, then, for silence. Looking back on that series of lucky chances, or narrow escapes, Jeroen felt confirmed in his persistent sense of being guided in this enterprise by an unseen power that fitted everything together, like Hegel's "cunning of reason" or Adam Smith's "invisible hand." He did not yet know the name of this power that was directing him but every now and again he felt its gentle pressure. What had prompted him, for example, to draw up a contract that had seemed at the time a mere touch of artistry, a perhaps wasteful embellishment? And the labor of printing the letterhead had been, in one sense, a waste; yet if he had not been moved to do that, how else could the group have learned that it had no cause for worry in the woman's wagging tongue? It was as if every "artistic" stroke had responded to a logic in the decaying capitalist structure. When a spearhead of revolutionaries brought a plan of subversion to bear on a bourgeois entity, that inner logic, uncannily, started to apply of itself, without priming.

Nevertheless, on Sunday afternoon, while Yusuf was watching *Schneeweiss und die sieben Zwerge* on the *Kinderprogramm* in the living-room and Carlos was napping, Elfride and Horst had passed an anxious hour or so at the kitchen window, alert to the danger represented by the woman's parents in Kampen, only half an hour's drive away. Who knew, after all, what story the daughter had told them? And if the old people were to turn up on an after-church ride with a bee in their bonnet of "keeping an eye on" the property, their failing eyesight could hardly miss the redoubt of sandbags that Carlos had toiled all morning to build, making efficient use of the farmer's potato sacks. But the Sabbath afternoon had gone by without a sign of an interloper. Jeroen, had he thought of it, could have put the comrades' minds at rest. From all the signs, as Elfride, a pastor's daughter, might have noted herself, these people were strict Calvinists, and their parents would be stricter. A born Lutheran from Hesse maybe would not know, but Dutch Calvinists of that persuasion did not joy-ride on Sunday or visit back and forth. In fact, the man of the house, though Elfride and Horst were unaware of the episode, had entered his first objection on learning that they were to fly on the Sunday morning.

Jeroen ought to have foreseen that. When poor Greet, all unsuspecting, came by with the tickets and the hotel vouchers, it had been too late to change. Everything depended on adherence to the schedule, which had the family's departure from Schiphol synchronizing with the Boeing's departure from De Gaulle and following, by eighteen hours, on the crossing of the border at Maastricht by the German-led detail. The man's sudden balking, at that juncture, could have been a real disaster. Luckily, he had allowed Greet and his disappointed family to persuade him to overlook, for once, the observance of the Sabbath: the fault would not be his but Hamburg's for setting an inflexible date. And on the way to the airport, as the woman pointed out, they could get the Gereformeerd service on the car radio.

Aside from this conscientious obstacle—the ultimate close shave—the family had given no real problems. Early Sunday morning, Elfride and Horst had arrived at the farmhouse in the by-now-familiar truck, explaining that the Dutch crew would follow: they had been held up in Amsterdam by trouble with one of the cameras; probably the family would cross them on the road. The woman, at Greet's suggestion, had prepared a list of instructions as to the watering of the plants, the regulation of the thermostat, disposal of the garbage, and so on. The Fiesta was already packed, and the man was worrying about parking it at the airport in a place where it would not be stolen —"too many lawless elements these days," he told Horst in broken German. Then came the transfer of the keys, and for an instant Elfride thought she saw a shade of doubt in the woman's eyes; clearly she would rather have Greet, who spoke her language, to entrust them to—that would be almost like "in the family." The man told her to hurry. Outside, the children, restless and eager to leave, were examining the truck. The older boy was pulling at one of the stickers. He called out something in Dutch. "Look, *moeder*, it comes off!" was what he was saying, plainly. He held up the sticker in his grubby little hand. Elfride caught her breath. She was sure she saw a funny, thoughtful expression come over the woman's face. But Horst was really a wonder. "*Ja, ja*, it comes off," he told the child in German, with a hearty laugh. "Now let's put it back, shall we?" Seeing his good humor, the woman scolded the child. "*Genoeg!*" she said—"That's enough." Then, to Horst, "Excuse it." Whatever she may have asked herself for a fleeting second, the importance of the stickers had not sunk into her mind. The Fiesta drove off, with the children waving from the rear window. In a few minutes, the back-up car waiting with Yusuf and Carlos was able to emerge from a side road off the highway. Supplies and the short-wave radio were swiftly transferred to the house. Werner, the driver, would head straight for the German border. The truck, stolen in Rotterdam, with the false Hamburg license-plate and altered serial number, had no further part to play; eventually it would be found by the police in the parking lot at Schiphol, where the young comrade assigned to fetch it had been instructed to abandon it after wiping off his fingerprints.

Now, two days later, Jeroen sat at the kitchen table before the short-wave set, holding an earphone to his right ear—the hearing of the left had been impaired by a beating he had got in a "Red Youth" demonstration in The Hague. The breakfast service was finished. The Air France people had washed up the coffee-pot and cleared off the paper plates and cups, which would be burned in the outdoor incinerator when the right moment came. He was alone. The kitchen had been declared out of bounds except to the Air France cabin crew and the two Dutch pilots. It had been decided to treat them as neutrals; they were working folk, with the usual pay grievances, and so, in principle, capable of being radicalized—Greet herself was a former KLM hostess, won to the just cause during a siege on the Cairo air-strip. In any case, their services were needed for the preparation and issue of food. Jeroen had elected to make the kitchen their command post because of its size, the unbroken view from the windows, and the privacy it offered during most of the day; it had sliding doors, which could be closed, as now, when important business was being transacted. Moreover, it pleased him to sit in a kitchen.

Werner's voice was coming through, clearly now, from Aachen. Still no news. Irritably, Jeroen put down the earphone and pushed the big set aside: he did not need to be reminded of the time difference; he knew quite well that it was only four in the morning in New York. Of course it was too early to expect a full report on the list of eleven parasites that Aachen had relayed to the comrades there; obviously museums and galleries would not open till ten, which would be four in the afternoon here. But there were other sources; newspapers stayed open all night. The names he and Greet had hurried last night to copy from the first-class passports must be on file in any newspaper "morgue." In that metropolis, surely, there were also students of art, critics of art, professors of art, with links to the movement who could be waked up for consultation. Some relevant information, however incomplete, should have reached the cell in Aachen by this time; the details could be filled in when the museums and art libraries opened.

But the names "Ramsbotham," "Tallboys," "Potter," "Chadwick," et cetera—with home cities added to avoid the possibility of confusion—had produced from New York, so far, only such banalities as "millionaire sportsman," "fat cat," "self-styled philanthropist," "extreme right-winger." Not a word suggestive of art patronage, to the point where Jeroen was beginning to wonder whether he and Greet had not made a mistake. Had they been too impulsive in departing, on their own initiative, from the agreed-on plan calling for the release of all first-class passengers? When they had got wind of a tour of collectors aboard the Boeing, it had seemed, at least to Jeroen, a challenge that could not be refused. Now, however, he asked himself if he and Greet had not over-reacted when she had hurried forward bringing word of "Giorgiones and Titians" belonging to a tour of millionaires traveling in first class: she had heard the little liberal woman say so. But that woman was an exaggerator, as they had since observed. Perhaps these people were not art collectors at all but just ordinary rich people who "owned" a painting or two.

To have seized a group of ordinary rich people, even millionaires, held no interest for Jeroen. Money, though it would have to figure on the list of demands, was the least of the commando's objectives. Furthermore, extorting ransom from a handful of plutocrats would fatally shift the emphasis: a jugular strike based on principle and aimed dramatically at the "superstructure," in Marxian terms, of Western capitalism would take on the appearance of another pinprick hardly distinguishable from run-of-the-mill criminality. Millionaires could pay "a king's ransom" and barely feel it, just as your rich bourgeois, held up on the street, surrendered his purse gladly, unlike the poor man—there was plenty more where it came from. To deal a blow at this society, it was necessary to take from it something it deemed irreplaceable.

That, at any rate, had been the concept behind the capture of the Boeing, known to be carrying an international committee of liberal cat's paws of the energy interests to investigate torture in Iran. The other passengers were of no concern—bystanders or civilians, to be sent about their business as rapidly as possible. "Excess baggage," as Horst had formulated it; for the coup to make its point, the committee must be *seen* to be the exclusive target. Seizing this body of self-appointed just men on an errand of mercy to the Third World struck at the core of the West's pious notion of itself. And to strike not at random but selectively, choosing showcase models of civic virtue whose price was above rubies and whom the West would have to save at any cost or renounce its image of "caring," was, of course, sacrilege. Without sacrilege, as history showed, there could be no terror worthy of the name. And the fact that these good souls were journeying on a patently selfless mission, in Economy class as befitted their social outlook, could be counted on to add to the horror and condemnation the deed would call forth. A re-action of universal shock and outrage was essential to the success of the design. There would have been nothing like it since the Olympic Games "massacre," and those were only athletes.

To the people's ear, the chorus of indignation would have a comic sound, for the West, in fact, set no value on concerned and high-minded citizens except when they could be used to further some purpose of its own. Had this committee perished in a plane crash, Washington, ordering a day of remembrance, would have been relieved, on the whole, to be rid of them, since its anti-Soviet interest required a simulation of friendship with the Shah, despite pressures from business elements hurt by the oil "squeeze" and desirous of a tougher line with him—this conflict of interests, out of which such a committee of innocents would tend to be born, was a typical contradiction of late cap-italism.

Yet a pretense of valuing its critics was still essential to the system in its present stage, and the price of maintaining the pretense in this case was going to be rather high. To save these sacred skins, the horrified West would have to accept an ex-change: for every just man, four people's army militants, to be released from the imperialists' jails. Having calculated the ratio with an eye to due measure, Jeroen had not believed that they should ask more. To ask more might decide the imperialists to refuse any concessions, on the ground that terror, knowing no bounds, could be met only with firmness. For the commando, there would then be nothing for it but to execute the prisoners.

In the new circumstances, however, that thinking was no longer viable. It had been natural to postulate the release of class-war militants according to a strict ratio, particularly for the German comrades, who had had Andreas and Ulrike in mind and Gudrun and Jan-Carl and the other Werner and Irmgaard. . . . But that goal, they would have to see, was no longer within reach of the commando. Study of the passports proved that, contrary to earlier and supposedly "sure" informa-tion, the venerable prelate from Köln was not among the pris-oners—Greet and Jeroen, in the Boeing, had already thought as much—hence, Bonn could sit back and smile at the fantasy of such a demand. Similarly, an American rabbi and Israeli stooge "guaranteed" to be with this committee was nowhere in evidence, so that the Zionist state could smile, too, at any ultimatum calling for the freeing of the Arab brothers it held. Bad luck for the Palestinian army, but it would have to be accepted. The whole position would have to be re-thought, in view of the current actuality, and larger demands conceived. It was a challenge to the imagination to find a truly radical approach. The old formula of a body-for-bodies exchange was too often unproductive, leading to killing for want of a better result. The enemy by his attitude, rather than proletarian justice, dictated your disposal of the prisoners.

In any case, killing was not a choice Jeroen cared to make except as a last resort. Killing the cat had been a botch, offensive to his workman's instinct; he had felt momentary pleasure in the act of taking aim, but using the poor creature to set an example to the passengers had surely been unnecessary. He blamed his nerves, which had been on edge as the pilot kept circling over Schiphol and it had begun to look as if they could not land. Killing accomplished little and with forethought could usually be avoided. As for torture, that was not envisioned. Elfride had been eager to give these liberals a taste of the conditions of detention suffered by comrades in the imperialists' jails. But solitary confinement, as at Stammheim, in a windowless box with a judas-hole and a blinding overhead light burning night and day, was clearly impossible in these living quarters which had not been designed as a prison. Perfect reciprocity—an eye for an eye—was an ideal that the revolutionary with his inferior means could not hope to achieve. Furthermore, the age of most of the hostages and their soft habits of life would make simple detention, with the inevitable crowding and inadequate toilet facilities, a species of harsh punishment that in their case suited the crime.

"Torture" in fact was the word they were already using to describe having had to sleep without blankets or mattress "like sardines in a can," one lot on the floor of the family living-room and the rest in the unfinished attic—those who had passed the night in the living-room objected to the bad air and those who had been sent to the attic protested the lack of heating. Posted with his rifle at the head of the stairway, Carlos had had to hear their grumblings and their intermittent snores. And now Greet reported that a petition was about to be presented by the pastor asking, on humane grounds, that any who wished it should be allowed to sleep in the helicopter; in the family room they were still disputing over the wording. Jeroen could have told them that they were wasting their breath. It was a rule of guerrilla operations never to disperse your hostages.

In the original plan, of course, excessive crowding had not been foreseen. The addition of twelve from first class to the nucleus of eight liberals was responsible. Yet if these people proved to be important collectors of art, then the difficulties of housekeeping and management created by their numbers would seem slight in comparison to the matchless opportunity their uninteresting bodies represented. If their collections were to contain a single Titian or Giorgione, their presence in the chosen plane constituted a windfall that Jeroen in his wildest dreams would hardly have dared to conceive.

Back in the Boeing, having brought him the incredible news, Greet, woman-like, had cooled in the face of his enthusiasm. All at once, she professed not to see the difference between a collector of paintings and any other Mr. or Mrs. Moneybags. "What causes you to think they are better, pray?" "Not they in themselves," he had answered. "What they have is better. Better than cars or yachts or 'securities.' Maybe not in our eyes but in the eyes of their society." "In *your* eyes, Jeroen," Greet had retorted. "I do not like to see you so excited." And in a moment she had added "I think I am sorry I told you." Faced with that wilful blindness, he had had to make her understand the uniqueness of the opportunity: finding this tour aboard put them within striking distance of dozens, perhaps hundreds, of priceless works of art. How they would manage to get hold of a few of those treasures was not yet clear to him. He would have to think, he had told her. But once they *had* managed it, no demand would be too bold. This society had two talismans: one moral and therefore hypocritical, honored by lip service, and the other material, honored in daily practice and most highly venerated in the form of works of art. In the interior of the Boeing, by one chance in a million, the pair coexisted, even if for the moment the art works were present only nominally, at a second remove. Such a chance would never arise again; if they let the collectors go, they would renounce a prize that would not be offered them twice. If they kept them, they ran no extra risk.

In the end, his arguments had persuaded her. The polder house, he had showed her, was one incentive the more, almost dictating their action to them. When again would they possess a stronghold with ample storage facilities, completely isolated and yet accessible by helicopter? It would not even be necessary for the helicopters bringing the canvases to land; their cargo could be dropped in the open field. In the event that large canvases were delivered—statuary, unless small, should not be attempted—the barn roof could be finished and insulated, which would be a job for the hostages.

Jeroen sighed. Thinking backward, to the great moment of decision in the Boeing, his mind was leaping too far ahead. Doggedly, he pulled the set to him and tried the Aachen frequency. Only static. Yet he could not make a serious plan until he knew what the collections, if in fact they existed, consisted of. There was no point in interrogating the prisoners, as Carlos had proposed: they would lie. And if there were no important works of art in the collections, it was hardly worth the effort. Better to get rid of the whole tour, though he could not think how. He would not accept dubious attributions or "school" or "follower" works. And no American stuff. His heart was set on the masters. He wanted Rubens, Rembrandt, Goya, Vermeer, as well as the Titians and Giorgiones, which may have been only a figure of speech. With American buying power in mind, he had been choosing, letting his memory range over the whole history of art. "You have gone back to your old love, Jeroen,"

Greet had reproached him on the plane. Now she slid open the door and, seeing him with the radio, she said it again. "Back to your first love. Be careful, Jeroen."

The accusation was partly true. In his young days in Amsterdam, when the word *"waarde"* had sounded in his brain, it had not once occurred to him to work to become rich so that he could own a fine canal house with pictures in it. His idea had been to consecrate himself, in poverty like a monk, to the value people called "art" by learning, if possible, to make some of it himself. As though to pay back a debt he owed for the joy his eyes were experiencing in the museums and along the canals. For a time he tried to teach himself by sketching in the Rijksmuseum and eventually also in the Stedelijkmuseum—he still loved Van Gogh as a person and as an artist. He went to night classes in drawing. But then he became interested in his trade union and began to give his evenings to union meetings and slowly he grew disillusioned with art. Next, moving steadily leftward, by a process that now seemed to him logical and as natural as the growth process in an organism, he joined the Party. There he got his only higher education—his parents had put him to work at the legal school-quitting age of sixteen. In the Party, too, he had learned to make prints and to letter; they paid for his going to classes and used his crude work in posters and handbills and sometimes in *De Waarheid,* their paper. He knew it was crude and was proud of that, for now the sole value he saw in art was that of transmitting messages to the people to incite them to action—at election times he painted wooden placards to be placed on the bridges urging the masses to vote for the C.P.N. He hated "art for art's sake," though he accepted the Party's teaching that in a classless society such a wasteful indulgence could finally be afforded. Then he became disillusioned with the Party and turned sharply against it. He saw that he had let himself be deceived: it was merely another part of the system of world-wide oppression—openly as in the Soviet Union or covertly as in Holland, where it served as a willing safety valve for the masses' discontent. He was ashamed of having had his work in *De Waarheid,* which did not tell the Truth, as its name pretended, but just a different set of lies. When he broke, he passed almost overnight to direct action. He became what was called a terrorist.

Now art, even the Party kind of making propaganda, lost all interest for him, except in the sense that a deed was a work of art—the only true one, he had become convinced. The deed, unless botched, was totally expressive; ends and means coincided. Unlike the Party's "art as a weapon," it was pure, its own justification. It had no aim outside itself. The purpose served by the capture of the Boeing was simply the continuance or asseveration of the original thrust; ransom money, the release of fellow-actionists, were not goals in which one came to rest but means of ensuring repetition.

Direct action had a perfect circular motion; it aimed at its own autonomous perpetuation and sovereignty. And the circle, as all students of drawing knew, was the most beautiful of forms. Thus in a sense he had returned to where he had started: terrorism was art for art's sake in the political realm. Some in the movement believed that their action would give rise to a new society, but this belief was an impurity. Jeroen was not even sure that the construction of a just society ought to concern a revolutionary; that dream had been dreamed too often. He thought Trotsky was right in his notion of the permanent revolution, right but insincere—in his day of power his ruthless repression of the sailors of Kronstadt had exposed his real attitude. Revolution, if it was not just a catchword, should mean revolving, an eternal spinning, the opposite of *e*volution, so attractive to the bourgeois soul. For the true revolutionary, the only point of rest lay in the stillness at the center of the circle, just as a wheel rapidly turning on its axis gave the appearance of arrested motion.

Such ideas were deeply troubling to Greet. She did not like to hear him state that the struggles of the Palestinian people were merely a parenthesis, to be closed without regret when they had served their purpose—"Your theories again." She was jealous of his brain, which she regarded as an untrustworthy

226

organ capable of leading him away from her and the others into a foreign sphere. As she sat across the table somberly gazing at him, he could read her mind. She was fearing that his interest in the group of collectors was a sign of softening or backsliding, that he would let himself be diverted by his old passion from the main end. There she was wrong. His "artistic" interest in them was of another sort; he was excited by the sheer beauty of the coup he envisioned. He had seen that they could be *transmuted*; it only needed the Midas touch of exchanging them against their masterpieces to turn their base substance into pure gold. The method of persuasion remained to be studied —whatever was best calculated to convince the collectors to accept the principle of paying their ransom "in kind." He foresaw a two-way airlift: crates of art descending, the "owners" ascending, to be shipped back home or to Teheran according to their mood. The transfer would put an end to the crowding and, far more interesting, it would render the farmhouse impregnable. Once the house contained irreplaceable masterpieces, any notion of taking it by storm would have to be abandoned by the imperialists unless they wished to pass for "barbarians" before the eyes of their entire "civilized" world. At that point, the commando could dictate its own terms and at its own good leisure; there would be no hurry.

Yet in the immediate time was pressing. It might only be a matter of hours before the disguise of the polder house was penetrated. The short-wave radio, indispensable as it was at this stage, was also a danger that had to be reckoned with. If the enemy were to pick up the "pirate" transmissions, the unlicensed frequencies could of course be spotted, and the authorities at both ends, having mapped the bearings, would swiftly close in. Here on the polder, the hostages were a safeguard, precluding an instant swoop, but the comrades in Aachen risked being surprised with their mobile transmitter by a cordon of police. Each transmission was increasing the likelihood of detection. The remedy was to shift to another set of frequencies, but there was a limit to how long that game could be played. Out of regard for the Aachen comrades, communications should be discontinued at the earliest possible moment. Yet to break off contact while New York was still to be heard from would constitute a defeat, and the Aachen cell, so far, agreed. For a while longer, Werner would keep trying and accept the risk, only moving to a neighboring frequency, by agreement, every third hour. The best hope was that the possibility of clandestine transmissions to and from the "criminal band" would be slow to occur to the authorities. And up to now there had been no discernible attempt at jamming—the usual warning sign. Yet unfortunately the absence of interference could read in two opposite senses.

There was nothing to do but stupidly wait. The fact that this morning no plane had yet come prowling overhead was at least a reassurance. The fools might be off on another track. Every hour the radio announced that an "energetic" hunt for the missing helicopter was in progress but gave no particulars. The evening news on television was bound to be fuller, if only in order to pander to the public's craving for thrills; they might even be shown the "dragnet" of search planes and police with walkie-talkies, or would it be merely interviews with the Defense and Justice ministers and the families of the hostages? Belgian and German radio reported a "security blanket," and of course there was not a hope of seeing a newspaper. As the hours passed, Jeroen grew unwontedly restless. To be marooned here with no news except that doled out by official sources was an experience he had not pictured in his planning. He felt cut off, left out of events and decisions that nevertheless should concern him as a prime actor—hardly, in that respect, in a better position than the hostages, who must be guessing and speculating too.

The final ridiculous touch was to discover this morning that the farm couple had had their telephone service suspended: the farmer had indicated to Horst that there was a coin box down the highway in case the crew needed to place long-distance calls. That was of no significance, so long as they had the radio, but the sight of the dead instrument on the kitchen counter was a sour reminder of the meanness and mistrust in the bourgeois nature, preparing petty frustrations for the foreigner in return for his generosity—what if the "crew" from Hamburg had urgently needed a doctor?

Adding to Jeroen's own frustration was the feeling that the comrades here were showing a certain reserve toward his plans for the collectors. He could count on Greet; she was loyal, in spite of her cavils. And in fairness he could not expect Horst and Elfride and Carlos to immediately share his enthusiasm; not having been on the Boeing, they had learned only last night of the abrupt revision of the program that had raised the number of hostages from eight to twenty. As for the Arabs, they had not yet had the collectors explained to them—there would be time enough for that when New York had pronounced—and had not been moved to ask; for them, the evidence that these additional people were rich was doubtless sufficient reason for their being here. It was depressing, though, that Werner, on being told late last night by radio of the unforeseen development, had responded almost with ecstasy (*"Wunderbar, nicht? Unglaublich!"*), while those here on the spot had had only neutral comments, as if to say time would tell. Nor had they warmed up appreciably as time had gone by.

It must be the waiting and watching him fiddle uselessly with the radio. Werner, in freedom, had the active part, telephoning New York, and on his own initiative making roundabout inquiries of a famous Aachen collector, who, however, knew only hyper-realism, post-op, post-pop, earth art, and the Americans who collected such *rommel.* Here the comrades were condemned to unemployment; they had nothing to do but eat and stand guard and rebuff the hostages' incessant demands for news.

Inactivity was the problem. From being masters of the situation, they were slipping into a state of dependency and powerlessness in respect to the outside world. The moment they got the information, good tidings or bad, it would be necessary, Jeroen decided, for the commando to assert itself and abandon this cat-and-mouse game. There could be no further need for hiding and waiting, maiden-like, to be found. An announcement from the command post would declare its location—why not? A flag might even be flown, boldly, from the roof. Making one on the Singer from the housewife's scraps of dressmaking material would give the hostages something to do. Some of the present precautions could be relaxed. There was no reason that the prisoners should not be permitted to go for short walks around the house, twice a day, under guard. For aerial reconnaissance to observe them at their exercise could do no harm. Jeroen did not agree that the headquarters should be regarded as a punitive re-education center—Elfride's idea, typically German. Contrary to what she said, it was not his intention to coddle the hostages, but last night's experience showed that given favorable conditions even the most unpromising human material was capable of cooperation.

The evening meal was being distributed when Aachen finally signaled that it was ready to transmit. Horst was monitoring the set, and the stewardess came running to bring Jeroen from the family room, where he stood looking at television. They were showing Royal Navy dredges dragging the Ijsselmeer for the helicopter—good entertainment; a few of the hostages, seated on the floor, were laughing and clapping. From the shadows on the screen, the time would appear to have been early afternoon, now several hours in the past. Just before dark, doubtless at the close of that costly and fruitless operation, a plane had circled over the farmhouse and disappeared into the sunset; the hostages had watched it through the pastor's binoculars. Now the house stood in darkness, except for the family room, lit by the television and a single lamp, the playroom upstairs, where the farm children would be doing their homework, the stairway, and the kitchen.

Jeroen seated himself at the table, fitted the gray rubber earphones on his head, took the pencil Horst was holding out to him, and prepared to write. The message was coming through clearly. The code they had settled on was simple, more like a shorthand used by children in a family to communicate among themselves when elders were listening than like the usual ciphers, which were child's play for the experts to "break."

Horst peered over Jeroen's shoulder as he wrote. "Your prognosis justified. Grandma Potter much better than was first thought. Dr. Van der Meer from Delft in constant attendance, also Dr. Tiziano but the one they call Big George unavailable for consultation. Sheer bosh that she cannot recover. Uncle Widderhintere's condition complicated by history of sporting activity. Keeps Duffy at bedside, also British specialists highly regarded in field, such as Stubbs, Ward, Marshall. The Gas fellow drops in from race track to see patient but Uncle Widder unwilling receive Ed's dancers in home. Since husband's decease, Cousin Margaret has mild religious mania, much attached to the Greek, sees visions in sepia of archangels but enjoys more colorful commerce with angelic monk and Italian primitive types, including older monk called Laurence." The next was unintelligible, then "Chadwick, *sagt Anna, hat 8 grosser kinder. . . .*"

With a sudden motion, Horst turned the radio off; he had heard a plane's motor. They listened. Out the window they could see a searchlight playing. Jeroen removed the head set and yawned. Let them come. He had heard all he needed. With the pencil he beat time to the beam of light dancing across the snow. He hummed an air from the hymnal—an old Dutch Resistance marching song—and wondered whether he would still be able to pick it out on the parlor harmonium. But Horst had not caught the mood. He frowned at the piece of paper lying on the table. *"Was soll das heissen, Jeroen?"* What the devil did all that mean? His heavy voice was plaintive.

Patiently Jeroen translated the message. There was a Vermeer in the Potter woman's collection, as well as a Titian, but no Giorgione, alias "Big George." In compensation, there was a Bosch. "Widderhintere" was Ramsbotham; he collected sporting art, including Dufy ("Duffy") and Degas racing subjects— no ballet dancers. "Cousin Margaret" was the big woman; sacred art was her field. She owned El Grecos ("the Greek"), sepia drawings by Michelangelo and Raphael (the "archangels"), a Fra Angelico, and a number of Italian primitives, unidentified except for Lorenzo Monaco ("Lorenzo the Monk").

The last passage to come through was hard to decipher, per-haps garbled: "Chadwick, *sagt Anna, hat 8 grosser kinder.*" Eight important pictures, but what? It was good that Horst found the answer. *"Sagt Anna"* equaled "Says Anne": Chadwick had eight Cézannes.

The search plane had completed its mission; the sound of the motors grew fainter as it gained altitude. The others, bursting into the kitchen, did not need to be told that the news was tremendous; they could read it on the faces of Horst and Jeroen. These collectors were the real thing. A Vermeer, a Titian, a Bosch, eight Cézannes—those were sufficient creden-tials. Yet, as always, there were some—the greedy Greet, in par-ticular—who were not satisfied, who had to know more. What was in the *rest* of the collections? Only four had been sum-marized. "Elfride, we must speak to Aachen again. They should finish their report to us."

She moved to the set. Jeroen held up a hand. *"Neen."* An-other contact with the comrades, he warned her, was not to be dreamed of at the moment. Supposing the search plane's radio had picked up even a small portion of the last transmission? She had not thought of that. There was a silence. The stewardess put in her head and withdrew. *"Wir haben das Wesentliche,"* Horst said. "I support Jeroen. Now let us have some soup." At the stove, Greet picked up the soup ladle and filled seven bowls: "Ahmed, what are you doing here? You should be on guard duty." She raised her bowl. "Eight Cézannes. I toast you, Jeroen." "To Werner," he corrected. "To the revolution." From now on, he could see, his leadership would be uncontested. Tears came to his eyes. He had proved himself.

Nine

It was their fourth day of captivity, and their second pent up in this farmhouse. The worst, Sophie thought, was not the crowding and lack of sleep or even the endless guessing based on ignorance but the fact that there was nothing to read. The only books were a kind of farmer's almanac, a children's encyclopedia, and the Bible—all in Dutch, naturally. Last night they had had the distraction of watching television, with Henk doing simultaneous translation, but this morning the screen was an empty gray, matching the weather and their tired minds. In Holland, it seemed, there were never any television programs in the daytime, when people were assumed to be at work—"Very civilized, Mynheer," gamely commented Simmons. "I could do without Barbara Walters, couldn't you, Sophie?" In the kitchen, the hijackers had a radio and they had let Denise, the stewardess, listen to Radio Belge while she was preparing breakfast. A development in the case, she heard, was expected within a few hours; there was a report that a message had been received from the hijackers but as yet no official confirmation.

Henk thought that if there were any real breakthrough, television, exceptionally, would be on the air with photo bulletins; they would not have to wait, like last night, for the evening news to show them that the Air Force and the Navy were still looking for them. In any case, since early morning there had been activity overhead, which offered the hope that their place of imprisonment had been spotted. Military planes passed and repassed, possibly taking photographs, but then flew away without trying to land. From the farmhouse windows the highway was invisible, and the men, when they went out to pee and relieve their bowels after breakfast, had heard no rumble of traffic that would indicate the approach of a rescue force. It was strange that in all this time—Tuesday and nearly half of Wednesday—not even the mailman or a traveling salesman had come up the entry road that led to the kitchen door.

After the milling and confusion of yesterday, the hostages were settling in, establishing routines alarmingly suggestive of permanence, though they did not see this themselves. Routines gave them a feeling of security, Sophie supposed; the first-class passengers must be used to having their wealth of time organized for them, as on cruises and "cures" and country house-parties. In the parlor today, by general request, Frank had conducted morning service. Now, warming to his role of pastor *cum* cheer-leader, he was trying to pick out Episcopal hymns on the old Calvinistic harmonium, which wheezed and groaned as if in dissent. It was a solo performance; invited to "sing-along," the others only hummed or beat time with a foot and eventually ceased to follow. Margaret, the big millionairess—they were on first-name terms this morning—had installed herself, like one administering a hint, on the horsehair sofa with the green folder "Torture and Illegality in Iran." It should have been reading time—study hall—for everybody, but the blue and green folders were the only fresh reading matter aside from archaeological guides to Persia, an English pocket Bible, *Wild Life of the Near East*, and the *Book of Common Prayer* that the hand baggage had yielded. The news magazines, *Vogues*, and *Harper's Bazaars* they had had with them in the Boeing had exhausted their usefulness during the long wait at Schiphol. In Sophie's carryall was an old copy of *Harper's* with an article by her in it which she had brought along as a credential, but she was too shy as yet to offer it—selfish of her, she feared.

Just beyond, in the family living-room, a checkers game was in progress, with coins for pieces. Using Eloise's manicure scissors, Johnnie was cutting photos from a Dutch illustrated magazine to make a set of playing cards. It was a sign of something maybe that the dread "Gretel"—whose real name proved to be Greet, short for Margaretha—had not seen fit to confiscate the scissors. The two gays from Antibes were playing "I packed my grandmother's trunk" with Beryl and the curator, their suggestion of charades having been rebuffed. Sophie had played it *ad infinitum* on rainy days, which was most of the time, in a Wasp girls' camp in Maine; the idea was to fill the "trunk" with unlikely and giggle-producing articles that each player had to name over in the correct order before adding a new one. Thus, this morning: "Sunpruf cream, a rosary, Muhammad Ali's jock-strap, Odorono, *Les très riches heures du duc de Berry*, Nixon's *Six Crises* . . ." For a while, the Senator had been refereeing but now he was showing Victor a match game, "Cannibals and Missionaries," that had been popular with navy flyers during the War.

Here in the parlor, as Frank pumped out "JEsus CALLS us O'ER the TUmult," those allergic to games in the morning were resorting to conversational gambits to make the time pass. "Are you related to the lovely old rose?" Beryl's mother inquired of Henk. "She means Dr. Van Fleet," interposed Margaret, looking up from her reading. "Of course," said Lily. Her soft blue eyes dwelt encouragingly on Henk. "A pure pale pink climber and a great New England favorite. One doesn't find it any more in the catalogues. Mother had it on a trellis outside the library door of the old house in Yarmouth. Ideal for cutting, like a hybrid tea. I believe there was a Mrs. Van Fleet too." "He spells it differently, Lily," Helen Potter ventured. "With a *V*." "*V* into *F*. A common New World corruption," observed Charles. "We Americans wrote down words as we heard them—phonetically, don't you see? But the great hybridizer, Dr. W. Van Fleet, can hardly have been 'family' to our distinguished young friend. The Dutch connection there would have been remote. His work was done at Bell Station, Maryland. And the family of climbers associated with him were of Japanese origin, the Wichuraiana—not your China teas at all." "Silver Moon," said Helen. "Dorothy Perkins. Now I ask myself who she was." It was astonishing to Sophie how much knowledge such "old money" people hoarded, like string-savers; its value, apparently, lay in its total uselessness and inapplicability to the practical world. "Ah, yes," fluted Charles, as if responsive to Sophie's thought. "Those old dooryard hybrids mean nothing to the rose fancier today. They were 'retired' from service years ago, like a line of automobiles. One cannot guess the reason; your Dr. Van Fleet was extremely hardy and free-flowering. But no doubt if one looked into it one would discover a Marxist explanation. The eternal profit motive." The Bishop, who had been dozing in a straight chair, opened his eyes. "Damn them!" he pronounced, fiercely, and then continued his nap.

Lily seemed disappointed. The hope of "placing" Van Vliet must have been brightening her empty morning. As a practicing lady, she was bent on pursuing connections; in her world, Sophie guessed, everyone had to be related, if only to a rose. The pursuit of connections extended "one's" boundaries; the poor souls did not wish to feel narrow in their outlook. This had led to a quite comical incident with the Tupamaro on the first night. "I am Carlos," he had said, introducing himself to the roomful of hostages he was to guard. At which Lily had risen from her couch of folded mink, as if from her tea-table, to receive him. "Not *the* Carlos!" she had breathed. But he too had to disappoint her. He was not the "most wanted," Number One terrorist, Vladimir Ilych Ramirez, but just *a* Carlos. Lily's graciousness had thereupon abated, but not so that he could *feel* an abrupt loss of interest; the cooling of her manner was gradual, a gentle drop in temperature that only another perfect lady could measure.

Now, to cover her little let-down on having failed to strike a sympathetic chord with the bright-cheeked deputy, she turned to Margaret and lightly tapped the green folder. "Is it interesting?" "Not exactly hammock reading," Margaret growled. Lily spied a second folder peeping out of Frank's briefcase. "May I?" She slowly turned the pages. No one spoke. Henk was studying the Flevoland listings in the regional telephone directory. Helen was dead-heading the housewife's plants, dropping the faded blossoms into an outspread Kleenex. Sophie, her loose-leaf notebook on her knee, was starting to keep a journal—it would be something to read tomorrow. Underneath the plant table, Cameron was busy with pencil and paper constructing a crossword puzzle; he was half hidden, as if in a rich tent, by the oriental rug that hung down over the sides like a table-cloth. At the harmonium, Frank had shifted to "Fairest Lord Jesus."

"Please!" Lily murmured, indicating the soft pedal. Margaret added her august voice. "Reverend Mr. Barber—Frank, I should say—do you intend to keep pumping at that melodeon all morning? Some of us here are musical." The minister jumped up from the stool, apologizing. In the quiet, they watched Lily read. "Have you come to the toaster thing?" Helen asked. Lily shook her head. Helen sighed. "Ghastly." They noticed that Henry was preparing to speak: his gray head and long spare body gave preliminary jerks and nods, like a wind-up toy starting to move—stage fright or alcoholic trembles? "T-toaster, my eye," he finally brought out. "It takes my sainted wife to believe that. I d-dipped into the bloody stuff this morning and, believe me, I could have found a better use for good p-paper outdoors." "Please, Henry!" said his wife. He started, and shook himself, like one awaking, and then began to mumble, nodding to himself. " 'Ladies present, Henry.' Must remember, Henry. Very important to remember, Pa always said." The Bishop was watching him with concern. The others averted their eyes. It was an embarrassing metamorphosis. The dignified old beau appeared staggeringly drunk, which was impossible—nobody had had a moment unobserved. Yet in a minute he recovered himself. The thick speech miraculously cleared, and he found his lost train of thought. "Yes, as I was saying, Lily, what I'd like to know is who gets this material out. It's not signed, you'll notice. Means nobody stands behind it. Anonymous hate literature is what it looks like, I'm afraid. People in our position ought to make it a principle never to read anything that somebody hasn't put his John Hancock to. Saves a lot of time too. On that principle, I never look at an editorial in a newspaper. Why should I have my mind poisoned by somebody I don't even know? And from what I've been told the Shah's a gentleman or as near to it as they make them in those parts. Helen and I have letters to him. That should say something."

Henk tapped his head warningly with a forefinger, and Sophie nodded. But the others were going to argue with this lunatic. "Now wait a minute there!" burst out the minister. "You're taking a very illiberal attitude. An ignorant attitude, sir. The Gospels aren't signed, and do you refuse to read them? Do you close your mind to Homer?" "I agree, Reverend," cried Aileen. "Why should we have to listen to this affluent nonsense? Does he refuse to read the Dow Index and the Stock Exchange quotations? They're not signed, but I'll bet he reads them *religiously*. Don't you? Come on, admit it!" "But he doesn't," said Helen. "Henry says a gentleman leaves the financial page to his broker."

"Does he leave it to his butler to shit for him?" called out Victor from the next room. Attracted by the raised voices, a group was collecting in the doorway. Carey stood in the center with folded arms and a look of amusement. Beside him appeared Harold, truculent as always. "What's going on? Was somebody in here talking about climbers?" "Climbing *roses*, Chaddie," said Eloise. "Now they're arguing about some silly report on torture." "What do you mean, 'silly'?" "What do *you* know?" Several angry voices were shouting at once. Ahmed, posted in the hallway, could be heard calling to Jeroen to come from the kitchen. Then Charles raised a pale hand.

"My dears, we do sound like a prison riot. And we don't want to be punished, do we? Although, with all this din, some of us might welcome a turn in solitary. Potter, dear fellow, our companions are a committee to look into these allegations. Or *were* a committee, I should say. No doubt you aren't aware of that. You don't wish to impugn their motives, I'm sure. When and if their report is made, it will of course carry their signatures. You need have no fear on that score. For my part,

I haven't had access to these particular documents, but friends abroad, knowing my interests, send me cuttings on affairs of this kind. The electric grill you mention is a matter of record. I believe I have even seen a diagram. One can picture it as a pop-up toaster or as one of those sandwich-like contrivances our countrymen use to carbonize beefsteaks at their 'cook-outs' —deplorable practice and quite carcinogenic, I'm told." A shriek came from Simmons. "Doesn't he slay you?" she said to Sophie. "Yes," said Sophie. It was true that she found Charles a rather frightening personality. He intended to shock, of course, but was it shock therapy he had in mind or some dreadful private joke? In any case, it was working here. The checkers players drifted back to their improvised board, and the bridge-players resumed their foursome: "Two no trump." In the parlor, the discussion moved on to cancer and a supposed cure for cancer. The Bishop produced his flask—a horn of plenty or pitcher of Baucis and Philemon—and offered a nip to Henry, who had begun to shake again. Soon the shakes stopped.

The episode led Sophie to wonder about the effects of deprivation if the present state of affairs were to continue long. What would happen when the Bishop's flask, which he must be replenishing from that hold-all, finally ran dry? Henry might get a rather high-priced cure, for which his wife would be grateful. But what about tobacco—Cameron's pipe, Henk's cigars, her own and Aileen's cigarettes? Most of the hostages were addicts of one kind or another, she supposed. With the older people, if it was not liquor or tobacco—Charles allowed himself a single Sobranie after meals as an aid to digestion—it would be pills. Yet the terrorists, who did not seem to have any of the usual vices or "dependences" themselves, would be in no position, even if willing, to cater to their captives' habits when private stores ran out. This could result in demoralization or, at best, a general fraying of nerves. The solidarity of the hostage group—such as it was—would not be proof against sudden fits of irritability such as they had just seen. With this in mind, Sophie was already rationing her cigarette consumption, so as to be able to share. In her bag were two cartons of Trues, designed to last three weeks in Iran, but in four days, thanks mainly to the harrowing time at Schiphol, one was half gone. Now, however, it should not be too hard to cut down; in these close rooms smoking seemed anti-social anyway. And yet, to her shame and surprise—she was used to thinking of herself as a both contained and generous person—she had felt something close to fury when Beryl, twice, had "borrowed" a cigarette to offer Ahmed. They said that extreme situations brought out the truth of one's character. Another cherished image, she realized, was a picture of herself as fearless which she had come to accept on hearsay: "You're so brave, Sophie." Would she have to discard that too? So far, she thought she could say honestly, she had not been really afraid. But so far nothing really scary had happened, and it was possible that when a test came she would discover, simply, that up to then she "had never known the meaning of fear." She replaced the cigarette—which would have been her fourth since breakfast—in the pack and took up her notebook again. "Eleven-thirty a.m., Flevoland . . ." She wrote on steadily, but there was little to record but her thoughts—only the occasional buzz of a plane overhead, the passage of a solitary heron and a flock of black birds with white bills that Henk said were coots from the Ijsselmeer.

Lily closed the folder and appeared to meditate on the contents. In the circumstances, being a slow reader was enviable: she had got two hours, Sophie estimated, out of roughly eighty double-spaced pages, which worked out to about two-thirds of a page a minute. She polished her reading-glasses with a chamois and restored them to their embroidered case. "Could the Shah be back of this, I wonder?" "Back of *what*, Mother?" Beryl had got tired of packing her grandmother's trunk and was staring out the window in the parlor. *"This,"* repeated Lily, waving a hand. She meant the hijacking, obviously. "Oh, Mother, don't be so stupid. How could the Shah figure?" "Very simply," Henk answered. "The idea is not stupid. Or at any rate I have had it myself." "Me too," agreed Sophie. To anyone with a political head it was by no means improbable that, if not the Shah in person, SAVAK, his secret police, had arranged for their committee to be deflected. As Henk was pointing out, collusion between "red" terrorists and "black" secret police was classical; it went back at least to czarist Russia. But by what route the insight had entered Lily's mind was a mystery. Had they "done" *The Possessed* at Saint Timothy's under an unusually thorough teacher? Sophie sought to imagine Lily in middy and skirt delivering an oral report on the ties between the Okhrana and terrorist circles such as Dostoievsky described in the novel. In any case, the insight, however come by, was impressive in a woman of her background.

But "awfully far-fetched" opined Margaret, and the Reverend concurred, though from a different starting-point, clearly. *She* refused to entertain the thought because it reflected on the ethics of the Shah, and Frank would not harbor it because he did not want to be "over-critical" of the terrorists. Whereas Beryl, more simply, scouted it because it had been voiced by her mother. It was an interesting study in the reception or, rather, non-reception of ideas. And still another factor was at work in these minds, as Sophie slowly recognized—the ineluctable factor of class.

Shah or no Shah, the first-class hostages, on the whole, resented any suggestion that the hijacking could have been aimed at passengers in Economy. They preferred to see themselves as the sole cause. And vice versa. "How can you talk such nonsense, Lily?" boomed Margaret. "I don't give a fig about the Shah, but it was *us* these people were after—no question of it." "But why us, dear?" wailed Lily. "Because we're filthy rich, Mother; that's why." "The Shah doesn't want our money," pursued Margaret. "He can buy and sell the lot of us. That's why he couldn't be behind this outrage for a minute. But the gang in there was after our money all right. They marked the plane down because they heard we would be on it. No one can tell me otherwise."

"I can, Madam." Cameron's voice, accompanied by a puff of pipe smoke, came like an oracle from under the table. "You confuse two notional sequences. Lack of training in clear thinking, I daresay. Let us separate the two sequences and examine them. Taking the premise that you were the target, I believe we can all agree that the Shah may be exculpated. As you say, he has no need of money, least of all dollars, of which you have a great many, if I can judge by my ears. But this premise cannot be assumed; it is what you started out to prove. Therefore, rightly, it should appear at the end of your argument, as the logical or persuasive conclusion. If we take the opposite premise, that the committee in Economy was the target, then things have another look. The Shah cannot be cleared of suspicion. We may decide that he was the priming agent that set the operation in motion, very likely with funds drawn from the secret-police budget—this was not engineered on a shoestring. The more we consider it, the more plausible it comes to seem that the committee was indeed the target. But again we are assuming what we set out to prove. Moreover, if we affirm that the committee was the target, this leaves us to explain your presence here, just as your belief that you and you alone were aimed at leaves you to explain *our* presence. It might be useful to think in terms of primary and secondary targets. In that case, the simplest hypothesis, and hence the one to be preferred, is that we were the primary target, that is, in essence the Shah's pigeon—though we may have been interesting to these anarchists for other reasons—and that you, *ab initio*, or at some later stage, came to be viewed as a prize in your own right."

"Bravo, Archie," applauded Henk. "Beautiful," said Sophie. "My God!" said Aileen, who had been yawning. "He's going to set that carpet on fire!" In fact a coal from the don's pipe must have singed the rug from under which his bristly head had appeared. There was a smell of burning wool. "Water!" called Beryl. "Ahmed, quick, bring some water!" "Dear me, no," said Charles. "You must smother it." After a minute, thanks to Charles's recipe, the incipient fire had been put out, leaving only a charred spot.

But the argument smoldered. "The Shah's a red herring," declared Henry. "I haven't seen a shred of evidence that connects him. Just a bee in certain bonnets and logic-chopping."

242

That was true, Sophie reflected. Henry continued, observing that he had the floor. "Let's take a look at what's under our noses. Put yourself in the shoes of these people here." "Who are you speaking to?" said Aileen. "You. You impress me as a bright lady with a tongue in her head. I'd like to hear your opinion. Assuming you were a terrorist, would you hold *you* for ransom or my wife? I've no doubt that you have many fine personal qualities that make you valuable to your associates, whatever you do in life, but let me state it bluntly: what do you *own?*" "Just the clothes on my back," said Aileen, preening. "These old rags from Filene's." "Well, then?"

She pursed her lips and grew serious, as though the educator in her had been called on to address this forum. "I'm important in what I stand for. My name counts. The half-dozen boards and committees I serve on represent the most vital currents in American opinion. I'm a *public person*, Mister Potter. You don't know what that means. Why, right this minute, I'll bet, my picture is on the front page of the *Times*, along with the Senator's naturally, and the Reverend's and Bishop Hurlbut's, I guess. And thousands of my alumnae are deeply concerned for my fate. You can't say that for your wife and her friends. They'll be lucky if their picture is in the society columns, which have blacks and Jews nowadays, in case you don't know it. I'm sorry, Mister Potter, but you don't *mean* anything in the world. And nobody is more on to that than a terrorist. All that these Baader-Meinhofs and so on care for is publicity, being spread over the front page. They're totally indifferent to money; the sensational million-dollar ransoms they demand are just headline-grabbers. Now who is going to get them more publicity, who is the public truly anxious about, our committee or your ridiculous tour? Add to that the fact, which is probably news to you, that they hate liberals even more than you do. Because they're serious and know that we're the enemy. We stand in their way."

Simmons's cheeks were flushed, making a curious color-contrast with her rouge; her eyes sparkled. She seemed earnestly moved, almost to the point of tears, as though the conviction she had of her importance were a religious matter—a cause she was pleading. But the collector group was offended, and the Bishop was shaking his head in sorrow, maybe at the prospect of another rift. Besides, it was unchristian, surely, to tell another human being to his face that he was nobody. Without being a sorrowing Christian, Sophie felt shocked and troubled herself. To her mind, it was a shameless performance, regardless of the truth of the assertions, which in fact somehow made it worse. She smiled comfortingly at Lily, who smiled back. Henry and Helen sat rigid. To make things worse, Beryl decided to weigh in. She turned on the finally silent Aileen. "I know you," she said rudely. " 'Thousands of alumnae'! You're 'Simmie.' You were the registrar at Lucy Skinner when they kicked me out. But you didn't have the war paint and the henna then. And you were no flaming liberal. Remember, Sophie?" "I didn't go to Lucy Skinner," said Sophie, glad to be able to stay out of this.

"The laughing cavalier!" suddenly cried Lily. She was indicating Henk. "I *knew* I knew that face. Don't you see it, Helen? A haunting resemblance. If you just add a tiny chin beard and mustaches." "What the hell are you talking about?" said Beryl. "Why, the Hals in the Wallace Collection, darling. The subject must have been an ancestor of yours, Henk." "Oh, Christ," replied Beryl. "Stop trying to create a diversion. Or stop being so obvious about it." Upon this, silence ensued. You could hear Aileen sniffling. At a meaningful nod from the Bishop, Frank installed himself once more at the harmonium and sounded a chord for attention.

"Let's try to sort this out. Does it really matter which of us is more important to these young men and women who are holding us in captivity? We each have our own *kind* of importance. Maybe we're symbols of things they don't like in the world of today. That's what I try to bear in mind. They don't hate me as an individual, I tell myself. They want to change the system of which we're all a part, like it or not. You and I, Aileen, as well as Henry. And I can't say that I blame them, though I may question their methods. Even there we mustn't be too sure. 'I bring not peace but a sword,' our Lord said. But the main fact to remember is that we're all in this together. We don't know why we've been chosen. Indeed, there is some mystery to it, I have to admit, as in God's inscrutable ways. Not that I mean to compare the election that has fallen on us with a divine intervention, although to some of His prophets the Old Testament Jahveh may have seemed like a holy terror."

"Oh, my God," muttered Sophie. But the good man was under a strain. It was not easy to play the peacemaker among these heathen. As for the habit of punning, that must be a tic, like the preaching habit which it seemed to go along with and which was maybe uncontrollable too. The poor fellow had been deformed by an unnatural occupation. "Lordy," he said, "there I go again. I can never resist a pun, my youngsters complain. Yes, but seriously, there may be food for thought there as to how these young folk conceive their mission, that Jeroen in particular. Strict Calvinist home, he confided in me when I was drawing him out. Well. Perhaps we shall eventually learn whether our carrier was singled out on account of the worldly goods of some of us or on account of the place some others of us occupy in the community. As we have been reminded, we have a bishop and a U.S. senator among us. Or chance, if there is such a thing—which as a Christian I'm taught to doubt—may have been responsible for our being gathered in this place together. Our captors may have struck at random, as the fisherman casts his net on the waters unwitting what the catch will be. Some passengers, as we have seen, were thrown back into the sea of ordinary daily life to go about their business like fish of no commercial value. And we have been retained. Whatever the reason behind that, we must look on our being here as a call. A call to deepen our faith and our brotherly love, which may be sorely tested. To extend our experience, launch our frail barks onto uncharted waters. Not everyone has the good fortune—yes, the good fortune—to be hijacked."

He paused, as though prepared for a stir of dissent. But no

245

one contested him. "To be shaken out of his complacency, dislodged from his daily unthinking rut. 'As of old, Saint Andrew heard it, By the Galilean lake, Turned from home and toil and kindred, Leaving all for His dear sake.' That is why I chose the dear old hymn just now. To show us that we have been given an opportunity. Through this unforeseen contact with our captors we can be enlarged." "I like 'unforeseen contact,' " murmured Henk. Sophie giggled. Yet there was merit in the minister's thought, if only it could be freed from the clerical gaiters it wore.

"We will be bigger people for it, if we will only let ourselves. Let us not brood over the mystery that has assembled us in this place or compete for precedence one over the other in our captors' eyes." "Hear, hear!" said Henk, clapping. "Amen," said the Bishop. But Frank had not finished. "Let us, rather, accept it as coming from God, whether we believe in a personal God or merely in some higher force. I am led to think of Jonah—"

"Excuse me, sir." Denise was standing in the doorway. "I do not like to interrupt, but some passengers are wanted in the kitchen. First Mrs. Potter, please." Helen rose and followed the stewardess. Her small pigeon-breasted figure appeared resolute. " 'The call,' " commented Aileen. Beryl grinned at Sophie. "Makes me think of being sent for to the headmistress's office." Sophie remembered. In the classroom, when the summons came, nobody ever supposed that the one sent for was going to hear anything good—the best hope was that it would be just a death in the family. It was the same here. Everybody avoided Henry Potter's eye, as if an execution were already taking place. "It'll be Ma's turn next, want to bet?" said Beryl. The smell of pea soup heating in the kitchen provided some wan reassurance. If lunch was about to be served, nothing very terrible could be happening in there. "Maybe they've taken her outside," muttered Beryl. "But why poor old Helen?" spoke up Henry. "Helen *first*," emphasized Margaret. "Don't worry, they'll have the rest of us on the carpet before long. 'Malefactors of great wealth.' Remember? He was the start of all this. I was a girl then, but Father knew it." "That doesn't answer my question, Maggie. Why my wife first? Why not Johnnie?" "Maybe just because we ask that," quietly said Sophie. "The aim of terror is to terrify, isn't it, and the trick there is to be arbitrary, *above* the rules of reason. Logically they should have started with Mr. Ramsbotham. It makes sense because he's the richest and a man. But if they acted logically, that would give us a handle on them." Henk agreed. "Maybe they drew straws, and your wife's was the short one. The point is for their actions to *defy* understanding. They're answerable to nobody and nothing—not even, as Sophie says, to the laws of reason."

"Quite," said Cameron, his head again emerging. "Yet if your conjecture is right, then you *have* understood and even given a name to a principle governing their behavior. That it answers to the name of 'arbitrary' still means that one can subsume it under a general law, in other words conclude that by and large one can expect aleatory conduct from them." "Well, I suppose that's some comfort, Beryl," Lily said cheerfully. Beryl laughed. "Can you define 'aleatory' by any chance, Mother?" " 'Dicey.' *'Alea jacta est,'* " supplied Henry, causing Margaret to shake her large head and sigh. "The ruin of a fine mind," she pronounced in a carrying bass aside.

"To understand that there's no understanding what they're up to," Lily mused. "And yet I have the funniest inkling. Maybe I'd better not say it. In case *they're* listening." "For heaven's sake, how?" said Margaret. "These rooms could be 'bugged,' " Lily retorted. "Quite true," said Henk, before Beryl could contradict. "I have been thinking that too." "Well, whisper it, then, Mother," prompted Beryl. "Just a minute!" said Frank. "Let's make assurance doubly sure." He began to play chopsticks energetically on the harmonium. Lily spoke into her daughter's ear. In turn Beryl whispered to Sophie: "The Vermeer." By the time it reached Cameron, it had become "Fear more." But most had understood. Though not as rich as Johnnie, Helen was the star collector: she owned a Vermeer.

The gravity of the first-class faces left no doubt as to the inference being drawn. It was as though Lily had voiced a collective thought that had lain too deep for words. The collectors sat with bowed heads, reflecting. Prompted by the naming of the Vermeer, each, evidently, was considering his own valuables. Even the outsiders were moved to sober reflection, like spectators watching a stranger's coffin pass. "Is it an important Vermeer?" Simmons whispered and, on being assured that it was, fell to pondering. It was not the occasion to tell her that there were no *un*important Vermeers; the parlor was silent, as if it contained mourners. In the next room, the games came to a respectful halt as word of the "inkling" leaked. Sitting with folded hands, Sophie was led to think of the death of Sapphire, she was not sure why. What did Victor's wickedly murdered pet have in common with a Vermeer of Delft except the color blue? Or—more to the point—that each was a rarity, a "pearl" of its kind? If Sapphire had been an alley cat, would she have got the same treatment?

Sophie had no idea of what might be in the rest of the collections, but the mere thought of works of art as legitimate prey for terrorists caused her sympathetic nervous system pain. If they could deliberately shoot a superb Persian cat—there had been *two* shots, she clearly remembered—there must be policy behind it. Sapphire had died as an advertisement of some unusual intention. That strange young man, Jeroen, might view himself and his band as apostles of "desacralization," which would be terror in a pure state, she guessed. In comparison, treating the lives of adult human hostages as bargaining counters seemed like normal, "civilized" warfare.

To her surprise, Henk was winking at her. He tapped his head again. Unwillingly, she saw what he was trying to tell her. To a rational mind, he meant, this was a nutty example of group-think: these people had become *possessed* by the notion that their art treasures were in danger, without asking themselves how that could be or considering it aloud as an objective proposition. They "felt it in their bones," and the feeling was so strong that it had gripped the whole body of hostages, not just the fraction that had personal cause for anxiety. Only

Henk, a Dutch skeptic, seemed to be immune. To judge by the silence, everyone else was just as suggestible as Sophie herself.

The first sight of Helen removed any uncertainty. Their bones had been right. The tribunes of the people had decreed that she could have her freedom in exchange for the "Girl in a Blue Cap with a Guitar." Henry's freedom would cost her a Titian. They had wanted the little Bosch, too—hardly bigger than a postage stamp—but mercifully it was on show in Los Angeles; she had a clipping from *Time* to prove it. The group had tried her and passed sentence, payment in kind, from which there could be no appeal. She had begged them—on her knees, literally—to take her whole fortune in the place of the "Girl" but without any effect. Snuffling and wiping her pale eyes, rejecting Henry's effort to quiet her and Denise's smelling-salts, she now took the entire "family room" into her confidence. Around her an eager ring formed, curiosity proving stronger than pity. Ransoming Henry, she told them, would not be so very painful; the Titian was studio work mostly, and she had never cared for the subject. But she would almost rather die, she had decided, than see harm come to the precious Vermeer—in perfect condition, with its wonderful crackle; when its near-replica, "The Guitar Player," had been seized from Kenwood House, she had suffered untold agonies, even though its "execution" by the vandals would have made her own unique. They had given her an hour to make up her mind.

Next Harold was tapped, then Johnnie, then Margaret, then Charles, and finally Lily. "Cheer up, Mother," counseled Beryl. "The pecking order proves that they don't know the value of 'fine English water-colors.'" For a perhaps evident reason the "boys" from Antibes were not being summoned to the bar. "'*Rien à déclarer.*' 'Nothing to declare,'" John, the younger, hazarded with a nervous giggle, as though apologizing for their luck. One by one, with increasing rapidity, the others rejoined their fellows: Harold was supported by the steward; Lily flew to Beryl's arms. Unlike Helen, they were keeping their own confidence. Whatever sentence had been passed on them was not for general consumption. Disregarding the compassionate eyes turned on them, they bunched in desolate twos and threes, like stately crows in a flock of starlings. Helen was finally persuaded to go into the parlor, out of the melee.

If it had been possible, Sophie would have fled the scene. She did not like the position of onlooker. It was obscene, like sitting in perfect health in a surgeon's waiting-room and watching the patients emerge. "They must resent us," murmured Henk. "If they're aware that we're here," said Carey. "Doesn't look much like it." In her own way, Simmons was respectful of their feelings. "We ought to go in and offer Helen our sympathy, don't you think? I was kind of mean back then." "You can try," said Sophie, unwillingly tagging along. The trouble was, it was impossible to sympathize in the true meaning of the word. You could not put yourself in the place of someone who owned a Vermeer—it was not a universal experience. You might be able to feel with a millionaire who had lost all his money; on a smaller scale, it could happen to you. But here the best you could do was to sympathize with the innocent Vermeer itself. To *tell* Helen you were sorry only marked the distance between you and her. But "Thank you, my dear," Helen answered. "I'm sure you mean it."

Soon the service of lunch intervened, breaking up the knots of collectors and generally loosening tongues. Discussion of the predicament of the few spread to the many. The greatest puzzle, it was agreed, was how the hijackers could have learned what was in the collections. "*Attributed* to Titian," they had said to Helen. Amazing. They were even up on the fact that she had arranged to give her Giorgione—pen-and-wash; unique— to the National Gallery. Most people thought it was hanging there on loan. That they knew about Johnnie's sporting art was peculiar too, surely. Stubbs was a "name," but how many hijackers had heard of Ben Marshall? Until a few minutes ago, Sophie had never heard of him herself. "Did you ask how they got their information?" The question was stupid; asking would have been a waste of breath. And not a word had been volun-

250

teered, naturally, that would give a clue. Jeroen, it seemed, had had lists in front of him which he consulted, leaving it up to the victim to affirm or deny. Poor Helen had begun by trying to disavow her Vermeer. "But it was all written down there—the size and the tiny restoration and the provenance." A tear fell onto her paper plate. "She could see that he knew," explained Henry.

"But what crime were you charged with?" interrupted Aileen. "I mean, specifically?" "Possession of art works 'stolen' from the people," answered Johnnie with a short laugh. "What can you say to an arraignment like that? That you bought them or had them left to you? To this kangaroo court, that's no defense. They shut you up by reading to you from the damn lists they've got—the evidence, as they see it. I must say, it's uncanny, finding they have it all there in black and white. Shakes a fellow up, almost makes him feel guilty as charged. Especially if he tries to hold anything back. Just to give you an example, I thought they'd missed out on my Degas, and so naturally I didn't call the oversight to their attention. Then damned if they didn't come up with it. Accused me of lack of frankness." Sophie nodded. It was cruel of them, she thought—a refinement of malice to let the collectors "prove" their guilt by denials and evasions and then face them with a full bill of particulars obtained from an unguessable quarter.

The suspicion that someone had informed was inevitable. During lunch it was vacillating between Charles and Warren, the curator. Or so Beryl, who was in on their councils, reported. "Wouldn't you know they'd want to hang it on a queer?" Beryl herself would have liked to hang it on "Simmie," but there was no way: "The hag knows nothing about pictures." The conchie minister, she said, knew about Lily's collection, but that was from long ago: "Most of the things Ma had then have gone on the block." The Economy class hostages had all been given a clean bill of health. "Ma pretends to be glad of it. Maybe she really is. Have you noticed that Henk likes her?"

But if Economy was excluded, it followed that the millionaires had to believe that the culprit was one of their own party or else that a tip had come from an outside source. You would have thought that they would have embraced the second theory, for their own peace of mind, but they were unreasonably slow in coming to it, said Beryl, and only through a process of elimination worthy of Sherlock Holmes. "The finger *can't* point to Eddie and John. They don't know any of us but Warren. And Warren, my God, is just an orientalist. How would he know about Johnnie's stuff?" The logical suspect, among their own number, was Charles, of course. He had come back from his interrogation crowing that he had been "let off scot-free"; his own explanation was that he had persuaded the gang that the few porcelains he still owned were too fragile to be moved unless he packed them himself. Yet it could also mean that he had been "singing" for his supper. "Harold was all for 'confronting' him. Whereupon the others decided that they didn't want to think that of him, really. You know why? 'Because we've known him all our lives.' That's what they call 'being fair.'" "Why don't they suspect you, Beryl?" They ought to, in view of Ahmed, Sophie was thinking. Beryl shrugged. "Because they've known Ma all their lives, I guess."

Anyhow, now they were leaning toward the "outside source" theory. It supported their faith in having been the sole motive for the hijacking. "This proves it to the hilt," proclaimed Margaret. "Before we ever left our homes, these people knew down to the last brush-stroke what was in our collections. This was planned months in advance, as soon as some revolutionary read in the Museum bulletin about our tour to Iran. But they had to wait till we got to De Gaulle because the security at Kennedy was too tight!" "Idlewild," said Harold. "But you're right; this clinches it. How could they have got the nuts and bolts on my Cézannes in this godforsaken hole? No way. The only puzzler is why they waited so long to spring it on us."

"Shouldn't we be helping Helen to think now?" said Lily, looking at her watch. "She has to decide very soon. But there's so much that she doesn't *know*, that none of us knows. What are they plotting to do with the Vermeer, with all our lovely things? They can't be thinking of bringing them here. I made bold to ask, but of course they wouldn't say. All they said was that if I wanted to return to my family unharmed I must make a tape instructing them to carry out orders for the delivery of my Samuel Palmer and my Turners and Cotmans—they didn't seem at all interested in Girtin, although he was so important. I had no need to know more than that, they told me. Just address the tape to a member of my family and precise instructions for packing and delivery would follow. But, as I tried to explain to them, since Joe died my only close family is Beryl. I wouldn't trust my sister-in-law, dear that she is, to know a Cotman from—"

"Personally I think I'd go along, Lily. That's the way I'm tilting myself. Play at being cooperative. I've pretty well decided to tell them that I accept. And with my Cézannes, I have more at stake. I'll just make one stipulation. That I direct the tape to my lawyer. Whatever I instruct my lawyer, he'll know that I'm under duress, so he'll have the sense not to play for keeps. With a relative you never can tell. My lawyer'll be smart enough to go through the motions of obeying instructions, in the interests of my and Eloise's safety, all the time being damn sure that the government isn't going to let him turn over a fortune in irreplaceable paintings to some reds representing these gorillas. The Treasury or the Attorney General will get a stay or an injunction or figure out some hokey-pokey. An agreement made under duress isn't binding. What do you think, Carey? You're a lawyer."

"I can't advise you," Jim said, rather stiffly. "But I can tell you the law. It's against U.S. policy to negotiate the demands of hijackers. If your lawyer starts negotiating at your instance, he will go to jail." "But he wouldn't *negotiate*. He'd fake and stall till the government stepped in." "It's not up to the government to do your lawyer's duty for him. He's an officer of the court. Of course he could arrive at some agreement with the FBI to seem to play ball with these folks, bait a trap with your works of art or reasonable facsimiles of them. . . . You're familiar with the scenario, surely."

"Well, fine. It adds up to the same, doesn't it? If I accept,

I've been a good boy, so far as the gorillas can see. And I'll have gained time. They're not going to shoot me as long as they think they have eight signed Cézannes in the bag. My lawyer'll need proof that I'm alive before he agrees to deliver. Even if they start getting impatient, they'll make up their minds to cool it." Carey sighed. "If you want to address the tape to your lawyer, I see no objection that Jeroen and Company can have. But you'll put your lawyer in a hell of a dilemma. He gets an instruction with your voice print on it. Is he supposed to carry it out or not? Either way, he's placed in a questionable position. Your instruction tells him to break the law. As an officer of the court, his first duty, then, is to report it. At the same time, being your lawyer, he will feel bound to respect the confidentiality of the communication. If we assume that he's scrupulous and reports it, not only does he ignore your express instructions, but he also, by the act of reporting it, frustrates any intention you may have of complying."

The warning was clear, Sophie thought, but she was not sure that Chadwick understood. Jim was being cautious, for reasons of his own, and for the first time she saw in him the quality that had disappointed so many of his followers. Simmons saw it too. "He just won't commit himself. Look at him, Sophie." He sat lounging on the floor, with his back against a wall and his long legs stretched out, and was idly tossing a coin. Sophie admitted that this show of detachment must appear cavalier to the millionaires. Yet the very fact that their treasures were at stake—to say nothing of their lives, probably, if they refused —might excuse his reluctance to pronounce. She wished Henk would say something; Jim's being a U.S. senator could be another element, not necessarily an admirable one, in his reluctance.

"What's the difference between my lawyer and a relative?" Harold demanded in his customary suspicious tones. Carey caught the coin and with his other hand covered a yawn. "Only that the relative is under no obligation to report a criminal communication of this nature. Otherwise the position is the same."

254

"So do you advise Helen to make the tape?" said Lily, anxiously looking at her watch again. "Sorry. I can't advise you, Lily. It would be improper on my part. I'll say this much." Slowly he got to his feet. "Any of you who agrees to make a tape under the existing circumstances will *not* be regarded as an accessory to a criminal proceeding. On that score, you need have no inhibitions. On the other hand, it would be unwise to think that the making of the tape is the easy way out. Having made it, you may find that you are bound to it. Or that our friends will require a promptness in compliance that you don't envision. Measures of an ugly sort may be taken to induce speed."

"But if we refuse," said Henry, "they'll kill us, isn't that the idea?" The collectors exchanged looks. "We had different impressions," Lily said. "*I* certainly thought so, but some of us weren't so sure. I don't believe the word 'kill' was actually used." "Not to me," said Johnnie. "It was more of a vague menace." Again, of course, no one had asked. "They left it to our imagination," said Harold. "Depends on how much you have." "They were *very* definite, though, about the deadline," Lily put in. "Each of us has an hour from the time he was dismissed. I wonder why." "Prolongs the torture," Henry suggested. "And on our side of the fence, I don't see the possibility of stringing the thing out, playing for time. We must give a Yes or a No." Charles giggled. "Why, by the bye, is it always assumed that time is on the side of the angels?" "Let's make the tapes," declared Margaret, rising. "Where's the harm in it? There's many a slip . . . I shall direct mine to my butler. I've implicit confidence in his judgment. One's children cannot be wholly objective. Remember that, Helen. Your eldest stands to inherit the lovely Vermeer, does he not?"

"No." Helen, who had been pacing the carpet with short unsteady steps, plumped herself down like a stout little bolster on the sofa. "No to *what*, dear?" cried Lily in a voice of alarm. "No, I shan't give them the Vermeer." "Oh, *Helen!*" the ladies reproached her in wailing chorus. "No," Helen repeated with a decisive wobble of her receding, indeterminate chin. "I don't *care* what they promise. Jeroen swore to me that not a hair of its head would be harmed. But I've no right to take his word for it. Any more than if it were a child. The painting will stay where it is, Henry. They can have the Titian if they want."

It became alarmingly clear that she intended to stick to her guns. Henry's reasoning was useless, and Frank could not shake her resolution, though he was feeling it his pastoral duty to try. Like anyone who has arrived at an immense decision, she had a look of being at rest, serene as a rock in the midst of the storm around her. Bearing out the prophecy that they could be "bigger" for their experience, her dumpy form seemed to have gained a full inch and not only in moral stature. It was a matter of posture, doubtless; her small muffin head was drawn up and her chest thrust mildly forward as she sat unmoving in the "place of honor" vacated by Margaret on the sofa. Perhaps she felt proud of the dauntless stand she had taken or pleased to be the undivided center of attention, but, if so, it only showed in a vague, bemused little smile, which she directed at those around her benignly and sympathetically, as though, from her present modest elevation, they were no longer quite in focus.

She did not turn a deaf ear to their arguments and objections but listened politely, with an evident effort at attention, nodding from time to time to show that she was following, as no doubt she did at her club when a lecturer dealt with a topic that was "interesting," although not directly to her. Facing her, Frank had drawn up a straight chair and kept hitching himself forward on it so as to be able to "reach" her. To the audience grouped around them he seemed to be giving a demonstration of his professional skills, like a doctor operating on a patient before a group of students. This was something he could not help, but the audience—or at least Sophie—could not help viewing it as a performance, that is, critically, forgetful of the earnestness of his purpose.

"Helen! You bear the same lovely name, 'torch' in Greek, as my own wife and daughter. Now let's think a little about this Vermeer. In the last analysis, it's a material object, isn't it?

Just oil and canvas handled in a certain way that you and I recognize as art. But that's relative, don't you agree? Depending on the culture we've been raised in. I mean, to an Eskimo or a Ugandan, the marks on that piece of canvas wouldn't say a darn thing. 'Beauty is in the eye of the beholder,' as the old saw had it. Well, isn't that pretty much accepted by art historians today? In art, we're responding to a set of conventions, the way we do in our clothes and the food we eat. Some creative spirits want to overthrow those conventions, and I don't say that I altogether blame them, even though I don't always understand what they're getting at. But that's beside the point. The point is that in our society we're making a shibboleth of art. We've learned that there's nothing sacred or eternal in our dress fashions and food habits. We've lived through several revolutions in those departments, with women wearing pants and men carrying purses and our young people cooking in 'woks' and eating raw fish like the Japanese. . . . Well, you know what I mean. But our attitudes toward art are still as rigid as they ever were, paradoxical as that may sound. We reverence art as something sacred, when we ought to be using it for our enjoyment as we do today with our clothes. Modern art hasn't succeeded in liberating man from the fetishism of Art with a capital *A*. We've come to worship a class of objects—paintings and sculptures—and we treat their creators as gods. If we all could be artists, as one day I hope we can, we wouldn't feel that way any more. We wouldn't look on art as precious property to be accumulated by any single person or society. Now, mind you, I think this totemism has a lot to do with the failure of organized religion. Despite church attendance figures, we've let ordinary humanity lose touch with the divine, with God. No wonder that the lucky few among us are tempted to put daubs of oil on canvas in His place. I say 'daubs' deliberately, Helen, to shock you. Remember, we've just agreed that to the Ugandan your Vermeer is no thing of beauty, and who is to say that he's wrong?"

"Yes, thank you, Frank. Very interesting. I know you mean well. And I suppose it's all relative, as you say. I've never cared much for African sculpture, though I know people who have a passion for it." Frank hitched himself forward another inch and made a gesture of entreaty. "Helen! Do you still know your Ten Commandments?" She nodded. "Well, recite me the First, then." " 'Thou shalt not make unto thee any graven image,' is that what you mean?" "Yes, dear Helen. 'Or the likeness of any thing that is in heaven above or in the earth beneath, or in the water under the earth.' This terrible experience should bring home to us the good sense of that commandment. Of course what was being enjoined against at that time was the fashioning and worship of idols. Secular art was unknown to the ancient Hebrews and indeed to most of the ancient peoples. And the special genius of the Hebrew religion was that its God was invisible, that is, immaterial, not to be represented or imitated in any material shape or form. The Incarnation, of course, was a radical break with that view of Him. 'And was made man.' Still, I wonder whether the old ban on representation didn't have more true wisdom in it than our own Church, reacting to the Puritan excesses, has been willing to admit. Did Moses foresee that the fashioning of images would be bound to lead to the worship of them? The story of the Golden Calf seems to point that way, doesn't it?"

"My wife's a Presbyterian," said Henry. "You won't find graven images in her church. But you're dead right on one point. She idolizes that Vermeer." Helen still wore her dreamy smile. "Did you ever happen to see it, Frank? It was hanging on show at Wildenstein's. For the Crippled Children. There was always a throng around it, wasn't there, Henry?" "I'm sorry," confessed Frank. "I missed it. I'm so darned busy with church work that I don't get out much to exhibitions any more." "Oh, well, then . . . If you had, you might understand." She was in love with the picture, that was obvious, though the minister did not seem to realize it. Moreover, there was a suggestion of tender reminiscence in her tone, a commemorative note, as though the "Girl" belonged to a distant, enshrined past, too far off now for tears. However the others were interpreting the ultimatum, Helen had clearly decided that she was on her way to a better world, leaving her dear possession behind.

Undiscouraged, Frank tried another tack. "Maybe we make too much of a cult of originals. Helen has had the privilege of living with one, but if she'd lived with a reproduction instead, nobody could take it away from her. If it happened to be stolen, she could always get another, exactly the same. Whereas when you lose a loved one, say a member of your family, there's no replacement. That's why, Helen, we hold human life sacred; the individual in each of us is one of a kind, loved by the Creator for the divine unique spark in him. Don't let your 'torch' go out. Your life is sacred to me, Helen, as it should be to you. You blaspheme if you think of exchanging it for a mere material possession, a thing whose value may be specious—in the sense of highly relative—as you yourself admit." But the Vermeer was one of a kind; that was the point he himself had just made, even if for him it would have done better to exist in the plural. It was odd that he did not see that everything he was saying about human life applied for Helen, equally—indeed more emphatically—to her "Girl."

"Leave her be, Frankie," gently spoke up the Bishop. "Let her follow her own counsel. We shall pray for you, my dear, and ask the good Lord to soften the hearts of these misguided young people toward you." "Helen Potter!" Jeroen himself stood in the doorway. "Come along now." Henk half rose, as if to intervene. "Stay where you are, Deputy," Jeroen said. "This affair does not concern you. You also, Henry Potter. Your wife does not need your company." With her short teetering steps, she followed him into the kitchen; Hussein with his pistol was at her back. The Bishop wiped his eyes. There went the stuff of martyrs. "Queen Victoria," whispered Henk, gravely approving. In fact there *was* a resemblance to the queen in her later years, something of pudgy royal dignity, that all at once had become visible.

"I suppose I might have offered to take her place," muttered Henry. "It wouldn't have done any good," the others assured him. "She's made her bed," said Harold. "Shut up, you," said

Sophie. The door to the kitchen was closed. Outside Hussein stood on guard, his pistol raised. Frank and the Bishop moved their lips in silent prayer. Carey swiftly crossed himself. "I can't bear it," cried Aileen, putting her fingers to her ears. For an eternity they waited.

Ten

Without any warning, toward the end of the afternoon, the television screen lit up. It was still Wednesday. Yusuf, very helpfully, got to work twirling the dials till the image would stay put. In the box appeared the farmhouse they were prisoners in, shown from several angles and surprisingly close up. The shots had been taken from the air: those military planes that they had heard zooming about this morning; sometimes, annoyingly, a wing got in the way of the picture. It was odd to have a bird's-eye view of your place of confinement, which you had never fully seen with your own eyes—on the night they had arrived it had been too dark. Now they were able to look down on the broad sloping roof—underneath was the drafty attic half of them had been sleeping in—the television aerial, the chicken coop and the rabbit run near the spot where the men peed. From above they saw a crisscrossing of canals and ditches, the highway they had landed on, and the big unfinished barn with its roofing of tarpaulin. Although the snow had melted, the camouflage job was still effective; examining it from a pilot's perspective, even Harold admitted to a certain satisfaction in the result of their labors, what the Sophie girl called "pride of workmanship."

Yusuf had turned up the sound, and Henk, who was found napping on the floor behind the sofa, was rushed to the screen to translate. They had missed the beginning while they were trying to wake him up, but they learned—what they could see anyway—that the long-awaited breakthrough had happened. It was the hijackers themselves who had taken the initiative. They had broadcast a message to the authorities announcing their location; the radio in the kitchen, it seemed, was a powerful short-wave sending and receiving set, which one of the Arabs—Yusuf probably—had known how to rig up to the TV aerial. Henk and Carey said that they had suspected that there would be a "pirate station" in the house—a pity that they had not come out with that sooner, when it would have cleared up some little misunderstandings. Anyway, the authorities, at first, had treated the message as a hoax, with the result that two whole hours had been lost. The message identifying the "command post's" position had come through shortly after two, according to the commentator, and now it was a few minutes past four.

The program, apparently, had started with a full list of the hijackers' demands; that of course would be the part they had missed. But now a spokesman came on the screen recapitulating the chief ones. First, an astronomic ransom—one and a quarter million dollars, half to be distributed among the workers and peasants of Surinam—for the return of the helicopter and its crew. Second, immediate withdrawal of Holland from NATO and breaking of relations with Israel. Third, liberation of all "class-war prisoners" from Dutch jails. Superficially, that one sounded more feasible: in a very liberal country like Holland, there could not be so many. But in fact it could mean anything, depending on the definition: the release of common criminals, for instance, if they were of working-class origin, which obviously most of them would be. The demand, Henk said, would be unacceptable as it stood to his government; several rounds of "clarification" might be needed before the ruling coalition could consider acting on it. Eventually a few fringe elements who by stretching a point could be regarded as political prisoners might be let out: e.g., small groups of squatters who had occupied canal houses and struck policemen seeking to evict them. . . . But in his opinion the *kapers* did not take this demand of theirs too seriously; it was on their list *pro forma,* to satisfy revolutionary protocol. The outcome for the hostages would surely not hinge on it. The same with NATO and Israel: he doubted that the terrorists really expected to change the foreign policy of the Netherlands by their "rhetoric"—his expression—of violence.

More to the point was the final demand: that a small helicopter with a one-man crew be supplied to pick up a bundle of tapes containing instructions from the prisoners to their families on how to bring about their release. This demand had a deadline attached to it. In less than half an hour from now, the pilot was to begin hovering over a designated spot, which would be marked by a flag and lanterns, thirty meters from the command post; at a signal he was to drop a cable. He was not to attempt to land, and any other craft entering the air space during the pick-up would be shot down. The tapes must then be transferred to a long-range carrier and delivered to the families of the hostages; under no circumstances should they be allowed to fall into the hands of the FBI or any other agency of the U.S. imperialist government. Failure to observe this condition would bring immediate reprisals. The Dutch military attaché in Washington would be held responsible for the prompt transfer of the tapes to the parties concerned. Delay or sabotage on his part would be viewed as an act of war, to be answered for in blood by the prisoner Van Vliet de Jonge, whose image in full color now flashed on the screen. . . . As he sat on the floor, fiddling with the knobs, they saw him chatting with the Queen at the opening of Parliament, addressing a crowd, eating a herring at a street stall. Then came some still photos of his wife and their children, poor little tykes—it was a surprise to learn that he was married to a Javanese beauty, slender, with sloe eyes. Henk's family vanished from the screen and were replaced by the Minister of Defense, a funny stiff old socialist, declaring that Her Majesty's government, mindful of the human factor, was bending every effort to meet the conditions laid down in the final demand: a helicopter of the Alouette II type was being dispatched, and a Lockheed Lodestar stood ready to receive the bundle of tapes. With a last sweeping view of the farmhouse, the special broadcast ended. Further news and commentary would be shown on the regular program at eighteen hours fifty-five, five minutes of seven.

As the image of their prison faded from the screen, the Chadwicks eyed each other. It looked indeed as though Senator Carey had known whereof he spoke when he said that making the tapes was not "the easy way out." He had tried to warn Harold in particular against that fatal cocksureness of his. It had been foolish of Harold, foolish of all of them, to imagine that the *"kapers,"* as Henk called them, would not do everything in their power to keep the FBI from interfering with their plan. As for "stalling" over the delivery of the paintings ("gaining time"!), from what they had just heard such tactics could cost Henk his life. Harold might not care if Henk was executed, but the others would. He was such good company, their "Laughing Cavalier," and he had a brilliant career ahead of him—they had not understood that till they saw him on television, though Charles had always said so.

No wonder Harold and Eloise were looking doubtfully at each other. After all, if he had not been so brassily confident of the harmlessness of making the tapes, the others might have hesitated. And there sat Helen, the living proof of how wrong they had been to listen to him. Jeroen and Company—so far at least—had wreaked no vengeance on her. She had made a tape with instructions to turn over the Titian as the price of Henry's head. That was all. No one had struck her or furiously twisted her arm. They had simply told her that they would be seeing her later. She had seemed almost let down when she came trotting back into the room. It was hard to believe that the band would give up on the Vermeer so easily; they would surely try again. But two hours had passed, and no new summons had come for her. If anyone had "gained time," it was she. Of course they had other business to occupy them, most importantly the helicopter, which was due any minute if the deadline was really going to be met.

The hostages in the parlor crowded against the western window to watch for it. In the dusk, they saw lanterns moving in the direction of the field. Nothing yet but a star—Venus rising—in the sky. "Watchman, tell us of the night," someone hummed, as a "sick" joke surely, for it was not signs of promise such as had appeared to the Magi that they were awaiting—rather, the reverse in the collectors' case. Still, one could not deny that there was something strangely thrilling in scanning the evening sky for the approach of a visitant from what seemed now like the other world. At any rate, it would be a break in the monotony. For some time, they had been hearing heavy thumps against the house wall: extra sandbags, the men said, being piled up around it in the event of an attack. At last Eloise's sharp ears caught the sound of the helicopter's rotors. There it was, hovering, a midget compared to theirs. They were able to watch the drop of the cable, but, disappointingly, the armed guards with lanterns patrolling cut off a view of the loading. Also it had become dark. They had only a glimpse of an indistinct object swinging upward to tell them that the pick-up was over. The little craft with their voices aboard immediately started to climb.

It was natural to feel despondent when it had disappeared. Only Harold, by bluster, avoided a sinking of spirits. He claimed not to feel that they had just said good-bye to their paintings—he still had faith in the FBI. According to him, the warning on television only meant that the FBI would have to be careful. They knew how to work under cover. If the Dutch tried to keep them out of the picture, they would have their own means. "Why, Maggie's butler could be understudied by an FBI man and not even the other help the wiser. Half the waiters and butlers passing trays of drinks and sandwiches at your red-as-a-rose fund-raisers are FBI plants. Like detectives guarding the wedding presents in monkey suits. If Gerry Ford knows what's good for him, they'll be careful." He patted his trousers pocket, where, one presumed, his billfold lay. The ladies sighed. How far away the time seemed when they were wont to tell each other that Harold and his wife—the first one —were "deliciously common"!

Johnnie shook his head. "No, Harold, my boy. If the FBI gets into it, they'll blow it. Sure as shooting." "Even if it means some of our lives," said Lily, sadly. "I'm awfully afraid you're right. It's a terrible commentary, isn't it?" "I never thought I'd reach the point of looking on the FBI as my enemy," declared Margaret.

"It only needs a weensy change in perspective, doesn't it?" That was Charles, being dreadful again. "A little bird tells me that we're not the enthusiasts for 'law and order' that we were a few days ago. It was that interesting third demand that brought it home to me. Why, my dear, I said to myself, if the whole criminal population of Holland were turned loose—every last cutthroat and child-molester and wife-beater—I'd have no objection as long as it meant that I'd be allowed to journey to Naqsh-i-Rustan with my ears and toes and fingers still safely about me. And since I'm a rational animal and not totally selfish, I hope, I found myself led to question the social utility of prisons. What difference would it make, Charles, I said, if in fact those criminals *were* all let loose? Very little, I concluded. Accepting such a prospect for my own subjective motives, rather than fearing it for society at large, allowed me to regard it objectively—a distinct gain, I always think. Till today, I confess, I'd tended to look on our penal institutions as a necessary evil. And, as for the second demand, can we honestly say that it would be a tragedy if Holland were to leave NATO and suspend relations with Israel? My own answer, I admit, would be prejudiced. As a pacifist, I hold no brief for NATO, and, though I'm not unsympathetic to Israel, I feel she could use a little lesson."

"Oh, *poor* Israel," moaned Beryl's "Simmie." "Would you take away her last friend? Well, I guess I would, if it was the only way of saving our lives. And you have to admit that some of her policies are open to criticism." "You see?" crowed Charles. He was right, one had to acknowledge: things did look different from a captive's point of view. One's dearest principles shrank in importance when weighed against one's freedom, till finally one began to ask whether they *were* so important, after all. Take the example of NATO: would Harold be such a jingo about the NATO forces as the first line of defense against Communism if taking Holland out of the first line would let them all go home in peace? France, come to think of it, he might tell himself, had left NATO years ago and the world had not come to an end.

"Yes," said Simmie. "And I'm starting to wonder about something else. Our famous free press. I know it's good that we have it and vital to a democracy. But in connection with your pictures, I ask myself . . . I mean, what's to stop reporters from interviewing all our families?" "Nothing," said Carey. "We can be sure that it's been done." "Well, then, when this tapes bombshell breaks, won't they be pounding at those same doors again?" Carey nodded. "Mmm . . . I take your meaning." But the others were left in the dark. "Explain," said Beryl. "Don't be so damned mysterious." "No mystery," said Carey. "Aileen means that this time some of the families will shut the door in their faces." "Yes. On the one hand, my Mamma will let them in and tell them that, no, she hasn't received any tape from me. They're bound to believe her. Mamma's a very truthful person. Anyway, in a small town like Fayetteville, everybody would know if she had. The same with your daughter, Jim. They'd seek her out in college, and she'd talk to them, wouldn't she, and tell them no tape? It would be like that with every one of *our* families, but with you people's it wouldn't. They'd refuse to see reporters for fear of saying something out of turn. So it would be easy to narrow it down and know who'd got a tape and who hadn't. Then it wouldn't take a genius to realize that every hostage who made a tape was an important art collector."

"Or just rich, Aileen," said Warren. "Well, the two go together," she retorted and then fell silent, as if the interruption had confused her. "In any case," said the Senator, helping her, "thanks to the press, the FBI won't have much of a problem running down the addressees of the tapes. The reporters lying in wait outside the stately homes will function as pointer dogs.

As for watching the families' movements, noting visitors, photographing them, trailing them, the press'll provide those services for Kelley's cops at no extra charge."

The collectors groaned in unison. The families had a right to their privacy in circumstances like this. Though no one, of course, wanted his works of art to be handed over to the *kapers'* accomplices, the thought that the press by its vigilance would stand in the way was very disagreeable. If one was willing to pay the ransom, that should be the end of it; press and government should stand aside till the deed was done. Granted, it was breaking the law, but there were times when the law was wrong.

It was true that great wealth, even relatively great wealth, got one in the habit of wanting one's own way, whatever the cost. Yet it was not an altogether bad habit to have formed. They were right to feel their hackles rise at the very idea of arbitrary interference in an affair that concerned no one but themselves. The paintings were theirs, so they should be free to dispose of them according to their own lights. Obviously, owning a masterpiece was a sacred trust—they all felt that, even Eloise with her pretty-pretty Laurencins—but how that trust should be regarded in an emergency ought to lie between one and one's own conscience. If the rich were staunch Republicans, that was not because they grudged a fair wage and decent medical care and playgrounds and the rest of it to the poor, nor even because they believed blindly in capitalism as the best system yet invented for creating wealth and spreading it to the workman and the small investor, but because they were accustomed to freedom and jealous of having it taken away from them by the government and the prying press. A poor man did not appreciate the value of freedom, never having had much; that was a sad fact and often not his fault.

Yet if one could not help waxing indignant at the prospect of reporters wantonly interfering with one's right to pay up, in another part of one's mind was a little prayer that some outside force—not necessarily reporters—*would* intervene to save the treasures that too weakly one had agreed to sacrifice.

Nobody knew *what* he or she wanted, really. For the *kapers* to have their way or not to have it? If they had their way, that would put an end to the torment at any rate. But to see them thwarted, gnashing their teeth like the villains they were, had greater appeal to the fancy.

Rescue, realistically, was the only hope. Of their own accord, the terrorists would not "go away," like a bad dream. A daring raid, under cover of darkness, might do it. Actually, quite a few of the party had been counting on the helicopter for deliverance: it had been tempting to picture a body of para- troopers springing from it heavily armed, overpowering the guards and calling on the leaders to come out of the house and surrender. Such had been his fond fancy, Johnnie confessed; others had imagined canisters of a paralyzing gas as well. But here again did one really desire that? The house was wired, all the way to the rafters, and these people were fanatics. At the very minimum, were a rescue force to land, there would be shooting. The hostages, one might argue, could lie on the floor, out of the line of fire. But there was that "human shield" tactic so familiar from thriller films. To think of one's frail body serving as a buckler for Jeroen's hefty frame made one recog- nize how inseparable one's interests had become from theirs, bound up together despite the evident differences for as long as this lasted; there was a name for that in biology: symbiosis. No wonder that when the helicopter appeared, it had been a relief, on the whole, to see that it was much too small to carry an army of flying Dutchmen—only the pilot and maybe one passenger could fit into it.

"Sophie," said Johnnie, "you're a journalist. What bright idea do you have for calling the pack off so that our families can do the necessary, if that seems best to them, to bring us back alive?" "The press isn't as unfeeling as you all seem to think," she answered in a low voice, interlacing her long fin- gers. "On its own, it can behave responsibly when it sees that the public's 'right to know' conflicts with military security or with the safety of individual lives. But it doesn't like to be dictated to or hear from others what its bounden duty is. It might help now, I guess, if an appeal was made to the papers to leave the families alone while negotiations are going on." "But who would make the appeal, Sophie?" asked Lily. "The Dutch, I suppose," said Sophie. "Through the military attaché." But she herself did not sound very convinced. "Surely it would come better from the families?" Margaret said. Probably it would, but how convey the idea to the families? They might think of it for themselves and they might not.

There was a dejected silence. "We're so helpless, aren't we?" sighed Eloise. "If only, over there, they could have the benefit of the thinking we're doing here. We could give them so many pointers." "I have an idea!" Aileen cried. "Why don't you make the appeal to the press yourselves? You could do another tape, with all your voices on it." They all turned to Carey. "Go ahead," he said. "I'm sure Jeroen *et al*. will be happy to air it for you." "You're being sarcastic," said Lily. "Do you mean we shouldn't?" "Suit yourselves, Lily," he answered. "But why so eager to make sure that our hosts get their hands on your pictures? Looks like you want to do their job for them. Kind of an auxiliary fire-fighting team of volunteers standing by with hook and ladder, getting your piece of the action." "But would an appeal *work*?" said Johnnie. Carey supposed it would, for the time being, with the big papers, till some small fry broke the embargo. Aileen burst in. "I've got a better idea. Sophie should do it." "Thanks," said Sophie dryly. "As a journalist you'll carry *much* more conviction," Aileen persisted. "Your colleagues will listen to you when they might not to a lot of millionaires. The voice of privilege isn't their favorite music. But as a fellow-worker, you'll speak directly to their professional consciences." But Sophie refused, point blank.

"Will you do it, then, Bishop?" The old man started. He had not been paying attention. "Do what, my dear?" His ruddy face had a purplish flush. Come to think of it, he had not been looking well since lunch time. "Make an appeal to the press, honey—" "Press?" He stared around the room. "Are there reporters here?" Sweat broke out on his broad forehead. "Hold it, Aileen," ordered the Senator, when he saw that her mouth was open, ready to speak again. He moved over to where Gus was sitting and took his pulse. Then his eyebrows went up. "Get Denise." He was unbuttoning the old man's shirt collar. "Is that better? Can you hear me, Gus?" The Bishop faintly nodded and tried to speak. His jaw worked. "Head." "Your head hurts, does it?" There was a feebler motion of the head and a facial sign like a wink. One eye was wide open and staring. He was having a stroke. As he twitched and fell forward, Frank caught him. "Shall we get him onto the sofa?" "Maybe better not move him," said Harold, joining himself to the purposeful circle around the sick old man. "Let's just take off his shoes." They unlaced the heavy brogues, and Frank chafed his feet in the thick socks. The right foot hung down, a dead weight.

"Stand back!" Denise was there now; she had been in the kitchen preparing supper. Having taken his pulse herself, she said it would be all right to move him, and Frank and Jim, with Harold helping, carried him to the sofa. He was breathing wheezily and seemed to be unconscious. Harold looked over the contents of Denise's first-aid kit and made a face. They had nearly forgotten that he had started out behind the counter, as a pharmacist—he had made his first million by "cornering" some new drug. "Is this all you've got?" he demanded. "I fear so, sir. Would you think to try the adrenalin?" "Are you crazy, woman? The worst thing you could give him. This is a stroke, see?" "There are *medicaments* in the frigidaire, sir." "Blood plasma, yes, plenty," said Ahmed, who had been hovering about anxiously. *"Voulez-vous que j'en cherche?"* Harold hooted. "Counter-indicated, I should imagine, Ahmed," put in Charles. "In my young years, I recall, blood-letting was a favored remedy for apoplectic strokes. Yes, I can still see the jar of leeches in Grandfather's sick chamber. We were in Seville, as it happened, when he was stricken while watching a procession of flagellants." Harold nodded. "Blood-letting would have taken the blood pressure *down*, which is what you have to do with a stroke. Adrenalin and plasma send it *up*." "And ice-bags," Charles continued, "were applied to the forehead. Could an icebag be improvised, I wonder?" Denise thought it could and hurried off to the kitchen.

Harold went back to studying the bottles and boxes in the first-aid kit. "Aspirin, anyway," he said. "May help some in dilating the veins. At least it'll relieve the headache. You heard him indicate that his head was aching? Normal in a stroke. Often the first symptom. Glucose—could there be any glucose in that frigidaire? But, hell, you'd have to administer it as an intravenous drip. No chance of that. In the old days they went in for camphor injections. . . ."

He had not stopped talking, thinking aloud evidently, when Greet appeared. She studied the Bishop, whose breathing was still noisy, and calmly removed his false teeth. Next she took his pulse. "You should raise his head and shoulders," she commented, letting his wrist drop. She had been an airline stewardess herself—KLM; trust Beryl to have learned that. Her eye went around the parlor with manifest dissatisfaction till it fell on the big Bible with its silver locks. "That will do," she decided. "Place it there, under the shoulders, and you, Pastor, add your coat." She showed Frank how to fold it. "Can he be flown out?" he asked, when his friend had been propped up in what to the layman appeared a rather uncomfortable position. But no doubt Greet knew what she was doing. One could not call her attitude kind, but it did seem very professional. KLM must give them more training than Air France did in handling emergencies. Or could she have taken a nursing course to prepare herself for enlisting in their "people's army"?

"This man cannot be moved yet. When he recovers consciousness, we will see." In her opinion, it was only a mild stroke. He was not in deep coma, and his pulse was better. In any case, he could not be flown out unaccompanied. They watched as her eye reviewed them. If Gus were flown out, what lucky person would be chosen to go with him? Frank was the logical selection, but, as Sophie had said yesterday—or was it only this morning?—that was not how these people's minds worked. The one thing you could wager on was that there would be no call for volunteers.

Harold held up a little ampoule. At last he had found something that interested him in Denise's kit. "Papaverine. Well, well." Greet took the glass container from him and inspected it herself. "A vaso-dilator," Harold told her. "Just what the doctor ordered. Miracle that she's got it. And of course she has the hypodermic." Greet dismissed his notion of a miracle. Papaverine, she said, was often found in flight emergency kits; it was to be doubted, though, that it was much more useful than aspirin for dilating the vessels. But she agreed that they should try it. "He may not be able to swallow aspirin. That girl, I think, is capable of giving an intramuscular injection." But there was only the one ampoule, and if Denise bungled the shot, it would be a great pity. Greet watched her busy herself with the syringe and a little bottle of alcohol. "No. Go to the kitchen and boil some water. I will give the injection myself." When the hypodermic was brought back in a pan of water, with a pair of tongs, she filled it. "Now turn him on his side and bring the trousers down." The Bishop's trousers were lowered, and his capacious underpants and flowing shirt-tail moved to one side, exposing his white buttock—the right one. Greet pressed his ancient flesh firmly between her thumb and forefinger and plunged the needle in. Then he was placed on his back again, with his trousers rebuttoned. Thanks to Denise's butter-fingers, there had been no avoiding a glimpse of his private parts.

Greet stood looking down at him for a minute and again took his pulse. "We have seen from his passport that the age of this man is eighty-three years. Were you unaware, Pastor, that he suffered from high blood pressure? Why have you brought him with you on your 'fact-finding' crusade? He should be in a home for the aged." She turned on her heel and strode out. "We will be giving you the icebag you have asked for."

Not many minutes later, the Bishop stirred. He was conscious and could talk a little, though his speech was impaired. That might be because of the missing dentures, the lack of which he noticed, asking querulously what Frank had done with them. Frank fitted them into the poor old mouth, which drooped on one side so that saliva ran out. The whole right side of his face seemed to be paralyzed, and his speech, though improved, was still thick. At first he did not know where he was and recognized only Frank. Gradually he took in a bit more of his surroundings. He sat up irritably on finding the Bible underneath him and demanded that it be taken away. Yet he knew it was Calvin's Bible, which showed that he was becoming less confused. His color was better, and he was able to swallow some of the liquids Denise fed him, holding his head up like a baby's. He complained of a "fierce" headache—a normal sequela, Harold said—and they brought him aspirin and a plastic sack with ice-cubes in it.

By night-time, he was almost himself again. They had moved him to the other sofa, in the family room, where he could watch television, which he followed remarkably well, considering that he seemed to have grown deafer in the last few hours and that his right eye, now blinking occasionally, was teary. The screen showed the helicopter, landing at a military airfield, and a crowd of reporters being held back by the military police. To the general surprise, he remembered about the tapes and about Helen, too. "Here you are, big as life," he told her. "The good Lord answered our prayer." They were not shown the departure of the Lodestar, if in fact it had actually left. But they saw the Minister of Defense again and clapped for him, like an old friend.

When bedtime came, Gus was tucked in for the night on the family-room sofa. They found his pajamas in his old tapestry carryall and put them on him. It was quite an event for one of their number to retire in proper night clothes, rather than fully dressed. Carlos brought him his own blanket and a pillow. Instead of going to the attic, Denise was to sleep at his feet, with Frank next to her. Just before "lights out," Elfride came in with a warm drink with a sedative in it. Horst had looked in for a minute, and all three Arabs had appeared to wish the old man a good night. Only Jeroen, in all this time, had not showed his face. It was his conscience reproaching him, Frank was sure. Frank was in a buoyant mood, having regained all his "pep" now that the Bishop was out of the woods, as he put it. Gus's stroke, he believed, was going to prove to be the blessed turning-point in this whole adventure. God's grace worked in mysterious ways, and He may have seen fit to try His servant with a little syncope in order to show these young anarchists the human havoc they could wreak through over-immersion in theory. "Over-immersion" was a funny way of putting it.

At any rate, Gus's own heart was touched by the attentions paid him. "You've been so good," he kept repeating in his still quavery voice to everyone who approached him. Well, he was a Christian and supposed to love his enemies, which meant seeing the good in them. In view of that, the others decided not to mention in his presence the little thing that had just happened: a few minutes ago, Helen was turned back as she was mounting the stairway clutching as usual her rubberized dressing-case to freshen up for the night. Her toilet privilege had been revoked. She could go outdoors with the men, Hussein told her, barring the way with the submachine gun he had taken over from Ahmed. In the shock of it, she had said no, she wouldn't, without considering her waterworks or the fact that it was dark outside so that no one would see her. Now it was too late. The single chamber-pot in the house had been placed where the Bishop could use it, and she would not want to do tinkle-tinkle and disturb him.

Thursday was nearly over. Twenty-four hours had gone by since the Bishop's *"attaque,"* as Aileen persisted in calling it—she had been talking French a mile a minute with Denise and Jean, the steward. There was no news yet on television, and the radio report was only that "negotiations" were proceeding through the Dutch Embassy in Washington. But on the scene there had been some changes—for the better, on the whole. Groups of hostages had been allowed to go out for walks, under guard and not too far from the house. Only Helen had been kept in, as a punishment, and Gus, on "doctor's orders"—he had taken a few, remarkably spry steps in the family room, refusing Frank's arm, but then had been made to rest.

Outside, since morning, a new sight had met their eyes: a cordon of special police in black uniforms with white braid around the neck drawn up in the fields perhaps five hundred yards off. They were an elite force, Henk said, called the *marechaussee*—something like guardsmen—and were used in state emergencies. According to Ahmed, the people's army had agreed to having them drawn up there, for its own protection. No sooner had the news gone on the air than curiosity-seekers had swarmed into the area. Last night the highway police had set up road blocks; the only cars permitted through belonged to people who lived here or worked in the pumping-station. But that had not stopped polder dwellers and pump men from hiking cross-country to have a look. It was to prevent that, partly, that the guardsmen had been brought in. A warning had gone out, too, against violating the air space immediately overhead. Yet the hostages on their walks today had seen civilian planes and a civilian helicopter. Most of them, Henk thought, had been chartered by the press and foreign television chains, but a few, surely, were taking tourists up for a spin over the area at so many guilders a head. It would not surprise him if a balloon were to appear. In fact, just before dusk, one group of hostages saw a glider. That was Holland, he explained; his countrymen were bound to turn the event into a carnival, with local-color touches. On the military's list of problems would be an invasion of skaters along the canals.

Every one of those aircraft carried photographers, one suspected. Frank, who had been allowed to bring his field glasses out with him, was sure he had caught sight of a telescopic lens pointing down at them from the helicopter. It was unpleasant to know one was being photographed by dozens of perfect strangers as one stumbled and slipped along the ruts of frozen fields with one's casual travel clothes looking decidedly the worse for wear.

The deterioration of one's appearance was one of the crosses of captivity that one had to bear with equanimity. They were all in the same boat, luckily, and yet, unluckily, not quite. The men's beards, for instance, grew at different speeds and some were coarser and spikier than others: Charles proved to be virtually hairless in the face except for his eyebrows, while Harold's jaw bristled with a thick pepper-and-salt stubble. Moreover, one had only to look at the men to realize how favored women were in comparison. Even there, though, there were degrees. Eloise, with her mirror and tweezers, managed to be impeccable, while Helen was a sight. She had had an "accident," poor dear, during the night, which had left a large spot that still showed, even when it had dried out, on the back of her dress, and all morning she had smelled of urine. One's olfactories could not help noticing, either, that Sophie was menstruating; being older, in these close quarters, had its compensations. The close quarters meant, too, that every little imperfection showed up as if in a magnifying mirror: the gray roots, for example, at the parting of Aileen's hair, a stye Beryl was getting, the boil on Victor's neck.

All were rumpled, and soiled as to collars and cuffs, though, again, not equally. Some looked "as if they had slept in their clothes," as of course everyone had, but a few were fortunate in the materials they had happened to be wearing. Henry's vintage herringbone seemed to be made of iron, and, until he had been stricken, the Bishop's tweeds had not showed a wrinkle or a spot. Henk's whipcord, too, was very wrinkle-resistant. As for Carey, he revealed his vanity every single night by taking off his trousers and sleeping on them to preserve the crease—like an actor on the road, he said—in his shorts and covered with his overcoat: he slid them under the rug, where they served as a mattress as well. No gentleman born could have done that.

The black-and-white *marechaussee* had field glasses, which they trained on the prisoners and their guards at exercise. To them, the differences in grooming and cleanliness so apparent to the hostages themselves were probably not visible. They would all look the same. But the guardsmen were less interested probably in the presentability of the hostages than in their health and morale, which would appear to be good. If the uniformed men knew the number of the hostages and could count, they might notice that two had not been taken out for an airing and report that to their superiors. But through their field glasses they might see, too, that relations between guards and prisoners were far from ferocious; perhaps in order to leave that impression, the amiable ones—Carlos and Ahmed—had been chosen as "chaperons." Nor would the impression be wrong. Inside the house, too, the atmosphere had lightened, leading one to wonder as to what could be the reason. Frank's theory that Gus's stroke had produced a change of heart had not won many converts; it was so obviously what a minister would like to believe.

During the commotion caused by the stroke, the idea of appealing to the press had been allowed to drop. This morning Aileen had tried to revive it, but she had been unable to compete with the distractions furnished by the cordon of guardsmen, the fresh air and exercise, and the continuing sideshow of airborne photographers and sightseers. With all these fresh sources of interest immediately at hand, they did not have time to worry about what might be happening in Washington and New York. Anyway, asking the press to stay away in a big country like America would be utterly futile if in a little country like Holland the authorities themselves could not do better than this afternoon's spectacle suggested. Far from being considerate of others' misfortune, people—not just the press ghouls —only wanted to batten on it.

This was borne out by the evening news. On the screen they were shown the line of men in uniform, the barriers across the highway, and, behind the barriers—what they would not have suspected—a throng of cars, bicycles, small trucks, and pedestrians. Merchants were selling smoked eels and herring from booths on wheels to the crowd, and, despite the temperature, there was an ice-cream vendor with cones and Eskimo pies. Some schoolchildren were flying a kite with a long tail. A reporter with a notebook jumped the barrier, and they watched the police chase him and capture him. On the canal next to the highway there were skaters, sure enough, in bright caps and scarves, that the police had to turn back too. It was like a national holiday. "The *kermis*," said Henk.

This day had seemed the shortest of any they had spent in

captivity. There had been no further mention of flying Gus out. That thought had fallen by the wayside, like the proposed appeal to the press. Gus himself did not want to hear of it. "I feel a power of good in me, Frankie," he said firmly, meaning— one gathered—that he had been filled with the spirit during his close encounter with the other world and intended to remain among them as the vessel of it. The staunch old soul must believe that the power of good stored up in him could move mountains.

For supper, there were *pannekoeken*—pancakes; Denise had made them as a surprise out of a mix she found in the housewife's larder and fresh eggs from the chicken coop. After supper, there were two "tables" of bridge, played with new cards John and Beryl had cut out and colored, using the children's crayons —the court cards, very amusing, had single eyes and two noses like Picassos. The match game Carey had showed Victor had caught on with some of the others, and a whole circle was concentrating on it. It was more of a puzzle, really: you had three matches representing cannibals and three representing missionaries, and the idea was to ferry them across a river in a boat that held two persons. The cannibals could never outnumber the missionaries at any stage, on one river bank or the other, or the missionaries would be eaten; all three missionaries knew how to row, and there was one rowing cannibal. Ahmed, who was on guard, came up to watch and suddenly put on a scowl. He decided that the game was racist. The real problem, he said, would be to keep the missionaries from enslaving the cannibals through the technology they brought with them, and the fact that the hostages had not seen that for themselves should show them how deeply racism was embedded in their culture. But, having recited his piece, the mercurial creature promptly came out of his sulk, took six matches—twisting the heads off of the ones that stood for missionaries—trotted them rapidly in pairs and singly back and forth across the rug, ending with two cannibals on the final trip and a winning grin on his brown face. He had solved the puzzle! Bravo for Ahmed! "You're the rowing cannibal, Ahmed," the Senator told him,

279

3 missionaries who can all row; 3 cannibals of whom only one can row.
A river to be crossed. 1 boat holding two persons.
The cannibals must never outnumber the missionaries on either bank of the river.

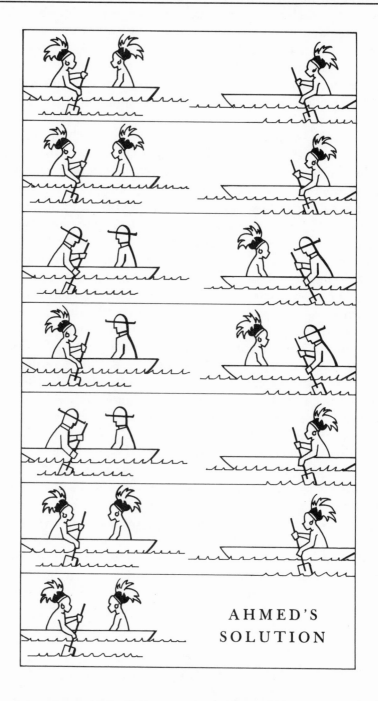

AHMED'S
SOLUTION

which was a risky kind of compliment. But the budding terrorist was pleased as Punch.

Before long it was toilet-time. Yusuf came on guard and ordered Helen out with the men. By now she was used to the humiliation. Then lights out. They were all hoping to sleep, after their time in the open, breathing in pure air. But it was not to be. The group in the living-room had just settled down when the Bishop's voice called for Frank. From the piteous sound of it they knew at once that something was wrong. They could hear Frank trying to comfort him. But it was not what they thought: Gus was not having a second stroke—he had forgotten the Lord's Prayer. In comparison, that might appear unimportant, but to him of course it was everything. He sounded frightened out of his wits. Before going to sleep, it seemed, he had wanted to say his prayers and all at once he could not remember how the Lord's Prayer began. In the dark now Frank was prompting him. "Our Father . . ." "Our Father," the old man repeated after him. But he could not go on by himself. "Who art in heaven." "Who art in heaven." "Hallowed be Thy name." "Hallowed be Thy name." It was terrible to listen to it. He broke off with a moan and must have put his hand to his head. "Does your head ache?" "No." He wanted to be left alone. There was silence, then he shouted in a terrible voice "My God, my God, why hast Thou forsaken me?" Christ's last words—awful. "There, now, you see, you remember *that*," Frank said, in a horrible effort to put cheer in him. "The other will come back in the morning, when you're rested. All of us get these blocks. Often on the things we know best."

From the doorway Yusuf pointed his flashlight into the room. In its beam they saw Gus sitting upright in rumpled pajamas, his fringe of white hair awry. "No, Yusuf," Frank said. "Turn it off, will you, please. We're all right here. Just a little wakeful." At last they heard the Bishop snoring, more wheezily than usual, but not enough, they decided, to send for Greet. During the night, he started up several times calling for "Rachel." He seemed to be asking her, whoever she was, for something. "Where the mischief is it? What have you done with it?" He was getting very excited. "What is it you're looking for, Gus?" Carey's easy voice asked. He had come to sit by him, to spell Frank for a bit. "Can't remember. Whatever it was, she took it away with her and hid it. She's always hiding things from me." "His mind's wandering," said Frank. "No use hoping to sleep till he quiets down again." "Tell her I need it. I have to have it now. I'm too old to put up with her tricks. You never loved me, Rachel. Don't you think I know that? You only loved my love for you." Then he fell to snoring again.

"Oh, my goodness," said Frank. "Do you think he really believed that all those years?" "He had doubts, I suppose," said Carey. "Being a religious man. But if she loved his love for her, she loved him." "Isn't that a sophistry, Jim?" Those nearest could not help listening; it was curious how the word "love" made one prick up one's ears even when one had passed the age for it. "But what about this whatever-it-is he thinks he's lost, Jim? Do you understand what he's talking about?" "His faith, I should think. She took it away with her when she died, and he needs it to meet her in Heaven." The sofa springs creaked. "That's it!" cried the Bishop, wide awake and chuckling. "Leave it to a Papist, eh, James? You darned fool, Frankie. I ordained you and made a good liberal of you, but even God Almighty couldn't make a spiritual man of you."

Some time during the night, the Bishop died. He must have gone quietly, for no one heard him. He was already getting cold when Frank touched his hand and knelt down to pray for him in the first light. There was nothing to do but wait for their captors to come down and take over. It would not be possible to bury him because the ground was partly frozen. Probably the best would be to have his body flown out. His friends could see to getting him out of his pajamas and shaved and dressed. These were labors of love that, by giving them something to do, would help relieve their feelings. Surprisingly, Charles was weeping big tears. But the one closest to the Bishop was not as broken up as one would have thought: Frank merely blew his nose from time to time and shook his head. It was as if he were still shocked or bewildered by the statements Gus had made during the night. In view of those, it was just as well perhaps that the old man had not lingered; he himself would not have wanted to live with his mind gone. And yet it was sad.

At last Jeroen and Greet came in to look at the body. Yusuf had brought them the news, but the only sign of life from them for what seemed like ages was the squawking of their radio in the kitchen. Now that they were here, they were very inhuman in their attitude. They pulled back the blanket and carefully examined the body. Then Jeroen ordered Jean and Denise to dress it—breakfast could wait. He would not let anyone help them and he did not want the body washed or shaved. Nor would he tell Frank whether they planned to announce the death soon—Frank was thinking of Gus's relations. "In our own time and in our own way. You will see," Jeroen replied and walked out. No one had had the courage to ask him what they were to do with the Bishop's things or any of the dozen questions that came to mind.

When the body was dressed and reverently laid on the sofa, Jeroen reappeared. "Sit him up," he ordered. The coins Denise had placed on the Bishop's eyelids fell to the floor. "Now open the eyes." Impossible to imagine what the purpose of this could be. Were they going to take his picture? The next thing they all knew they were being pushed into the parlor—Denise and Jean too. When the door was slammed on them, there was scarcely room to breathe. As they stood there, pressed together, swaying at the slightest motion and bumping into the plants, a rattle of gunfire came from behind the door. Then the door was opened, and they were allowed back into the next room—a privilege they could have done without. The Bishop's body lay slumped forward on the sofa, riddled with bullets. Along his vest buttons were holes darkly oozing blood. Hussein was recharging the submachine gun. At a nod from Jeroen, Yusuf and Carlos carried the corpse out, dripping blood onto the rug.

"Was he *alive*?" shrieked Lily. Henk shook his head. "So you think a dead man has no blood in him?" Jeroen said, with a peculiar satisfied smile. "Then why have you done this terrible thing, Jeroen?" cried Frank in a voice of anger, which broke into wild sobs. Jeroen went on smiling. "The deputy has guessed, I think." "You had bad news," said Henk. "No pictures," agreed Carey. "Well, that was to be foreseen." He turned to the others. "They must have learned, first thing this morning, that Washington refused." But the others still could not make a connection. "The application of force was indicated," Carey dryly hinted. Henk nodded. Then Sophie saw. "You were going to shoot a hostage," she told Jeroen. "Beautiful!" "And, my dears, they've done so, haven't they?" fluted Charles. "Most economical of you, Jeroen. My compliments. You have seen the use of leftovers in your revolutionary broth." That was a dreadful way of putting it, but at least all now understood. From their own point of view, callous as it sounded, it was providential that the Bishop had died during the night, allowing the revolutionaries to find a "use" for his body. It had saved them the work of having to shoot a live hostage. If he had waited to die until later in the day, one of the people in this room—which?—would already have been executed.

Jeroen stood there listening, neither confirming nor denying. "You will now eat breakfast," he commanded, as Denise entered with the usual *"ontbijt"* on the pastry-board she made do with for a tray. When he was gone, they found that they were hungry: it was well known that death quickened the appetite. While they ate, the television screen lit up. A spokesman from the Ministry of Justice was announcing that a message had been received from the hijackers: a first hostage had just been executed, and the assassins now called for a helicopter to come and pick up the body. It must arrive within a delay of no less than two hours and observe the same conditions as before. The execution was to be understood in the context of legitimate ransom demands accepted as such by the prisoners themselves that Washington had criminally rejected. The identity of the hostage was not known, the spokesman added. Then the Minister himself came on the screen, appealing to the hijackers to take no more lives while Her Majesty's government continued its efforts to find a peaceful solution. No avenue leading in that direction would be left unexplored. That was all.

It left a good deal to be mulled over in the long morning ahead. "No avenue will be left unexplored," for instance—what did that signify? Henk thought it meant that Den Uyl was appealing to the Vatican and to the NATO allies to put pressure on Washington. The announcement that a hostage had been murdered would make his task easier.

"It won't wash," predicted Johnnie. "An autopsy's bound to show that poor Gus died of a cerebral incident." "We don't *know* that," Frank pointed out. "It might have been a heart attack. He had a heart condition, you know." Johnnie kept his patience. "Whatever he died of, it'll be easy enough for the experts to establish that the bullet wounds were sustained after death." "Not so easy," said Harold. "Rigor mortis hadn't set in, you notice. So there'll be no way of fixing the order of events prior to the onset of death. The cerebral accident or heart failure could have been a *result* of the bullet wounds or of just plain fear when he saw the Thompson aimed at him." He sounded like quite a different person when he was in his own element. "He *didn't* see it," objected Henry. "Jeepers, man, *we* know that, but the medical examiners won't. And the fact that we can sit here debating when we witnessed the whole thing shows what a free-for-all the pathologists'll have with the autopsy. Hell, there are likely to be *two* autopsies, one here and one when they get him home. This is Dutch soil, no?" "There will be a *lijkschouwing*, certainly," Henk agreed. "Before the body can be released. And the body may be held, in expectation of a trial, if the cause of death is in doubt. I am not sure of the law." "Well, that's your answer, Johnnie. Meanwhile there's a corpse full of bullets, which will be all the prima facie evidence Gerry Ford needs to get his ass moving on the pictures."

"And yet we know better," sighed Aileen. Others sighed with her. It would be maddening to watch the terrorists get away with their hoax—that was the only word for it—and be unable to speak out and expose the deception. And yet should one be anxious to expose them? As long as they succeeded in palming off the dead Bishop as a live hostage they had ruthlessly shot down, there would be no pressing need, surely, to select another candidate. Not till Washington refused again, and would it, with all those international pressures? It was only one's feeling for the truth that objected.

Frank's missionary mind had been elsewhere. "Don't you think that we should have grounds for rejoicing, as well as sorrow, in what we have witnessed? To me, the most interesting fact is that Jeroen and his comrades were unwilling to take human life." "Unwilling or just kind of reluctant?" said Carey. "Loath," suggested Aileen. But, whatever the shadings, Frank was basically right. There was no denying that Jeroen had chosen *not* to shoot one of their number. And if he was truly unwilling to kill a fellow-creature and kept finding excuses not to—why, after all, had they spared Helen?—then there was no great reason to be afraid of him, which should be cause for re-joicing in itself. Yet in fact it left one strangely uneasy.

Frank might be glad, piously, for Jeroen's immortal soul, but the general reaction—if one could judge by a few comments —was more complex. If they could be sure that this proclaimed revolutionary was incapable of killing anything more than a cat, they would be relieved for selfish reasons, but he would go down in their estimation. Over these days they had formed an "image" of him which they would have preferred to keep intact. He seemed so hard and resolute, yet fair in his own way—an enemy one could respect. And since one was in his power any-way, it was preferable to look up to him. As Margaret said, a Jeroen who was "loath" to take human life was too small for his boots. "Your class still has warrior values," Henk commented, seeming amused. "I don't see it that way, Maggie," Harold ob-jected. "Don't you think we'll have to hand it to him for getting away with murder if he pulls this stunt off?" That was the slick business man speaking, and "murder" was scarcely the appro-priate word. Yet it was interesting that Harold, of all people, should come to appreciate a hijacker and precisely for qualities valued in the business world. Of course Jeroen was bright as a button.

It was interesting, too, to learn that one had warrior values. Captivity was bringing out new facets in everyone. On the sad side, Helen, with her poor weak kidneys, had turned into something pathetic and repulsive, like an animal clawing at the door to "go out." The admiration she had won for her willingness to die for her "Girl" had evaporated when Jeroen denied her the privilege. To be fair, that was clever of him. Now even Lily's exquisite manners were finding Helen rather hard to take. In the end, Jeroen would get the "Girl" anyway was the general prophecy.

On the cheerful side, Lily was blooming: there was more to her mentally than had ever been suspected, least of all by Beryl. And Beryl herself was different. But, above all, there was the adventure of getting to know oneself, which was like making a new acquaintance. In the usual social round, there was so little time for that. Until deprivation showed them, they had not realized how many hours they spent changing their clothes, going to the hairdresser, the dressmaker, having the *masseur* or the *masseuse* in. Bathing twice a day, as the men did—in the morning and after squash—took up a good half-hour in itself. Not to speak of shaving and using the sun lamp—Johnnie. Then changing your books at the library or having your chauffeur do it: had anyone ever counted the hours consumed by that? Naturally they all fretted now over the absence of these time-takers and complained of being bored. Yet there *was* the compensation of having, for once, leisure—the last thing, come to think of it, that the so-called leisure class enjoyed—to contemplate one's navel, study one's reactions and those of one's friends, probe into human psychology, which could be disappointing, embarrassing, but also plain fascinating.

This morning, in addition, they could profit from the unusual quiet. With the Bishop dead, games, which tended to become noisy and argumentative, were of course not to be thought of, and Frank could not tune up on that instrument. Out of respect, even conversations were subdued—no shouting matches. And probably there was small prospect of being taken out for exercise, at least while the helicopter was expected.

* * *

287

The Bishop's body, they learned, was in the shed; quite soon, though, the guards would be taking it outside to be ready when the helicopter appeared. As the time drew near, Frank, brave man, asked if he could hold a funeral service. Surprisingly, the *kapers* raised no objection. They would allow Frank and the Senator to carry their friend's body to the field, escorted by Jeroen and two guards. Frank could say the last rites over it, provided that he limited them to precisely five minutes; the mourners were not to attempt to linger but must return at once to the house. At Henk's request, another concession was made: he and Charles could accompany the cortège too and remain for the service. But no one else need apply.

A handful of hostages hurried into the parlor to watch from the window. Most of the first-class passengers, however, felt it more seemly to stay behind. "Eloise, sit down," Harold ordered. "What makes you want to rubberneck?" But Lily, armed with a clean handkerchief and wearing her black cashmere over her shoulders, refused to be deterred. "I think we should all mourn for him. It was so sad about his faith. I'm sure he got it back, though, in the watches of the night." Beryl raised her eyebrows but with a sigh she joined her mother, and gradually others followed till the gloomy little parlor was full.

Frank had left the Book of Common Prayer, marked with a red place-ribbon, so that those who wanted could take part in the service. After "I am the resurrection and the life, saith the Lord," he was going to use Psalm XXVII, "The Lord is my light and my salvation; whom then shall I fear?"—very appropriate—and lastly some verses from the fourteenth chapter of the Gospel of St. John, "In my Father's house are many mansions"—very appropriate too. He had timed the selections, pacing up and down: three minutes. That would leave room for the Lord's Prayer—some wondered about the tact of that— and the responses. He was fussed by not having his round collar and dickey with him for the occasion; they were at Schiphol still, in his suitcase.

They watched as the procession came round the end of the house: Carey and Henk as pallbearers carrying the body on their shoulders, followed by Charles and his walking-stick, and with Frank in the lead. The three terrorists stood on the sidelines, their weapons lowered. Despite them or perhaps because of them, it was very moving. Cameron opened the window a crack, and the voices of Henk and Carey could be heard chanting in Latin as they marched along, keeping step: *"Requiem aeternam dona ei Domine. . . ."* They had good strong voices, Henk's a pure tenor and Carey's a rich baritone. Then the voices faded. The body was set down on the open ground with not even a blanket to cover ·it; Frank made the sign of the cross and began to recite the Scriptures. He did not attempt to sing, and his voice was too broken to carry. But in the parlor they followed him, some looking on at the book and some reciting from memory. A few simply moved their lips or stood with bowed heads. They could tell when he came to the prayer because the group in the field knelt down by the body, but in the parlor, after a moment of indecision, everyone remained standing. In the doorway, Sophie—hesitant because of being Jewish, probably—finally joined in with the last "Amen."

When Cameron closed the window, most were in tears. Outside, the mourners were turning back to the house, no longer keeping step. Without the body to support and accompany, like an offering, their number seemed to dwindle, and they looked pathetic in those flat fields under the sad gray sky. The illusion they had given while the Bishop was with them of a band of early Christians chanting and professing their faith in the wilderness had vanished; the composition, so like a frieze, broke up, and they could be four hoboes, almost, unshaven, in unpressed suits, heading for shelter in a barn. It illustrated the value of ritual and the need for forms. There were no clods of earth to throw into the grave by way of farewell, because of course there was no grave. Frank had performed the regular burial service, which was the best he could do under the circumstances no doubt, but without grave or coffin this was like a mere sketch, a cartoon, of Christian burial.

Those remaining at the window watched Jeroen stride back to the house and tried to make out what the Arabs left behind were doing. In fact, the pair of them were packing the Bishop for shipment; using what looked like two large potato sacks, they were stuffing the white head and the shoulders into one and the feet into the other. By shaking the Bishop down, they made the sacks meet in the middle, around his waist; then they used another sack to truss the package up and they finished with some rope. During the shaking down, the Bishop's silver flask fell out and went into Yusuf's pocket. Finally, they shouldered their weapons and waited, scanning the sky. The helicopter was strangely slow in coming. There was a general move out of the parlor. Few had the stomach to stay and press Frank's hand, tell him "Very inspiring," and so on, or to witness the Bishop's ascent. Yet those who lingered at the window were rewarded in the end by a touching scene.

It was Sophie who first noticed the big dark bird hovering in the air, almost directly above the Bishop's remains. She grasped Henk's arm. "What is it?" "A gull?" suggested Lily. Henk shook his head. "A buzzard, I think." Carey crossed himself. "Not a vulture?" wondered Lily. "Only in zoos," said Henk. "But it's too *soon*," argued Frank. Henk shrugged. "Maybe. Look!" Another big dark bird, of the same family, had joined the first, hanging motionless with wings outspread. "Buzzards, all right," declared Cameron. "Twa corbies, eh? But it *is* too soon, man, for the creatures to sniff carrion." "They're waiting," said Henk. "He bled, Archie," Carey added. Johnnie reached for the field glasses. "Don't look!" cried Sophie, covering her eyes. "I can't bear it. They're going to strike!"

It must have appeared so to Ahmed, too, for, as they watched, he began to wave his short arms and thrash his body around to frighten the buzzards off. He was acting as a scarecrow to protect the Bishop. Except for the two motionless birds, the sky was empty. Below, far away, was the cordon of guardsmen. The only movement on the ground, as far as the eye could see, came from Ahmed, whirling and waving his arms. Yusuf stood by, doing nothing. Now the birds were turning in a circle above the body. Ahmed picked up a rock and threw it at them, then another. "Why in God's name doesn't he shoot them?" cried Frank. "Saving his ammo," said Carey. Ahmed was aiming another rock upward, with a motion like a baseball pitcher's, when the birds, as if coming to a decision, wheeled about and flew heavily away. The helicopter appeared. Perhaps it was the noise of its rotors and not the angelic Ahmed that had scared the buzzards off. Sophie burst into tears as though from relief and flung herself on Henk, fervently kissing him. Then, still crying, she kissed Jim and Lily. But it was sallow little Ahmed that they would have all liked to hug for showing simple respect for the dead. In their emotion, of course, they forgot the obvious fact that the Bishop would not *be* dead, bundled up in potato sacks and a prey to hideous scavengers, were it not for Ahmed and his ilk.

Eleven

He was just as glad, on the whole, not to figure in the batch of hostages scheduled for release today or tomorrow, depending. The Congress was still in recess; he had no wife waiting for him; the company here was congenial, and he was curious as to what would happen next. The release of the first lot hung on the delivery of the first consignment of paintings, which were presumably in transit, having left Dulles yesterday in the Dutch diplomatic pouch. Washington must have finally caved in, under the combined pressures of the Vatican, the World Council of Churches, the Archbishop of Canterbury, the Quakers, sundry ambassadors, and the hostages' well-heeled relatives. But nothing in this shifting world was certain; the "qualifying" hostages already eyeing their watches might be counting their chickens too soon. An amusing wrinkle would be if the carrier winging toward them with their El Grecos *et alii* were hijacked by professional mobsters.

Barring the unforeseen, however, a helicopter should arrive within the next twenty-four hours and unload the canvases. The hostages had already been warned that a careful inspection would follow, to determine that the paintings were genuine, corresponding anyway to attested photographs the relatives had been ordered to provide. If the inspection found nothing suspicious, the hostages would be permitted to embark. In short, an on-the-spot horse trade, transacted while the helicopter waited and the national guard looked on.

To give himself credit, Jim had surmised, fairly early, that this was the plan. It made sense. The exchange of flesh-and-blood hostages for painted images, eidola, had a number of advantages that the strategic genius of Jeroen would perceive. In the first place, eidola did not have to be fed. They would take up less space than their owners were doing, and they did not ask questions or require watching. With reasonable care, they would not fall sick. More important, upon their arrival the polder farmhouse would become impregnable. Any thought of taking it by storm in a pre-dawn raid would become unthinkable to the Dutch authorities, who otherwise might accept the risk to innocent lives entailed. After all, in investing a target, civilian casualties were largely unavoidable, viz., "We had to destroy the hamlet in order to save it." If a hostage or two got killed, it had to be seen in the perspective of the greater good of the greater number. But works of art were a different type of non-combatant, not to be touched with a ten-foot pole by any government respectful of "values." It was in the nature of civilians to die sooner or later, by preference in bed, but also in car crashes, earthquakes, air raids, and so on, while works of art by their nature and in principle were imperishable. In addition, they were irreplaceable, which could not be said of their owners. Once the paintings were here, Jim reckoned, the farmhouse would be safe as a church. Guards could almost be dispensed with; all the authorities needed to know was that within the walls a man was standing ready to activate a fuse.

Finally, the masterpieces would not only guarantee the security of the command post; they would be replacing their owners as hostages. Threats to execute one or all of them would have more powerful leverage than threats to execute one or all of the present company; the very notion of such an infamy would cause a thrill of horror to run round the civilized world. And Henk's unlucky prime minister would find himself in a worse fix than before. Inhibited from resorting to force to dislodge the barbarians, he would be reduced to begging, since what, realistically, did he have left to offer in a peaceful trade-off? Bombarded with ultimata by the enemy, he would be under crossfire from his own troops. On the one hand, he would be told to stand firm against "blackmail." On the other, if he showed undue Dutch stubbornness in the face of a menace to art, he would bear the brand of "philistine" writ in large letters across his socialist forehead; the entire circuit of Philistia would rise to apply the hot iron. The lesson to be derived—well understood by Jeroen—was that paintings were more sacrosanct than persons.

It had been short-sighted of the Dutch not to see that. The use of art as a weapon had been conceded by them to the *kapers* with no perception, seemingly, of the consequences. And yet there were recent precedents, just across the Channel, that should have been instructive—put a terrorist next to a work of art and you got an infernal new chemistry, as scarifying to "civilization" as the nuclear arm. But it had not occurred to The Hague, evidently, that the hijackers would insist that the paintings be flown to the polder. So far as could be judged from television, the reaction of official circles had been one of the purest surprise. But what had The Hague been expecting? To transfer them by armored truck to a New York bank vault in care of the Weatherman account?

The collectors, too, had been unprepared for the news that the paintings were coming here. For days they had been voicing puzzlement as to what the hijackers were going to "do" with their lovely things, as though the only function of a world-renowned painting was to enhance the furnishings of a drawing-room or proceed finally, through a tax write-off, to the wall of a museum, duly labeled "Potter bequest." That, Jim sup-posed, was immortality to them: a vision of future museum visitors bending to read a label. It had failed to penetrate, apparently, that art was negotiable tender; they were privileged indeed not to have seen their holdings in that cruel commercial light when every secretary knew that pictures were the soundest investment, a hedge against inflation, and so on. Even now, they had not quite grasped that the substitution of their "things" for themselves represented an immense improvement in the *kapers'* position. Instead, they were already worrying about where and how the paintings were going to be kept and pronouncing it "quite insane" of Jeroen to have dreamed of bringing them here, with no humidifiers, no curtains to be drawn against the sun, no proper thermostat to maintain an even temperature. And the poor little Potter woman was still busy wondering why she had not been allowed to die for her Vermeer, unable to accept the idea that any sane hijacker, given the slightest hope of ultimately laying hands on her canvas, would be satisfied to leave her her unrewarding life. Her case, in fact, suggested that it had probably not been necessary for all of them to make the tapes—at any rate not so precipitately.

Now most of the Croesuses would soon be going home, the Potter woman included. The withdrawal of the toilet privilege had done it; following on Gus's funeral, they had revoked Henry's too. When his wife learned that the stately old duffer had been forbidden to go outside with the other males, she had capitulated. Both were on today's list for release, which meant that the bruited Vermeer would be aboard the helicopter when it turned up. The Chadwicks, unfortunately, were remaining; dear Lily and Beryl, too, by way of compensation. The rumor was that these four would be in the second batch; there had been some question or mix-up about the delivery of their holdings.

Like him, Henk and Sophie were content to stay; they were looking forward to seeing the Vermeer unpacked. Jim was curious to see it himself, but he was looking forward more to simple peace and quiet and room to stretch his legs. There was also the fact that supplies were running low; Aileen had told Greet that they should ask for a food delivery as well, and Greet as always had been unreceptive to advice. Aileen said the prisoners should have a Suggestion Box, so that their ideas could get a fair hearing—hard to know whether she meant that seriously. In any case, with eight fewer mouths to feed, the strain on the larder would be somewhat relieved.

Rumor—in other words, their friendly Tupamaro—also had

it that tomorrow or the next day the Dutch airmen would be allowed to fly the German helicopter to freedom. If so, that would liberate the barn and reduce the total of hostages to thirteen—a manageable number, though Lily was superstitious about it. It looked as though the ransom money had been paid or promised. There had been no word of it on television; instead, the box had spoken of the expected release of some *"kabouters"* in accordance with Demand Three. It seemed clear that out in the busy world things were moving along nicely, so far, although Greet had voiced displeasure at the *kabouter* announcement. Those were middle-class elements, she said, calling themselves "goblins" and living in a childish fairy-tale of non-violent pranks; to release them was to violate both the spirit and the letter of the important third demand.

Still, the fact remained that eight hostages were fairly certain to be freed within the next hours, which showed that the government's concessions, by and large, were meeting the commando's requirements. Strictly speaking, half the number would have satisfied the terms. Old Charles and Warren and the two "boys" from Antibes had been thrown in as a gift, it would appear. Warren owned no art, and Eddie's collection consisted of erotic prints from near and distant lands—"just a *potpourri,*" he explained with a withered smile—while John's only holding was a collection of rare cookbooks. They were going to be set at liberty without any pretense of exacting a *quid pro quo*—an injustice keenly felt by Aileen. The case of Charles and his porcelains was slightly different; they were letting him go on his say-so, and now he was regretting it. "I'm hoist with my own petard, James," he lamented. "I should have dearly loved to stay on with your brave committee, like a rump parliament, to the bitter end. So short-sighted of me. But that gorgon won't hear of it. I don't eat much, I said to her, and my conversation is good value, they tell me. But no. I have made my bed and I must lie on it."

"James" would be sorry himself to see him go. It was a punishment prettily designed to fit the crime, for Charles, of course, had conned them: his porcelains, he had been confiding, were by no means as breakable as he had let on. These people had the art of punishment. It would "kill" Charles to leave now with his "whole" winter ruined, and to see himself separated from the anointed band of liberals seemed to be hurting the most. "Do I deserve to be sent packing with my millionaires, James? Well, I suppose I do. Yet I'd hoped there was a saving difference." Jim was noncommittal; he trusted there was a credit balance in the Recording Angel's books—Charles would have an account marked "Special." But, apart from the wound to his feelings, he was probably well out of this business. Whatever he believed, his age and sybaritic habits did not fit him for a long internment. And, insofar as the future was legible, that was surely what was in store for the communion of saints.

On that subject, "James" had come to have second thoughts. He could not see that the trumpeted arrival of the paintings was going to solve anything. A brilliant coup, a stroke of genius, whatever you liked, nevertheless, when and if it happened, it would be unproductive in terms of final ends. The bleat from the sheared sheep "What will they *do* with our beautiful things?" had merit, on reflection. Unless he planned to open a gallery in the barn, there was nothing Jeroen *could* do with all that art. Well, he could hold it for exchange. Jim had been pointing that out to himself and others as if it were a self-evident proposition, needing no demonstration. But the longer he pondered it, the less reasonable it appeared. Exchange against what, exactly?

Safe-conduct? But that was already assured. Money? But if they wanted money—beyond the "price" of the helicopter—it would have figured in their demands. Having chosen, in lieu of it, "priceless" works of art, they would hardly be satisfied at this point to convert them into packets of currency, however portable. Liberation of comrades in Israeli jails? No doubt they would be glad to see that but they must be aware that it was chimerical—they lacked what Aileen called the "*atouts.*" The fact that a gang in Holland was holding some art works was of no concern to the Israelis. It might be different if the people's army had got hold of the original Ark of the Covenant and Aaron's rod and phylacteries. No. It came down, unfortunately, to Demand Two. And Demand Two was non-negotiable. Den Uyl could not and would not take Holland out of NATO or break relations with Israel at the beck of a terrorist's will. And a demand of that type left no room for maneuver or compromise: offering to cut down the NATO forces by a quarter and being prepared to settle for a third; agreeing to reduce the Embassy staff in Tel Aviv over a period to be discussed. The Netherlands' foreign policy could not be turned around to suit a few gunmen by the present team at bat; that would require a whole new ballgame and some funny new uniforms. What Demand Two, in fact, implied was Jeroen's seizure of power. It would be interesting to know whether Jeroen himself understood that. Did he suppose he could build a power base on a single hijacking?

Jim strolled to the window and stood looking out. For a moment, he wondered whether he ought to discuss this with Henk. But that cheerful nature was already on record to the effect that Demand Two was "*pro forma.*" Jim shook his head. "Think again, Henk," he silently adjured. "Review the bidding and try to explain the pictures." Retracing the steps of his own reasoning, half-praying to find a false one, he arrived at the same starting-point: what end was served by bringing the pictures here? Well, they guaranteed the security of the command post; so far, that figured. It was demonstrable and would be demonstrated in the coming days. But reason could not rest there, although his own had been quite pleasantly doing that, like Aeneas in Dido's arms, till jarred, just now, by a doubt. Impregnability, my friend, he had told himself, was not an end in itself. It must serve an ulterior purpose. For the *kapers* to stay holed up here impregnably for an indefinite period argued a great aim in view.

Staring out at the improbable, man-made landscape, he chuckled. They were plump in the middle of Nowhere. A diverting vision appeared to him, of the polder as Jeroen's crazed kingdom, the farmhouse as his castle, his *feste Burg* (if it was not a sin to quote Luther), and the barn, hung with masterpieces, his royal picture gallery. He would be Lord of the Waters, and the committee would be his serfs, tilling the reclaimed land, making the sea floor bloom, maybe erecting a mountain or two, never to be manumitted, *et in saecula saeculorum.* They would breed, with each other and with their overlords, and produce the New Man. The fancy continued to tickle him, and he did not consider it altogether wide of the mark. Demand Two was irrational, and, if Jeroen did not know that, he was mad.

But would he be having the pictures flown to him, with another consignment to follow, unless he intended to persist in it? Otherwise, having achieved the majority of his ends, he would be calling for a plane to fly him and his cohorts and whatever trophies they desired to keep to an air-strip of his choice, there to prepare himself to strike again and yet again at the "system." Electing that scenario, he would become a hero and a legend and perhaps disappear eventually like Prester John into the African continent. Here he was, instead, resolutely painting himself into a corner, or so it looked, if the decision to return the NATO helicopter was a sign. He intended to dig in for the duration with a skeleton crew of hostages and stand firm on Demand Two. The pictures would make him that much more intractable. The fact of having obtained them against all likelihood, abetted by Providence in the shape of the Bishop's death, was apt to imbue him with a feeling of irresistible strength. The pictures were a misfortune, for unless he ceded sooner or later to the unbudging piece of Dutch reality represented by Mr. Owl, there was no way for this story to end.

Sophie held up a penny. He shook his head. "No sale." His thoughts were too queer and gloomy to worry her with yet. Time would tell, and the exercise of reason could lead a man astray. For example, he had been considering only Jeroen— the brain of the undertaking and *qua* brain transparent, like a chess opponent whose intentions are manifest though the power to counter them may be lacking. But there were seven others among the hijackers who might be developing intentions of their own.

Besides, Henk and Sophie were in love. Analyzing Jeroen and his eventual aims no longer excited them except as a game or pastime which they could take part in as a duet. Love gave them a shorter perspective: seize the day. He wished them well and would be happy for them when finally—today or tomorrow —there would be fewer onlookers. But there was no way for that story to end either. Henk was married; there was no chance here for them to be alone, and afterward an affair was unlikely. Jim could picture a single tryst—*ite missa est*—in a KLM-style twin-bedder in the airport hotel on the day release to real life took place. But of course Henk's wife would be meeting him. Now they could only touch hands as he lit her cigarettes, and he could take her arm on walks. No detail of this "tragedy" (actually an idyl) was missed by the chorus of sympathizers, which professed itself "sorriest" for Sophie, watching openly for her reaction when his wife appeared on television, noting the trembling of her hand when he held out fire for her True cigarettes. The spark that passed between them when their fingers met was likened by one of the chorus to the divine spark passing between God and Adam on the Sistine Chapel ceiling. "Probably friction from the rug," Jim suggested, although privately he did not doubt that the sexual electricity between two such handsome creatures, one at the grave pole of being, one at the merry, could be referred to God's creation.

He could marry Sophie when this was over. The idea had occurred to him, but he was not really tempted. He admired her aquiline beauty and sympathized with her tenseness; it would be a proof of loyalty to Henk and cement this experience. But he knew that he could never marry a journalist without asking her to give up her profession. He could not have a wife running around the world and exposing herself to danger while he sat reading the headlines in the Senate Office Building. A notoriously brave woman was a handicap to a political man. Yet during these last days his mind had been turning on marriage at least semi-seriously for the first time since Eleanor had died. Maybe it was a survival instinct: sketching out a future for himself with a woman by his side "tied him down" to having a future.

Strange as it might seem, he had been considering Lily. Any single man in public life, he guessed, had an occasional pipe-dream of marrying a rich widow. Jim did not blame himself for it, though he feared it sprang from his indolence. As a clever lazy war veteran, he might have had the makings of a fortune-hunter in him, had he not married young. Now, with Eleanor out of the way, he was a "catch," he discovered; his fan mail was replete with offers of marriage, filed under "Matrimonial," in the "Inactive" drawer. Though the thought recurred idly when he contemplated his campaign debts, he put it aside. The woods were full of available widows of inde-pendent means, but he could be thankful that his requirements were inordinate—God's grace, he reckoned, at work against the old Mammon. She would have to be pleasant to look at, with the hair color Nature gave her, pleasant-spoken—what his mother used to call a real lady—good company, capable of good works, no friend of the bottle and no enemy either, mature but not too old. There were few, if any, rich relicts answering to that description—St. Bridget of Sweden, who fitted (give or take a few visions), had passed on a long time ago. In short, it was a pipe-dream: Q.E.D. He indulged it, knowing the field: fund-raising dinners had taught him how little in deportment and personal attributes the rich had to offer and how much they demanded in the way of attention for the bounty of a four-figure check.

Yet here was Lily, who filled the bill on all counts and had the additional endearing attribute of being slightly absurd. At first sight he had typed her as an "older" woman, that is, beyond the age, but recently he had been trying to estimate how old she actually was. If you gave Beryl thirty-seven or possibly thirty-eight, then, assuming her mother had had her at the age of twenty, Lily would now be fifty-seven or fifty-eight, scarcely older than he was himself. And society buds in those days married early, so that she could have been eighteen, fresh from that social school of hers where they taught Dostoiev-sky along with riding-to-hounds, when she went to the altar (Episcopal)—which would make her nineteen when Beryl was born. Her skin was still fresh and smooth, except for a few perplexed lines across her pretty forehead; it was only the gray hair that put age on her, but he applauded her for not dyeing it, and, hell, his was nearly white. Nor was she a dim-wit, despite the initial impression. Her "inklings" were worth pay-ing heed to, as Henk, too, had observed—she had made quite a conquest of Henk. That her collector friends and her daughter rushed to correct her every time she opened her mouth with some dreamy suggestion was an argument for her intelligence. It sounded as if her associates had been sighing over her for years. He got the sense, too, that her collection was regarded as a triumph of taste over buying power, i.e., that she was not quite as moneyed as the rest of them—all to the good; he would not want to marry a great smelly fortune and its bodyguard of tax-dodging lawyers. The attraction Lily exercised on him could have something to do with his feeling for the weaker party in any confrontation of forces. In her group here, she was a minority needing defense in its right to be heard. Henk had the same reaction, natural in a democrat, if not in the *demos*. Which reminded him: in the event of their marrying, something would have to be done about that society accent, which would not go down at Grange suppers; an elocution teacher could see to it—the voice itself was a nice soprano. The only drawback was Beryl.

"Funny bunch, aren't they? What do you make of Lily?" "Why, I like her," answered Sophie, having duly weighed the question. "She's much the nicest of them, isn't she? Henk says she reminds him of some pale pink rose she described that isn't grown any more. Its name was Van F-l-e-e-t." Spelling that out seemed to please her. "I'll miss her and Beryl when they go. But of course they're another world. If we met them again in real life, we'd have nothing to say to each other, would we? Except about *this*. Perhaps we should hold reunions, like the press corps that served in Vietnam. But those things are always grisly—total flops. You've been through some experience together which gives you the sense that you have something in common. But when you meet again, you find that you've all reverted to type. The thing that held you together is gone, and you discover that you don't even have the same memories of it. It's better not to try, I think."

She was talking of herself and Henk, obviously. Jim lightly took her hand. "You don't agree with the Rev, then, that some of us can be changed by the opportunity we've been offered?" "He least of all." She laughed. "A few of us maybe *think* we've been altered. But we all have to revert. It's a law of nature. Like in the plant world, with the perennials going back to the original sick magenta. Frightening. Have you ever been to a college reunion? Or a veterans' reunion?" "I'm a politician," he said. "And I'll see *you* again, Sophie." "That's different. We have a *reason* to see each other. We work the same side of the street. It's not a complete accident that we were on the plane together. Your being on that committee was pretty much why I came along. I always wanted to know you. But the rest is fortuitous, mainly. We've been thrown together like marbles shaken in a bag." "And yet connections came to light," he suggested. "You knew Beryl. Beryl knew Aileen. Charles knew Henk's grandfather. And I knew *of* Henk." "You *researched* him," teased Sophie. "I wish I could read his poetry, don't you?" "You could learn Dutch," he said. "When you know German, it's not hard. I find I understand quite a bit."

Sophie smiled. "Remember *'haast hebben'*?" She was dreamy —her first words of Dutch "taking her back," like a yellowed dance program. Then her tone changed. "You never learn a language unless you use it. Anyway, the committee's a unit. And the millionaires are another. Oil and water. I think we deserve credit for having mixed as well as we have. That's Henk, mainly, on our side, and Lily, I suppose, on theirs. They've both been well brought up. But Lily in real life would be unbearably conventional, wouldn't she? Otherwise why would Beryl have declared a revolution?" She had touched on a vital point. "I prefer Lily," he said shortly. "Well, I've

303

known Beryl longer," said Sophie. "But I admit I wouldn't seek her out as a friend. She has no real interests, that's her trouble. Having been brought up in an arch-Republican family, she's rebelled by being totally a-political. And she hates art and books; Lily's a great reader, it seems." Jim pricked up his ears but he only remarked: "Arch-Republican? I should have thought of Lily as a swing-voter." "You know what Henk says?" Sophie went on. "That they're the common-law criminals —the millionaires, I mean—and we're the politicals. Do you see?"

Jim saw indeed. It was an interesting idea. On the model of a Soviet labor camp, the common-law criminals—murderers, thieves, and such—would be serving short sentences, while the political offenders would be in for long stretches, often till their health broke, or in dire cases, like the poet Mandelstam's, till death intervened. In the scales of "people's justice" as weighed out here on the polder, a similar distinction seemed to apply. The millionaires—ordinary pickpockets and highway robbers—would be going home, having paid for their crimes. But conditions for the committee's release, individually or as a unit, had never been "aired" in any communiqué that had reached their ears. Not a *quid* or a *quo* vouchsafed. From time to time, their likenesses appeared on the screen—always Henk and himself—accompanied by the comment "So far as is known, the deputy [or the Senator] is still alive." As in the Gulag, a blanket of silence covered the politicals' fate; for all the world knew, they could in fact be dead. Confronting himself over and over on the screen—mainly on the '68 campaign trail, preaching to the unconverted, suffering the little children— Jim got the eerie feeling that he *had* died, at any rate politically, some time back and was watching the pages of a memorial album turn.

When the collectors were gone, it might be the committee's turn finally to learn what they must give—or see given *for* them—in exchange for their freedom. But the itch to know in Jim's case was far from overwhelming. He feared he could guess. Would their release in fact hang on Demand Two? If

Henk was right, it would be artistically appropriate—meet and just in the *kapers'* eyes—for the fate of the "politicals" to be sewed up with that demand, political as a stick of dynamite. Moreover, like Charles's banishment, it would constitute a punishment suited to the crime. Their crime as liberals—he believed he could confess for all—was, *primo*, to support the Atlantic Pact. Critically, and with this or that reservation, nevertheless, *grosso modo*, they were for the "shield." *Secundo*, they were for the survival of the Jewish state; any reservations they had put on record as to Israel's policies could be shown to stem from the belief that her current behavior was suicidal. To be instrumental in the dismantling of NATO and the ostracism of Israel would be a torture worthy of SAVAK. Perhaps, like the Potter lady with her picture, most of them would rather die than stand by as helpless spectators while such a deal was arrived at in their interest.

Jim pulled himself up short. That would never happen. There was no cause to fear it. But what if constraint were put on them to make a bunch of tapes urging the acceptance of the second demand? That could be in the cards. And what would he do if "invited" to make a tape? An uneasiness took hold of him as he foresaw the argument that might edge him into consenting. It was what he had just told himself for the *n*th time: that Demand Two was unacceptable. Whatever pleas the eminent hostages might make, Den Uyl and his Cabinet would have to stand firm, stoppering their ears like the sailors of Ulysses. Hence it could do no harm to make a tape. He was *free* to make a tape, in all good conscience, at the bidding of his own intelligence, which reminded him that a hundred tapes could not alter the outcome. So then? His uneasiness only grew deeper. Something in him was opposed to making a tape—perhaps the old Christian yearning for martyrdom or just an addiction to truth-telling. He was wary, with reason, of his brain. Not that it misled him; its assessments were generally dead-right. It was not clouded by self-interest or prone to "rationalization." But it had deterred him, too often, from action by showing him the futility of it. That had happened after Wisconsin. Now it could prompt him to *embark* on an action by the same type of demonstration. He might allow himself to do a distasteful, base thing secure in the private knowledge that it could have no effect. The operative word was "base." It was an ordinary matter of honor. He guessed that an honorable act—or abstention from action—was always needless, wasteful, uncalled for. The requirements of honor had to buck the assessments of intelligence. And in James Augustine Carey, he acknowledged, laziness and intelligence could be accomplices. The easiest thing would be to make the tape.

.

They were finishing lunch when the pictures came. In custom-made flat wooden cases that fitted their dimensions and were going to be a job to open. In the shed, the hijackers went to work on them with hammers and pliers, and Ahmed promptly smashed his thumb, reopening the six-day-old wound. Chadwick's offer to help had been turned down, but he was allowed to stand around kibitzing. As on the first night, revolutionary discipline had relaxed; the collectors wandered in and out of the shed, expressing anxiety over the paintings that were no longer theirs. They were anxious, more selfishly, over the slow progress of the uncrating; by the time the pictures were vetted, the sun might have set, and the pilot of this helicopter did not want to take off in the dark.

The first case to be opened produced a surprise. The picture that was emerging, to Jim's inexpert eye, did not look like an Old Master. In fact, it was a good-sized Cézanne. Soon Harold's Cézannes, all eight of them, were sharing wall space with a kiddy-car and the family bicycles. Someone had blundered. But they were carried into the family room and stacked against the wall; Harold set them up, one by one, in front of the TV set to be looked at. "Of course you're seeing them without reflectors," he explained. To Jim, they looked like every Cézanne he had ever seen, only more so: there were the apples, Mrs. Cézanne, that mountain near Aix, pine trees with red bark growing in red earth, some pears with more apples and a white pitcher, the card-players, and what Harold said were the first oils of "The Bathers." Jim glanced at Lily. The feeling he was getting of *déjà vu* made him wonder whether they were not high-class copies—had Harold been stung or had that lawyer of his pulled a fast one? She read his thought. "Rather standard, aren't they? But he's not an adventurous collector. You'd almost doubt they were real, they're so 'classic,' so much what one's conditioned to expect. But they are, you know. You see how the paint is laid on, very characteristic. Dear, clumsy Cézanne." "Couldn't draw, of course," boomed Margaret. "Look at that arm." She pointed to a nude figure among the bathers. "Completely out of drawing." Jim was impressed.

A large envelope containing documentation had come with the shipment. Jeroen took a long time studying the photos and transparencies and comparing them with the paintings. While this was happening, a number of the hostages, Jim himself and Lily included, returned to the shed. They were in time to see a long narrow painting of a horse race unpacked. Jim would not have recognized it as a Degas. "Oh, yes," said Lily. "He did a great many of those. I believe he was mad about racing. Lovely, isn't it? Johnnie has an eye. Do you think that's Long-champ—see the stand there? Or did it exist in his time?" "I can't tell you, Lily," said Jim. "I only know Aqueduct." "That's a joke, isn't it?" "Yes." There followed a huge landscape with precipitous gray cliffs and a sunlit meadow below on which sheep, very small, were grazing. "The Ward," Lily said. "Nearly as grand as the one in the Tate." "I like it," said Jim. "Notice the waterfall?" Then came an artist he recognized—Winslow Homer—and another—Dufy—and half a dozen "sporting" subjects: stags locking horns, a lion and a tiger fighting, two boxers in a ring, an archery contest, a horse in a stable with a groom and a cat—Stubbs, said Lily—a game of horseshoes, a horse market at a country fair. "Thomas Hardy," said Jim. "Oh, no, I don't *think* so," said Lily. "Maybe a Morland. Oh, I see, you mean *Hardy*. Yes. *The Mayor of Casterbridge*." That was a good recovery, he thought. He frowned. "What the hell is this one?" Lily put on her glasses and bent down. "That must be a mistake. It's a print. Not very old either. 'Elephants Wading,' it says." "Where's the tie-in with sport?" "I don't really know, Jim. Johnnie's idea of sport can be rather all-embracing. Still, in India, in the old days, didn't the rajahs hunt elephants? I seem to remember that." He saw that if he stuck with this lady he was going to learn a good deal.

Jeroen meanwhile had declared himself satisfied with the Cézannes. The inspection of Johnnie's works was more cursory, to the point of offending Johnnie, who stood by, eager to show the provenances and present photos for comparison. Jeroen, he complained, should not be approving them in bulk like a job lot. The Stubbs Arabian, for instance, would repay examination—the market these days was full of journeyman "Gimcracks" and "Herods" being offered as Stubbses. "Well, I oughtn't to blame him. You have to remember that until recently sporting art was put below the salt—a reaction against Landseer and good old Rosa Bonheur. I was a pioneer, along with Mellon, when I started my collection." "Mellon?" Jim queried. "Paul," Lily whispered. Johnnie was continuing. "People thought those things had no standing as art, belonged in a club or a trophy room. All that's changed, thanks, if I may say it, to my labors."

"He gives this talk," Lily explained softly, "whenever he shows his collection." "Shut up, Ma," said Beryl. Johnnie raced on regardless; he needed no spurring. "I've promoted it with the serious investor the way I would a stock, commissioned monographs, underwritten college lectures. I'm offering my alma mater a Ramsbotham Chair in the Visual History of Sport. The result is, we're beginning to see fakes—the surest sign, of course, of the impetus we've given. Up to now though —here's the funny bit—we've had no success in interesting the collector crowd in dog subjects. Nobody wants dogs except as accessories in a conversation piece or a fox-hunting scene. Though there were many fine artists once upon a time who made a pile in dog portraits. Take old Maud Earl. How do you explain that?" No one had a suggestion. His "job lot" was consigned to the parlor, and he was a free man, cleared for take-off as soon as the rest were ready.

Henry's Titian—a man in black armor—also passed muster. There remained several smallish cases. "Those are Margaret's things, I suppose," Lily said. "Though I remembered the Greco as bigger." When the cases were pried open, a cry rang out. "My Marie Laurencins! Oh, shit, Chaddie, what have those horse's asses done?" There were six of them, and one much like the next: the same doe-eyed misty maidens that Jim recalled from his early days. They were easy to like. In fact, when he was young, Marie Laurencin had been his favorite modern painter. He guessed that was because he had always been able to spot her, like a Stutz Bearcat. He had liked Redon and Rouault for the same reason. But from Lily's little cluck of disappointment, he judged that the artist had "dated."

Margaret's art had been left behind somehow. A quick check with the pilot confirmed that it had not been sent on from Dulles —so far as he knew. Evidently the signals had got crossed: Chadwick's Cézannes had been meant to come in the next shipment, and Eloise's Laurencins had not been meant to come at all. It was reassuring in a way to see that life among the terrorists was just as liable to foul-ups as normal government activity on Capitol Hill. But the alarming discovery was that the Vermeer was missing too. It was definitely not in the helicopter; to satisfy Jeroen, Ahmed and Carlos went out and searched, though there was no place it could be hiding.

Jeroen was angry. For the first time, he let his displeasure show. He did not appear to mind so much about Margaret's stuff; it was the Vermeer that his heart had been set on. He shouted that there was a plot among the imperialists to hold it back. In reply, he was canceling all departures. The helicopter would return empty. "Carlos, tell the pilot he should go." The moment, plainly, was critical. The collectors cowered before the vengeful giant, as if before their eyes he had turned into a cruel ogre. The whole crowd was looking to Henk, as if trusting him to mediate. But abruptly Greet intervened, playing, for her, the unusual role of pacifier. She spoke with Jeroen in

Dutch. "She reminds him of the food supply," whispered Henk. They debated. At length Jeroen squared his shoulders, accepting, it seemed, her arguments. "You will go now as promised," Greet announced. "The armed proletariat keeps its word." The Chadwick couple, she said, would replace Helen and Margaret, the total remaining at eight. There could be no question of letting Henry remain behind. "You are to tell the imperialists that this is our last concession. We will tolerate no more delays and evasions."

The sun was setting when they boarded, for first they had to undergo a search, pronounced very humiliating by Eloise, who had been stripped by Greet and Elfride. The point of the search was not clear to those remaining. "Pure sadism" was Aileen's verdict. To prevent the smuggling out of information, Henk thought—a plan of the house, for example, with some indication of the wiring system. Jim could not see that. The collector group on its own was capable of drawing a plan, describing the sleeping arrangements, guessing at the location of the fuse-box, and so on. Henk shook his head. Of the eight that had been freed, only Charles, he reasoned, had wit enough to provide useful information, and Charles would have an over-supply of it, very apt to mystify the authorities. "No, Jim. Our *kapers* are fearful only of you and me. They look on us two as their peers. '*Weerga,*' we say." In his belief, the *kapers* feared that he and Jim, between them, might contrive to send the authorities not only plans and diagrams but political counsel—advice on the timing of an attack, analysis of the leadership structure of the commando, recommendations on negotiating tactics. . . . "Inscribed on the head of a pin?" Jim inquired.

It was true that, in their place, Jeroen would have been doing just about that. Taping tiny spills of paper covered with writing —doubtless in code—to Eloise's underwear. But he himself had not once thought of spiriting out a message of any sort, let alone one of a para-military nature. Nor, evidently, had Henk. There was no need of messages, written or oral. The returning hostages would report that their fellow-captives when last seen were alive and well, which was all that mattered to the families. More significant for the authorities, they would report that Gus had died a natural death. As for hints on negotiation, Jim had none to offer; in the last hours he had come to see the situation as hopeless, barring, as ever, a miracle. Jeroen had moved into a no-win position and apparently did not know it. And if Henk had a clever formula in mind for breaking out of the deadlock, he would have mentioned it. There was no information lying around here that could not be transmitted by direct word of mouth. Aileen must be right; pure sadism was the explanation. Or else it was something the *kapers* read in a terrorist's handbook: frisk captives prior to release.

Jim was struck, though, by the notion—which had not occurred to him—that the *kapers*, i.e., Jeroen, regarded them as their peers. If it meant simply that on both sides there was a sound sense of power and its leverage—Jeroen a gifted tyro and Henk and himself old adepts—the idea, though novel, was not especially interesting. But it could imply something else: a mutual recognition. That tied in with a thought he had been pursuing—till interrupted by the arrival of the pictures—that the situation of a terrorist in terms of achievement of ends was hopelessly circumscribed. He was limited by the *status quo ante* that in principle he was setting out to topple. People liked to say that terrorism "could not really change anything." And unfortunately that was the fact. The demands it was able to see satisfied were demands in keeping with the established value system: turnover of money or equivalent goods, supply of transport, distribution of food to the poor. Even the freeing of the occasional "class-war prisoner" fell considerably short of amnesty and was more like parole; the liberated comrade nine times out of ten was promptly re-arrested, on suspicion of recidivism, i.e., on sight. The same with safe-conduct; it saw the undesirables safely out of the country, at which point they became fugitives with a price on their heads, obliged to take cover in semi-friendly countries where as terrorists they found no employment. All in all, an unprofitable exercise of juvenile energy and imagination. And yet they kept trying.

But what had his own career of bucking the system netted in the long run? A few immediate gains compatible with the *status quo ante* and no fundamental change. He could claim the fall of Johnson and the tempering of the war in Vietnam. But the fall of Johnson had eventuated in Nixon (which had to figure as a debit), and the war in Vietnam would have been winding down anyway. The establishment dipped into its provident fund and gave what it would not feel the loss of to dissent burning its draft card. He had been as much of a millennialist in his hopes as any "misguided" terrorist. Observing that, he laughed, feeling a real fondness for Jeroen. What Greet liked to call the armed politics of the underground—their euphemism, he guessed, for terror—was only the kid brother of minority electoral politics, with the same old Achilles heel.

Coming out of his abstraction, Jim looked around him. Night had fallen, and they were alone with the paintings. Mrs. Cézanne in a blue apron was propped against the TV set, and the Titian "Gentleman in Armor" was opposite, behind the davenport. The ever-silent Yusuf was on guard. Contrary to expectations, the house felt lonely. Maybe Harold was right that the paintings needed reflectors, for the longer Jim stared at them, the more disappointing they seemed. Longer acquaintance was not helping him to see "new treasures" in any of these canvases, as Lily had promised him it would. The contrary, almost, was true. Probably a trained eye was required. He was relieved anyhow that the Marie Laurencins had been sent back to the shed. Johnnie's collection, stacked up in the parlor, he found the most rewarding. There was something to look at in those pictures beyond pictorial "values"; some of them even told a story, or you could make a story out of them, and the animals were great, particularly the "Stags Fighting." He also liked the fact that, as far as he could judge, the horse in the Stubbs, though a breed you did not see now, had its bones and muscles in the right places—Lily said Stubbs had written a book on the anatomy of the horse. By contrast, he was more and more bothered by that arm on one of the "Bathers"; he wished

Margaret had never mentioned that it was "out of drawing," for now he could see that himself; in fact it was the only thing he *could* see in the picture.

He had no doubt that he was reacting like a philistine, like the two Dutch pilots, who seemed to be made highly uncomfortable by the pictures, walking up to study them with heavily knit brows, shaking their heads and turning away, then drifting back, unable to resist having another look. Like him, the pilots were more at ease with Johnnie's pictures. Not Yusuf, though. It occurred to Jim, measuring Yusuf's inflexible frown, that he was asking himself whether the chief had not gone loco.

Art had a disquieting power of producing social embarrassment; Jim was familiar with the symptoms in Eleanor. In museums he had noticed that it caused people to make silly remarks and then laugh self-consciously, as if the pictures, which knew better, could hear them. It could not be just ignorance; displays of armor and mummies and natural-history exhibits did not have that effect. And even he was prone to it, for all his self-possession. If you were alone with art long enough, as here—or when he used to wait for a girl he knew on a bench in front of "An Old Woman Cutting her Nails"— you began to get the feeling that it was looking right at you. Like the reproduction in his grandmother's parlor of a trick painting of Jesus whose sorrowing eyes seemed to follow you: the Hound of Heaven. Lily said there was a room in Mantua with a frescoed horse whose eyes moved when you did. Jim had missed that—and a lot else—in Virgil's burg while wandering along the Mincio with the Ninth Bucolic in hand: *"qua se subducere colles incipiunt."* Fortunately, anyhow, he did not sense the apples eyeing him—what worried him there was that he could not find anything especially clumsy in the way they were painted.

All these ghostly and somehow demanding presences were unnerving in the quiet house. It would be better when Mrs. Cézanne was replaced by the seven o'clock news—live. He found it impossible to ignore them, though, according to Beryl, that was what collectors did. "They hardly ever look at them.

Ask Mother." There was some truth in that, Lily admitted. One of the boons, then, of being a collector was that you felt at home with art to the point of not noticing its presence; it was just part of the furniture.

"If you don't look at the stuff you own, what gives you the right to have it?" Victor. The paintings must have been getting at that touchy customer too. With his sprouting beard and blackheads and the boils on his neck, he looked noisome, as if he were coming to a head; during exercise, he had been playing with the rabbits, and he had rabbit hairs all over him. "The rest of the race isn't all that jaded." "One isn't 'jaded,' Victor," said Lily. "I think one's constantly aware of one's beautiful things—what's the word?—subliminally." "But tell us something," demanded Aileen, whose hackles were also up. "What do you gain as a person by living with your 'beautiful things'? Has it made you any different? Would it make Jim and me any different? Can you pretend that any of that beauty has rubbed off on Harold and Eloise? Why, Harold could be a museum guard, for all the good that being exposed to Cézanne has done him." "Harold's rather a new collector," observed Lily. "And Morgan and Frick?" "But is art meant to be morally improving?" objected Sophie. "Think of Goering." "Well, leave out morals for the moment," Aileen agreed. "Show me *any* result. Really, having been with this tour of yours for a week now, I wonder. . . . I can't see what this vaunted ownership has done for you. Well, all right, there's Charles. I guess it's made him kinkier than he might have been." "They don't claim to be art authorities or scholars, Aileen," Sophie said. "Art authorities would be worse," said Beryl. "Poor Ma's just having fun."

"So art gives pleasure to man, can we agree on that?" said Frank. "It's like God's own delight in His Creation." Lily nodded. "Genesis. 'And, behold, it was very good.' I often think about that." "Come off it," Victor retorted. "Is that why they take schoolchildren to museums? Stop dodging the issue, you folks. We all know in our gut that art educates. In other societies, they're aware of the power it has of speaking directly to the masses, teaching them to be better socialists, better citizens. The trouble is that with us it's fallen into the wrong hands. Forget the speculators. I mean you proud possessors that claim to have a corner in it. This isn't the eighteenth century. The concept of the collector is so rotten by now that it stinks. Why, Yusuf here instinctively has a better appreciation of those apples than all your museum boards. Cézanne painted for *him*; he's been hungry and knows what an apple means." All eyes turned inquiringly on Yusuf, whose scowling features betrayed no interest even in hearing his name. "I want to get this on record," Victor went on excitedly, raising his thin voice and striking his fist into his palm. "In my considered belief, Jeroen and Greet had a great idea in liberating these pictures from their plushy jailers. The more I've seen and heard here, the more I salute them for that."

This harangue, coming from that quarter, caused less of a stir than Victor had probably hoped. "Has he been drinking? Where did he get it?" Aileen whispered. "Why, the man's a common agitator," Margaret exclaimed, not deigning to lower her voice. "Kind of an *un*common agitator," Jim said, behind his hand, to Henk. Lily had overheard. "How interesting that you say that," she murmured. "Why interesting, Lily?" "Well, I don't like to say it, but I had a little theory of my own." "Oh?" They moved behind the TV set. "I rather thought, Jim, that he might be connected with—well, with certain initials. . . ." "You mean—?" She meant CIA.

"What made you think that?" "Oh, little things. He seemed different from the rest of your committee. As if he didn't quite belong. None of you knew him before. Then that mushroom look he has. The man from underground. I don't mean to be snobbish. There are a number of well-connected, brainy men in that organization. In fact, Beryl and I have letters to one in Teheran—a cousin of a cousin. He's quite out in the open, attached to the Embassy. But this cousin said that Teheran was *full* of them, open and not so open. They have a kind of investment in the Shah. That made me wonder, too. Then I couldn't help noticing that Victor drank more than was good for him.

They say that's a characteristic of agents. The strain of the life they lead. The constant deception . . . But of course none of that's *proof*."

"No." He pondered. "Have you mentioned this to Beryl?" "Surely not. She'd laugh at me." "Well, don't. I've no more knowledge than you have, Lily, but if what you think is true and word of it gets to the Committee of Public Safety here, well, we could witness a real execution. Or if it isn't true, for that matter." But it *was* true, he felt confident, and it alarmed him for Victor that Lily should have spotted it. His own case was different; he was a pro. It had become evident to him, some time back, that Victor must be an agent. He had all the earmarks. Starting with the cover: half the university specialists traveling around on grants in the Middle East were working part-time or full-time for the Agency. Jim had nothing against that; as long as they confined themselves to information-gathering, they served some sort of purpose. Moreover, it stood to reason that the CIA would try to plant a man of its own on the committee, to observe and report back via the Embassy cableroom or maybe even to obstruct the committee in its work. As far as that went, Cameron could be an MI-5 plant, although Jim doubted it. Britain's interests were not so tied to the Shah, and Archie appeared to be what he seemed: a burry don with no secret drawers about him. Jim doubted, too, that either of them would have been reporting directly to SAVAK, which would have made for an interesting time in the Shah's country, almost as lively as a hijacking. In any case, the hijacking had made the entire question immaterial. Jim had mentioned his thought to Henk, he could not remember when—while they were still at Schiphol, he believed—in confidence, naturally, on a no-action basis. The cat by then had died, and Victor, they agreed, was at present more to be pitied than subjected to any form of ostracism. They had not spoken of it again.

But that outburst, just now, was troubling. If he was trying to curry favor with the people's army—which was certainly what it had sounded like, given the raised voice—Victor must be in a bad state. Somehow, presumably, he must have come to fear that his captors were going to get wind of the CIA link-up. Jim knew how such a fear could grow in a nervous mind; he had clients like Victor years ago when he was still practicing law. Every day that passed, far from calming him, would appear to increase the danger. And he had no one to share his worry with, no one to laugh him out of it, show him that it lacked any basis in reality. . . . Or did it? "Wait a minute, Carey," Jim said to himself. Victor might have reason. That college where he taught in upstate New York might be swarming with envious colleagues only too eager to denounce him to the nearest "underground" news sheet—Jim doubted that Victor was very popular. And a story like that could be picked up and sent merrily out on the waves by an early-morning newscaster who found himself short of hijacking copy. From that point on, world-wide diffusion would depend on the conscience of journalism, often pretty elastic. Anything damaging to the CIA was considered newsworthy these days, whoever got hurt in the process. Hell, the revelation, duly supplemented by CIA denials, could have been carried *already* by the news services. "Over" then to Radio Moscow, and back to Ostberliner Rundfunk, coming home to roost finally on the *kapers'* short-wave aerial, crowing like the Pathé cock.

Jim's imagination, he observed, was quite equal to supplying extra fuel to Victor's, should it stand in need of it. And he had no difficulty in picturing the sequel: the "trial," the confession, the sentence, the bullet-plugged body dumped in the field without benefit of funeral service. The only question was, would poor old Victor have the stamina to wait to be accused? Unable to stand the suspense, he might decide to anticipate the workings of revolutionary justice and accuse himself, claiming to have been "re-educated" by his current experiences. That way, he might hope to be pardoned, though Jim, in his place, would not be too sanguine. To maintain credibility, the *kapers* needed another execution.

As he glanced at Victor, pale and silent, squatting by the sofa, his arms wrapped around his chest, Jim was feeling sympathetic vibrations. What had been passing through his mind was a troop of mere possibilities, but the possible by definition was a thing that was capable of happening. The idea suddenly gripped him that he would have to save Victor. He did not know who or what had made him Victor's keeper. Perhaps it was a caprice—the old bottom-dog business—or Victor's increasing resemblance to a bum calling out the Salvation Army in him. Or his obligation as a senator to a putative federal employee. Anyhow something would have to be done to rescue Victor from the fear he was in, before he did something on his own that was bound to be ill judged.

If only there were some way of getting him out of here . . . That was the best hope. Invalided out maybe? On the next departing whirlybird. He asked himself whether Victor was capable of playing sick. He looked sick enough already—doubtless because of bad conscience and attendant lack of sleep. He was a hysterical type, certainly, and that type was gifted at working up symptoms. With a short inner laugh Jim pictured Victor receiving the stigmata. But of course nothing could be done without his cooperation. Jim sighed. He had no choice but to be frank with him, confront him with his guilty secret or—correction needed—the secret Jim was imputing to him. And if he denied having any problem? Or wept and playacted while admitting it? Jim was not in a mood for dramatics.

To his relief, Victor came clean almost from the start. It was as though he had been hoping that Jim would confess him. "Apologies, Senator, for that goofed-up performance. I figured you'd understand. I was trying to plant the idea that I was getting ready to defect to their side. I thought that if I seemed to be willing to serve in their ranks, they might figure that there was a lot of information I could pass on." He raised his eyes, forcing Jim to meet his look. "Actually, I don't know a damn thing. I only had the one contact, the same one I met every time. You knew right away, didn't you?"

"No. Not right away. I expected there might be a Spook with us but I hadn't yet settled on you. The cat threw me off."

"Funny. I thought you knew that first morning on the plane.

318

When you made friends with Sapphire. I decided you were trying to show me you were sorry for me, didn't blame me too much. You're a tolerant guy, Senator." "I'm an indifferent man, Victor. That's my secret. Enough of these boyish confidences. What we want is an action plan. These folks aren't indifferent. Before anything rough happens, you and I have to get you out of here. Do you know how to fake a temperature?"

Victor did, and he could make his pulse race. At once he was full of energy. "When shall we start? Shall I stretch out on the floor now?" Jim interposed a caution. "Let's not tip our hand too soon. We don't want Greet giving you a thorough physical tonight." For the time being, he proposed, Victor should merely let it be known that he was not feeling too well and wanted to be left alone. Victor nodded. "Then tomorrow I can suddenly be worse." "Tomorrow *morning*?" Victor was racing his engine. They ought to be careful with their timing. Victor should not have to play sick for too long; he was not a convincing actor, judging by the recent performance, and it might overtax his abilities to keep up the pretense. "Let's aim to find out, first, when our pilots are slated to go." The acute phase, if Victor could manage it, should be arranged to coincide, as if providentially, with a helicopter waiting in the wings. "But I already know that," said Victor. "Tomorrow. Carlos said so. They're just waiting to clear the flight landing with the Germans in Aachen."

Tomorrow morning, then, Jim agreed. "Denise can take your temperature and report it to Greet. She'll examine you and order the Royal Air Force to take you aboard. And she won't waste much time in the process. Hell, you might have a contagious disease." The promise of action—*any* action—was enlivening. But Victor, all at once, before he had even started, developed cold feet. A discouraging personality: Jim wondered how the Agency had managed him, but they had experience with unstable types. "Maybe it's too soon, Senator," he argued. "We don't *know* that Dirk and Pieter will be shipping out tomorrow." "We don't. But you just said that we had good reason to think it. And you'll have to be ready to get onstage with your act." Their roles had reversed in the course of a half-hour; Jim was impatient to begin, and Victor was hanging back. "I'm afraid, Senator." "Fine. Let's see your teeth chatter. But don't overdo it for now." Victor lay down on the floor. "I need a bar of soap."

Jim laughed aloud. It was the old army game, popular with draft dodgers till the medics caught on; it had been used in the Navy too, he acknowledged, by scared young pilots hoping to duck out of a mission. A bar of soap was placed in the arm-pit, secured, usually, by adhesive tape; he had never understood the chemistry of it, but in a few hours the body temperature went way up. "How long will you need to have it there?" "Two or three hours. All night will be OK." "Can you manage with-out the adhesive?" Victor thought he could if he did not move around much. "But can't you pinch some from Denise's kit?" he wondered. "Better not, my friend, if you think you can get along without it. Adhesive leaves marks." "They come off with ether." "No." Jim was enjoying himself and he was sorry to see his confederate lapse so readily into a state of total depend-ency. He did not even have soap of his own. Jim passed him a fair-sized bar of Ivory in a Statler Hotel wrapping from his inactive shaving kit. "Laundry soap would be better," said Victor. "Well, you'll have to make do with what's available. Be grateful it isn't Camay."

During the night a hand tugged at him. "Senator?" "What is it, Victor?" "Don't you want to try it yourself? That way, we could be shipped out together." "No. Nice of you to think of it. But two would tax credibility." "Well, you could leave me here." Jim wondered whether he meant that. "Thank you, Victor, but I'm in no special danger that I know of. You're a case all to yourself. Say, what about the pulse?" "Oh. Well, I'd need pepper for that. A *lot* of pepper. I don't see how we could get any. They never give us pepper." "Well, forget it. When Greet comes to examine you, you won't need pepper to make your pulse race." "That's true." It was good to know, at any rate, that Victor had some respect for limits: he could have proposed that Jim raid the kitchen for him. Essaying to fall asleep again, Jim set himself the puzzle of what war Victor had dodged—too young for Korea, too old for Vietnam. Korea, he concluded.

"Do you mind if we talk a little?" Reluctantly, Jim moved nearer, renouncing sleep for a second time. "I want to tell you something. Jim—do you mind if I call you that? My mission in Iran. I was only going to report back to the Agency. I couldn't see how that could hurt your committee. You were going to hold a press conference anyway." Not in Teheran, brother, Jim observed to himself. But he let Victor go on. "You won't believe it, but I *identified* with your committee. I would never have agreed to sabotage what it was trying to do. Like this afternoon. I really hold to what I said about art. I came on strong because I meant it. On that one point, I share the hijackers' credo. It just so happened that I was able to play up to them without compromising my integrity." In the darkness Jim grimaced. "Maybe you *ought* to defect, Victor."

Victor's voice brightened. "Do you think so? It's true that underneath I have an ambivalence about them. But I'd never really fit in. They'd never really accept me." "Victor, the Apostate." "Why do you have to mock, Jim? It's been so fatal to you as a leader. And you're better than that. But I want to go back to what I started to say. When I took the assignment to work my way into your committee, it didn't feel right to me. I can confess that now. I didn't see the harm in it, but it rubbed me the wrong way. Sailing under false colors with a group like yours that I respected. You don't know it, but I'm a scholar in my field. I met Aileen once at a scholarly gathering, though she doesn't remember it. But there was the free trip to Iran, where I could brush up on my subject in my spare time, and then there was the chance of associating with you people on equal terms. . . . Well, you know how it is."

"You were tempted," agreed Jim. "But my conscience must have bothered me finally. Over Christmas, I did some heavy

321

drinking, and, like a lot of compulsive drinkers, I have an allergy to alcohol. I can't handle it. Well, you know what happened. I blacked out in my hotel room and if it hadn't been for Sapphire I would have missed the plane at Kennedy." That detail was new to Jim. "Yes. My unconscious must have wanted me to miss it. Anyway, I've been punished." He waited, as if expecting Jim to complete his thought. "Sapphire?" "Of course. I killed her, Jim." "Strange. I had the impression that Jeroen killed her." "You're mocking me again. You know what I mean. I had no business bringing her. It was my insecurity and selfishness. Because I wanted company, somebody to be with me that loved me, whatever I was or did. She didn't want to come. Sapphire hated traveling, hated the cage. So I let her out." He groaned. "For humane motives, Victor." "Not entirely. I've gone over and over it, Jim. No. She got on my nerves, clawing at the cage and wailing. That began to undercut me. It was a reproach, telling me I shouldn't have brought her. And I was still drinking. When I drink, I can't stand any authority telling me what to do. If I hear of a rule, I'm bound to break it: observe the green light; no smoking in the toilet. All that stewardess had to do was tell me that I should keep *'Minou'* in her cage. *So I let her out.* I tell myself that at least I could have kept her in my lap. Why didn't I? Because I didn't care, really, whether she prowled the aisles and disturbed the other passengers. I *liked* the idea. And that stunt she has—had— of hiding. The manhunt they put on for her. That was really rich!"

"But the second time? With the hijackers?" "I don't remember. Maybe I was half-asleep. And how could I expect a hijacker to shoot her?" His voice rose suddenly, sounding shrill and aggrieved, as though someone was accusing him. That was where examinations of conscience tended to end—in a burst of pitiful anger. The Church was right; confession to a priest, carrying absolution and penance, was wiser. Poor Victor had run the gamut of emotions. The sequel, now, would be tears. No doubt he was right in blaming himself about the cat, but then everyone here, surely, had something to answer for that would make the present event appear like the workings of justice. "Let's catch some sleep now," he urged, and returned to his pallet.

He was disturbed, for the last time, by Archie. Oh, Christ. Archie wanted to tell him, while the others were still asleep, that he had slipped a folded plan of the house and surrounding ground, with a sketch of a practicable tunnel, into Eloise's vanity-case, under her powder-puff, camouflaged by a thick layer of face-powder.

Twelve

Henk could have told them not to depend on the release of the big NATO helicopter for the execution of their plan. Morning had scarcely broken when he learned from the downcast pilots that they would not be going today. Carlos had wakened them to say that their departure had been put off indefinitely, and Pieter was taking it hard: his wife in Sneek was due to have their first baby at any moment. Henk commiserated but saw no ground for appeal. The *kapers* must have their reasons. Having consoled the pilots with philosophy—the child would be born anyway—he was startled by Jim's reaction to the news when it reached him finally during the breakfast service. "Jesus!" he swore, and let his cup of coffee spill over on Denise's tray. What was it to Jim that a young father would not see his wife through her labor? Then, during the toilet "break," Jim and Victor enlightened him.

He was glad to be taken—though a bit late—into their confidence. He would have been sorry to be left out. In return, he sought to put fresh cheer into them. Their idea was sound. They had only to be patient and wait for the next opportunity, which might come sooner than they guessed. As material encouragement, he offered to contribute a fresh bar of soap and some snuff, to bring on sneezing. And as it happened, luck was with them. The sparkling film of hoarfrost had not yet melted in the morning sun rays when a small helicopter put down in the field.

Welcome as the sight was to him *qua* duly inducted conspirator, he could not help reckoning the cost to his government of these repeated arrivals and departures. He pictured the Tweede Kamer in late session tonight—the billiard-green leather, pew-like benches and the gallery filled to capacity as his friend at Defense rose beside the Speaker to answer questions from the rightist fractions on the "squandering" of oil reserves during the national emergency to "coddle" a handful of impudent terrorists. And the daily siphoning of the precious fluid—the life blood of the "system"—must be gratifying to the *kapers'* pride. A pity, he thought, really, that no means had been found to convert earth gas to high octane fuel.

The new helicopter seemed to have been expected. It brought a case containing Helen's Vermeer and a small fair man with gold-rimmed glasses, recognizable to Henk at a hundred meters as his countryman. The unexpected was Charles, emerging gleefully from the freight bay and stretching his long legs. "Here I am," he shrilled, entering the family room with unruffled composure despite the pistol at his back. "Don't be tiresome, Hussein. I shan't try to escape." He looked around him happily. "How nice to be back. I always wanted the experience of being a stowaway."

Like many of the old man's boasts, this proved to be somewhat fanciful. To be accurate, he had come as a hitchhiker. "This delightful gentleman, Mr. Van der Kampe—your compatriot, Henk—was kind enough to give me a lift. Yes. We met by good luck at the heliport, when I was feeling frightfully down-at-the-mouth. Scarcely knowing what to do with myself, yet unwilling to turn tail and go home. Mr. Van der Kampe is from your incomparable Rijksmuseum, Henk. We found many friends in common. He explained to me as we chatted that he had been sent for to vouch for Helen's Vermeer. If I divined correctly, the suggestion came from our friend Jeroen. Indeed, one can fancy it as an imperative. Naturally Mr. Van der Kampe was somewhat apprehensive as to the circumstances he might find here. I was able to allay his anxieties, and we became thick as thieves."

Henk's eyes turned to the Rijksmuseum expert, who had remained impassive during this account of himself and his mission. He had set down the briefcase he carried and stood, trim feet together, like a mute exhibit being presented by Charles. Yet surely he understood English—which of the tulip-people didn't? "But how did the two of you come to meet, really?" cried Sophie, voicing Henk's own mystification as she looked from one to the other. "Why, my dear, he recognized me!" The small precise-featured Dutchman gave a small nod. "While I was having a cup of chocolate at the little bar they have. He saw me on television, imagine!"

Henk and Sophie exchanged a smile. They had all seen Charles on television last night. On the seven o'clock news program and, as an encore, at eight. He had actually spoken a few quaint words of Dutch. "You were a hit, Charles," said Jim in his easy tones. "Far outshining the rest. And, yes, I agree, quite memorable. Wouldn't you say, Lily?" "Oh, by all means. The star. We were proud of you." "But where *was* this bar?" Aileen asked. "My dear, I can't tell you exactly. At the military airfield, where we landed." "And they let you stay all *night* at a military airfield?" "I *hid*!" said Charles. Henk lifted a questioning eyebrow; he was acquainted with that heliport. "In the toilet for a time, if you must know. Then there was a jeep that I had noticed standing outside, which became rather chilly, I must say." "An *empty* jeep?" "Oh, no. That would have been careless of them, wouldn't it? There was a young soldier in a greatcoat asleep at the wheel." "And then?" "And then, my dear, let's just say that I have a way with me. In the end, the junior officer in command was most accommodating; you Dutch are so helpful to foreigners. Imagine if one had been in France. The only bother was that he was eager to furnish me transportation to Amsterdam. But I managed to stay put, resorting to what they call 'delaying tactics.' And the young men coming on duty had seen me on television. Some of them asked for my autograph. I expect they thought I was some figure of the stage or screen. In return, they were most informative. I learned that Helen's picture had been left behind. It had stood there all day. Anyone could have stolen it."

He broke off and eyed Van der Kampe, who was examining the Titian with the aid of a loupe. At Charles's prompting ("Do have a look at the splendid Ward they have in the next room"), he moved on into the *beste kamer.* Charles waited. "Well," he continued, lowering his voice, "I was not quite so guileless as I led *him* to believe. Hussein, would you mind shutting that door? At my age, one must be careful of drafts. Thank you. To go on with my story: I was forearmed, you see, by my young informants. Being assured that the picture was there emboldened me to hang on. When Mr. Van der Kampe appeared, one of my young acquaintances, guessing my interest, nipped into the toilet, where I was taking evasive action, to tell me that orders were for that gentleman to embark with the painting. Not being familiar with art matters, he could not say why. But I intuited it and I posted myself at the bar, trusting that a conversation between us would open. When it did, I offered myself as his guide. We agreed that he would pass me off, should the deception be necessary, as a fellow-authority. From our Fine Arts Museum—between ourselves, shockingly weak in Dutch seventeenth century, but who would know that here?"

Sounds from the shed announced that the Vermeer's case was being opened. At a sign from Jim, Henk, drawing Sophie with him, joined Van der Kampe in the parlor. He had no great yearning to fraternize in Dutch with this *landgenoot,* but it was important to Jim to know how long, roughly, the authentication was going to take. In short, how soon he would be returning to Amsterdam. Victor needed to be ready.

Though content to be enlisted in the rescue operation, Henk, on reflection, did not share Jim's sense of Victor's peril, which was based, he thought, on a misreading of the *kapers'* mentality. He doubted that CIA agents in the present circumstances were an endangered species needing protection. Almost the contrary. As the *kapers* would view it, if he read them right, he and Jim, even Sophie, were key imperialist agents operating under the cloak of liberalism and more deserving of execution by a people's firing squad than a rank-and-filer like Victor, were he to be exposed. In the scale of things, Victor would be judged to be a mere tool exploited by the bosses for his language skills and his Middle East credentials, and he had only to confess to be given a second chance. Redemption would be easy, as often happened with informers. To an observer, that seemed obvious. Yet the wretch, being fearful, was unwilling to take the chance. He preferred to be saved by his Great White Father, the Senator.

In any case, Henk was happy to do his share. It would be their first act of subversion. Like a schoolboy, he was almost offended when his snuff was refused. He had agreed, of course, to say nothing to Sophie, and Jim, he noticed, was keeping his distance from Lily this morning. Wisely, Henk considered, for that observant lady was likely to detect his suppressed excitement and remark on it wonderingly in public. One of the conditions of the game of skill they were playing was that anyone not in the secret had to be looked on as a potential enemy.

Entrusted with the vital mission of sounding out Van der Kampe, Henk felt honored and slightly apprehensive. He was a scout, obliged to step carefully lest an over-heavy footfall or the crackling of a twig give his purpose away. On entering the room with Sophie, he had experienced a kind of stage fright; he swallowed to moisten his dry throat. Danger was an exhilarant. He had lost all sense of proportion, he told himself, for the slight risk they were running was as nothing in comparison with the permanent danger that surrounded them, whose effect was mainly depressing. He supposed the difference was that this danger was of their own choosing—they were courting it, you might say, like a woman.

Van der Kampe would not say how long it would take him to pronounce on the Vermeer. He seemed irritated by the question. An irritable fussy little man, the worst type of Netherlander, and made nervous, evidently, by the guns—he did not appear to have noticed the highly visible wiring—and by the mixed company he found himself in. He was a snob, *natuurlijk*, and the apparition of Charles in full traveling regalia at the heliport must have led him to expect better things. "Of the old school, that one," he said to Henk in Dutch with a pale purse-lipped smile. The rest he found harder to catalogue. Mrs. Potter, he understood, would be traveling back with him in the event that he could certify her painting. Her husband was standing by in a hotel in Amsterdam—in the bar, Henk imagined, and not with a cup of hot chocolate. He saw that the uneasy fellow was taking Margaret, who retained some semblance of grandeur, for the owner of the Vermeer. "One of the great old fortunes, my 'guide' let me know." Henk redirected the authority's deferential gaze. "Not *that* lady!" Van der Kampe exclaimed, shocked. "We're prisoners," Henk reminded him. He felt embarrassed in front of this stranger for the state of Helen's dress, as if she were an aunt or an even nearer relation.

Van der Kampe excused himself. He had forgotten their state of duress. And now he understood (he said) why Henk had been anxious to learn when he would be returning to Amsterdam. "You will be wanting to send messages to your wife and children. By all means. Lose no time, please, in penning them. I shall be more than glad to deliver them to your home." Henk felt Sophie stiffen beside him at the words *"vrouw"* and *"kinderen."* But Van der Kampe's field of vision, on the whole perhaps fortunately, did not seem to include Sophie. If Henk were to mention that the feminine shape opposite him bore an uncanny resemblance to the Empress Theodora in the Ravenna mosaic, Van der Kampe, he supposed, would explain that that was not his "field." "Your address, please, and may I offer you pen and paper?" Henk reflected. "You *must* write," said Sophie. For a moment, Henk could think of no message to send that would not be heavily humorous ("Greetings from Flevoland") or a lie ("I miss you and think of you constantly"). In the end, he wrote "I am well. I amuse myself and I send you my love. Greet Elisabeth." "Who is Elisabeth?" said Sophie. "The wife of Den Uyl." To shake off the thought of his family, he moved to the window, where he had a good view of the helicopter. There should be room, he estimated, for another passenger.

Mrs. Potter was a small woman, and Van der Kampe was not much bigger. With the Vermeer out of the way, one of them and Victor, supine, ought to fit quite easily into the cargo bay.

Van der Kampe begged pardon. He had to answer a pressing call of nature. Unaware of the privilege, he was shown to the toilet. Leaving Sophie behind, Henk strolled into the family room. He made an affirmative sign to Jim. The expert, he had concluded, would make short work of his expertise; he was in a state of terror that now seemed to be gripping even his bowels. Henk suddenly realized that the man must believe that it had been an act of great bravery to come here. And in his vanity he perhaps still suspected that he had been brought here on a ruse and was going to be held hostage.

Carey was tackling Denise. "Come here, *chérie*. Mr. Lenz had a bad night. He looks damn sick this morning." "*J'ai vu*," she agreed. In truth Victor looked terrible. He lay huddled in a chair with red spots on his high cheekbones and his forehead the color of a young Leidsekaas with cumin. "Should we take his temperature?" Aileen proposed. It was wonderful how valuable at times an interfering woman could be. Denise's thermometer read 39.5.° "What's that in Fahrenheit?" someone asked. Sophie answered from the doorway. "103.1." Henk was pleased to think of a computer with flashing lights swiftly adding, subtracting, multiplying, inside that noble head. "I *knew* those boils were unhealthy," Aileen observed. "Shouldn't you give him aspirin, Denise? At least he'll feel more comfortable. Temporarily, they'll bring the fever down. Oh, poor Victor."

Jim held up a hand. "Whoa there, Bossie. Not till Greet has a look at him. What do you think, Henk?" Before he could answer, Aileen had reversed herself. "No, Denise. Better not. It could be something serious, and the aspirin would mask it. We might have *known* something like this would happen. Could we ask to have a doctor flown in? When I think of the darling Bishop . . . He might be alive today. *You* ask, Henk. Jeroen listens to you." "It might be more to the point," Jim commented, "to fly old Victor out." "But would they ever

330

agree to that?" Lily asked. "Why not?" said Henk. "They could put him on the helicopter with Van der Kampe." "Now *there's* a thought," cried the Reverend. *"Chapeau,* Henk," said Aileen. "Actually they'd be criminals not to." "They *are* criminals," said Lily. "Still, perhaps one *should* remind them of Gus." "I wouldn't advise it," said Jim. "You don't want to put their backs up. Let them decide for themselves what's to be done. The main thing is for Greet to look at him. And let's not get too worked up, Aileen. He may just have some little bug, a touch of flu." "With 103.1?" Aileen retorted. "Why, we could all catch it!" Ahmed felt Victor's forehead. *"Très malade,"* he decided. "Well, go tell your boss-lady," said Beryl.

A distraction, however, occurred as the painting was brought in. Van der Kampe seemed to be still in the toilet. Jeroen himself carried the canvas to the parlor and ranged it against the west wall, where the light was best. In the family room, Victor was helped to the sofa and left to himself while the rest of them crowded in to see the "Girl."

She wore a blue cap—more like a coif—over sandy corkscrew ringlets that looked as if they had just come out of curl-papers; her long full jacket was yellow taffeta trimmed with ermine, and her billowy skirt was white with dark-blue panels. She held a guitar on her lap; she was touching the strings with her right hand, and her head was turned sideways as if she was looking toward someone, maybe her teacher, for a cue. Or else there was a spinet in the next room, and she was both looking that way and listening for a chord to tell her to begin. There was something uncertain in her attitude, and she held the guitar awkwardly. Her high-colored cheeks, stiff curls, and big Dutch nose had a provincial, teenager look. Henk did not think that the "Girl" could have been much of a musician. He felt sure she was a Vermeer, though.

He did not know the painting. He was certain that he had never seen it in reproduction. But it must be very similar to the Vermeer that had been stolen by terrorists in London. That was maybe why Jeroen had been so interested in it: he was copying those Irish extremists or competing with them.

Henk remembered the photos and daily news stories in the English press and his own keen concern for "the hostage," whose fate had been more avidly followed than if she had been a live maiden. It was "only" a material object, as the pastor had said of this one a few days back, yet—possibly for that reason—there had been an aura of sacrilege about that riveting event. When a strip of the canvas had been mailed to a newspaper, it had been, for Henk at least, like the martyrdom of a Christian virgin as depicted in his old *Calendar of Saints*—Agatha, his mother's name saint, having her tender breasts slashed off by fiendish pagans.

Sophie was staring at the painting. Her brow was furrowed, and her narrow jaw thrust out in deep American meditation. She was asking the canvas to "say" something to her—something profound and important that it had never told anyone else. Henk waited. "It's a weird thing," she said finally. "It makes me think of old studio photography. She's all dressed up to have her picture taken, and the photographer has arranged the lighting, pulling back that curtain from the window so as to let the sun's rays fall just right on her features. He's adjusted the folds of her dress and tilted her head, running back and forth to the camera to see how she looks in the lens. He's not satisfied; she needs something to do with her hands. But he has an idea: that prop guitar he keeps in the studio. He puts it in her lap and shows her how to hold it. Then he ducks under his black hood. 'Wait for the birdie.' Click."

Henk was amazed. What she had noticed was there, certainly; she had made a true observation about Vermeer. "The *instantané* effect. 'Click,' as you say. You will never find that in a Rembrandt. Rembrandt never 'catches' his sitters in a single flitting instant." "Fleeting," said Sophie. "Rembrandt's sitters, you mean, have been there for centuries, like his trees?" "Something like that. Vermeer, I think, Sophie, is always painting time. That's the meaning of all the musical instruments and the clock in the 'View of Delft.' You know it?" "I saw it once in Paris. At the Orangerie. I noticed the clock too." Henk felt extraordinarily happy. "You are right, this picture is weird," he told her. "*Raar,* we say in Dutch. Because it says to you that it is posed while at the same time it is telling you that it is a snapshot, a split second of arrested motion." "You think that's on purpose?" "Yes. It points to a contradiction. There is pathos in it. The grotesquely overdressed young girl, with the pearls round her neck—" "Do you suppose she could be Jewish, Henk?" He studied the "Girl"'s features again. "The nose," prompted Sophie. "And those dark popping eyes. Plus being overdressed." "All that is Dutch," he consoled her. "We are much like you, Sophie—a merchant race with overdeveloped noses and—"

"Please!" They stepped back. Van der Kampe was finally ready to examine the canvas. He neared it, drew back, got down on one knee and looked up at it. Doffing his spectacles, he took a big magnifying glass from his briefcase and held it close to the canvas, where there appeared to be a signature, then moved it slowly across with his bare eye squinting through the lens. Henk was reminded of the feeling of having a doctor's head pressed against your chest as he listened to your inner organs. The only sound that came from the Rijksmuseum clinician was of heavy breathing as he knelt before the work. Finally he put his cheek to the surface and blew softly.

"He's dissatisfied," whispered Sophie. "Oh, God. Poor Helen." "It's not that," said Henk. "He doesn't like to give an opinion under these conditions." "Because he thinks Helen's life might depend on what he decides," assented Sophie. Henk shook his head. "This gentleman thinks of his career, of his professional standing. As he explained to me, he would normally never consent to do an authentication 'off the cuff,' without the facilities of the Rijksmuseum laboratories." "No talking, please." "Come," said Henk, guiding Sophie into the family room. What he saw there reassured him. There were still red patches on the invalid's cheeks, and Jim and Denise were with him.

In the laboratories—Henk reflected—the painting could be subjected to x-rays, carbon tests, and so on, by the men in white under Van der Kampe's authority; he would never be under the necessity of using his own unaided judgment in making an attribution. No wonder he was so uneasy; physical fear would be heightened by professional fear arising from lack of practice. It was probably years since he had arrived at an independent judgment of a work of art. "Like doctors today," said Sophie. "They're afraid to diagnose a case of chicken pox unless they can send samples to the laboratory. They don't like house calls either. I suppose, for him, this counts as a house call." She pondered.

"But what made him come, then?" Henk gave a short laugh. "His patriotic duty, he would tell us. In fact he's a high civil servant depending—you will smile, Sophie—on the Ministry of Culture, Recreation, and Social Work." "You mean they put pressure on him?" Henk did not know. The most effective pressures on such a type were those he would exert on himself. "They had only to suggest to him that in the event of his refusal they would regretfully have to turn to his younger colleague of the Mauritiushuis in The Hague." Van der Kampe could never permit that. That the other should appear in the world press, not to mention Eurovision, as the Netherlands' leading authority on Vermeer of Delft! Undertaking a dangerous mission in the sensational hijacking case, decorated by the Queen, maybe even receiving a knighthood . . . Sophie nodded. "But if he's so scared for his career, will he give an honest opinion?" "You don't know Hollanders. 'Without fear or favor,' as he would put it." "I wish he'd hurry." "He will not be hurried. Although, as you see, he is burning with impatience to leave. Even in these unsuitable conditions, he is determined to live up to the 'highest professional standard.' "

Jim, too, was becoming impatient. "Can't you light a fire under him? Christ, how long can a man's body maintain an artificially induced 103° temperature?" But Victor's hand was hot, and his teeth were authentically chattering. Henk seated himself at his bedside on the sofa's edge and became aware of an unmistakably soapy smell. It would be wise, he suggested, to get rid of the evidence before Greet was summoned. Victor fumbled in his clothing and handed over a sticky remnant of soap to which a few pale body hairs clung.

In the *beste kamer,* Van der Kampe had declared himself ready to pronounce. Greet ordered the room cleared, leaving herself, Jeroen, Horst, and Elfride in the auditory. In the doorway Henk protested. Mrs. Potter, he argued, had a right to be present and to have a Dutch-speaking witness to translate for her. "And you volunteer, Deputy?" Greet was sarcastic. He was a lawyer, Henk retorted, and there was no one else on hand to represent Mrs. Potter who had a knowledge of Dutch. "The truth is, you are curious," said Greet. Nevertheless she allowed both him and the owner to stay.

Horst shut the door, and Van der Kampe took a stand before the canvas. He had set his briefcase on the harmonium and from time to time, as he spoke, he took neatly stapled documents from it for reference. At his request, to avoid distractions, the Ramsbotham collection had had their faces turned to the wall. Except for the ever-present pistol in Greet's bulging bosom, there were no weapons in the room, and it might have been a seminar for a group of picked students. Charles's walking-stick served the expert as a pointer; all he lacked were slides. From the harmonium stool, Henk translated. There was a small restoration, the speaker indicated, of the left-hand fingers and some signs of an earlier over-painting in the landscape hanging on the wall behind the subject. The glazes were in unusually good condition. Though the signature seemed to have been added by another hand, the painting appeared to be an authentic work of Johannes van der Meer, probably executed in the last years of the artist's life. Possibly on commission from a client familiar with the Kenwood House "Guitar Player" and desirous of owning a work of the same kind. Photos and transparencies were produced from the briefcase and passed from hand to hand. Jeroen accepted the expert's magnifying glass. Beside Henk, Helen preened. "Just what the authorities at home said."

It was evidently not a replica, Van der Kampe proceeded,

but might be described as a variation on a theme. The Kenwood House painting (consultation of papers from briefcase), dated approximately 1667, was generally identified with a work known to have been in the hands of the painter's widow following on his death. A picture of like description figured in the Amsterdam sale of 1676. Conceivably, that was the present work. Or possibly the canvas here was to be equated with a work that figured in Lot 4 in the later sale, of 1696, as "A Young Lady with a Guitar." The notion of two closely allied "guitar" works of the master—one believed to have been lost—had often been put forward. Helen nodded.

Van der Kampe offered photostats of documents for inspection and stepped back to the canvas. With the stick, he indicated the source of light, a window on the right almost entirely masked by a blackish drapery, as in a camera obscura, thus permitting the sun's rays—the stick moved—to irradiate the subject's face and upper body and the wall behind her with an effect of stage lighting. This treatment was also found in the "Guitar Player"—Henk obediently held up a photo enlargement—and supported a late date, as did the thinness and fluidity of the paint. In the absence of scientific tests, nothing more could be said. The painting had all the hallmarks of a late Van der Meer, but this could also be seen as a suspicious circumstance. Without chemical analysis of paints and canvas, forgery should not be ruled out. One could postulate a master forger of the nineteenth century, active during the period of Van der Meer's "rediscovery," or a current forger with access, through a clever dealer, to canvas dating from the seventeenth century. The painting was either a genuine Van der Meer of the second rank—a certain lack of freshness was to be noted, deriving possibly from diminished inspiration, often found in near-replicas done to order—or it was the work of an anonymous imitator endowed with undisputable genius. The speaker personally inclined to the first hypothesis, but in any case it was a work of museum quality.

He promptly picked up his briefcase and, gesturing to Horst to open the door, went briskly into the next room. Helen fol-

lowed him. Her stout little body was quivering with indignation. " 'Second rank'! But if it's a forgery it's a work of 'genius.'
Oh, no, sir, you contradict yourself!" In Henk's view, there was
no contradiction, but Van der Kampe did not dispute that with
her. He stood polishing his spectacles, ready to depart. "It's
had all those tests he speaks of," Helen went on, beginning to
sniffle. "And passed them with flying colors." "In the States,
madam. But professionally, you see, I cannot take account of
that. Were you to offer it to the Rijksmuseum, we should have
to submit it to our own testing processes, even though, as I've
indicated, I've no personal doubt that it's genuine. Someday,
in fact, I should be greatly interested in doing a monograph
comparing it with the Kenwood House canvas. I'm quite often
in New York, and if you'd allow me to call on you and study it
at leisure—" He was stopped by a burst of tears. The pompous
fool had forgotten that if his validation was accepted she would
no longer have the painting. "Pray forgive me. How tactless of
me." He glanced at his watch. "In any event, if you will be
staying on a few days in Amsterdam, I shall take pleasure in
showing you our Van der Meer archive. Your husband as well.
Fascinating insights were gained in our restoration clinic at
the time of that unhappy incident—you recall it, of course—
the canvas hacked from its frame while on exhibition in Belgium. Irreparably damaged, we feared, when we first recovered
it."

" 'The Love Letter.' Yes. Quite some time ago." Her mind
hopped like a bird onto the new topic. "I always asked myself,
did the museum pay a ransom?" "Madam, as a distinguished
collector, you know very well that my answer must be a negative. But, as I was saying, it will be an honor, one day when we
meet again—" " 'When you meet again'!" Margaret burst out.
"Why, she'll be going back with you. I gather you've won her
her freedom, though you took your time over it, I must say."

Greet looked to Jeroen. "We are satisfied, Mr. Curator," he
said. "You and Mrs. Potter will proceed at once to the helicopter. Carlos!" "And you will be going too, old gentleman,"
Greet ordered quite fiercely, handing Charles his walking-stick.

"Carlos, take him along." "Can you wait a minute?" said Aileen. "Victor's sick. There, on the couch." "We are busy," said Greet. "I will look at the prisoner later." "He has much fever, Greet," put in Denise. "*Très malade,*" said Ahmed, making his own teeth chatter. "Could you send for a doctor maybe?" Jim said in a meditative tone that won Henk's full admiration. "I guess that aircraft out there might pick one up if a message was sent ahead." "You will leave decisions to us, Senator. We are masters here. I will look at the prisoner, Jeroen." Denise stood ready with her thermometer. Greet shook it down and inserted it roughly under Victor's tongue. "39°." Her thumb went down on Victor's limp wrist, taking his pulse. "Fast. But not so fast as the fever would propose. Is there a history of tuberculosis?" Victor licked his lips, and his eyes turned to Jim, who made a dissuasive motion with his head. Henk agreed: the fewer lies the better. "Not that I know of," said Victor. "*Vreemde,*" she said to Jeroen. "She says it is strange," Henk reported. Greet and Jeroen eyed each other. They murmured together in Dutch. Henk crossed his fingers, touching the piece of soap in his pocket. He caught the words "*uit*" and "*weg.*" They were telling each other, evidently, that it would be best to be rid of Victor. Henk nodded affirmatively to Jim.

It looked like clear sailing. Only one little reef remained to be crossed: was there room, after all, in the helicopter? When estimating the craft's seating capacity, Henk had overlooked Charles. Van der Kampe, who had been listening impatiently, had his own word to add. He was not prepared to have his return flight compromised by the extra burden of a sick man. "I wish to put my foot down," he said loudly. "What is now proposed is for us dangerous. I do not like it. They have promised me safe-conduct, Deputy. Four besides the pilot is an overload—too many."

"Goody!" Charles cried, with a clap of his hands. "He can have my place." Greet looked to her partner. Jeroen shrugged. More hurried Dutch undertones. She was angry. In a way, Henk sympathized: to let the incorrigible old man stay in defiance of her orders would undermine her whole conception of discipline. But Charles, as he had said, had a "way" with him. Jeroen overruled her. Once again, from the parlor window, they witnessed a departure to freedom. Seeing Victor safely stowed in the freight bay, Henk and Jim breathed easier. "Wouldn't you know, they forgot to search them!" observed Aileen, clicking her tongue.

The following day brought Margaret's collection. No expert accompanied her El Greco "Saint in Ecstasy," her tiny Lorenzo Monaco "Virgin and Saints," her sepia drawings by Raphael and *sanguine* by Michelangelo. Jeroen, however, was satisfied, and they were put in the parlor, replacing the Ramsbotham collection, which was stacked in the shed. "What your museum needs is an annex, Jeroen," Jim commented, as Margaret took her leave. But with Margaret, Charles went, definitively—he had gained only a day of grace. Next to go were Dirk and Pieter and the NATO helicopter, which was pushed out of the barn with surprising ease. Of the collectors, there remained only Lily and Beryl. This, as Henk and Sophie decided long after, had been the happiest time. There was not so much work for Denise and Jean; chicken and rabbit appeared on the menu. The *kapers'* mood was still indulgent; everyone got toilet privileges, and the men were allowed to shave. There were walks twice a day for the entire company, with only one guard, and pairing off occurred as a matter of course: Jim and Lily—on rainy days under the Bishop's umbrella—Aileen and Archie—fast friends by now— Henk and Sophie, and, in the rear, the pastor and Beryl, unluckily not so well matched. The pastor's binoculars were a godsend. Thanks to them and to Henk's instruction, the hostages learned the shore birds of the Netherlands; as Lily said, that was something they would have in common all their lives. In the house, Frank conducted morning service as usual, which somewhat appeased his longing to be shepherd to the flock. But when he sought by example to introduce grace before meals, the practice was discouraged. There were no more arguments—

only lively discussions often lasting till late in the evening and usually touched off by the paintings that confronted them at every turn of the head.

Afterward it was sadder. The departures of Lily and Beryl appeared in retrospect to have been the turning-point. It was odd to have Lily replaced by her water-colors, which uncannily resembled her. Airy clouds, mountain peaks at sunrise, cottages, ancient bridges, country-church spires, hay ricks, lichened castles, they represented Nature and the works of men in their least terrestrial aspect—they were gentle English "inklings." In their tasteful "neutral" frames, they were ranged upstairs in the children's playroom, and Jim, using the excuse of going to the toilet, frequently went up to look at them. He was communing with her spirit, he said. She had kissed him on leaving and cried a little, producing the chaste handkerchief—still immaculate—that she had used for the Bishop's funeral. Henk and Sophie, trying not to watch, could not make out what her real feelings were. "Come on, Ma," Beryl interrupted. She had already said good-bye to Ahmed and given him her address in New York. With Lily and Beryl, Jean went. Now they were only seven.

The realignment that followed was inevitable. With Jim bereft of Lily, Henk and Sophie saw no choice but to close ranks around him. Once again, as at the start, they were a threesome, Sophie between the two men. Jim's efforts to join up with Aileen, leaving them alone, were seldom successful. Having "lost" Jim to Lily, Aileen was determined to keep Archie to herself, and Archie, when Jim joined them, tended to detach himself and gravitate toward the also bereft and quite pretty Denise, mismatched with the pastor, who could not speak French. It was jackstraws, said Sophie: when you pulled out one —Lily—the whole house came down. In any case, the reduction in numbers made being alone in this confined space all but impossible. Lovers lost themselves best in a crowd.

This became cruelly apparent at night, when the lights were turned off. The attic was no longer serving as a dormitory; for sleeping, the hostages were divided between the *beste kamer* and the family room. By Aileen's decree, Sophie was on one sofa and she herself on the other, with Denise curling up in a chair. The men were assigned to the floor, and Henk was farther removed in every sense from Sophie than he had been when the room was packed with bodies and they had lain side by side often, sensing each other's breathing as they listened to the older people snore.

Would they ever make love? For his part, he was unable to imagine its happening now, as if on a public stage. Sophie was bolder. The other day she had wistfully mentioned the attic. "Do you think Ahmed . . . ?" She meant would Ahmed let them use it some night when he was on guard. "For a few minutes or all night?" he had answered dryly. Impossible, he had told her, with seven *kapers* bedded on the floor below, the creaking stairs, and the unlucky other hostages waking, perhaps, and missing them. He would not want to restrain himself to a quick noiseless act with Sophie; she was not a whore you went upstairs with while your friends waited below. Finally, it would seem wrong to him to joy in her hungrily when the others were not so favored. It might have been different when Lily was still here. Not that she and Jim, at their age, would have been likely to have a go themselves. But they had formed a kind of couple. No, he would not attempt it and, if he did, he would probably be impotent or at any rate dissatisfied.

Yet when he spoke of a future meeting it was Sophie who drew back. "You could stay on in Amsterdam," he pointed out. "No." On the polder, she said, she would have no scruple, because the polder was a separate world. It could not be mistaken for real life. On the polder, they could love each other and be sure of a clean ending: death for either or both or release, which would cut the thread. She did not want their love to be "messy," that is, clouded by his thoughts for his family, deception, stolen meetings—"the usual when the man is married." She was right, he recognized, as far as Amsterdam went: he was too well known to register in a hotel with her or even to go up in the lift to a room she would be waiting in. And The Hague would be worse. Indeed, thanks to the present adventure, there was no corner in Holland where they could hope to hide. And, once restored to his family, he could not promptly leave them and his work to fly off to meet her in Avila or Assisi or a chalet in the Austrian Alps. But Flanders might be possible.

"Do you know Bruges?" he said. "No. But no," said Sophie. "The people there would know you. Anyway, what would your plan be? To meet me for overnight?" She could stay on, he said, and visit the museums, and he would come back to her. "Bruges is nice. You could even take a train to Gand for the day." "Ghent," she said. " 'The Mystic Lamb.' I've seen it. And when you came to Bruges, Henk, what would you do? Leave a friend's telephone number where you could be reached, I suppose. Then clear it with the friend so that he còuld call you at our hotel in case something happened at home. A government crisis or one of the children sick." He had not sufficiently reflected. Sophie laughed. "I can see you've never had a serious affair. Not overnight, with hotels and friends covering for you." "And you have?" "It sounds so, doesn't it? Yes. But this is different. I think I truly love you, Henk. I wouldn't like to watch you behaving shabbily. To be honest, I think you'd find it quite hard."

Unfairly, he had been angry. Her resistance had struck the vein of obstinacy in him. In the bathroom mirror, he saw that his jaw was set in moody lines of determination. He resented the mention of the attic—a substitute, such as you might offer a child. He was jealous, of course, as well. It irked him that a one-time affair with a married man (or several) should prejudge her relation with *him*. Yet gradually his irritation subsided. He was being wilful himself, he perceived. Moreover, she was righter than he. It was absurd that he should be sad because she refused to meet him in Bruges. The local outlook, after Lily's departure, made nonsense of such a quarrel. As soon debate whether she would accept a rendezvous in heaven—on a cloud—which seemed closer to hand.

Negotiations, he had learned, were at a standstill. Jeroen himself confirmed it, with a curious show of pride. And Jim had not been wrong: they were serious about their Demand Two. That was the sticking-point. Holding valuable live hostages and invaluable works of art, Jeroen believed himself to be an irresistible force. He could not see that Den Uyl was an immovable object. "Talk to him, Henk," Aileen begged. But he had already shown the lot of them, point by point, why it was impossible for Den Uyl to agree. Greet had listened intently; Henk had felt he was half-convincing her. Horst and Elfride were noncommittal; the Arabs and Carlos could not follow the presentation, and Jeroen calmly smiled. "You will see," he predicted.

It was now a true siege. As in the Middle Ages, the opponents faced each other across a neutral terrain, each counting on the force of attrition to sap the other's morale. Inside the fortress, supplies were running low. But the *kapers,* so far, had declined to ask for a food drop. That would be a sign of weakness, Greet told Aileen. There was still flour in the larder, dried milk, a little cooking fat, and some legumes. The rabbits had been sacrificed at the rate of two a week, but the hens were being hoarded, for their eggs, until they ceased to lay. A share of the new-laid eggs was replaced under the hen each morning with the idea of hatching chickens. "How long does it take," Sophie wondered, "for a chicken to be big enough to eat?" Archie had the answer; he had grown up on a sheep farm in Aberdeenshire. Three or four months. That gave them the measure of the *kapers'* determination. In view of this, it was lucky that the farmer had left a good supply of chicken feed. "We'll be eating it soon ourselves," Aileen prophesied. "Not so daft," said Archie: chicken feed was readily digestible, having a high protein content, considerable fat, and roughage. There were no crops yet, naturally, in the farmer's new-planted fields, but the binoculars had shown ducks swimming in the distant canal, and the whir of pheasants had been heard. This inspired Ahmed and Hussein to talk of foraging out for game, taking a hostage along for protection. But the leaders were doubtful about a dispersion of forces. Up to now, this had differed from a medieval siege in that there had been no sorties and no attempt at scaling the ramparts, which were reinforced nevertheless from time to time.

As the unchanging days passed, the hostages came to perceive that the world outside was diminishing in reality for them. Staring fixedly out the parlor window, Henk no longer "saw" the *marechaussee* drawn up in the field. They had become part of the scenery. He supposed he was aware of them all the time "subliminally," like Lily with her collection. If he looked out one morning and they were not there, he would notice them, he hoped, as an absence. Just as he had ceased to pay attention to the air traffic overhead and perceived one day with an effect of surprise that it had stopped; the sky was empty except for an occasional patrol plane. In a parallel development, the world was becoming oblivious of *them*.

On television, the polder "ordeal" figured more and more rarely. The descent of Lily and Beryl, in their furs, at the heliport was a kind of grand finale—though the fond audience in the family room did not guess it—before a curtain dropped. Now nights in a row went by without the obligatory shots of the farmhouse and the accompanying bulletin read by a spokesman from the Justice Ministry. The farmhouse returned briefly to a stellar place on the screen when the *boer* himself and his *vrouw*, back from the Balearics with peeling sunburns, were interviewed in the house of relatives in Kampen. ("The old country," they both called the mainland, where they were staying, which made Henk smile, translating—that was how the polder settlers thought of Holland.) Hearing them tell their tale, the captives, as in a cinema flashback, were able to reconstruct the early part of the story, its infancy, you might say. Its humble birth, in the mind of Jeroen, remained obscure.

The couple's testimony led the police to an abandoned truck with a false Hamburg license-plate in the airport parking lot. This was the first clue, the spokesman explained, that the police had had to work on; there was hope now of finding the gang's accomplices. But the trail, evidently, was cold. The truck—stolen, of course—was shown on an evening program, and then no more was heard of it, or of the *boer*, who had spoken feelingly of his winter wheat crop. The story, like the year, was at a dead point. "I wonder what happened to Archie's tunnel," Jim inquired with a dry laugh one night.

Consciousness of being buried, like a small item in a newspaper, was affecting the *kapers* too. Their fading from the news, to be replaced by other raiders, kidnappers, bombers, could not fail to worry them. To maintain their ascendancy, they would feel bound, soon, to execute a hostage. Or so Henk feared and he supposed that Jim was sharing the thought—Archie too, perhaps. The external signs were ominous: frequent sounds of argument from the kitchen, with Yusuf's voice dominant—sometimes plaintive, sometimes shrill. Present policy, obviously, was being questioned. It was natural that some of the commando—the less intelligent—should be spoiling for an action. Jeroen, heavy-browed and silent, as if marking a withdrawal, was spending more and more time shut up in the parlor with the Vermeer. Ahmed now and then softly knocked and joined him. When on guard, Ahmed seemed depressed.

But executing a hostage would be a mistake, from their own point of view. Henk believed he could show that much to a few of them, at least to Greet and Jeroen. It was not a point of principle, on which Jeroen would balk, but a point of praxis. Having resolved to speak, Henk waited till he could find the two alone. The moment came after lunch on a Sunday—their fourth in captivity, unless he was losing count—when Denise had finished washing up and Carlos, a "friendly," was on guard. Carlos carried his message, and the kitchen door was opened. The pair sat at the table. Greet was darning Jeroen's sock, and his big white foot was bare. The others were above, presumably napping.

"You have something to tell us?" "Yes." He had determined to come straight to the subject, and she had spoken Dutch—from her, a good sign. They had been discussing the execution of a hostage, he told them. They showed no surprise that he knew. It would be an error, he said—a *fout*. *"Waarom?"* That was Greet, not sounding, as so often, sarcastic but as though she were more than curious to know his reasons. Jeroen's reaction could not be seen; he was bending down to put the sock and heavy boot on. If they killed a hostage now, Henk explained, it would be like a signal to the authorities to strike —a pretext certain elements in the coalition would have been waiting for to employ "strong measures." "Van Agt," said Greet, naming the Minister of Justice. "There must be much public pressure," continued Henk. Killing a hostage would clear the way, which had been blocked by Den Uyl's scruples. "They will storm the house. You cannot prevent that." Jeroen held up a hand. "You are right. We cannot prevent that. But there are comrades here who do not believe they will storm it. They say, look at your Bishop. There was no reprisal. To the contrary, we gained our way. You recall that?"

That had been in the early stages, Henk pointed out, when the policy of peaceful negotiations had had the upper hand. "But now it is late, Jeroen. My government is tired; the people are tired. They feel this has gone on too long. But they will be patient and wait a little longer if you do not kill." Jeroen nodded. That was his view, he acknowledged, and Greet's. "But maybe we see that, like you, because we are all Dutch. Though we are enemies, we have a similar political understanding of this country. We Dutch are not fond of bloodshed. Mr. Den Uyl is not fond of bloodshed. We are of one mind on this. But the others . . . Even Carlos." He sighed. Not Ahmed, said Greet. He was loyal to Jeroen; he loved him. But the others . . . Jeroen sighed again. "Because the imperialists did not retaliate when we gave them your Bishop's body, they are sure the imperialists here are weak. If we shoot a hostage, they say, the imperialists will see we are serious and concede us whatever we demand. They say the imperialists will not storm the command post for fear of heavy casualties."

"Among the hostages," Henk corrected. "Again, that was true at the start. But not any more, if *you* kill." Greet interrupted. "They have learned to accept the assurance of casualties. That is the weakness, evidently, of too long confrontation. I have told you so, Jeroen." "And they are stronger," Henk added. "You are only eight. If they lose eight men storming the house, for them it is only unfortunate. But you cannot lose eight. Even six, even five. Those who do not die will be taken prisoners. As for us, some will die, but that, too, is only unfortunate. A tragedy, people will say. But that is literature." "They will not willingly harm the pictures," Jeroen suddenly objected. "That was true, too, at one time," said Henk. "But no longer, I imagine. Now, if you force them to strike, they will *hope* not to harm the pictures. Or only a few."

"So what do you advise? An action is necessary for the comrades' morale." The Arabs, he said, were failing to grasp the importance of the second demand, the part, that is, concerning the NATO forces. They were interested only in Israel. "We will be frank with you, Van Vliet de Jonge. Yusuf has been a problem. He believes that we deceived him, that we promised to liberate the Israeli prisoners." "And you did not?" "We saw this idea was invalid, though I confess we had considered it for a time. To liberate Israeli prisoners, you must strike directly at Israel. At the outset we believed that world feeling might be capable of forcing Israel's compliance. But we came to recognize our error. Solidarity, even among those of the same interests, is unnatural in the capitalist world. You saw how Washington sought to block the agreed-on delivery of the paintings. But Yusuf is too undeveloped to understand this. He suspects we betrayed the Palestine liberation fighters to enrich ourselves with Western art."

In any case, Yusuf was a source of disaffection. He was intent on revising the demands and on starting to kill hostages to enforce the one close to his heart. "He has a cousin, you must know, that the Israelis are torturing." And he had half won over Hussein. "But the Germans?" That was different, Jeroen said. The Germans and Carlos, more developed politically, were in full agreement with the demands as they stood. But they, too, were arguing that it was time to kill a first hostage. "So you are outnumbered." "Not altogether. Among themselves, the comrades disagree on the timing and order of the executions. The German comrades prefer to go slow and to start with you, Deputy. The Arab comrades would start with the

Jewish woman." Henk felt himself turn pale. "You need not be afraid," Greet said with a smile. "This dissension means that we are still masters. But you must offer us a solution."

There was no solution, Henk thought, and, before long, Jeroen would see that. The woman already knew. Surrender with promise of safe-conduct might still be acceptable to the authorities but not any longer to the comrades, he judged from what he had heard. Some, at least, among them were on a suicidal course. In his clever planning—admirable, the touch of the German "television team" that the *boer* had told of!— Jeroen had overlooked the time factor. For all concerned, this had gone on too long. Nevertheless he pondered. If there was no visible solution, there could be an immediate alternative that would take the edge off their hunger for executions. A substitute could be offered, as in an old story. Instead of a hostage, why not a painting? One not sufficiently "priceless" to seem a flagrant provocation. A Marie Laurencin? As he spoke the words, he felt a strange sorrow, as though he were condemning a frail living thing—a moth or butterfly—to death.

Jeroen and Greet nodded. He had chosen well. "We shall tell the comrades that this is our decision." The door opened. Horst and Elfride entered. "Ah," said Horst in German, "you are instructing the prisoner to tape an appeal? Excellent!" Henk closed his eyes. He had hoped to avoid that stupid imperative. But the Germans, evidently, had been conferring too. They had decided that a plea from the deputy might work as well, for the time being, as an execution; finding him there persuaded them that the other two had come to the same conclusion. Henk shrugged and looked at Jeroen. It could have no effect on The Hague, but, if Jeroen wanted it, he would do it. He had enlisted, he saw, as Jeroen's ally and Greet's in their contest with their own dissident elements. That was the result of having been taken into their confidence; he would do whatever would help them. An hour ago, if ordered to tape an appeal, he would have cheerfully refused, not desiring to sound like a fool or a coward to his governmental colleagues. And when it became known that he had made a tape for transmission—should that be Jeroen's will—his fellow-hostages would be surprised and shocked. They would not have expected that of him. Even if he did not immediately tell them what he had done, there would be no way of concealing the fact from them: tonight he would be back on the screen—still campaigning or talking with the Queen in her feathers at the opening of Parliament—as his craven words were registered on the sound track. He felt sad in advance for Sophie. She would not know what led him to it; that a majority of the *kapers* had been calling for executions was a fearsome thing he must keep from her.

"And what, pray, am I to beg of my government?" Acceptance, of course, of the second demand. "You will add," said Elfride, "that if they fail to give a positive response, acts of justice from our side will commence." Jeroen met his eyes; he, too, shrugged. This must mean that he, too, saw the futility of it. "You will state in your own words what the comrades require." In the end, the tape was dispensed with. With the four standing over him, he sat in a chair and spoke directly to the short-wave radio. Though the idiot words were shaming, when he had finished, he felt satisfied, rather proud. He had been careful to keep his voice light to obviate the suspicion that he had been tortured or drugged.

Horst and Elfride went out. Jeroen and Greet remained with the radio. "You expect a response?" said Henk. "You ironize, Van Vliet de Jonge," Jeroen answered, without hostility. "You do not believe there will be one." "In any case, negative. I have told you why already. Nothing has changed." "I would like to hear again," Greet said. Wearily, Henk repeated the arguments demonstrating the impossibility of the second demand. As he spoke, he felt compunction for Jeroen; if finally he was convincing him, brute force of reason was killing a long-held dream. He was sorry for that; it would have been wonderful if the brave fellow, single-handed and by sheer persistence, could have taken the Lowlands out of NATO. He would have gone down in the national annals like William the Silent or the boy with his finger in the dike. "You have only your will on your side, Jeroen. Den Uyl has reality—the power of circumstances. *His* individual will does not count. You see a battle of wills but you are wrong. It is your single will against the inertia of facts. Holland will not send the NATO forces away unless many facts change and evolve, of their own weight, independently." The woman was nodding. Jeroen only stared at the silent radio. He drew a deep breath. "It is exercise time," he said. "You will go out with the others, Van Vliet de Jonge. And you also, Greet. Everyone must have exercise today. I order it."

Henk's conscience misgave him. Jeroen's voice was dull; there was the lead of despair in it, and his arms hung heavily by his sides. With a violent gesture, he had turned off the radio. It had been wrong to discourage the dream without offering something in its place. "Look, Jeroen, here is another thought. Why not sensibly ask for a food drop? They will accept, because of the hostages, and the mood of your comrades will soften. Hungry men are prone to mutiny. Then we can think together of what is to be done." "He is right, Jeroen," said Greet with a sigh. Jeroen smiled. "Thank you. You are a man of good will. I have seen that. It is a pity that your lot has been cast with the class enemy. Yes, we will consider, as you say, what is to be done. Yet if we give up our second demand, what is left? Nothing." Henk was silent. "You have not killed anyone," he said finally. "That is in your favor." "If we surrender, you imply. . . ." "He implies that the imperialists will allow us safe-conduct out of the country," said Greet. "Since you've committed no capital crime," Henk agreed. "It is likely that they will concede that, yes," said Jeroen. "But to Yusuf and Hussein unbelievable. They have another mentality." "With food, they may be less suspicious," Henk argued. "And you can impress on them that many capitals will be proud to receive your band, now that you are famous." "Thank you. While you are having exercise, I shall be thinking." He moved to the door. "Carlos!"

Only Ahmed remained behind, to be with Jeroen. He would not be dissuaded. It was a sunny cold afternoon. They saw a flock of snow buntings around the house, and in the field near the canal the binoculars showed them mallards walking in pairs, like couples on a Sunday outing. "And it *is* Sunday," cried Aileen. "Isn't that funny? Do you suppose they know it?" Henk welcomed her chatter. "You were in there a long time," Sophie had said to him as he was helping her on with her coat. "What was it?" "I was advising them to ask for a food drop." "Oh, glory. And will they do it?" "I don't know. Jeroen is thinking." They walked briskly in threes and twos—Sophie with Henk and Jim, Aileen with Archie and the dominie, Horst and Elfride with Carlos, Denise with Greet, Hussein and Yusuf bringing up the rear. "We look like a procession," Aileen called out. "It's the first time, isn't it, that so many have been out together. I wonder what it means." Henk wondered too. Any departure from custom had a significance, they had learned. It was the first time, also, that Greet had left the house, and evidently she did not feel easy.

"We shall return now," she announced abruptly, seizing Denise's arm and wheeling about. Cries of protest arose. "Oh, Greet, that's not fair," remonstrated Aileen. "Jeroen *said* we were to have thirty minutes. We all heard him. And we've only been out ten." "Another five," pleaded the pastor. "It's such a wonderful day. You need the fresh air, Greet. It'll put roses in your cheeks." Greet did not bother to answer. With big strides, almost running and pulling Denise along, she was on her way back to the house. "What's got into her?" said Archie. "She's gone white as tallow." "She's jealous of the Vermeer," Aileen said. "Haven't you noticed? She hates it when he shuts himself up with it." But suddenly, as if stampeded, they were all rushing toward the house, Greet in the lead and the Germans just behind her. Henk felt Yusuf's rifle at his back and irritably pulled away. He and Sophie were the last into the shed. As they stumbled in—Sophie's boots were bothering her—they heard a fearful yell: Jeroen. *"Uitstappt!"* "Get out!" "Berserk," estimated Archie. They could not see Jeroen, but those ahead —who could, apparently—were turning back in a rout, choking the narrow entry hall, when the first explosion came. A second explosion followed, then a third. Wood and plaster were falling. As if transfixed, Henk watched the profile of a painted stag's head with a big baleful eye alight on his own head; he brushed it off. His last action—at any rate, that he remembered —was flinging himself on Sophie, to shield her from a huge piece of jagged glass that was hurtling toward them through the air. Then something—a timber or window frame—hit his skull with a loud crack, and he "knew no more."

Envoi

Aileen and Frank were taking the plane—KLM—to New York. They had been the only ones to survive without serious injury when Jeroen blew himself and the house up. Most had been killed instantly: Jeroen and Greet, Archie and the Senator, the Germans, Carlos, Denise. Two of the Arabs had died from burns before they could be evacuated; the cookstove, run on propane, had caught fire. Ahmed had died two days later in the hospital; his lung had been punctured by a falling joist, and transfusions could not save him. Sophie was in a *kliniek*, having lost an arm. Henk was at home now, still in bed; he had had a concussion and gone into deep coma. For a time it had been feared that his brain, if he lived, would be affected. He had also lost a good deal of blood from splinters of glass that had pierced his neck and hands and had had to be removed by surgery.

He and Sophie had been unconscious and bleeding badly when the military were finally able to enter what was left of the house, in time to put out the fire, which had spread beyond the kitchen to the entry hall and was just licking at the stairway. Frank and Aileen, making their way through the debris, had found the two of them under a pair of children's bicycles before the guardsmen came and had not known what to do: whether it would be more dangerous to move them or to wait for help. They had lifted the bicycles off them and waited, with Frank praying his heart out and Aileen counting to a hundred, while they smelled the smoke and listened to the nearing crackle of the fire. Outside there was nothing but rubble, which had had to be partly cleared before the stretchers could enter. All the pictures had been blown to pieces, except for Lily's water-colors—though sections of the floor had caved in, the upstairs was not much damaged, apart from broken windows. In the yard, even the chickens had perished. Yet Frank and Aileen, though dazed and shaken and temporarily deafened, had emerged with only superficial cuts and bruises. They had been strong enough to visit the mortuary and identify the bodies, and Frank, after a physical, had been allowed to give a pint of blood to Ahmed.

Identifying the bodies had been an ordeal they could not yet describe. Some were horribly dismembered; they had known Jim Carey principally by his silver hair. Yet Jeroen, who had been at the very center of the explosions, as if in the eye of a hurricane, had hardly been touched, so far as one could see. His glasses had been broken, and his chest had been crushed by a beam, but that was not visible under the sheet. On the slab he looked peaceful, though he must have died in a fury of rage, because his orders had been disobeyed.

They had learned from Ahmed what had happened. In the hospital he had been too weak to have visitors, but he had talked to them on the medical helicopter that had come to take the living to Amsterdam. And he must have talked to the police at some point, since the whole story was in the papers. Frank and Aileen had read it in the *Herald Tribune* and in the London *Times* while staying at the house of the U.S. Consul General, who had contrived to keep the press away. They had brought copies to Sophie, for when she would be up to reading about it; the amputation had caused her a great deal of pain, and she was still under sedation. The stories had carried all their pictures and a drawing of the interior of the house showing the wiring system and where the fuses had been. The *Times* had found an old photo of Greet in her KLM hostess uniform, just like the two girls today. But they did not have a good picture of Jeroen.

In the medical helicopter, Ahmed had been very sad. It was not just that so many lives had been wasted, though he was sorry about his comrades and had shed tears when he heard about the Senator, who had encouraged him to recite Arab poetry. Rather, it was that he had wanted to die himself—a warrior's death—with Jeroen. Jeroen, he said, had not decided on the spur of the moment. He had been thinking of it for a long time. He had not told Ahmed, but Ahmed had known. He had come upon him one day in the parlor with the detonator—no bigger than a little pencil—in his hands, sitting there quietly with the Vermeer. But even if Ahmed had not seen the detonator, he would have understood what was in Jeroen's mind. Greet had begun to guess too, he thought, because she loved him, though with a woman's love, which was more interfering than a brother's. She had always mistrusted the paintings. Bending to catch Ahmed's words, Aileen and Frank had nodded. It must have been a sudden suspicion that had driven her back to the house that fatal afternoon, to frustrate Jeroen's design.

He had planned to die alone with the "Girl" he had fallen in love with—like a bride, Ahmed said. After the others had gone out walking, he had sent Ahmed away too, ordering him to follow them and not linger around the house. But Ahmed had been determined to die with him; it was a privilege he wanted for himself which the others would not share. He had crept back through the front entrance, which no one used, and observed Jeroen's arrangements: the time device ticking to activate the battery, and the sticks of dynamite wired to the joists as usual—Yusuf had tested the wiring, as a matter of routine, that morning. Hiding in the pantry, Ahmed had known that he would not have long to wait; Jeroen would have timed the blast to allow ten or perhaps fifteen minutes for the others to be well away. But Greet, woman-like, had destroyed her man's plan and herself as well. Absorbed in his thoughts, Jeroen could not have noticed them returning across the field. The first Ahmed knew of it, in the windowless pantry, had been the sound of voices, a door banging, and in the same moment, a fierce startled yell from Jeroen. Yelling angrily in

Dutch, he had sought to drive them back, out of the house, where they had no business. But they had not understood, losing valuable seconds in mystification, though in fact that had not mattered. It had been too late anyway.

"I can't get that picture out of my mind," Frank confided as they unfastened their seat belts. "Him standing there with that wild look and his arm raised, to expel us, like the angel with the flaming sword, at Eden's gate, you know. It was all so darned Biblical." "Lot's wife," Aileen said. "Greet. Turning around in that field to look back. Lot's wife was disobedient too. A pillar of salt. Could you *face* Greet's remains in that mortuary? Barely identifiable." Frank shook his head to dispel the memory. "I keep thinking of Samson, Aileen. I guess that comes the closest to our big strapping fellow. . . ." "Pulling down the temple," she agreed. "On himself and all the Philistines. But Jeroen didn't *intend* to kill anybody but himself. I think we have to accept that. Himself and the pictures. It was more like suttee in a way."

The hostesses circulated menus. "I still don't understand what drove him to take his life," Frank resumed after a cursory look. Henk, they had discovered, took the blame on himself. When they had visited him—sitting up in bed and mournfully eating a piece of smoked eel—he had told them about his last interview with Jeroen. Even then, it seemed, he had sensed that he was doing wrong to make him see that their enterprise had no future. It was true, but he should not have demonstrated it, not at that juncture, when Jeroen's own people had been turning against him. He had let his love of reasoning carry him away. Frank had tried to reassure him: according to Ahmed, Jeroen was going to blow himself up anyway. Henk had been interested to hear that, but he still held himself responsible; whatever Jeroen's intentions, their talk had been the precipitating cause. "You think you triggered it," Aileen had summed up. He did not take to her verb, Henk had answered, making a wry face, but, yes, he was persuaded that the impulse to sudden action had come from him. Despair—the ultimate sin against the Holy Ghost—had resolved Jeroen, and he had been the source; he had despaired *for* Jeroen, and Jeroen had known it. He had not had the right to take hope away.

"It was peculiar, Reverend," Aileen said now. "I suppose he can't help blaming himself for Sophie's arm. He hasn't seen the poor girl yet, of course. But, aside from that, from the way he talked I almost got the feeling that he *sympathized* with his *kapers* and their project. As though he grieved for them and wished for their own sake that he hadn't disillusioned them. That's crazy. You have to take hope away from dangerous criminals, show them they can't win, don't you?" Frank guessed that was true. "But Henk's conscience may tell him that he should have added some positive suggestion. I wonder myself why they never thought of surrender. Wouldn't that have been the logical thing?" "You've said that before," Aileen reminded him. "But I don't see Jeroen as the type to surrender. Can you picture him marching out with a white flag? And the Arabs were planning to kill us all anyway—the *kamikaze* idea. Henk said so. If Jeroen had tried to surrender, they would have started shooting, don't you see? I wish we'd asked Ahmed about that."

"The *needlessness* of the slaughter," Frank continued after a moment. "I keep coming back to that. It must trouble Henk too. I gather he feels that if Jeroen had been left to himself he might have planned his own destruction better, not to endanger other lives." "He tried. We have to give him that," said Aileen. "He put too much faith in technology," Frank decided. "Modern man. I ask myself, Aileen, why didn't he use a plain old-fashioned gun? That rifle of his. I wish somebody would clarify that for me." Aileen sighed. "Here they come with the cart. Let's order a drink." "You mean I ought to use my imagination," said the Reverend. "But I'm a down-to-earth sort of cuss, if you can believe it of a man of my calling. In temporal affairs I have to have my *i*'s dotted and my *t*'s crossed." "Ahmed explained it," she said. "As much as anyone can. He empathized with Jeroen."

"*C'etait un poète, madame,*" the poor Arab, very dignified,

357

had told her in the helicopter, choking out the words as he tried to raise himself on the stretcher. They had not realized then what had happened to his lung. He meant, apparently, that Jeroen had designed a poetic end for himself, like a Viking's funeral. He had intended to go down with his ship ablaze. *"Il fallait tout détruire."* All his plunder. *"C'etait un homme du Nord, vous savez. Je l'aimais beaucoup. Je l'ai compris. Même sa deuxième demande."* To a Palestinian, she could see, NATO was not all that important, but Ahmed had gone along, knowing that to Jeroen his second demand meant everything. *"Mais les tableaux, Ahmed. Pourquoi?"* Like a muezzin, he repeated: *"Il fallait tout détruire, tout sacrifier."* But Jeroen had loved the pictures, she protested, or at least the Vermeer. Why, then, destroy them? One must sacrifice what one loves, Ahmed had answered. *"Le geste sublime d'un grand révolutionnaire."* Blood rose to his lips; he spat and before their eyes lost consciousness, falling back onto the stretcher.

The hostess reached across the Reverend and set a bourbon on Aileen's tray, beside a plastic glass filled with ice-cubes. "Civilization," Aileen commented, winking back a tear. "Poor Ahmed. I grieve for him, I must say." She unscrewed the little bottle. "He was the only one in the end who didn't want to kill us. Not counting Jeroen and Greet, of course. *That* was a surprise, wasn't it? I mean, the change in Greet." "We were all changed, Aileen. Don't you sense it in yourself?" She considered. "Not really." She raised her eyes to his and lifted her glass. "Cheers. No, I don't feel changed and, frankly, I don't notice any difference in you. We're the same as ever. Maybe that says something. We're the ones that nothing happened to, physically or morally."

He was startled. His face fell. "That's a harsh judgment, Aileen. And a snap judgment. You'll learn better when you've digested this experience. I'm still struggling to encompass it myself. Maybe we both have a bit of 'survivor guilt,' which in your case leads you to fear that there may be a lack of depth in yourself if you're alive and well when the others—" "There *is* a lack of depth and in you, too. Well, we have to live with that. We're two-dimensional, Reverend." "But, Aileen, surely you feel sorrow." "Not much. Only superficially, like with our cuts. Yet you could say"—she laughed—"that I lost two matrimonial prospects in the great explosion. Did you know Archie was a widower? His wife died of cirrhosis of the liver. An alcoholic, isn't that terrible?" "But who was the other? Why, good heavens, you must mean Jim. A great tragedy, that, and for the country. He had so much to give." "He'd given it," she said shortly. "There was nothing left. It was obvious. That page had already turned."

Frank felt chilled. Women of her age with the misfortune of being childless could have an unnecessarily bald way of passing judgment. They drank for a time in silence. "After lunch," said Aileen, brightening, "shall we look at Sophie's journal? There's not much left of it, but it will help pass the time." Pages from Sophie's notebook had been found in the rubble, blown to the four winds; the authorities had come upon a few, semi-intact, in the rabbit run. They had been turned over to Sophie after Aileen had identified them. "Poor Sophie," Aileen said. "She wanted me to destroy them. But I made her see that they constituted a valuable document. Somebody might want to use them for a history of terrorism or she might use them herself if she decided to write a book about the polder events." "That could be a good project for her," Frank admitted. "If it didn't stir up too many memories . . . With her handicap, I suppose she can dictate." "I told her that. But she wants to be re-educated to do everything with her left hand; she even thinks she can learn to type with it." "They have special keyboards," Frank remembered. "So much is done nowadays to help victims of accidents to adjust to the machines we all depend on." "Well, she's brave," Aileen said. "Wasn't it strange to hear her laugh about the wooden arm she'd get with movable fingers?" Frank thought that she had been on a "high" that day from the opium or whatever it was they gave her: she had also

spoken, gaily, of designing bathing dresses for herself that would
have balloon sleeves and full skirts to go with them—she had
always loved swimming, she told them.

The original of the journal was in Aileen's briefcase. Sophie,
on her "high," had offered to donate it to the Lucy Skinner
library, and Aileen had taken her up on it. A photostat was
going home to Connecticut with Sophie's parents. There was
nothing intimate in it, Aileen said; she had seen that when she
identified it for the police. It had looked like a mixture of
scraps of overheard conversations and Sophie's own thoughts.
Many pages had been lost; others were too tattered and stained
—with water and probably blood—to be legible to anyone but
Sophie. Yet of course it could not fail to be interesting to those
who had lived through the events. When the trays had been
cleared off, Aileen got it out. "Now here's some conversation."
They bent over the sheets.

E. You never miss a chance to make fun of us for being capitalists.
C. A missionary to the heathen, that is my role. My upbringing
and tastes, you see, didn't fit me for evangelizing the masses.
E. . . . made his first killing in pharmaceuticals. Squibb bought
him out because he had a corner in one of those mycin drugs . . .
money he borrowed from friends in local rackets. . . . They had
a pool, and Harold was the brains. But if some baby was dying and
couldn't get the drug because Harold was pushing the price up?
C. My dear, it doesn't do to dwell on the origin of a fortune. . . .
Some are older than others so that the smell of the buried bodies
isn't so fresh. My own small holdings go back to the textile mills—
horridly sweated immigrant labor, mostly Portuguese. One could
even say that the newer money is somewhat cleaner.
E. (brightening) Do you really think so? But you have so much
culture. It frightens me to hear you talk sometimes. I feel so ignorant
and inferior. And I know that Chaddie and I can never catch up.
It's no use for him to own the Cézannes and me my poor Marie
Laurencins—very unadventurous of me. I ought to branch out but
I'm afraid to. Owning them doesn't give us any real satisfaction
except for Chaddie's ego. What's the use of owning them if you
don't know what to say about them when people come to see the
collection. You feel you don't own them at all. You just have them

there for other people to look at. Chaddie doesn't have the time of course, but I've been to art appreciation courses in our museum. It's a woman's job to understand art. Division of labor, he says. But I appreciated the pictures more before I took the courses. They only made me feel stupid. For instance, our teacher said that Cézanne was a bad draughtsman and tried to illustrate it with a pointer in that "Man with a Pipe." I couldn't see what he meant and when I went home and told Harold he was furious and said I could drop the course. I guess if I'd been able to tell him why Cézanne was a bad drawer he would have been even madder. When I do learn anything in the class he says I sound like a parrot.

C. Mmm.

E. . . . want Harold to turn over the Cézannes to them. They don't care about my Laurencins. Do you think he should agree? No, I shouldn't ask you. For you it's not the same. When I listen to you talk, I have the feeling that you own art with your mind. It won't make any difference to you if you have to turn over your collections. You'll still own them in your head, the way you do masses of things that don't belong to you, that you've just seen once, in a museum or somewhere. But Harold and I wouldn't. If he lets them have the Cézannes, that's it. He'll have nothing to have any pride in any more. Though in a way it would be a relief. Let me tell you, he actually bragged to me because they wanted his Cézannes and not my things. He said it proved he had more taste.

C. In your Harold's place . . .

"That's all of that," Aileen said. "I wonder when it was. Now here's a different bit."

Mrs. Tallboys (gracious). Are you related to the rose? A lovely old pink climber. You don't find it any more in the catalogues. Dr. Van Fleet. Mother had it on a trellis outside the library door. . . . F-l-e-e-t.

"That was much earlier," Aileen decided. "I'm surprised to see she was keeping the diary then. Well, you don't need to read it. We all heard it anyway. What made Sophie write it down? She seems to have been fascinated by those people. But I wouldn't think they'd make good copy, would you? But here's something about you. 'F. keeps wanting to have serious discussion of terrorism.' " But the rest of the page was gone.

"Let's look at her own thoughts. We *know* pretty much what the rest of us said but we don't know what she was thinking. I always wondered what was going on in that head." "Should we?" "I told you, there's nothing private. Not a word about her and Henk. And, after all, she *gave* me the journal. If it worries you, we can stop. There's quite a long stretch here without any stains or torn parts. See, it starts with me."

Aileen's question: what can art "do" for you, can it make you a better person, etc.? To the second part, evidently not. Collectors, dealers, museum people, art experts worse class of person generically than dentists or plumbers, say. Was it always so? Probably. Isabella d'Este, François Ier, Medici popes. Leave reasons for this aside for the moment and consider first part of the question. Does art have *any* effect on person who lives with it? Yes, it may. "Rub-off" from constant exposure to beauty can develop taste, e.g., Lily. That is, teach the art of acquisition. The "connoisseur" merely a highly trained consumer. "Lily has an eye," "Johnnie has an eye," they say of each other. Eye an organ of appropriation: Charles. A sensitized eye may make up for slender means; tastefulness substitutes for money. But all this essentially a circular process—familiar association with beauty enables one to recognize, i.e., seize on, more of the same. Ownership of works of a. qualifies a set of well-to-do persons—at any rate in principle—to be "discriminating"; to that point, it's educational. *Great* means not strictly necessary, may even be a handicap: millionaire's eye can afford be "lazy," relying on pack of seeing-eye dogs—Berenson, Duveen—to do work for it. But for collector *some* means or family history of them v. important. Art and wealth boon companions. Sad but so.

Returning to second half of A.'s question, isn't that part of the reason that experts, dealers, curators, fall into same bag as collectors —like them, snobs, reactionaries, materialists? Even poor Warren has itch for spending names, pathetic triviality. His specialization means corrupting contact w. trustees, donors, etc., as on this journey. Lives "high" when w. his Croesuses, gets familiar, over-familiar, w. butlers, limousines, first-class travel, w'd surely have been presented to Shah & Madam Shah. At home a church mouse and must feel contempt for ignorance of most trustees, donors, he fated to accompany to view treasures. V. bad for character. "Servants of art" form obsequious priestly caste.

Yet perennial association of art and wealth not whole explanation of seeming evil effect of art on moral fiber of its devotees. Visual art (see above) excites cupidity, desire to possess, also touch, finger—my mother a trial on chateau tours; exclusive enjoyment everybody's dream. Strange this should be so? Concerts and stage plays v. different. Communal. Who would want to be sole audience for symphony or stage play? If no one else in hall, w'd be sorry for actors and musicians. But no one wishes to share painting & statuary w. mob of strangers. My ideal: to be alone in Venice Accademia or w. chosen friend. Perhaps problem is that visual beauty always incorporated in an object (Rev. Frank deplores). How share an object between many in limited span of time? Judgment of Solomon. Books? Must be alone—or undisturbed anyway—to read a book. But a book, though an object, exists in the plural; no displeasure felt if others are reading it at identical moment.

Back to A.'s question, first part. Put it another way: can an aesthete ever be a good man? Strongly doubt it. Cf. Kierkegaard on inferiority of aesthetic to ethical. H. says pronounced Kerkegor.

Artist himself not aesthete. Workman, rather. Artists notorious for lacking taste. Able appreciate "hand" of fellow-craftsman or predecessor, but taste prerogative of amateur. Artist often unrefined, rough individual; unlike his product, out of place in collector's salon.

Sophie! Are you saying art is good for nothing? In fact bad, like radium, for people regularly exposed to it? V. bright and clever, but you know better. True, if you judge art by human types attracted by its "aura," you're bound to condemn it. But forget collectors and other parasitic growths on the noble tree. What about works of art —the Parthenon—that have always belonged to general realm of onlookers, gods, supposedly, and men? Frescoes in churches and statues standing in public squares. Cathedrals. Skyscrapers. Whoever commissioned them—cardinals or Seagrams or the city fathers—by now they're part of the social fabric. Surely they're art as it was meant to be. Sacred artifacts owned by nobody and by everybody that passes by. A lot of them (Chartres) visible from a long way off. But they can be tucked away in a cloister (Moissac) or even in an oratory shown you by an old nun. The point is, they've become assimilated to whole family of natural objects—mountain ranges, harbors, stands of trees—that have settled down to live with us too. Of course they "do" something for human community; they're pillars holding it up. But also living members. Come to be seen often as protectors, esp. in old cities. Like lares and penates of Roman house. Perhaps represent eternity, on account of remarkable endurance. Anyway they "concentrate the mind wonderfully," as Dr. J. said of hanging. And there's no question of taste, fine discrimination, involved. Everyone understands they're wondrous without being told. Cf. the first rainbow a child sees. With them it doesn't matter whether their "owners"—clerics or Union Carbide—notice they're there or pass them by oblivious most of the time. Here "just part of the furniture" no sacrilege as no religion of art involved. Not there to be worshipped by idolatrous possessor but to be lived among by the many. In fact the term "art" may be out of place in this context. Art merely the medium, the element, by which the sacred, i.e., the extraordinary, is conveyed.

Written in another hand across the bottom of the page was "You romance." She must have showed the journal to Henk. The next entry—probably some pages were missing—had no connection with art.

. . . These very different from guerrillas I've interviewed. Except Carlos. I almost feel I know him. Hussein & Yusuf wary, a bit like some of the Laos I visited in their cave "command post." But more hostile. Of course circumstances different; in Laos I was treated as a "friendly." Bolivia too. And my old friends in the mountains saw themselves as patriots bent on liberating their country—a limited objective.

A. keeps calling *"kapers"* fanatics. Yes, but what does it mean? 90% of the population is a fanatic: look at "Chaddie," who's less of a collector's piece than I like to think. Frank is a fanatic on keeping an open mind. Wish we had a dictionary so I could see what word comes from. "She's a fanatic for neatness"; same as French *maniaque*. Doctrinal fervor certainly implied, which gives a chill to others. Yet Jeroen not particularly insistent on strict observance except in vocabulary: "imperialists," "people's army," "people's court." Vocabulary his hair shirt. Or monastic "habit." Otherwise quite open to reason. Ahmed a doll. Fanaticism linked to abstinence. Abstention from alcohol, tobacco, sex, forbidden books, forbidden thoughts. *There's* the distinction: H. and J. not madly tolerant but enjoy thinking, take pleasure in play of their minds. Jeroen's hair-shirt vocabulary keeps his mind pure of thought. But he's intelligent, H. says, so must have temptations. But I suspect he takes the urge out in planning; planning comes from his will, and his mind then gets a permit to exercise. True of any puritan; revolutionaries today as the last puritans. Do he and Greet have sex? H. and J. think not any more.

A gap followed; then she was writing about museums.

Problem of art for the masses. Museum = private collection opened to public at certain hours & under certain depressing conditions. Public there on sufferance, unwelcomed, continually watched and chided. Guards' happiest hour ten minutes before closing time when they can start throwing people out. Note difference between this and usual attitude of sacristan or verger, eager to open and explain. Must distinguish between the many & the masses. Many good, masses n.g. Museum is crowd-drawer and conceives mission as such. Attendance figures plotted on rising graph. Growth statistics, cf. industry. Greater growth, less individual member of crowd can see what he came to look at. Most drawn by curiosity anyway; museum promotion, presence of guards, searches, no briefcases or umbrellas, locked cases & cabinets, restraining cords to hold public back all convey thought of museum as fantastic treasure trove. People flock to see treasure.

Since undemocratic restrict attendance to so-called qualified persons, solution would be to get art out of museums whenever possible. Malraux had right idea when he took "valuable" statues out of Louvre and set them up on the grass, where any bus-rider can look at them: traffic jams become boon. Evidently this not possible w. paintings. But lots c'd be returned to point of origin—churches, monasteries, town halls, shrines. Sh'd apply to other works too, e.g., Elgin Marbles. Interesting w'd be to "unmake" Barnard Cloisters, repatriating component parts. Such a reparations policy (aegis UNESCO?) w'd have same appeal as returning Maine to Indians. Suggest it to Senator as campaign plank for '76: promising vote loser. But it w'd be just and bring about much needed redistribution of art works. Not only Europe; Asia & Africa w'd benefit. Could Jeroen add it to demands? All right, a whimsy, but *something* will have to be done soon, as w. pollution. Decentralization the watchword. As for educating schoolchildren, what was wrong with copies and casts?

The other hand had inserted a question: "The horses of San Marco?" And Sophie had put in her answer: "They can stay."

Special problems w. modern art. Went from painter's studio to dealer or straight to collector. Hard to find a "home" to return it to. Artists' studios torn down. But statuary—Arp & Brancusi—sh'd be placed somewhere outdoors, where it can have air around it and breathe. Henry Moore "King and Queen" & other big pieces "naturalized" like daffodils in Hampshire landscape. Why not more "earth sculptures"? America big enough & empty enough to accommodate whole cities of sculpture, esp. in the desert. Great Salt Lake? Dakota badlands. Stonehenge c'd give hints.

Again pages seemed to be missing. Then came two—blood-stained but partly legible—that Aileen remembered watching Sophie write.

Friday. Lily's pictures came today. Show perfect taste, like everything about her, including her name—Tallboys. She was born Bocock, I learned. *Re* her water-colors, I mean not just that they're exquisite in themselves but that they show restraint in her as a collector. Somehow it's proper to collect water-colors—not grabby. Anybody has the right to own a few. Some limit like that ought to have been respected in collecting. Maybe in her case it just a happy accident because she's poorer than the others. Johnnie's collection rather appealing; at least it reflects his interests. But private collections . . . Must go public. Happening anyway. A few c'd be maintained as illustrations of history of taste. Preferably in little castles & hunting lodges . . . But without guards—only guides & not too many. Identification of art with lucre to be discouraged. Then fewer tourists w'd come in bus loads to see it. (Did I write that before?) *Correction.* "Art & money boon companions." Holds mainly for easel paintings & things like reliquaries, drinking cups, etc. Things which actually were a species of furniture. Furniture (*meubles, meubelen* in Dutch, H. says) movable by definition. Frescoes, monumental sculpture, bas-reliefs, altar panels, town-halls paintings are stable, cemented into place & time. Celebrations, *vide* triumphal arches. Lots carted off in war . . . pillage. But that felt as desecration, contrary to original intention. Whereas church vessels & easel paintings almost "made" to be stolen.

4 p.m. L. and B. left. Still light. Days getting longer.

The remainder of the page and the succeeding ones were badly torn and defaced. "No use trying to read those," Aileen said, unexpectedly bringing her handkerchief to her eyes. "But here she is, still writing about art. Do you want to go on? We'd better hurry. They're going to show the movie."

. . . dissatisfied my distinction mobile vs. stable despite germ of truth. Try art as treasure vs. art as celebration. Easel paintings treasure, hoarded by owner for solitary enjoyment. Cf. Jeroen w. "Girl." Find that disturbing but "Girl" disturbing too. Wonder if I'd want to live with her. She *too* compelling, like "Mona Lisa." Doubt she w'd be "good" for one in long run. "Feasting" one's eyes: miser's banquet. Mme. Cézanne better for soul—piece of Nature. Cézanne atypical as easel painter; hence failure in own time. Yet whole museum effect here uncanny. We forced to live w. paintings. As punishment? "Girl" consummate example of sin of West; fetish of art as commodity—denial of Marx labor theory of value. Trouble-maker maybe. Arabs don't like her. Upset by pictures here. Islam forbids images. But what about figures in carpets? Only animals, I guess. Awful no books to consult, but awful we so dependent on books. Punishments inflicted here weirdly suited to our bourgeois crimes: forced feeding w. art, deprivation of books, esp. dictionaries, encyclopedias, histories—West's cabbala. I feel it as lesson.

She appeared to have let several days pass before the next entry.

Today Ash Wednesday, Frank tells us. Fast and pray. We fasting all right; *kapers* too—no distinction made. Must collect thoughts again. Ask self central question: why Jeroen wanted pictures. Well, good "investment" for him; improve bargaining position. But also lend artistry to design—flourish of mockery of capitalist values. Yet much ambivalence in him, surely. Loving the thing you hate. You hate it because you love it. In an evil world—"system," he w'd call it—the beautiful gets ugly, like a fallen angel, and must be cast out if fresh start to be made. Yet God loved Lucifer better than all the others.

Thinking this, I am sorry for Jeroen. Greet too. I almost wish them luck. Idealists, I know, are dangerous, but the claim of the ideal (Ibsen) has to be felt or else. . . . Or else the world, our deteriorating world, will continue on its course by sheer inertia. Inertia is taking over, right here; you can sense it. The effort persists but only of its own momentum, beyond Jeroen's control, I think. He must act soon somehow to end that. And Henk's *marechaussee* out there—the reality principle—don't have to act. Only wait. Oh, dear. What can happen? I w'd give an arm, as they say, if this thing could end grandly, the way Jeroen w'd wish, whatever that is by now.

"Good Lord!" Frank smote his brow. "Very chilling," agreed Aileen. The hostesses had been pulling the blinds to darken the cabin. Now the lights were switched off. "That's all there is anyway," Aileen said. "Do you think that was the last thing she wrote? Well, let's not dwell on it. Too painful. At least she's alive." In the dark, she shook down the sheets of the journal. She must have sensed that Frank's shoulders were heaving, for she waited. Then she went on in her usual bright voice, as if kindly not noticing the fight he had been having with his emotions.

"I was hoping she'd put down more about terrorism, weren't you? She actually fell for it, that's clear from the end. But it would have been interesting if she'd analyzed the state of mind that brought her to that point. Nobody's going to care about her views on art. Pure Radcliffe term paper—all the right references, with the obligatory New Left twist. Poor Sophie. That isn't her field." "What?" said Frank. "Oh, sorry. I was thinking about Gus. It's funny how it hits you. Something about those torn pages set it off maybe. But you were saying that art wasn't Sophie's forte, wasn't that it?" "Never mind, Frank." "No, it's good to keep our brains occupied. But about art and Sophie, I'm really no judge, Aileen. I must say, though, I was impressed by how much she knew. Her European background maybe. This has been my first trip abroad." She gave a little screech and patted his arm. "Better luck next time."

His shoulders heaved again—with appreciation of the joke. "I must remember that, for my youngsters. 'Father's first trip abroad.'" He had not seen the risible side. But he was laughing too hard; she was eyeing him with concern. "Seriously," he continued, "there was another thing. . . . I was interested in what she had to say about idealists being dangerous. That hit home. I'm a confirmed idealist, as I guess you can tell. And to be honest with you, Aileen, I had a sneaking sympathy for Jeroen myself. You're a bit too hard on Sophie there. I never felt that he and I were all that far apart. If his gifts could have been turned to a more progressive purpose—gradual betterment of the old society . . . Platitudinous, yet how else can you say it? And we shouldn't be afraid of platitudes. But Henk put his finger on it. You remember, the other day when we visited him and he said that Jeroen had fallen into despair—the ultimate sin against the Holy Ghost? That's true of so many of our young people; they're driven to violence by despair. I see it with the blacks; we must act to give them hope, Aileen." "Do you want to watch the movie or sleep?" she interrupted.

David Niven was on the screen wearing a tropical helmet. He seemed to be in Malaysia or Indonesia, having problems with native guerrillas. They had not rented earphones—Aileen said she never did—but they were able to follow the action quite well. They certainly knew about guerrillas, and watching television plays in Dutch night after night had taught them to do without words. It had been good mental training, the Reverend Frank acknowledged, glad to be reminded of the need to count their rewards.